UNTITLED, Nude

UNTITLED, Nude

a novel by

Carol Doumani

Wave Publishing
Venice
1995

ISBN 0-9642359-6-X
Library of Congress Catalog Card Number: 94-61117

The text of this book was set in Bembo,
a facsimile of a type face cut by one of the most
celebrated goldsmiths of his time, Francesco Griffo,
for Aldus Manutius, the Venetian printer, in 1495.
The face was named for Pietro Bembo, the author
of the small treatise entitled De Aetna in which it first
appeared. Through the research of Stanley Morison,
it is now acknowledged that all old-face type
designs up to the time of William Caslon
can be traced to the Bembo cut.
The present-day version of Bembo was introduced by The Monotype Corporation, London,
in 1929. Sturdy, well balanced, and finely
proportioned, Bembo is a face of rare
beauty and great legibility
in all of its sizes.

Composed by Gamut Publishing,
Cohoes, New York
Printed and Bound by The Haddon Craftsmen,
Scranton, Pennsylvania
Designed by John Deep

To Roy, who has made this book and all things possible.

"Art can never exist without naked beauty displayed."

William Blake

UNTITLED, Nude

Federal Bureau of Investigation

J. Edgar Hoover Building
Washington, D.C. 20004

Robert M. Johnson, Program Director
National Stolen Art File

April 16, 1994

Mr. David La Salle, Vice President
Century Insurance of America
Fine Art Division
1830 Santa Monica Blvd.
Los Angeles, CA 90066

RE: Lot # 1427K.2 - M, The Michelangelo Giant

Dear Mr. La Salle,

I understand that you have been newly appointed Director of the Fine Art Division at Century, and have requested an update on the above noted case. Enclosed are copies of the pertinent historical documentation in our file. Because the material herein is voluminous, let me summarize it in brief.

The artwork known as the Michelangelo Giant is a sculpture carved of Carrara marble, 6.1 inches high, 1.4 inches wide, 22.07 ounces in weight (see photograph). Current value in U.S. dollars is estimated at $42,000,000.

We have determined that this statue, thought to be the work of Michelangelo Buonarotti of Florence, was carved sometime between the years of 1498 - 1502. Supposedly it was a study, a maquette, carved while the artist was idling his time in Carrara, waiting for the perfect marble to be quarried for his statue of David, commissioned by the Medicis, which was completed in 1504.

When he left Carrara, Michelangelo was said to have given the figure to the Chiesa della Madonna, where it sat in obscurity, virtually unappreciated, until April of 1978, when it was reported missing. Since there was neither provenance nor other material documentation of its existence, it was impossible to retrieve, and was considered lost until June of 1990, when it was discovered among the ruins of a fire at the Far Hills, New Jersey estate of Mafioso Giovanni Alberti.

All that remained after the blaze which cremated the Mafia boss and seven of his closest associates was a fireproof vault filled with priceless works of art and antiquities. It is believed that Alberti stockpiled this black market collection not because he loved art, but as political collateral, to be exchanged for favors or to use as negotiating tools should he ever be held for ransom.

At any rate, it fell to us at NSAF to locate the legal owners of the many works of art, the Michelangelo Giant among them. For some reason, the Italian Government failed to step forward at this time to claim the Giant. Because we have no facility for long-term storage of such priceless artworks, in 1991 the statue was turned over to your client, the J. Paul Getty Museum in Malibu, California, where it was displayed briefly, then stored with the rest of the Getty's vast cache of antiquities.

You may or may not be aware that the Giant had been in the hands of the Getty for only a few months when suddenly, through diplomatic channels, the Italian Government cried foul, insisting that the artwork rightly belonged to Italy, and that it be returned.

However, because the Italians could not document its previous ownership or prove its theft, the Director of the Getty, Dr. George Lambert, fought extradition, insisting that his institution had sufficient legal claim to the artwork. In his letter to the Italian authorities (enclosed) he pointed out that it was impossible to verify that the Giant had ever belonged to the church in Carrara in the first place, that, indeed, since Alberti was of Italian birth himself, he could have been the rightful owner!

The case was highly publicized in the art press, but eventually bogged down in legal hassling. It wasn't until March of this year that the Giant again made the news when, as you know, it disappeared from the vault of the Getty.

I'm sure you are aware of the theories as to its current location. Some accuse us at NSAF of forcing the Getty to return it to the Italian Government, although both the Getty and the Italians deny this. Others are certain that the Catholic Church planned and executed a heist, though of course Papal authorities vehemently object. Still others feel the Getty has merely moved the Giant to a safer locale, until the furor dies down.

Because of the diplomatic urgency of this issue, we have been authorized by the Secretary of the Treasury to encourage the Getty to offer a reward for information leading to the recovery of the Giant. Although it would be up to you, as their representatives to determine the amount, we suggest an award of one percent of the value of the sculpture, which would be $420,000, as we have found that the higher the enticement, the greater the chance of ferreting out an informant.

Should you require further information, please feel free to contact our office.

Sincerely,

Robert M. Johnson
Program Director

cc: Mr. Elliot Faulk Harrington
CEO, Century Insurance of America

I

I

ONE

H E HELD THE BLADE to her throat, and with icy precision made a slash just under the chin. There. It was done.

His excitement now coming in shallow breaths, he set the blade aside and raised his hand to the cut, delicately massaging the gouge with his fingers until what had been a hole softened into a curvature just a fraction of an inch deep. He stood back to judge the effect and smiled. It was perfect.

Pleased, Nick closed his eyes and let his hand trail down her throat to her breast, feeling in the subtle swelling what a musician experiences when he touches the strings of his instrument. His hand completely engulfed the cold, firm mound, drawing music from it, a tingling sensation in his fingertips that shot through his body like an electrical charge. For a moment he felt a dizzying rush of joy, a sense of ultimate bliss that he recognized as creation. Just a fleeting glimpse of the muse, and then it disappeared.

He opened his eyes and looked around, hoping to recapture the spirit, but to his surprise, Julia wasn't there; he was alone in the studio, alone and aroused, with his hand pressed against the unfinished clay statue before him.

He groaned in frustration. Julia was constantly pulling this stunt, evaporating into thin air when his back was turned. At first he'd been patient, explaining that he needed his model there in the studio, that her physical presence was essential to the process even when he wasn't looking at her. But she'd ignored his pleas, and after a while he'd realized that the disappearing act was intentional, her way of getting the upper hand. God, he hated being so dependent. But what choice did he have? He was trying to draw life out of a block of clay. Without a flesh and blood body for inspiration, he might as well sculpt fruit.

"Julia? Hey, babe, I need you. Please?"

Desperation crept into his voice. When his creative juices were flowing he was obsessed with her. She called it love, but he knew obsession was just part of the process of his art. How could he sculpt a perfect likeness unless he absorbed every detail of her body — inhaling her breathy sighs, bathing in the sweet sweat trickling down her back, tensing from the muscle spasms in her arms and legs when she held a pose too long, spasms which intensified when he explored her most intimate secrets.

"Julia!" he bellowed, angry now at being ignored. "I mean it!"

"Christ, Nick, go suck an ice pick. I'm getting dressed," she yelled. "And you should too. You know how pissed off Francis and Margaret will be if we're late."

He gritted his teeth in exasperation, and began looking for her, following the sound of her voice. Finally he saw her at the far end of the studio. She was wearing a black lace bra and G-string, prancing around on four-inch spike heels. Another power play.

"Just work with me a few more minutes. With all the egos in that crowd, they'll never notice if we're a little late."

"The party's in your honor. Of course they'll know."

Who gives a shit, he wanted to shout. But then his eye locked onto a flaw in the Figure, a bulge in its thigh that he knew from memory wasn't on Julia's flawless left quad. He picked up the fettling knife and started to shave it down, joyfully losing himself again in creation.

Work was his opiate, his salvation. It was better than sex, more potent than drugs, more essential than food, family, or money. And if you asked him why, he'd only shrug and tell you he was an artist. He couldn't explain it in words. He could only show you through what he created. And he created bronze statues of the female form.

As he scraped away the excess clay, he remembered back fifteen years, when all he could afford was wood — crude, cheap, and temporal — his sculptures more craft than art. But even then he'd made only statues of women. They were tiny figures, some less than six inches high, each a perfectly proportioned miniature person he could shape to fit his fantasies, giving them big lusty tits or tiny prepubescent swells with nipples the size of bee stings, legs as long and straight as the Ventura Freeway or asses dimpled and soft as a Botero. All of this had been within his power to create, and it still was, except it was much more difficult in bronze. The metal was much less forgiving and the processes infinitely more time consuming.

But the market for bronze was huge, and ideally he could sell five or ten castings from a single clay maquette. It wasn't that he cared about the money. As long as he made enough to keep working he was happy. But it took a fortune to run the foundry, and it seemed like he was always in debt.

The thigh was looking better now, smooth and sleek with just a hint beneath it of the musculature that Julia worked so hard to build. When he was working and she was wandering around the

studio nude, listening to music, doing her exercises, he could watch
her forever. Her body was as close to perfect as he'd seen. But still,
the details drove him crazy: the place where her thigh met the
crease of her buttocks, the arch of her foot, the texture of the skin
on her ear lobe. If he could just get it all into the statue, then he'd
be happy.

"Goddamn it! Where's my other earring?"

Julia appeared in the archway that connected the studio to his
living area. She was completely dressed now, wearing a flirty yellow dress that hugged her torso and flared out into a sunburst just
a couple of inches below her crotch. What had happened to the
black bra and G-string? This sheer minidress couldn't conceal
them. She must have worn them just to turn him on. And guess
what? It had worked. He stared at her, fettling knife poised, just
drinking in her beauty.

"Come on, Nick. Take your prick out of your hand and let's go."

Irritation flared inside him. As gorgeous as Julia was, she had a
coarseness that kept seeping through into his work, destroying the
purity of his image of her. If she would just keep her mouth shut
and allow him the illusion! But the attitude was always there, getting in the way.

"If you knew what a pain it is schlepping every damn thing back
and forth from my apartment to this dump," she continued to rant.
"I feel like a traveling salesman. Are you listening to me, Nicholas?"

Nick turned back to the Figure, tuning her out. But her tirade
had provoked the attention of his Schutzen-trained German Shepherd, Attila. Sensing animosity, the dog tensed and growled softly,
his throat vibrating with menace. He didn't trust Julia; he never
had. He kept a wary eye on her now, maintaining a dignified distance as he'd been trained to do, but ready to intercede if she
threatened his Master.

Julia moved into Nick's line of sight, standing next to the unfinished statue. Side by side the resemblance was dazzling. But Nick
could see that he'd gotten the line of the jaw wrong. So he angled
Julia's head slightly into the light and began gently reworking the
Figure's profile.

"You're not listening to me! You never pay attention to anything but that stupid statue." Julia stamped her foot like an indig-
nant child. "Here I am, a live, hot body, aching for a little attention.
And you can only get off on that slab of clay. Who do you think
you are, Michelangelo. Fat chance. The only reason people buy
this stuff is because tits and ass sell. *My* tits and *my* ass. You're nothing but a . . . "

"Shut up! Shut the fuck up!" With a cry of release Nick plunged
the knife deep into the mouth of the Figure, gouging a ragged, gaping hole between the clay lips.

Julia screamed and raised her arm and rushed forward to punish
him for this desecration. But Attila leapt to his feet and was instantly
at Nick's side, growling through bared yellow teeth, eagerly anticipating the command to attack. Julia froze.

"Call off your damn dog," she shrieked.

And Nick did, with a brief sideways motion of his hand. Fighting
against instinct, Attila sat, but continued to growl. "What is your
problem, Julia?" Calm now, after his outburst, Nick's voice made
a mockery of gentleness.

"I can't find my other earring," she whimpered, backing away
from Attila's bared teeth.

"Then just wear one," Nick said, letting his controlled anger
press against her in place of the knife. "You'll start a trend."

"No I won't. I'll look ridiculous," Julia cried. "People will laugh."

"Well, at least they'll be paying attention to you. That's what
you want, isn't it?"

They stared at each other in open hostility, neither willing to back down. Then the silence was pierced by a three-note whistle, the sound Nick's friend Willie Wilson used to tell the world he had arrived.

Unaware of the drama he was upstaging, Willie sauntered into the studio as though he owned it. As usual, he was dressed in vintage clothes from the B'nai B'rith Thrift Shop. On most people, the windowpane suit, green socks and lemon yellow tie would have looked gaudy. On big, black Willie, they were art.

Attila, however, wasn't impressed. Or he was set off again by the derelict odor of the used clothing, because he forgot that Willie was Nick's oldest friend, and sprang forward in full frontal attack. Instinctively, Willie dove under one of Nick's work tables.

"Attila *FREEZE!*" Nick shouted, and the dog skidded to a reluctant halt inches from Willie. "Come here, boy."

"Jesus H. Christ! Give the mutt a 'lude!" Willie cried, brushing himself off.

"Sorry man. But you know you can't come up behind me like that. When he senses a threat, he reacts." And then with a pointed look at Julia, Nick added, "And so do I."

"Nicky," she cooed sweetly now that there was an audience, "it would be so much easier if I could *live* here, instead of all this traipsing back and forth. I'm tired of living out of a suitcase. I feel like Willie Loman."

"I don't want a roommate, Julia. All I want is to work and to be left alone." How many times had he uttered this line? However it began, it always came down to this.

"Well, I'm tired of playing second fiddle to your work," she wailed. "God, doesn't anybody fall in love anymore?"

Nick was silent.

In frustration Julia turned to Willie. "Willie . . ."

"Love? Don't look at me." He shielded his face with his hands. "I've been exposed, but I'm not a carrier, I swear."

"You are both pathetic worms!" Julia swept past Willie, dismissing him with a melodramatic flourish.

"The earring, Jules," Willie said, reaching out to flick the crystals dangling from her ear as she passed. "It's *so* juicy!"

"Stuff it," she snapped, and flounced out of the studio.

"Stuff this," Willie muttered, brushing his hand over his crotch. "Why do you put up with it, Nicky boy?"

Nick shrugged. "For the work," he said, and Willie nodded understandingly.

Nick watched Willie circle the statue, examining it with a critical eye. Normally he didn't let people see his sculptures until they were finished. It was like serving someone a half-cooked steak, or stripping off your clothes and pointing out the pimple on your ass. But Willie was different. They'd been friends so long he knew Nick's work almost as well as Nick did.

"It's good," Willie said at last, "except the mouth looks a little German Expressionist." Then he frowned. "But something's missing."

"I know, and damned if I can find it." Nick threw a sheet over the clay. "Let's get out of here." He started for the door. Willie began to follow, but stopped to pick up a small cluster of crystals from the floor — Julia's lost earring. He held it up triumphantly, then clipped it to his right nostril. "How does it look, my man?" he asked, shaking his head to get the most from the dangling beads.

"Like you tried to snort a line on a cold day in Nome. Come on, let's go. I have to tap dance for Thornton's guests."

"You get paid yet?" Willie asked.

"No, but it's peanuts to Thornton. He's not going to stiff me."

"That's exactly why he'll stiff you. Because he's so goddamn rich and famous he thinks he doesn't have to pay. Like you should be honored just to have your statue in his collection. He does it all the time." Willie shook his head, and the crystal earring in his nose tinkled softly. "I keep telling you, man, you should let a dealer handle your stuff. It's the only way to do business. You should talk to my guys at Rave."

"They're bloodsuckers and you know it."

"So find someone else. How about L.A. Louver or Margo Leavin? If you want to go for the big time, you can't do it alone. Trust me."

Nick put his arm around Willie. "I do trust you. That's my problem."

TWO

CONSTANTINE UTTRELL was not surprised to find the party's host, Francis Thornton, holding court in front of the new Rothko. Granted, it was an impressive piece of art, and he'd paid Con a fortune for it. But, Con thought with disdain, a man of Thornton's wealth and position should be less obvious. Clearly the painting was impressive enough to draw attention to itself. Why not let people discover it on their own?

But subtlety wasn't Thornton's style. In addition to being one of the most voracious art collectors in California, Thornton was known to be a ruthless entrepreneur. Con respected this because in his own business as a private art dealer he operated the same way, going straight for the kill, damn the expense and the body count. If a client wanted a specific piece of art, Con would go to whatever lengths necessary to procure it. If he couldn't buy it, he improvised.

With disgust Con watched Thornton puff on his Cohiba cigar and blow smoke directly at his $650,000 investment. Didn't he know how destructive smoke was to the delicate oils? Con considered telling him, but rejected the idea, preferring to stand by and watch Thornton destroy something for which he'd paid so dearly.

Then Thornton saw Con, and waved him over. Con would have loved to avoid this confrontation, but it was inevitable; Thornton expected him to kowtow, and he'd do it because he'd just put $200,000 of Thornton's money — his commission for this sale — into his Swiss bank account. And, because there would always be more art to sell.

"Good afternoon, Francis. Lovely party," Con said, discreetly standing downwind from the cigar.

Thornton puffed in silence, letting the smoke escape from his mouth like steam from a boiling pot.

"The Rothko looks splendid, doesn't it?" Con asked politely.

"Does it?"

The hackles rose on Con's neck. He sensed trouble, but before he could intuit the cause, a matronly woman interrupted. Con pegged her as an aging art groupie, the kind who volunteered as a docent in a museum, or opened an art gallery the size of a closet in a suburban strip mall. In the '70s menopausal women had pawned themselves off as interior decorators in order to distract themselves from their shriveled wombs. But in the late '80s and '90s they'd begun invading the art world, calling themselves 'consultants,' and selling schlock to their friends. It was much more lucrative than decorating homes, and far less work.

"Mr. Thornton, Jeanne Parsons from the Contemporary Museum in Dallas." Con smiled; he was right again. "I must compliment you on your new Rothko. It certainly is a find."

"Then you must compliment Con Uttrell, my dealer, because he found it for me."

Con didn't like the emphasis with which Thornton infected the word 'found,' but he bowed to the woman, masking his concern with gentility.

"Well, I must say it is a gem. And I dare not ask how much you paid for it — certainly well over half a million."

"Well over," said Thornton, eyeing Con like a beetle he was about to step on. Con could feel perspiration forming in his armpits, and hoped that his immaculate white Versace suit would not betray his anxiety.

"Think of us in Dallas if you ever want to talk tax deductions," the woman babbled on, oblivious to the undercurrents of the conversation which were threatening to drown Con. "The powder room is this way?"

Thornton nodded and watched the woman walk towards it. He kept his eyes on her as she tapped on the door to the powder room and then stepped through it.

"Oh! I'm terribly sorry, I . . ." she gasped, backing out the door, stumbling in her haste to retreat, and rushing away down the hall.

Thornton's thin lips contorted into a sneering excuse for a smile. "Our Duane Hansen. You must see it." What could Con do but follow Thornton to the powder room and look in.

There, poised in front of the vanity mirror, were the extraordinarily lifelike figures of a man and a woman. Every detail, from their polychromed skintone to their polyester clothing, was utterly realistic. The woman sat on the sink, skirt hiked up, arms and legs outstretched to encircle the man, who faced her, his pants around his ankles.

Although Con admired Hansen's craftsmanship, he disdained the work as ephemeral kitsch; once you got past the shock value, it's humor started to ebb. Con couldn't imagine living with one of these pieces, any more than he could imagine living on a permanent basis with another human being. Besides, *he* hadn't sold Thornton the Hansen. Who had?

"Quite lifelike, Hansen's work, don't you think?" Thornton was saying.

"Marvelous," Con lied politely.

"I've been standing by all afternoon watching my guests discover it. It's fascinating to see who is fooled into thinking the statues are real people." He paused and turned to face Con fully. "Or, for that matter, who is fooled into thinking that Rothko you acquired for me is real art."

"I'm not sure I follow. . ." Con sputtered.

"You can drop the act, Uttrell. I'm aware that the painting is a forgery, which is bad enough. But the fact that it is not a very good forgery, my dear fellow, is insulting to say the least."

Con felt the blood drain from his face. How could this have happened! Thanks to the new laser scanner his man was using, the Rothko was a masterful reproduction. Con had even seen to it that he'd gone to the considerable trouble of adding egg yolk to the paint, the way Rothko had, to give the oil that ethereal sheen.

"I gave you the authenticating documents," he managed to choke out. "The provenance . . ."

"Come off it," Thornton spat. "Even an imbecile knows better than to believe what's written on a piece of paper. You've overestimated yourself, Con. Or even worse, you've underestimated me. I want to speak with you in private. Come."

And without another word, he spun on his heel and walked down the hall, toward the elevator that led to the upper floor of the annexed building. Panicked, Con considered making a dash for safety. But then he reconsidered. Thornton must have something besides bodily harm on his mind, or why would he have waited to stage this confrontation after the article about his purchase had been published in *Art News*, and while his house was full of guests? With reluctance, Con followed Thornton down the hall.

Like most people of wealth, the Thorntons guarded their privacy and went to great lengths to establish impenetrable public façades for the media. So in flagrant defiance of the local building codes, the small elevator in the new Frank Gehry wing was the only access to the private living quarters. Con squeezed into the car, forced to suffer the indignity of Thornton's Bijan cologne, and Thornton imprinted his hand against the control panel, activating the elevator.

When the door opened on the upper floor, Con was not surprised to see a Neo-Nazi goon with an eighteen-inch neck waiting. He fell into step behind Con and they followed Thornton down a thickly carpeted hall to a metal door with no handle.

"Hans, if you please," Thornton said to the goon. "I've forgotten my glasses." The behemoth stepped in front of Con and deactivated the security system. Then he stepped back and allowed Con to follow Thornton into the room. The door closed behind them with the whoosh of an airlock.

When Con first met Margaret and Francis Thornton and saw their home, he immediately pegged them as typical Beverly Hills art afficionados who 'acquired' what the critics told them was important and valuable, rather than 'collected' out of passion for beauty.

But now, entering this inner sanctum, Con realized that he had grossly misjudged them, that the guise of the wealthy but naive collector was rather a *dis*guise. For inside the room was an array of art the likes of which Con had not seen outside the intimate private museums of Europe, more precious because it was not displayed, but meant to be enjoyed by only a select few. A Rembrandt, several Renoirs and a Van Gogh, two Degas ballerinas and a trio of Rodin busts were the first few pieces that caught his eye. But the collection was not limited to paintings and sculpture. The rugs on the floor were antique silk Keshans and Tabriz woven of gossamer silk, the sort which would grace the palace of a Saudi king. The furniture was Louis Quatorze, meant not to be sat upon, but admired and preserved. And yet clearly Francis Thornton was using it. There were ancient urns from Greece and Italy holding masses of flowers, and Pre-Columbian fragments used as paperweights. He was sure the Bible on the table was a Gutenberg.

Indeed, it was a feast for the senses, the collection of a connoisseur with deep pockets, large and esoteric appetites, and a very discerning eye. But what captured Con's attention was the small stone statue that Thornton was cradling in his arms. It was only six inches high, barely larger than a can of cola, but it towered over everything else in the room.

"The Michelangelo Giant. You have it." Con's voice dropped an octave in awe. "Of course."

"Of course," Thornton replied, pride of ownership glinting in his beady eyes.

Con was incredulous. Had Thornton masterminded the theft of this priceless statue, or had he purchased the Giant on the black market? And if he had bought it, how much had he paid for this piece of stone, a work purported to be worth more than forty million dollars?

Con did not have to wait long for his answer. Thornton said, "There is no point in asking me how the Giant came into my possession. That is my business. But I will tell you this. I need to have it transported to Japan in utmost secrecy. I want you to handle the shipment for me. It must be moved within thirty days. Do you have any problem with that?"

Con was too overwhelmed to speak.

THREE

TORY HARTMAN watched her mother scrutinize her face in the Lincoln Town Car's rearview mirror. She'd commandeered it when they'd gotten off the freeway on Sunset at least ten minutes ago, and she was still staring into it. Didn't she ever get tired of admiring herself?

"I can't see a damn thing," Charlotte Hartman whined, squinting at her reflection.

Then why do you keep gawking, Tory thought, like you'll turn into Catherine Deneuve or something.

"You could wear your glasses," Arthur Hartman suggested, resisting the temptation to twist the mirror back into place. It always irked him when Charlotte used it to primp while he was driving. But after eighteen years of marriage, he knew better than to interrupt his wife when she was performing the sacred rite of putting on her face. "You didn't forget them, did you?"

"No, but they make me look like Whistler's Mother." Charlotte sighed, and with amazing dexterity for someone who couldn't see, slashed a streak of cerise across her mouth.

Tory waited for her father to supply the litany, and then mouthed the familiar words along with him.

"You always look like the Mona Lisa to me."

Tory rolled her eyes, glad no one else was around to hear this bogus comedy routine. Hopefully, when they arrived, she could ditch Charlotte and Arthur before they embarrassed her. She didn't know the people who had invited them to this art thing, but from the looks of the neighborhood, they had to be way-loaded. Charlotte would probably be falling all over herself to make a good impression.

At last satisfied with her own appearance, Charlotte slipped on her glasses and turned a critical eye to her daughter. "Tory, for heaven's sake, sit up straight. You know how linen wrinkles. I don't know why you insisted on wearing that raggedy thing. I told you to wear your Laura Ashley."

Oh, go puke, you fashion mutant, Tory thought, and defiantly scrunched lower in the seat, her eyes finding her mother's in the rear view mirror. "I'm seventeen, not seven," she grumbled aloud. "You can't tell me what to wear!"

"As long as I'm paying the bills, I think I do have that right."

Mother and daughter stared at each other in the mirror, their hostility palpable. Reflected side by side, both faces were attractive, but strikingly different. Charlotte was composed and picture perfect. Her relentlessly blonde hair and finely chiseled features were static and two dimensional, like an airbrushed model in a magazine ad. She was forty-two, but with effort and in the right light, she could pass for thirty-five. She was proud of her attractiveness, and spent a great deal of time and money to maintain it.

Tory hated her looks, so she compensated by trying to camouflage herself with flashy makeup, exotic hair colors and cuts, hats, dark glasses, and trendy jewelry. But whatever she did, she always

felt like a geek, and she looked different every time she saw her reflection in a mirror, as though she were still in the process of evolving. And despite strenuous though sporadic diets, she always felt fat.
Men seemed to stare at her anyway; she didn't know why. To her
own eyes, she looked like a blob with stringy hair and zits.

Today her hair was dyed a color called 'Lucille Ball.' It was as
unnaturally red as her mother's was blonde. The cut was shaggy and
unshaped, brushed forward to cover a pimple on her forehead. Her
face was angular, with strong cheekbones that made her eyes stand
out, and a wide, sharply defined jawline which contrasted the slen-
derness of her neck like a rose in full bloom balanced precariously
atop its narrow stem.

"I made an appointment for you with Dr. Mason on Thursday,"
Charlotte said.

"The gynecologist? What for? Do you think I got pregnant from
taking a picture?" Tory's voice was full of rancor. "I hate to disap-
point you, Mother, but we didn't do the dirty deed. I'm still a virgin."

"Victoria!"

"It's true. At this rate, I'll still be a virgin when I'm your age."

"Arthur, say something!" Charlotte demanded.

"Dad!" Tory leaned forward to plead her case. "Tell her. I want
to be a photographer. I need to experience life to take good pictures."

"Experiencing life does not include photographing that boy in
the nude." Charlotte closed her eyes to erase the image that had
been replaying itself since she'd come home Friday afternoon and
found Tory bent over the supine body of the McMurphy boy. The
only thing separating Tory's head from his genitalia had been a
35mm camera.

"This is so insane! It was for a class assignment. If you're going
to go ballistic, blame Mr. Lempke."

"I find it hard to believe that a teacher at the Westridge Day School would condone that kind of assignment."

"It was a study of anatomical motion. Everyone had to choose some body part," Tory tried to explain.

"And look what you chose!" Charlotte cried in triumph, satisfied that her point had been made.

"It was his leg," Tory insisted.

"And a few other closely related organs that just happened to get into the picture."

"Mother, he was wearing a jock stra . . ."

"I don't want to hear about it," said Charlotte, clapping her hands over her ears, careful not to disturb her helmet of beige hair. "Now for goodness sake, sit up straight and pull the hair out of your face. You look like Michael Jackson."

"I wish!" Tory sat up to get a better look in the rearview mirror, but Charlotte asserted control by twisting it back to its original position facing Arthur.

"Honestly," she said to him, loud enough for Tory to hear, "I wish you'd act a little more concerned about our daughter."

Arthur shifted uncomfortably. He'd felt awkward talking about Tory ever since the night he'd passed her bedroom door and caught a startlingly erotic glimpse of her clad only in a bra and panties. "She's a good girl," he said, hoping it was true, and knowing he wouldn't have a clue what to do about it if it weren't. "Maybe you're over-dramatizing the situation."

"Your seventeen-year-old daughter was taking photos of a boy in the nude! Don't you think that sounds just a little suggestive?"

"I'll admit it's a switch. In our day, the boys were the ones trying to take pictures of the girls," Arthur chuckled, hoping for a laugh from Charlotte.

He got one from Tory. Her dad was dorky, but at least he wasn't

as bad as the Wicked Witch of Westridge. Tory had been so em-
barrassed when Charlotte had barged in on her and Brad in the
middle of their Kodak moment, raving like the 'Madwoman of
Chaillot.' As if Brad could care about Tory. He was doing Lauren
James, for God's sake, and she was a cheerleader who looked like
Michelle Pfeiffer's kid sister. The only way he'd even looked at
Tory was through the lens of her camera, and it had taken a lot of
effort and planning just to get him to do that.

And now this scuzzy business with the gynecologist, Dr. Mason.
Well, maybe Tory could flip it in her favor. She'd been dying to be
fitted for a diaphragm, in the unlikely event she ever needed one.
Once she was alone with the doctor, she could talk to him about
it. Certainly her mother wouldn't come into the examining room
with her . . . or would she?

"There it is, see the valets?" Charlotte pointed to a driveway
crammed with luxury cars of every size and description. Reluctantly, Arthur turned the bulky Lincoln in, wishing he could self-
park, but knowing Charlotte would never stand for it. He pulled
to a stop and allowed the valet to open his door.

"Treat her gently, eh?" he said to the boy, who hardly looked
old enough to drive. But the valet ignored him and gunned the car
in reverse down the drive. Arthur winced and followed his wife
and daughter up to the front door where a short line had formed.
He looked around.

Although the property was extensive, the façade of the house
was unimposing, no gates or uniformed guards in evidence, only a
low stone wall and a couple of off-duty policemen checking names
on a list as guests arrived at the door.

Arthur was surprised. Like everyone else in L.A., he knew Francis and Margaret Thornton because of their wealth, their social stature and their standing in the business community. He would have

expected a mansion at the end of a long, gated drive, not this non-descript though sprawling ranch style house with an abstract two-story addition tacked onto one end. Either the Thorntons weren't as rich as the public thought, or they kept a low profile. A very low profile.

Well, it was fine with Arthur. The less interesting the house and the party, the sooner he could ease Charlotte out and get home in time to watch Monica Seles play Martina Navratilova in the Australian Open. Still, he couldn't resist taking a dig at his wife. "You didn't tell me we'd have to line up for the honor of paying homage. Do you think we should have brought some sort of tribute? A fatted calf? A golden sepulcher?"

"Hush, Arthur," Charlotte whispered. "You know I've been dying to meet this artist Nicholas Stone. That alcove in the foyer would be a spectacular place for a piece of his sculpture. And Mr. Morris from the museum said his work is still reasonable."

"Reasonable is a relative term, Charlotte," Arthur felt compelled to add. He made a comfortable living as Director of Inspection and Control at Los Angeles International Airport, but the Hartmans lived as well as they did because of Charlotte's trust fund, a fact that had always rankled Arthur.

MARGARET THORNTON, doyenne of the West Coast art scene, was greeting guests just inside the door. She was an imposing woman of sixty-two, her handsomeness the sort which could be purchased at Ferré, Chanel and Valentino. She was to Rodeo Drive what her husband was to Wall Street: a savvy player and a big spender.

"Mrs. Thornton, I'm so honored to meet you," Charlotte gushed, myopically extending her hand to the Thorntons' social secretary, who was standing discreetly back with a clipboarded prompt sheet.

"*I'm* Margaret Thornton," Margaret said, taking Charlotte's proffered hand. "And you are . . ."

"We're the Hartmans, Mrs. Thornton," Arthur interceded. "I'm Arthur. This is my wife Charlotte and our daughter Victoria."

Charlotte stepped in front of him. "It's an absolute thrill for us to be invited, Margaret, to actually experience your collection. We've seen so many pictures of the house, and since I joined the Women's Council at the Museum, well you're just like a legend, and this house is practically a shrine . . ." Charlotte babbled on, groping for the right words to impress and flatter Margaret Thornton.

"Did we meet at the Museum?" Margaret murmured, leaning back so she could hear her secretary whisper, "Customs official at LAX. He helped get the new Giacometti into the country."

"Yes, of course," Margaret remembered, although that didn't explain why Francis had invited him to this party. But she graced Arthur with a smile nevertheless. "Mr. Hartman, it was so kind of you to help us resolve that little situation with the Giacometti."

"It was my pleasure. We don't often see such a fine work of art, Mrs. Thornton." He chuckled. "Mostly we get those velvet paintings coming in from Mexico."

"Well, it's finally installed in the garden. You must visit it in its proper setting." Out of the corner of her eye, she noticed Francis returning from the annex, with Con Uttrell in tow. She frowned. Such an unpleasant man. What were he and Francis up to?"

"Francis, dear," Margaret waved him over. "You remember Arthur Hartman, the gentleman who handled all that Customs red tape with the Giacometti. Why don't you show him how lovely it looks in the garden."

Arthur and Thornton shook hands. "My wife Charlotte and my daughter Victoria," Arthur introduced.

Thornton acknowledged the ladies with a nod and turned his attention back to Arthur. "Good to see you again, Art. I've been reading that the Feds have been all over you since that Michelangelo statue disappeared from the Getty. Your boys must have their work cut out for them . . ."

"Dad, I forgot my camera in the car. I'll catch up with you," Tory said, and slipped away before either of her parents could object.

She found the Lincoln parked half a block from the house, under a low-hanging shrub whose thorns had made hairline scratches in the immaculate hood. She slipped past the bush to retrieve her camera from the back seat, and as an afterthought, shrugged out of her jacket and threw it into the car. She knew Charlotte would be furious, because the bodice of her dress was sheer to the point of transparency, and even though the dress was full and loose, there was no hiding the curves of her hips and bosom.

Tory wasn't trying to be suggestive; in fact her main fashion goal was normally to hide as much of her body as she could, under as many layers as possible. But she'd seen Lauren James in a dress like this, and had splurged on it with the Easter money her grandmother had sent. The fact that her mother hated the dress had been an added bonus.

Tory hopped over the low stone wall and went around the house to the garden, wandering through the party crowd, hiding behind her camera. Not that it made her inconspicuous. If anything, she drew curious stares as she aimed and shot her photos. But having the camera gave her a purpose and made it possible for her to circulate without feeling obligated to speak to anyone.

Besides, there was so much to see and photograph. In addition to the abstract sculptures of metal and wood dotting the lawn, the landscape itself was awesome. Forty-foot pines surrounded the yard, blocking out the neighboring houses and creating the illusion that the Thorntons' property was a meadow amidst a dense forest. Flowers bloomed everywhere, spilling carelessly out of their beds in colorful masses. On closer inspection, Tory saw that this effect was contrived. The garden had been carefully manicured to convey the impression of nature run wild, yet another work of art.

A flagstone path meandered through the flower garden to a pond of abstract shape and unknown depth. Three black swans glided over the surface in a chevron formation, causing the water to undulate softly against a tall rectangle covered with a large white cloth. Tory moved toward it to investigate.

ON THE PATIO overlooking the garden, Nicholas Stone had been cornered by two attractive women. Despite their rapt attention to him and their obvious sexual posturing, Nick was ignoring them, taking in the whole garden scene through his mirrored glasses, searching for escape.

"How do you choose your models?" Lisa, the brunette, asked him.

"I don't. They pick me," Nick said impatiently. People always asked him this, as though he could tell them in twenty-five words or less how his eye determined what was interesting and from what raw materials he created art. Didn't they know it would be impossible to articulate, even if he understood it himself?

"Why do you always call them 'untitled'?" the redhead named Bettina persisted. "It seems so . . . impersonal."

"That's the point," Nick replied, his expression deadpan. "I see," Bettina said, not sure what she saw.

"Do you always work with them . . . in the nude?" Lisa probed.

"No, I'm dressed," replied Nick dryly. "Usually."

The girls giggled. "You know what I mean," Lisa insisted. Nick sighed. Yeah, he knew what she meant, this yuppie groupie who was predictably offering herself up on the exalted altar of art. He used to get off on such attention. But lately it had become a pain in the ass. He was about to tell her so when he saw Julia approaching, and decided to pull her chain.

"I take photographs and videotape. But I work mostly with my sense of touch." He ran his fingers lightly up Bettina's arm. "I like to know my models from the inside out, to feel their muscles erupting through their skin." He paused. "If you know what I mean."

"I'd like to," Bettina murmured.

"Too bad Nicky's completely consumed with *my* statue," Julia interrupted, moving to Nick's side. She saw Nick's hand, securely wedged between Bettina's plump triceps and her surgically augmented bosom, and glared at her. "We've been locked up together for months trying to get it perfect."

Bettina returned Julia's stare, her eyes narrowed into green slits. "That would be a challenge."

"Slut," spat Julia.

"You're calling *me* a slut? Go look in a mirror," Bettina spat back. "If you've got a strong stomach."

While the girls were distracted, Nick moved away, disappearing into the crowd and resurfacing at the bar to drown his ill ease in expensive Scotch. It wasn't just the women; he was tired of the whole art scene. Always the same posturing sycophants with the same hangups and ego trips. Is that what art was ultimately about?

He remembered when he had been a struggling art student at San Francisco State University. What he wouldn't have given then to be invited to a party like this, let alone to be the guest of honor, unveiling a sculpture for which he'd been paid $62,000.

But now that he was here, he ached for the days when he had been able to live for his work and not concern himself with posturing and politics. He had liked who he was then.

On the other hand, he was enormously proud that this elite group of collectors had gathered today in his honor. And if he hadn't played the game and won this level of success, he would never have been able to afford to work in bronze. It was a daisy chain, he decided, sucking the last of the Scotch off an ice cube. And he was helplessly shackled to it.

Then his eye glimpsed something out of place in the predictable art party tableau — a young girl at the pond's edge, camera raised to photograph one of the swans. Nick watched her kneel with the unselfconsciousness of youth, positioning herself for the awkward shot. Automatically, his artist's eye accumulated details: the nonchalant way she gathered her flowing skirt together and hugged it between her knees, the glint of sun on her hair, picking up red and blond highlights in the jumble of sloppy curls, the essential naiveté of her expression, juxtaposed to the pretensions of the other guests. In the way she leaned forward, he saw a potential for grace which her body had not yet grown into, and his gut wrenched with a deep yearning, for what he did not know.

"Christ, Nick, can't you at least wait until they reach puberty?" Julia's voice brought him back to reality.

Nick didn't bother to look at her or reply.

"On the other hand, she's probably too young to know what the word 'lecher' means," Julia continued, twisting the knife.

"It's tired, Julia. Give it a rest," Nick said.

"Don't you dare walk away from me!" she hissed as he did just that, knocking her elbow as he passed, splashing red wine down the front of her yellow dress. She gasped in horror.

Nick just smiled. "Amazing. That stain looks just like the Sam

Francis Thornton's got in his den. Did you see it?" And he was gone.

The girl didn't see him approach because she was intent on getting her shot, leaning out over the water for the right angle. He was struck by how much she resembled the swans she was photographing, the arch of her long, fragile neck, the downy hair feathering her bare arms. Her unconsciousness of her own fledgling beauty took his breath away.

"Don't fall in," Nick cautioned.

"No way," she replied. Her voice, high and girlish, tickled his ears.

She snapped the shutter and repositioned herself to get a different angle, ignoring him. He did not like being ignored.

"How do you like the party?" he persisted.

"It's kind of like going to the Museum," she answered, still not taking her eyes off the swans. "Just a bunch of people looking at a lot of boring art."

Nick smiled. He couldn't have put it better himself. "You don't like art?"

She shrugged. "I like photography better. Art is too old-fashioned."

Again, a silent dead end. Annoyingly, she still had not looked at him. He groped for something clever to say.

"Are you for hire, or do you only do it for free?"

Oh gag me, Tory thought and finally looked up from her camera lens. What she saw was a man twice her age, ancient compared to the guys she knew, but youthful looking nevertheless. Although he was gaunt to the point of being scrawny, there was something sexy about him, and he was staring at her so intensely that his hungry eyes seemed to devour her limb by limb. He was slouched against a willow tree, his large hands hanging loosely by his sides. But in a creepy way, she could imagine them touching her, exploring her body, and without realizing it, she took a step away from him.

"I'm not from *Buzz*, if that's what you mean," Tory replied, trying to sound indifferent. "I'm taking pictures for a contest at school. The winner gets a summer scholarship to this photography school in Paris."

"The École Photographique?" he asked.

"Yeah," said Tory, surprised he knew the name.

"Well in that case, why don't you try the shot from over here? The light will be better," he offered nonchalantly.

"That's okay. This is fine," Tory replied.

"If you shoot it from here, you'll be able to maintain the proportion and the proper depth of field. From there the bird's head is going to come out bigger than its body."

"Maybe that's the shot I want," Tory said stubbornly, but she got up anyway, and let him guide her into place. Through the viewfinder she saw that it was indeed a much better shot, but she was distracted by his powerful hands gripping her ribcage, and she couldn't concentrate on taking it. His strength made her feel fragile, and her heart was beating a lot harder than it should have been. Finally she willed herself to snap the picture. Then she stood up.

"Obviously you know a lot about photography," she murmured.

"I know how to look at things," the man replied smugly. "I'm Nick Stone."

Tory shaded her eyes to get a better view of him. "Am I supposed to be impressed?"

He frowned. "How old are you?"

"Less than half your age."

"Give yourself a few more years. When you grow up you will be."

"Yeah? Think how old you'll be then."

Pleased with her put down, Tory flounced away from him, for-getting she was standing on the edge of the pond until it was too late. She felt herself begin to slip and managed to maintain her bal-ance just long enough to throw her camera into the grass before she fell backwards into the pond with an indelicate and noisy splash.

The pond was not deep and Tory was not in danger, but she was mortified to see that her clumsy stunt had drawn the attention of the entire party. She sat there dumbly, half submerged, dying of embarrassment as a crowd gathered.

And then Nick was wading into the water, sacrificing his trousers and his shoes to save her. He extended his hand. A peace offering.

Tory considered for a moment, but what choice did she have? She grasped hold. As their hands touched, their eyes met. Some-thing like a current passed between them, and then it was gone.

Nick pulled Tory up from the water, allowing himself, as reward for his chivalry, a long, quenching drink of her body. Soaking wet, her gauzy dress now hugged her body like a second skin. Through it he could see that her figure was strong and youthful and prickled with gooseflesh. He marveled at her nascent sexuality, so thinly veiled by the awkwardness of youth. It was not erotic, but highly sensual, and he felt a rush of passion.

He helped her out of the pond, and the guests who had gathered around applauded in delight. Francis and Margaret Thornton made their way to the edge of the pond, and Francis faced the crowd.

"We had in mind a much more dignified unveiling, but in light of the situation, we are pleased to reveal 'Untitled Nudes of the Fountain' by Nicholas Stone. Margaret, dear, will you do the hon-ors?"

With a flourish, Margaret Thornton pulled the white cloth off of the rectilinear bronze relief, which depicted three emerging female figures, their limbs entwined.

"I'd ask Nick to turn on the fountain, but I think he's had enough water for one day," Thornton chuckled. "Neville, if you please. . ."

The butler turned the key that started the flow of water, and it cascaded down over the bronze relief, bathing the figures in a waterfall which in turn trickled into the pond. The guests' applause drowned out Arthur Hartman's gasp of surprise as he led Charlotte through the crowd.

"Arthur, what is it?" she asked. "I can't see without my glasses."

"It's Tory," he managed to say.

"What do you mean?" Charlotte's voice quivered with apprehension.

"Tory is in the pond," he repeated.

Charlotte considered this for a moment. "Why?" she asked.

"I have no idea," Arthur replied.

FOUR

T HE ANGRY QUACKING of the ducks awakened Rosiland Weeks for the third morning in a row. That was the price she paid for living on Linnie Canal in Venice, a neighborhood of waterways left over from the '20s, when entrepreneur Abbot Kinney had realized his personal fantasy and built an Americanized version of Venice, Italy, complete with gondolas and a pseudo St. Mark's Square.

These days all that remained were the canals, now filled with brackish water and garbage, and lined with ramshackle houses, which, due to logic peculiar to the L.A. real estate market, were valued at up to $500,000. When Rick divorced her, in lieu of alimony he had signed over the deed to the little shack on Linnie Canal — termites, crumbling foundation, leaky windows, mortgage and all. Roz loved the place and had worked hard to keep up the payments. But sometimes she would have been glad to swap her eccentric abode for a sterile one-bedroom with an acoustical ceiling in Encino.

It's those damn joggers, she fumed, dragging herself into the bathroom. They think that just because they're up at dawn, revved and ready to face the world, everyone else on their route should be as well. She climbed onto the toilet seat and cracked open the high window. Sure enough, there was the perky blonde with Julia Roberts' long legs and ridiculously short shorts, who stopped on the bridge every morning and threw crusts of bread to the ducks, who squabbled like real estate agents fighting over a new listing.

Beside her was her constant companion, an adoring fifty-something man who anointed her with looks so passionate they could have melted Barrow, Alaska. Watching these two together always made Roz realize how lonely she was. In the ten years since her divorce — had it really been that long? — she hadn't always been alone, but she'd never recaptured the feeling of oneness with another person she'd experienced during her marriage. Still, she kept looking for it. And currently, she was looking in the direction of her art teacher at night school, an Indonesian with the mellifluous name of Adrian Ambulu. So far he'd kept his smoldering Asian eyes on her drawings, and their conversation had been about their mutual love of art, not about the art of love. But it was only the middle of the semester; she was still hopeful.

When the joggers were gone, Roz stepped down and summoned the courage to confront her reflection in the magnifying mirror. She'd hardly slept the night before, and it showed on her face. Striated, saggy, swollen — middle age brought with it a whole new set of adjectives.

Oh, she knew she was being too hard on herself. She looked great for forty-five. But the problem was, as a single woman Roz had to compete with twenty-two-year-olds like the blonde jogger for the available men. The only cost-effective way she could keep herself emotionally stable and in fighting trim was to live the life of a nun on Pritikin, which she usually did. So what had precipitated the chocolate chip cookie bake-and-binge last night?

Oh, right. It had been that cop who'd pulled her over for speeding on Venice Boulevard on the way home from work. She'd been annoyed because she knew she hadn't been going more than forty. But it wasn't just the ticket. When she'd rolled down her window to give the guy her license, she'd nearly been knocked over by the smell of his cologne. Aramis. Her ex-husband Rick's cologne of choice.

And that had triggered a depressing trip down memory lane, because when they were married, Rick had been an L.A.P.D. mountie too, just as young and dashing as the cop writing her up, with curly, black hair and a luxurious moustache and — oh, shut up, Roz.

So she'd wallowed in it all night, pitying herself for having been dumped at thirty-five and still carrying a torch at forty-five. The cookie binge had only been the tip of the emotional iceberg.

Well, this morning there was just one thing to do — get herself over to the gym and have a good workout — Stairmaster, weights, sauna, the works. Good for the body and the spirit. She'd be late for work, but she could finesse that.

THE OFFICES OF Century Insurance of America occupied the thirty-second and thirty-third floors of a triplex of office buildings on Santa Moncia Boulevard overlooking the San Diego Freeway. Usually it gave Roz a lift just walking through the huge rosewood doors into the granite and glass reception area. She was the only one of her siblings who could boast a college degree or a job in business, and after her divorce she'd worked hard to achieve them, working nights at Val's Pharmacy to pay for her classes. It made her proud that she had graduated and gotten the job at Century all on her own, without financial support from a husband or family. But today, aware of how late she was, Roz slunk past the receptionist's desk and through a doorway which led to a maze of hallways and cubicles, to her own work station, a windowless office across from the Xerox room, which she shared with another staffer. He looked up when he saw her.

"Hey, Roz," he said, "better late than never."

"Hey, Nelson." Roz shrugged out of her coat and looked around for her mug. After the workout she'd put herself through, she craved caffeine. "Is there any coffee left?"

"Just dregs. But I've got some Red Zinger if you want."

Nelson was twenty-four, one of those acne-ravaged, brainy nerds who seemed to have all the answers. How he had ended up at Century investigating insurance claims, instead of in a think tank somewhere inventing the next generation of computer magic, was anyone's guess.

"So where've you been?" he asked, handing her the tea bag.

"At the doctor," she lied and crossed the hall to get some instant hot water from the Sparkletts tap.

"I hope he gave you a written excuse for missing the meeting this morning," Nelson called after her.

He was picking absently at a particularly virulent pimple on his left cheek when she returned.

"Who?" asked Roz purposely turning her back. She liked Nelson, but had a hard time looking at the angry red pustules on his face.

"The doctor, dummy. There was a staff meeting at eight with the new veep La Salle, in case you forgot."

"Shit," said Roz. She had forgotten.

"Oh, and he wants to see you. He told me to tell you the second you came in."

Roz groaned. A one-on-one with a newly appointed veep, especially after missing his first staff meeting, was not her favorite form of torture.

"Why does he want to see me?"

"Are you ready for this? The scuttlebutt is that "Ocean Park, Number 84" has surfaced."

"You have got to be kidding!" Roz gasped. The Richard Diebenkorn painting was one of a trio of contemporary masterpieces stolen from the mansion of Eva and Gerald Stein in Sherman Oaks. It had been the first case Roz had been assigned to when she moved into the Art Recovery Division last fall. Although other smaller cases had come and gone, Roz had not been able to pick up the trail of the Diebenkorn or the other two Stein paintings. She had surmised that professionals had stolen them and were wisely storing the canvases until the art world forgot about them, at which time they could be safely bartered.

"Have they made an arrest?" Roz asked. It would be nice to close the case, especially since the Steins were breathing down her neck, demanding compensation. But damn it, she wanted to be the one to find the paintings.

"No, but they've got their eye on someone," replied Nelson.

"Who?"

Nelson milked the moment, loving the fact that he had Roz's complete attention. "What's it worth to you? Dinner, maybe? How about 72 Market Street? I hear they have this fantastic new French chef."

Roz wanted to hear the news before she saw La Salle so he wouldn't think she was completely incompetent, but her gorge crested at the thought of staring at Nelson's pustulant craters across a dinner table. "Nelson, either you tell me now or I'm going to find out from La Salle in about two seconds."

"Con Uttrell," he said, his voice husky with rejection.

She digested the news. Of all the art dealers in town, Con Uttrell was both the most famous and the most infamous. If he did have the Diebenkorn it would be nearly impossible to pin the theft on him, because he was so well insulated. "Thanks, pal," she said, smiling at Nelson. But he wouldn't look at her.

She started for the door, then stopped, feeling guilty for being rude to Nelson. She knew a thing or two about fragile egos, and besides, an evening out would do her a world of good. "Let's compromise. I can't do dinner, because I'm starting Ultra Slim Fast. But how about a movie?"

Nelson brightened visibly. "Friday night? They're showing 'The Little Tramp' at the Nuart."

"You got it," she said, vowing to be a sport even though she hated old movies. Then she turned her attention to the heavy door at the far end of the hall which led to La Salle's lair.

ALTHOUGH HE WAS ONLY thirty-one, sitting behind a massive mahogany desk equipped with all the right brass accoutrements, David La Salle looked every bit the company man.

But he was on his way out and he knew it. This lateral move into the Fine Arts Division had been, in his opinion, a step closer to the door. Nobody took this Division seriously. Art was simply too difficult to safeguard, and too costly for most people to insure. And when insured art did disappear, it was almost impossible to find. Take the Michelangelo Giant, for example.

He picked up the confidential file the FBI had sent him, and pulled out a photograph of the sculpture, taken when the piece was given to the Getty Museum in 1991. The small stone statue was not very impressive; it hardly seemed big enough to merit all the attention it was being given, especially when there was no way to document its authenticity. Sure, it was old, but was it really the work of the master sculptor himself? La Salle was doubtful.

And yet the powers that be at Century were giving the case top priority, meaning he and his staff were supposed to work at full tilt, though in strictest confidence, with La Salle reporting their findings right to the top, to Mr. Elliot Faulk Harrington.

La Salle, however, had other plans. If he was being pushed out, he was not leaving empty-handed; he would take the $420,000 reward for himself. Fortunately this break in the Stein case had bobbed to the surface at just the right moment. If he could keep his staff burning the midnight oil on it, he could go after the Michelangelo alone.

There was a knock on the door. His secretary entered. "Ms. Weeks is here."

"Send her in."

He didn't like this Weeks woman, was aching to terminate her. Like so many single women over forty, she could be strident and oversensitive. And worse, she reminded him of his mother. But her file said she was a good worker, that she carried her own weight. Unless he had due cause to let her go, she could slap a wrongful dismissal lawsuit on Century faster than you could say equal opportunity employer.

Hell, he was stuck with her so he might as well accept it. But she was just too damn smart for her own good. If she got wind of the reward on the Michelangelo she might beat him to it. He had to keep her off balance, by getting her to concentrate on Stein. He closed the FBI file and put it in the top drawer of his desk.

ROZ STEPPED INTO her boss's office with no small amount of trepidation. She knew he didn't like her, despite the fact that her work had been praised in semiannual employee evaluation reports. Her guess was that he was one of those young pseudo liberals who paid lip service to the concept of equality between the sexes, but who secretly despised any woman he was not attracted to sexually. It was a variation on the old theme of sexual harassment — either they were sticking their hands up your skirt because you were beautiful, or they were ignoring you because you weren't. She wondered how La Salle would feel if she declined to work with him just because he was balding, overweight, and notorious for his bad breath.

Regardless of La Salle's sexist attitude, she was treading a thin line this morning since she'd been over an hour late to work and had missed a staff meeting. Roz decided the only thing she could do was to kiss ass and hope for the best.

"Mr. La Salle, I'm very sorry to be late," she said humbly. "I had a . . ."

"No need to explain," he interrupted. "Sit down, please."

Roz would have preferred to stand, to make this audience as brief as possible, but she realized he wasn't leaving it up to her. She chose a hard-backed chair facing his desk, pulling it close enough to hear what he was saying, but far enough away to be out of range of his fetid breath.

"I want to talk to you about the Stein Case," he began, smiling magnanimously. "There've been some new developments and I'm counting on you to be the one to close it."

FIVE

NICHOLAS STONE'S studio. This is Leslie. Oh, hi, Randy. What's up?"

Leslie Woods wedged the phone between her shoulder and her ear so she could sift through Nick's morning mail. As usual it was rife with bills and past due notices. The cost of operating the studio was enormous, and despite Nick's growing success, he simply could not produce enough work to get ahead. Plus, he was hopelessly extravagant. When she tried to talk to him about a budget he looked at her as though she were speaking Greek. She couldn't understand how he could concentrate on his work with the specter of financial disaster hanging over his head, but somehow he was able to block it out — the sign of a true artist.

Maybe that was her problem — she was too easily distracted. She printed "FOCUS" on a slip of paper and tacked it on the wall above the desk as another line began to ring.

"Randy, can I call you back? It's crazy this morning." She hung up and punched the second line with a pencil to preserve her fingernails, which were filed into blunt, two-inch long talons.

"Studio?" she said, her inflection making it a question. "Yes, this is his secretary."

It was a woman wanting to talk to Nick about a private commission. Leslie wrote down the name — Mrs. Charlotte Hartman — sketched a dollar sign next to it, and then wrote the message. She reached across the office and tacked the note next to the door so Nick couldn't miss it.

Her small cubicle was barely larger than a closet. A heavy metal door on one side led to a hallway which connected the studio to an alley. On the other side, an archway led into Nick's studio, so anyone coming to see Nick had to get by Leslie first. Strips of colored silk fabric less than an inch wide dangled from the top of the arch to the floor, blocking her view into the studio but allowing sounds to travel freely from her office to Nick's work space. Fortunately, the studio was enormous — a warehouse really — and he generally worked at the far end. But she kept earplugs in her drawer for those times when the noise of the solderers and welders got to be too much.

Above her desk was a small, barred window that overlooked the alley and beyond to the littered cement walkway called the Venice Boardwalk. Carnival-like on the weekends, it was nearly deserted on this grey Tuesday morning, save for the stray dogs and the homeless contingent, who apportioned the contents of the trash barrels in peaceful coexistence.

The phone rang again. At this rate she'd never get her work done. "Studio?" she snapped. Then her annoyance melted into decorous civility. "Oh, hello, Mr. Uttrell. How may I help you? At your house this evening? Nine o'clock. I'll tell him. I'm sure he'll be there. Thank you."

Leslie barely had a chance to jot this down in Nick's Daytimer and take a sip of her tea, which was by now as cold as the cement floor, when there was a knock at the door. She swung it open and confronted a man and a woman, he carrying a camera, she a tape recorder. "Can I help you?" Leslie asked. "I'm Zelda Stevens," the woman said, and when Leslie didn't react she added, "From *Art Scene Magazine*." She let this sink in. "And this is my photographer Pablo. We've got an appointment with Nick Stone at eleven."

"Yes, I know. He's expecting you," Leslie replied coolly. Nick was such a private person. He hated to be interviewed, but publicity was a necessary evil. Art didn't sell itself these days. Some artists even hired publicists to keep their names in the columns. So she forced a smile and stood aside to let the team from *Art Scene* enter.

"Can I get you some coffee or tea or anything?" she asked.

"No, thank you," said Zelda. "We're on kind of a tight schedule. If you don't mind letting Nick know we're here."

"Have a seat. I'll be right back." Leslie disappeared through the silken curtain.

Although the studio was as familiar to Leslie as her own apartment, she always felt a little thrill of pride when she entered it. Nick was the most famous person she'd ever known personally. Working for him didn't pay as well as what her friends called "McJobs" — service work in restaurants or retail stores — but the prestige of being employed by a famous artist was a plus on her social resumé.

She plowed through the clutter of plaster casts, fragments of sculpture, derelict furniture and lighting, and statues in various stages of completion, the discarded ruins of Nick's unflagging energy and fertile imagination. She gave Attila's head a pat as she passed him. He was chained on the far side of the studio, calm, but watchful of Julia, who stood on a small platform fully lit against a white wall, her back to the dog and to Nick. Julia was completely naked, save for a pair of state-of-the-art headphones. She swayed to some unheard music, occasionally singing the words aloud, something about love, rejection and resurrection.

Watching Julia move, her perfect body a vision of erotic grace and harmony, Leslie felt a stab of resentment. She knew for a fact Julia gorged herself like a truck driver, but she never gained an ounce because she stoked the fires of her metabolism with liberal doses of cocaine and daily workouts at Gold's Gym. Leslie sighed. She would love to have the money to support a white habit and the time to hang out with the gang at Gold's under the supervision of a personal trainer at $40 per hour. Maybe in her next life.

She turned to Nick and her expression mellowed. His gaze was fixed on the clay figure as though he were sculpting it with his eyes, so consumed by his creative muse that he was oblivious to the real world. To Leslie he was the perfect man, an amalgam of masculine strength and feminine sensitivity, contained in a body that both excited her and aroused a maternal instinct. But most of all, she was awed by his talent. Everything he looked at turned into art. She knew the ecstasy of having him bestow his attention on her, and was convinced that she had become more beautiful under his immaculate eye.

"Why do you wear your hair so long? You have such a beautiful neck," he had said. And she'd gone into the Hair Gallery that evening for a drastic asymmetrical cut she'd loved instantly. When he'd told her the spike-heeled shoes she wore distorted the proportions of her body, she'd invested in six pairs of flats and found that all her clothes looked better. And she'd started wearing black when he'd told her it brought out the luster of her skin. The luster of her skin. How many men would notice a detail like that?

"Nick?" Leslie whispered, not wanting to startle him, but aware that it was her job to keep him grounded. After all, the people from *Art Scene* were waiting. He didn't respond.

"Nick," she repeated, louder this time, touching his shoulder.

He whirled to face her, distracted and angry, then softened when he saw it was her. She responded like a puppy, wriggling with gladness, basking in the spotlight of his attention.

"The reporter and photographer from *Art Scene* are here."

"I thought that was next week."

"I reminded you yesterday," she scolded gently. "That's why I put out the clean shirt for you to wear."

They both looked down at the shirt he was wearing. It was beautifully pressed but already sporting a streak of clay across the chest. Nick's mouth widened into the goofy little boy grin he used to get on a woman's good side. It always worked with Leslie. She picked up a rag and dabbed at the shirt, successfully replacing most of the clay with a large wet spot.

"What're their names?" Nick asked.

"The reporter's Zelda, and the photographer is some guy named Pablo, I think. Are you ready for them?"

Both Nick and Leslie glanced at Julia. Her perfect breasts swayed voluptuously, and the rest of her lithe body followed as she swung around to face them, still wrapped up in her music.

"Yeah, bring 'em on."

Leslie nodded and trotted back to her office.

Nick turned back to the clay. He was restless. The work was not going well. The Figure had no heart, it was just a cold, sterile shell. He looked at his tools: a small, dull riffler, a flat-edged chisel, scrapers, etching whistlers and needles, and finally selected his favorite, the fettling knife. He hefted it like a dagger, flipping it from hand to hand. He looked at the emerging sculpture, then past it to an abstract target drawn on the wall fifteen feet away. He raised the knife, aimed, and threw it. It whizzed past the statue and stabbed the target dead center, twanging with the impact.

Julia removed her headphones. "Goddamn it. I thought we were going to work."

"Today, this is how I work."

"Fine." Julia stepped off the platform and picked up her robe.

"Where are you going?" Nick asked, the exasperation clear in his voice.

"Today, this is how *I* work."

"Julia, *Art Scene* is here to photograph us," he said, an appeal to her vanity.

"Why don't you do your Jim Bowie routine for them?"

"Julia!"

"Go suck a big one, hon. I'm through for today."

Nick grabbed her arm. "Hey, you split now, you don't come back."

"Oh yeah? How do you expect to finish without me? It takes two, remember? Just like fucking." She jerked her arm free and stared defiantly at Nick, both of them oblivious to Leslie, Zelda, and Pablo, who were winding their way through the studio.

"How will I finish it? Like this," Nick replied.

Savagely, he ripped the knife from the wall, and with a sweep of his arm sliced the support line which held the head of the clay figure taut to its brace. Then, using both hands, he shoved it to the floor. It landed with a sickening thud, face down. Nick nudged the clay with his foot, turning it so that the smashed face stared up at him. "It's finished," he said. And then he gave it a brutal kick in the mid-section, his heavy boot leaving a painful cavity in the bosom.

Julia reacted as though he'd kicked her. "You are a maniac!" she screamed. "A fucking maniac!" She threw herself on him, clawing at his chest, her nudity making a parody of her vicious attack. Attila leapt to his feet barking wildly, straining against the chain which kept him tethered.

"Why don't we wait in the office?" Leslie suggested, trying to shield Nick and Julia from Pablo's camera.

"Are you serious?" Zelda replied. "This is cover material. Pablo, get a picture of the statue, right where he kicked it."

THAT EVENING NICK SAT slumped against the wall in the darkened studio smoking a joint, reflecting on the Figure, still lying like a mangled corpse on the cement floor. He took a dry suck on the roach and looked around for a match to relight it. He wasn't in the mood for a party.

Evenings at Con Uttrell's were usually a lavish mélange of Hollywood stars, art world talents, and business leaders. It was a sign of status to be invited, and the first few times Nick had attended the convocation, he'd been excited to be included.

But eventually attendance had become an obligation. Predictably, he would resort to excesses of drink and drugs to get through the night, and the next day would be clouded in a fragmented haze of the who, what and when of the night before. But Con Uttrell was an important arbiter of talent. He could make or break a career, and Nick couldn't afford to offend him, especially if his finances were in the mess Leslie kept telling him they were. To decline the invitation would be to slap fame in the face. Although Nick knew that someday he would do just that, for now, as much as he hated it, he had to bow his head and endure the social indignity of jumping at Uttrell's command.

Nick sighed and got up to shower and dress. His living area — a bedroom and a bathroom connected by a hallway to the north end of the studio — housed a bed, a table, four derelict chairs, a small refrigerator and a microwave. It was hardly the lap of luxury, but Nick couldn't have cared less.

His personal demands were simple: food, shelter, warmth, and sometimes companionship. He didn't need or want creature comforts and was not impressed by wealth. As far as he was concerned, the only thing money could buy was freedom, the freedom to do his work.

Nick stripped off his work clothes, leaving them in a dirty heap. Then he stepped into the shower. Julia's armory of expensive bath products had disappeared, and there was a new bottle of shampoo, something herbal, with no animal by-products, he read off the label. Leslie's work, no doubt; she had tactfully erased all traces of Julia.

Julia. Why was he so unlucky in his choice of women? As usual he had thrown himself into a relationship with her with explosive passion and mind-numbing absorption. He had been entranced by her beautiful body, revelling in the way she animated it with erotic heat. To look at her and to touch her was to summon the muse.

At the beginning they had hidden out in his bedroom for days at a time. He had explored every inch of her, his hands memorizing the nuances which he would later translate into clay. But something had gone wrong in the process, some vital synapse had broken. The muse had withdrawn, not suddenly, but in gradual increments, so that he didn't miss it until it was gone and the clay figure was left spiritless and inert. As beautiful as it was, and as perfect a likeness of Julia, it simply refused to come alive under his touch.

So eventually he had lost heart. And then everything had started to go sour. He had become resentful of the time the relationship took from his art, disinterested in sex. Julia had retaliated by making demands, expecting more from him than he was willing or able to give, until finally, as always, he'd exploded.

It had happened a dozen times before. Usually the whole drama played itself out in a matter of weeks or months. Julia had lasted longer than most, but he'd known the end was coming; he'd just been waiting for it to arrive. And now it had.

He let the water cascade over him, drowning the thought of her, and bringing to mind the young girl who had fallen into the pond at the Thorntons. The memory stirred inside of him, a tingling sensation, a sense of renewal. He recognized the feeling, it was a manifestation of his creative fire, sparked by a new muse. Who was she? What would it be like to sculpt so young a model?

He raised his face to the nozzle and felt the water pound against his eyes. It was impossible. He didn't even know her name. And even if he could get it from Thornton, how would he ever convince her parents to allow her to pose for him?

Ah, but it was such an enticing thought. It excited him just to imagine how he would translate her young body into bronze. She was beautiful, but it was more than that. All the women he allowed into his life were beautiful. But they often had nothing else to recommend them. Once one of his friends had commented that Nick's women were merely walking photographs, nice to look at, but having no more depth than a piece of glossy paper. It hadn't bothered Nick then. He was, after all, a visual artist. It hadn't occurred to him that beauty should have to justify its existence in any other way.

But after seeing the girl, how her spirit shone through her movement and her shy smile, he realized he was seeing a deeper beauty, one that wasn't just physical. That had been the problem with Julia. When he'd tried to plumb the depths of her soul, he'd found her to be as shallow as a wading pond. And it had shown in his work.

Today the reporter from *Art Scene* had asked him if his art wasn't really about his search for love and the ideal woman. His response had been characteristically brusque. "My work isn't *about* anything. It just is."

But thinking about it now, he knew that the reporter had been right. He was looking for something, something to fill a void inside himself. He threw himself into his work with each new model, be-lieving in his heart that she was the one who would provide the synergy between his talent and the rest of his life. It's just that he'd never called that feeling love.

And Julia certainly hadn't been the ideal woman.

Walking out of the studio, he passed through Leslie's office and saw the pink phone message she had tacked on the wall by the door. He pulled it loose and held it up to the light.

"Mrs. Charlotte Hartman $$$, mother of girl in pond at Thorntons ??? Call about commission. 818-555-2505."

He smiled. If that wasn't fate lending a helping hand, he didn't know what was. She was the next one. She had to be. He thought about smoking another joint to celebrate, but decided against it. At Con Uttrell's parties, it was always best to keep your wits about you.

SIX

CON STOOD at the top of the stairs surveying the room full of guests. He had, in part, built his reputation on these extravaganzas, but that didn't mean he enjoyed them. Like almost everything else in his life, they were machinations staged to increase his wealth and power. And like almost everything else, they succeeded brilliantly.

No matter what the media reported about belt tightening and the restraint of the '90s, Con knew that his guests relished the opportunity to indulge in gratuitous excess, a chance to deny the reality of a recessionary economy, AIDS, and dwindling natural resources. In the fantasy world Con created, people still wore fur, ate meat, engaged in illicit sex acts, and abused their bodies with drugs and/or alcohol. And they loved every minute of it.

Tonight Con himself abstained. He had other things on his mind. He circulated through the living room politely avoiding contact with any of the revelers, but making sure everyone was well taken care of.

Although the house was tastefully and expensively furnished

with contemporary designs from Knoll and Donghia, it contained little art, no paintings or sculpture, only a few scattered decorative pieces — a lifesize rhinoceros made of leather, and a white marble chess set on a black marble table. If a guest questioned Con, wondering if it weren't unusual for an art dealer to own so little fine art he would reply, "I don't have a collection for the same reason I never married — my tastes are too varied to make a commitment to any one thing." It wasn't the truth. He had plenty of art. But, like Thornton, he kept it for himself.

He walked through the sliding glass doors that opened onto an enormous balcony cantilevered over a pool, which itself was cantilevered over the dimpled hills. Beyond, and as far as the eye could see, the lights of the city shimmered, a panoply of stars. He'd paid a fortune for this house, a masterpiece of architecture designed by John Lautner, all curves of poured concrete with burnished Brazilian mahogany detailing. The spacious living room lent itself well to his extravaganzas. Better yet, the secluded canyon location — a deterrent to some prospective buyers who still had nightmares about the Charles Manson murders of the Seventies, which had occurred in a similar sort of mid-Beverly Hills isolation — was a plus to Con, who preferred to distance himself from prying eyes. He installed a monstrous gate at the foot of the narrow quarter-mile private drive that led up to the house, and at parties stationed the valet parkers there, offering a shuttle to the house.

This allowed him to screen his guests in advance of their arrival. A security guard at the gate carried a walkie talkie whose mate was permanently attached to the belt of Con's current assistant, Bryant Norris. So if one of the great unwashed, the press, or, God forbid, some law enforcement agent, tried to crash the party, Bryant would get the call several minutes before the visitor arrived, in enough time to advise Con.

As Con watched the shuttle wind its way up the drive, his mind considered the problem of transporting the Michelangelo Giant out of the country. In itself it was not insurmountable; he'd often moved illicit art pieces from one country to another. What disturbed Con was the knowledge that he was not calling the shots. He did not know Francis Thornton well, but well enough to be wary of his unspoken motives.

First, why did Thornton want to send the sculpture to Japan? The obvious answer was that he was selling it to some outrageously wealthy Asian. But Con doubted that this was the case. Thornton himself was outrageously wealthy. He wasn't going to jeopardize his reputation for a few paltry millions. Con knew that the statute of limitations on art theft in Japan was only two years. After that, a piece of stolen art could be legally purchased by a third party. Perhaps Thornton had arranged for the Giant to be held by an intermediary from whom he would, in time, regain ownership.

But why go to all that trouble to legalize his ownership? If he wanted to keep it for himself, he had it already; if he wanted to sell it for profit, he could do that now without the paperwork. No, it wasn't about money. He must have another reason for wanting the Giant shipped to Japan.

Con looked at the city lights undulating beneath him. From his vantage point he could make out the Sanwa Building and Sony Pictures, the old MGM studios. Despite the worldwide recession and the recent decline in the Nikkei Index, Japanese conglomerates seemed to own half of California, and they were still buying. Jesus, they had so damn much money already, what more could they want?

Then it dawned on him. What did people want when mere wealth was no longer an enticement? They wanted status, to own something no one else had, such as a priceless work of art. Perhaps

Thornton was using the Michelangelo as a bargaining chip in a business transaction, offering the prestige of its ownership to cement a relationship which could be translated into millions or billions in future profits. Think of the fellow who was awarded the franchise rights to Toyota in North America or Mercedes Benz in Saudi Arabia. Somebody handed out those prizes. And that somebody must be above mere wealth.

The more Con thought about this, the more sense it made and the more uneasy he became. It was one thing to deal with two-bit thieves and black market fences, and quite another to get in the middle of a billion dollar deal. But what choice did he have? If he refused Thornton or failed to get the job done, Thornton would destroy him.

At this moment Bryant appeared, walkie talkie fused to his hand. "Excuse me, Mr. Uttrell, Nick Stone is on his way up."

Con shook himself back to reality. "Take him to my office. I'll be there shortly. Anything else I should know?"

"Fiona and Inez are looking for you. They've got a new girl — one of their cousins from Oslo — they want you to meet. She's some kind of chess freak. And Suzanna's here with Barry."

"I don't want him doing any crack."

"I know. I already told her. She says he's clean tonight."

"And Roman Polanski writes nursery rhymes," Con snapped sarcastically. "Keep an eye on him."

"Yes, sir."

Ten minutes later Con pried himself loose from the cousin from Oslo, and hurried down the outside stairs to his office. He didn't see the girl pick up a marble chessman, wrap it in a handkerchief, and put it in her pocket. Nor did he know that she'd been promised $100 to steal one of the pieces, $200 if she made sure it had Con Uttrell's fingerprints on it.

Con's office had its own entrance beneath the main house, off the pool patio. Previous owners of the house had used this space for storage because it had no windows. But Con had immediately seen the benefit of having his office completely detached from the house. He rapped twice and the door swung open. Con nodded his greeting to Rocco, the latest in a long line of bodyguard/butler/chauffeurs, and entered.

The room was well-appointed, and like the rest of the house, contained no art. The only remarkable feature was a huge glass terrarium which stretched across most of one wall. In it, a large grey snake patterned with black-edged diamonds oozed across a patch of sand toward a helpless mouse.

Con joined Nick Stone beside the enclosure and watched the snake slither toward its prey with a nonchalance that illustrated the cynicism of nature. At first the mouse was blithely unaware that its brief life was about to end. It rooted through the sawdust and branches, sitting back on its tiny haunches to nibble at a morsel of cheese, the picture of contentment. But an awareness of danger fell over it like a shadow, and when the mouse turned and saw the snake, now only a foot away, it panicked and tried to escape. Tiny claws scratched desperately on the tempered glass. Razor-sharp teeth gnawed at the metal cornerpiece that held the front and side glass panels at right angles. When these pathetic attempts failed, the mouse darted for shelter beneath a small branch and hovered there, pathetically obvious and vulnerable. Although it had the mouse completely at its mercy, the snake did not strike. Instead it waited in sinister patience, prolonging the poor creature's agony.

"He's a pit viper, sub-species fer-de-lance. Very venomous, deadly in fact. A killer by instinct." Con's tone was respectful. "But as you see," he continued, "I have trained him not to strike until I give the command."

"What good does that do?" These were the first words Nick had spoken.

"It is always important to be the one in control, my dear Nicholas. Now, watch."

Con blew sharply on a small silver whistle and instantly the snake struck at the mouse. Then its jaws unhinged and its mouth yawned obscenely open, like a cartoon character who manipulates his anatomy to fit the needs of the situation. It devoured the mouse in one swallow.

Con and Nick watched the bulge which was once the mouse travel slowly down the length of the snake. "He is so well motivated by this whistle that I can make him defy his instincts and strike at any object, even if it is not edible. Watch."

Con opened a door in the glass and threw a silver dollar into the enclosure. The snake's head whipped around to the sound of it falling, and then with surprising agility heaved its bulk so it was positioned in front of the shiny metal. Once again, Con blew the whistle and the snake reacted, easily closing its lipless jaws around the coin, creating a second, smaller bulge which slowly followed the mouse down its intestinal tract.

"Can he digest that?" asked Nick.

"I suppose not," Con replied, "which makes him an unusual sort of piggy bank." Opening a low, locked drawer in his desk, he withdrew a silver-capped vial of rock cocaine. "Refreshments?"

"Not that," Nick replied. "But I'll take a brandy."

Dropping the vial back into the drawer, Con moved to the bar to pour two brandies. He handed one to Nick and cradled the other in his own hands as he settled into the crocodile chair which was his throne.

"I have a proposition for you, one which I trust you will find advantageous."

Nick looked at Con squarely. "If it's to my benefit, why all this snake and mouse crap?"

"Merely to remind you how the world operates."

"Meaning that even if this 'proposition' or whatever you want to call it isn't in my best interest, I have no choice but to go along with it?"

Con smiled, pleased at the way Nick was playing into his hands. "But since it *is* in your best interest, I'm sure you will want to co-operate."

"I'll decide that," Nick replied.

"Very well." Con paused, taking a sip of his brandy. Then he spoke in carefully modulated tones. "I have a client, a foreign collector, who has expressed a desire to purchase a piece of your art for his collection."

"Who is it?" Nick asked.

Con had anticipated this question and had a ready answer. "He prefers to remain anonymous. You see, he is very well known, and fears his reputation would be inhibiting to a young artist."

"I'm not that young."

"In the international marketplace, you are indeed a babe in arms," Con said, relishing the opportunity to deflate Nick's ego. "The man is eccentric, to be sure, but he has one of the finest private collections in the world. And for some reason, he wants a piece of your work. You should be flattered."

"I would be if I didn't think there was some sort of a catch involved." Nick considered for a moment. "What does he want?"

"A bronze statue. One of your female figures. At least four feet above the base, with a width of fourteen inches."

"Sorry. We seem to be out of that size. Perhaps you could interest him in something smaller," Nick snapped, outraged that a sophisticated patron would be so exacting. This request sounded more like it had come from an 'I need a blue painting to go with my wallpaper' kind of a person.

Con ignored the sarcasm. "We discussed a six-digit sum."

"Does that mean $100,000 or $999,000?"

Con smiled. "Do you think your work is worth a million dollars?"

"It's worth whatever some asshole is willing to pay for it," Nick responded.

"He's willing to pay $150,000, which is, I am aware, more than double what your most recent work fetched on the open market."

"But this isn't the open market," Nick persisted.

"I didn't realize you were in a financial position to turn down a commission of $150,000," Con said, purposely repeating the figure for emphasis.

Nick wasn't, but he wondered how Con Uttrell knew it.

"How much of that do you take?"

A smile oozed out of Con's mouth and he shrugged. "One-third. A very reasonable fee."

"Not bad for a fifteen-minute meeting," Nick said.

"One of the benefits of having my connections," Con replied, taking another sip of his brandy. "There is one stipulation. Timing. I need to deliver the piece to him in one month, thirty days."

"But that's impossible. Bronze takes time. I can't work that fast. I don't even have a model right now."

"What happened to Julia Richaud? I was told you were completing a statue of her."

Nick shook his head. "Not any more. I killed it this morning. I'd have to start from scratch."

Con frowned. The whole scenario was predicated on the fact that he'd heard Nick had a statue already in the works, near completion. This setback would definitely slow things down. But he'd already set the ball in motion. He couldn't withdraw the offer now without arousing Nick's suspicion.

"Well, then, get yourself another model. Fast."

"It's not that easy."

"Of course it is." Con snapped his fingers and Rocco handed him an envelope, which Con, in turn, handed to Nick.

"Nicholas, here is the first five thousand. Buy one."

SEVEN

TORY HELD HER BREATH as she watched Brad McMurphy study the photos she'd taken of him for her class project.

"These are totally awesome," he said at last. "You're good."

"No way," Tory beamed, thrilled but embarrassed by the compliment. "Anyway, thanks for posing. You've got a great bod," she said, audibly stroking it.

Brad grinned and tore his eyes away from the photos to look at her. "Yeah?" he asked.

"Definitely." She thought about the bulging muscles of his torso and his lean, hard legs, the first male body she'd seen up close, close enough to touch. But she couldn't imagine touching him! She had been grateful to hide behind the camera lens and just look without appearing obvious.

Then she flushed, remembering that other muscle, the one Brad had kept straight-jacketed in a jock strap during the shoot. She'd wondered whether it had hurt it to be smashed and stuffed into the strict elastic of the jock, or whether it had been comforting to Brad to have his ego pressed so tight against him. Her thoughts had been a confusing jumble and Brad's sexuality a mystery only hinted at by the black curls of pubic hair which had escaped from the jock when he stretched his torso.

And then it had started to move! She'd tried not to stare, but she'd been positive she'd seen a twitch, and then the elastic material of the jock started to expand, like a magic trick.

And that's when her mother had burst in, spoiling everything.

As though he could read her thoughts, Brad leaned back on his Jeep, tilting his pelvis toward her, taunting her with the bulge in his skin-tight bicycle shorts. He raised his hand toward her breast and Tory drew in a throaty gasp which sounded to her own ears like her heart shouting "yes, yes!" But he was only reaching for the camera. She had forgotten it, hanging around her neck as justification of her story that her only interest in him was as a subject for her photography. Brad held it in both hands, running his thumbs back and forth over the lens. Tory knew that his oily fingerprints would be difficult to clean off the glass, but she was mesmerized by his rhythmic strokes, as though he were caressing her body instead of the molded plastic camera case.

"Maybe we could have another session some day," Brad said, "do some close ups." He pushed the button which activated the zoom, and the lens became tumescent. "Oops," he said, grinning.

Tory's body burst into flames. "My mom would kill me," she blurted out, immediately hating herself for sounding so infantile.

"We could do it at my house," Brad pressed, tugging gently on the camera strap to pull her closer.

Their bodies were almost touching. Tory's mind raced ahead, imagining Brad's lips on hers, his hands reaching under her skirt and tearing off her panties and then, at last, relieving her of the humiliating burden of being the oldest living virgin at the Westridge Day School.

"My mom works nights and my dad's never home," he whispered in her ear. Tory could smell the liquor of Gatorade on his breath, and she was thinking she would forever consider that odor an aphrodisiac, when Brad continued, "Maybe you could get some shots of me and Lauren together, know what I mean?"

Lauren. She had completely forgotten about Lauren, and she'd assumed Brad had too. Brilliant, Tory — he doesn't even know you exist! Devastated, she took the camera out of Brad's hands and let it thump against her chest.

"Look, I've got to go. Biology test tomorrow." She stepped away. "You can keep those; they're extra," she added, motioning nonchalantly to the photos in his hand, although it had cost her two weeks' lunch money to have them developed, enlarged, and reprinted.

"Thanks. Hey, but I mean it. Any day after practice. Lauren's through with cheerleading at five."

"Yeah, I'll think about it."

"I'll even pop for the film," Brad called after her.

But Tory was already running into the house, slamming the door behind her. How gullible could she be! Brad McMurphy interested in her? That's a laugh. But she felt more like crying. She was leaning against the door trying not to when the maid appeared.

"Missy Tory, why're you slammin' the door like that?"

"Sorry, Radiance," said Tory. She ducked her head to avoid having to look the maid in the eye and came face to face with the long crepey line of cleavage that seemed to start at Radiance's Adam's apple and plummet into her uniform, probably all the way to her navel. Gross, but probably better than having no cleavage at all, Tory thought.

"Where's Mother?"

"She's out back in the lath house with her midget trees. You don't be botherin' her now; she's expecting company."

Radiance and Tory always called Charlotte's bonsai collection her 'midget trees,' and winked at each other when they did because it drove Charlotte crazy.

"I won't. I'm going to go for a swim," Tory replied. Maybe she could work off some of the pent up frustration left in the wake of Brad's visit *and* build up her bustline. "Do you know where my suit is?"

"On the deck chair where you left it last week," Radiance said. She was pretending to be angry, but Tory saw the indulgent smile in her eyes and knew she wasn't. She gave the maid a hug and headed for the pool.

CHARLOTTE EYED the tiny red maple with satisfaction. Every branch was wired at just the right angle, every leaf standing in perfect symmetry. If she'd bothered to think about it, she would have realized that she had turned to pruning the dwarf trees, stunting their growth and forcing their branches into stylized patterns of her own design, at just the time four years ago when it had become clear she would never be able to mold Tory into a clone of herself. Even at thirteen, Tory had outweighed Charlotte by fifteen pounds. She had shown no innate tendancy towards the poise and grace Charlotte felt were her own best qualities. And she was distinctly unwilling to be the dutiful daughter Charlotte wanted her to be.

So, unconsciously Charlotte had rechanneled her energy into the miniature trees, which either responded to her machinations and matured into her vision of them, or died. Not that she hadn't kept trying with Tory. But at least with the bonsai she had a fighting chance. And they provided her with an artistic outlet.

That's why she had decided it would be most appropriate for Nicholas Stone to meet her here to discuss the commission she was going to propose to him. Here, he could see her surrounded by the product of her own artistry. And the lath's scrim, which blocked the sun, would also provide cover from Radiance's prying eyes.

Besides, she wanted him to agree to the commission before he saw the inside of the house and the rest of her art collection, such as it was.

She'd grown up in the old Victorian and later it had been her inheritance from her parents — she and Arthur would never have been able to afford to live in such grandeur otherwise. As it was, every penny of Arthur's salary went towards maintenance — of the house, the grounds, and appearances. Rarely was anything left over for art.

Nevertheless, she already knew where she would enshrine a statue by Nicholas Stone — in the foyer. There, it would be the first thing guests saw when they entered the house, setting the tone, coloring the atmosphere with the patina of good taste. But that was only a minor part of her reason for calling Nicholas and inviting him to come to Westridge.

The main part was the way he had looked at her when they'd been introduced — after Tory's fiasco at the Thorntons. That had been what made her pick up the phone. His eyes had inspired romantic fantasies which had been smoldering inside her ever since. Oh, Arthur was a fine and faithful husband, and she would never stray too far from her marriage bed. But every once in a while she needed a flirtation to reaffirm her desirability, to make her feel alive. Thinking about Nicholas Stone certainly made her pulse race. She'd lain awake all night imagining how arousing it would be to model for him, to be his muse, his lover . . .

Listen to me, she giggled. I sound like something out of Danielle Steele.

An instinct alerted her, and she pulled the scrim aside, squinting toward the house. A blurred shape was crossing the lawn. Was it Nick Stone or the gardener? She slipped on her glasses and saw that it was Nick.

She had just enough time to remove the glasses and give her hair a quick pat before he pulled back the scrim, ducking slightly to enter under the bar that held it.

"Mrs. Hartman?" he asked uncertainly.

"Charlotte, please," said Charlotte, extending her hand.

"Nick." He said, and took the hand, not so much shaking as consuming it. Charlotte savored the strength of his grasp and the erotic contrast between the callouses on his palm and the velvet softness of the back of his hand. She didn't want to let go, but decorum dictated that she must. After all, he had only just arrived.

"I hope you don't mind if I just finish up a few things here," she said.

"No problem." Nick settled on a bench and picked up the tree closest to him. "You make this?"

"Only God can make a tree," Charlotte replied automatically, the flippant response she always gave when someone asked her about her bonsais. "But I do love having my way with them," she said gaily. He cocked his head to one side as if to be sure the double entendre was intentional.

It wasn't. To cover her embarrassment, she picked up a young evergreen, as yet untrained, and jerked it roughly from the soil. The limp, white roots dangled like flaccid appendages, knots of dark, damp soil clinging to them. With a snip of her shears Charlotte castrated them to a uniform length.

Nick winced. "Doesn't that kill the tree?"

"Not at all," Charlotte replied. "I trim the roots to inhibit the growth, then I wire the limbs. That way I can train the tree to grow any way I want." She smiled at Nick, artist to artist. "The same way you create your statues, molding the clay into the shape you want."

"Only the clay isn't alive," Nick pointed out, staring at the tree. "I would never presume to improve on nature." He ran his hands lightly over the feathery branch tip of the small evergreen, letting the immature pine needles tickle his skin.

Charlotte sensed disapproval in Nick's tone and answered quickly, "I didn't mean that I'm trying to improve on nature. It's more that I'm trying to release the true essence of 'tree'. An idealized version of the original. Wouldn't you say that's what you do with your models?" "Release *my* true essence," she begged him silently.

"No. My goal is to make my figures as realistic as possible," he said, answering her spoken question instead of the plea she was making in body language. "What I try to do is make a likeness, perfectly copying the original in every detail, to capture the spirit, flaws and all, to preserve my vision of the figure at that moment in time. Forever."

"That is truly inspiring," Charlotte said, wishing her own beauty had been frozen in time, before age had begun to extact its toll.

"Mrs. Hartman . . ."

"Charlotte, please."

"Charlotte. My secretary said you wanted to talk to me about a commission . . ."

Charlotte would have preferred another few minutes of foreplay. But now, figuratively speaking, he'd leapt into bed, and she had no choice but to join him there. "Yes, you see our collection, right now it's modest, but piece by piece . . . and to have one of your statues would be . . . of course they must be frightfully expensive, but a small one . . . I'm sure I can convince my husband . . . he's not an artiste like you and me, but when I explain to him what a good investment . . . anyway I do have a bit of inheritance from my father tucked away, enough for you to get started if you can, if I can . . ."

Charlotte knew she was blathering like an idiot, but there was something about the way he was staring at her. Was it possible that despite the difference in their ages he could see her beauty? That he was attracted to her? She preened before him, feeling a warm light surround her body.

"I will make a statue for you on one condition. If I can use your daughter as my model."

"Victoria?" She couldn't have heard him correctly.

"I didn't know her name," he said. "Victoria." He let the word rest on his tongue.

Charlotte felt as though she'd been slapped in the face. "You want my daughter to pose for you?"

Nick nodded.

"But she is so young and . . . unformed." "What about me?" her heart cried.

"I know. That's why. That's the quality I want to capture. Since the party at the Thorntons', she's constantly been in my head. There's so much beneath her surface, so much beauty shining from the inside. It hasn't awakened yet, but it's in there. I can see it. And somehow she's even more beautiful because her loveliness is still untapped."

Charlotte was amazed at the transformation that came over Nick as he described her daughter. His eyes were fixed on the little evergreen tree, but she could tell he was not seeing it; he was seeing Tory. His hands played over the branches of the tree with such sensitivity that Charlotte blushed, imagining them stroking her own skin, or, God forbid, Tory's. "She's only a child!" she blurted out.

"How could you think I would let her pose for you in the nude!" She drew back, embarrassed by her outburst.

Nick seemed unfazed. "I understand your concern, Charlotte, but I can assure you there's never been any trouble with any of my models. This is my work. I take it very seriously."

"Please don't think I was questioning your motives," Charlotte said defensively. "It's just that Tory is so young for her age. She's terribly shy of her body, and I'm certain she would be horrified at the prospect of letting you or anyone . . ."

"I'm making a one-of-a kind piece for an important foreign collector and I need to start immediately, so I'd like to make you an offer. Of course I will pay Tory, but if you'll give her permission to pose for me, I'll also give you and your husband my artist's proof."

"Artist's proof?" asked Charlotte.

"The sample casting of the statue. I usually keep them for myself, but in this case I'll make an exception. You said on the phone you were interested in buying a piece of my work. I will give you this for free, a portrait of your daughter, as beautiful and untouched as she is right now."

"I just don't know," said Charlotte, the word 'free' ringing in her ears. She had never dreamed of having a full-size bronze statue of Nicholas Stone's because she knew the cost to be prohibitive. But how could Arthur object if he didn't have to pay one cent? Of course he might be uncomfortable at the thought of Tory posing for this man in the nude, but she was certain she could convince him, in the name of art, his beloved daughter, immortalized in bronze!

Nick went on, "I usually do editions of six or ten when I make a full-sized piece. But there will only be two of these. The collector's and the proof, yours. So it will be that much more valuable."

"I can see that it would. But I'm sure Tory would refuse," she said with disappointment.

"Could I talk to her?" Nick asked. "I don't want to push you," he continued over Charlotte's silence, "but I'd need to start immediately."

"Well, I suppose it wouldn't hurt for you to just feel her out — I mean that figuratively, of course," Charlotte blushed.

"Of course," Nick replied, and he smiled.

TORY WAS BREATHING HARD, as she swam the last lap. Only five circuits and she was pooped. She hated her body for its weakness. No wonder Brad McMurphy looked right through her. Maybe she should take steroids, build up some muscles. But no, hadn't she read that steroids made you more masculine? That'd be just what she needed.

When her hand finally touched the tiled lip of the pool she stopped kicking and floated, allowing her body to undulate with the gentle lapping of the water, a human lily pad.

"Hey!" a male voice rippled through the water.

Tory raised her head and through the blur of chlorine saw a man leaning against the diving board. It took her a moment to catch her breath and recognize him — the artist from the party! How dare he watch her float like an inflatable raft! She didn't know if she was more furious at him for appearing unannounced to spy on her, or at herself for getting caught looking like a whale.

"What are you doing here?" she asked, clinging to the edge with both hands, feeling uncomfortably wet and foolish.

Nick towered over her. She had to crane her neck and squint upward to see his face. "I came to talk to you," he said, and reached out a hand to help her from the water. "Haven't we already played this scene?" His eyes twinkled.

Tory pushed away from the edge and floated into the center of the pool. She would have loved to get out of the water, but no way was she going to let him see her in her ratty old bathing suit. "You didn't answer my question," she said, treading water.

"Well, I'm here for two reasons, actually," he said, squatting down so that he was closer to her. "First, your mom called me and asked me to come."

"What for?"

"She wants to buy a piece of my sculpture."

"She didn't tell me about it," said Tory, although she knew she would be the last person Charlotte would tell about an art purchase.

"I only talked to her this morning. You were probably in school."

Tory paddled in silence for a moment, hoping she wouldn't die of exhaustion before this conversation was over. "What's the second reason?"

"I wanted to see you," Nick said simply.

"Me?" She was incredulous. "What for?"

Nick smiled at her the way he had at the party, not as an adult to a child, but as a man to a woman. "Couldn't we talk better if you got out of the pool? You must be getting tired."

Tory weighed her options. She was exhausted and she couldn't go on paddling forever. But to let him see her like this! Again he seemed to read her mind. He picked the towel up off the lounge and held it out to her.

Tory swam to the side and hauled herself out of the pool, using one hand on the ladder and the other to grab the towel and wrap it around her body.

"So, what did you want to see me about?"

"I wanted to give you this." He held out a crumpled brown paper bag. "Sorry about the gift wrapping."

Tory was leery, but curiosity won out. She anchored the towel under her armpits and took the bag, and from it withdrew a camera lens. She examined it, holding it gingerly away from her body as though it were radioactive.

"It's a bifocal zoom. I thought it might come in handy next time you want to shoot portraits of swans."

"Awesome!" She'd never even heard of a bifocal zoom, but it sounded very professional, and very expensive. But she knew she couldn't accept it, knew instinctively that presents as costly as this came with ulterior expectations attached.

Finally, reluctantly, she held it out to him. "Thanks, but I can't take it."

"Why not?"

"My parents told me never to accept gifts from strangers."

"Don't think of it as a gift; think of it as an apology."

"For what?"

"For letting you fall in the pond at the party."

"It wasn't your fault. I slipped."

"Yeah, but I distracted you." He looked at her for a moment. "And don't think of me as a stranger. After all, how many men have seen you soaking wet?" He gave her that smile again.

Tory blushed furiously. "I can't take it, really," she insisted. Since he wouldn't take the lens from her, she set it down on the table.

"Come on, how are you going to win that contest without the right equipment?"

Tory snorted with contempt. "Even if I did win, my parents

would never give me the money for the plane ticket. I'm a prisoner here, or couldn't you tell?"

"Pay for the trip yourself."

"Yeah, right, with what, Monopoly money? The airfare is over a thousand dollars.

Nick shrugged. "I'll pay you twice that if you'll pose for me." He waited to let this sink in. "I want to make a statue of you."

"Right."

"I mean it." She watched his mouth move; the magical twist of his lips somehow made her feel hot and cold at the same time. "Do you think I'd drive all the way to West-fucking-ridge just to talk to Charlotte?" he asked.

Tory smiled despite herself. She'd never heard anybody use the word "fucking" in the same sentence as her mother's name.

"Since the party I can't get you out of my mind," he continued. "And that's how I know I want to sculpt you. That's always how it starts."

"How what starts?"

"The process. My process. Of creating my art."

Tory drew the towel closer around her. Even though she was out of the water she felt like she was drowning, and she didn't know how to save herself. She only knew that she had to hang onto something or be swept away.

Nick didn't seem to notice. He continued talking, his eyes luminous. "People ask me all the time how I choose my models. And I can never tell them, because I don't know. Something just happens. I'll see a woman, maybe not even up close, maybe just someone at the beach or across the room in a restaurant. And then, hours later, days even, I realize I'm still thinking about that face and that body."

He stopped short, staring so intently at Tory she felt like he was seeing right through the terry cloth of the towel, through her wet saggy bathing suit, even through her skin, to her innermost being. What surprised her was that she didn't feel shy or embarrassed anymore, but incredibly excited by his attention, powerful, and womanly.

But she was no dummy. She knew when he said the word "pose," making it sound as innocent as "stand" or "sit," he was talking about her taking off her clothes. In front of him, in front of the whole world.

No way! She'd be too freaked. And her body was too repulsive. But she couldn't let him know that. She busied herself screwing the new lens onto her camera and took the easy cop-out.

"My mother would never let me do it."

"She already said okay. She said it was up to you."

Suddenly Tory felt like one of those acrobats in the Cirque du Soleil, working without a safety net. Was he rousting her? Charlotte was the Virgin Mary. She'd never allow her to pose in the nude. Or would she? "I don't believe you."

"Ask her," Nick said.

"I'm sure! This is too much. I don't believe it," she sputtered. Then she looked away. "I mean, I'm not exactly Brooke Shields or anything, in case you hadn't noticed."

"If I wanted Brooke Shields, I'd ask Brooke Shields," Nick said. "You're what I want. There's a spirit I want to capture. It's in you. I can't explain it. I can only feel it. I want *you*."

Tory didn't know what to do, where to turn, how to deal with this. So she held up the camera, focused on Nick's face, and took his picture.

EIGHT

PORTRAITURE IS a unique art form, in that it creates a pro-
vocative relationship between artist and model, juxtaposing
the artist's desire to capture the spirit of the model realistically, and
his need to idealize the model physically by imposing his own sen-
sibilities on it. This is particularly true of nudes."

Roz tried to concentrate on what the teacher was saying. But she
was having a hard time tonight. Normally Adrian chose a middle-
aged woman to pose for his "Drawing the Nude" extension class
because, as he explained, the contours of a mature body were more
obvious, easier to capture.

But for tonight's class he had brought in a young man, a very
handsome young man, a graduate of the University of Washington,
who was taking a year off to hitchhike across the United States before settling into his family's salmon fishing business in the North-
west.

Now he stood nude in front of the class, holding a pose which
fully exposed the glory of his anatomy, as well as a small but perfect
tattoo of a snake's head on his left buttock. Roz felt a pang of desire

and let herself fantasize. No Nautilus and Stairmaster for this kid; the constant treadmill of the road and weight of a knapsack had shaped the rippling muscles of his abdomen and his rock-solid thighs. The tattoo aside, he was a living version of Michelangelo's famed marble "David," and was he living!

Roz glanced at the drawings of the students around her. The men on either side seemed to be having trouble depicting the model's genitalia and buttocks, as though they were embarrassed to focus on another man's private parts. Instead of drawing him as he was, they had created caricatures of the boy, variously exaggerating and minimizing body parts, abstracting reality. On the other hand, the woman in front of Roz had drawn a fairly good likeness, but it was lifeless.

Roz returned to her work, letting the visual feast before her guide her hand, translating her emotional response into a pencil sketch. Suddenly she felt the weight of Adrian's presence behind her, and she sat back to look at the sketch through his eyes. With mortification she saw that raw eroticism had seeped into the thin leaden pencil lines. Somehow she had unintentionally invested her sketch with a quality of sexual readiness, and she was sure this was as apparent to Adrian as it was to her.

She reached for the large gum eraser which lived on the right side of the easel, always ready to excise her mistakes, but before she could apply it to the paper, Adrian grasped her hand, holding it captive as he said, "Okay, everybody, time's up for tonight. I'll expect you to have your portfolios of the quarter's work ready for me in two weeks. If anyone has any questions, I'm available for a few minutes now, or by fax or phone in my office tomorrow morning. Thank you."

The other students began to stretch and collect their supplies, chatting loudly to make up for the two hours of silence they had just endured. When Adrian finally released Roz's hand, she felt as though there should be a red scorch mark where he had held it, so intensely had she felt his grip. "Your drawing is very good. What were you going to change?" he asked.

"I dunno," said Roz, knowing she could never explain how embarrassed she was to have her own sexual hunger so obviously recycled into her drawing.

"I think this is the best work you've done," Adrian continued. "You've a tendency to use the eraser to censor your work."

"Isn't that what it's for?"

"To an extent. But it's holding you back."

"I just don't like to make mistakes," said Roz.

"Nothing you can draw is a mistake. Whatever appears on paper is true and incontrovertible." He looked back at her drawing. "You seem to have a natural affinity for the male form."

Completely rattled, Roz blushed and began to gather up her things. She mumbled her thanks and something about having to get home, and started for the door.

"Rosiland, wait," Adrian called after her. "I'm sorry if I embarrassed you," he said. "The fact is you are very talented. All of your work this semester has been good, getting better each week. If you have time, perhaps we could talk about it over coffee some evening."

Roz stared at her Reeboks, thinking how long it had been since a man she was attracted to had asked her out. But now that he had made the overture, she was afraid. Of what? Of bursting the bubble of her infatuation by seeing the real person? Of ultimate rejection?

Or had it just been so long since she'd been with a man (four hundred and eighty-one days since her last relationship had ended, but who was counting?) that she'd lost the knack? It wasn't too late; it couldn't be. All she had to do was look up at him and say, "I have time tonight." And she did.

Two hours later, Roz and Adrian were the only customers left at Eddie's Twenty-Four Hour Diner, a coffee shop within walking distance of the warehouse that served as the headquarters for the Extension Program's art classes.

Roz watched Adrian nurse his bowl of yogurt and berries. The way he ate intrigued her. He seemed to be using the yogurt as an erotic art form. Each bite changed the configuration of the mass, and it was creating these shapes that seemed to be the point — food as art rather than sustenance. If he'd been twenty years younger, Roz would have told him to stop playing with his food. But as the minutes ticked by, she became more and more entranced with his frozen sculpture. The white mass in the bowl now loosely resembled a mini-Matterhorn, or a silicone-enhanced breast. Anyone's in particular, Roz wondered.

Adrian smiled at her. "Tell me about your job," he said, stroking the yogurt with his spoon.

"I work for Century Insurance, investigating art thefts," Roz replied. "I was promoted from auto claims last fall."

"Isn't Century the firm that insured the statue that was stolen from the Getty a few weeks ago, the Michelangelo?"

Roz nodded. "To the tune of about $40,000,000."

"Well you've got your work cut out for you."

"Actually, I don't know who's handling that case. They've been keeping the investigation quiet. Anyway, it's a little out of my league." She told him about the Stein case, her need to retrace the path of the Diebenkorn painting, which was poised to reenter the marketplace through private dealer Con Uttrell. Adrian had heard the name.

"The problem is, Uttrell is so well insulated. I can't get anyone who knows him to talk to me, and I can't get to see him myself. I'm stymied."

Adrian thought a moment, looking at her. "He's an art dealer. What if you approached him as a buyer?"

Roz smiled. "I think you're overestimating my bank account."

"You don't actually have to buy anything, do you? All you have to do is look like you can afford to — the right attitude, the right clothes. You know what I mean."

It was an interesting idea. Roz giggled, trying to imagine David La Salle's reaction if she itemized a shopping spree on Rodeo Drive on her expense report.

"What's so funny?" he asked.

"Nothing," Roz said. "Would you like to see where I live? It isn't far."

"THIS IS MAGICAL, it really is."

Roz and Adrian stood on the bridge which spanned Linnie Canal. Like vaseline on a camera lens, the moonlight softened the view before them, airbrushing out the cracked and buckled walk along the waterway, the murkiness of the water, the homeless man asleep in the bushes. Even the derelict façade of Roz's house took on an aura of rustic charm.

A formation of ducks glided beneath them. "It looks even better from a boat," she mused.

"Do you have one?"

Roz shook her head. "Before. Rick and I . . ." She paused. "It sank with the marriage," she said, remembering the satisfaction it had given her to punch a hole in the dinghy and watch it go down. She looked into the water, imagining Rick's face reflected back at her, and shivered. Taking his cue, Adrian put an arm around her shoulders. Roz found a piece of a cookie in her pocket and threw it into the water, gratified to see the image of Rick fracture and dissolve into a series of ripples.

There was a noise beneath them, a rustling in the weedy brush banking the canal, and then a series of phlegmy coughs.

Adrian tensed. "What was that?"

"Probably one of our local homeless. There's a whole community of them in Venice. Every so often we get one or two living under the bridge."

"Doesn't it scare you?"

"You get used to it. They're part of the local color, kind of like the artists. They don't hurt anyone, and they stay hidden pretty much, because the police will take them in if anybody makes a complaint."

"You should be careful," Adrian warned sternly. "You never know who's going to turn out to be a psychopath."

"You sound just like my ex-husband," Roz said.

Turning the key in the lock of her door, Roz suddenly realized that maybe she should be more careful, bringing a strange man into her home. It was the '90s after all, and like Adrian said, you never knew who was going to turn out to be a psychopath. What if he got violent? What about AIDS? What about modesty?

But the gentle pressure of Adrian's hand on hers helping her to turn the key reassured her. It was not the touch of a homicidal maniac; it was the touch of an artist.

"I hope you're not expecting Versailles," she said brightly, too brightly, a dead giveaway to her nervousness.

"I'm not," he replied, "I'm expecting the Garden of Eden."

His lips on the back of her neck made her feel hot and cool at the same time, an exquisite torture which obliterated her anxiety. It had been way too long since a man had kissed her like that.

She closed her eyes and let her entire consciousness focus on his mouth as it blessed her shoulders and softened the knot of tension at the top of her spine. She could feel his hands pressing her arms against her body, not to restrain her, but to give ballast to the caressing progress of his lips over her body. With each kiss, another shred of resistance dissolved.

Okay, she thought, I'm in your hands. Please be gentle. She closed the door behind him and double bolted it.

Roz had never made love to an artist before. With his attention focused so intensely on her she felt deliciously sexy, even beautiful. She thrilled at the thought that his sure hands, removing her clothing piece by piece, were releasing her essence, the way a sculptor carves marble from a slab to release the art within.

Finally she was naked. Adrian quickly stripped off his own clothes and stood in front of her, nut brown, sleek and strong and lean. And ready for action. She waited for him to join her on the bed, but instead he stood apart in the dark, his erection insinuating itself like a third presence in the room. She was confused. Did he want her to come to him or was he waiting for something to happen? Had he changed his mind? God, it would be much easier if men just let you know what they expected.

Then he took his right hand and grasped the turgid thing, locking a masturbatory grip on it. Maybe this was some sort of performance art, a one-man show, and she was the audience. She began to get the creeps. There was something off about the way he was involved with his own body, leaving her to fend for herself.

Finally, and it was not a minute too soon, he loosened his grip and walked toward the bed, his erection bobbing ahead like the baton of a drum major. The closer he got to Roz, the bigger it seemed, until he, it, was one inch from her nose. If he jammed it into her mouth she swore to herself she'd bite it off. There was a

thin line between consenting sex and date rape when you were unfamiliar with a guy's routine. And she would not be forced to do
anything she didn't want to do. She braced herself for the thrust.

But instead he handed her a condom. "Better if you do it," he
said. "I can't seem to get it on without my glasses."

NINE

C ON WOKE with a start. He had dreamt he was being buried alive, the sensation of being in an airless coffin so real, so terrifying, that it took him a minute to catch his breath and realize that the probable reason for the dream was the fact that of the two bodies in bed with him, one was draped across his abdomen, pressing down on his diaphragm, and the other had flung her arm across his face, virtually blocking the passage of air in and out of his nose.

Con disentangled himself and got up to relieve his bladder, cursing as he stepped on the sequined bra top of one of the girls, strewn along with an assortment of other clothing across the floor of the bedroom. He despised untidiness. The place looked like Frederick's of Hollywood after an earthquake.

He kicked the clothing aside and limped into the bathroom. Maybe he was getting too old for this life. He used to be invigorated by the youthful bodies of the young women who fawned over him. He remembered the times, pre-AIDS, when the bedroom acrobatics would go on for days, three, four girls at a time, satisfying him alone or in pairs. These days they only made him feel every one of his fifty-four years. And his private parties were becoming more and more rare.

Con let himself out the side door and walked down to the pool. He eased himself into the tepid water, enjoying the way it enveloped and soothed him. The irony that he would rather be here, exercising his body in the solitude of his pool rather than in the company of his bedmates, was not lost on him. But he pushed the thought to a far recess of his mind and concentrated on completing his exercise.

No sooner had his hand touched the edge of the pool at the end of the twentieth lap, than Bryant appeared with a steaming pot of coffee, *The Los Angeles Times* and *The Wall Street Journal*, a portable telephone and Con's habitual breakfast of Metamucil mixed in a tall glass of freshly squeezed orange juice and seventeen vitamin pills.

"Any calls?" Con asked.

"Just the office, confirming today's schedule. You've got a meeting with a Caroline Van Patten at eleven-thirty, lunch with Ed Ruscha at Patina at one, and a three o'clock with your accountants. And I got through to Mr. Thornton's secretary. The name of the Customs official you met at his party is Arthur Hartman. Do you want me to set up an appointment?"

"No, I'll call him myself."

On the way to town, Con thought about the Van Patten woman he was due to meet at eleven-thirty. Although he rarely saw strangers, this woman's request had caught his attention.

"I'm looking for a Diebenkorn, something from the Ocean Park series," she had said when she'd called the day before. "I've been told you might be able to help me find one." Emphasis on the word 'find'.

Could it be a coincidence that an unknown woman would inquire about such a painting when only days ago one had come into his possession? In a normal situation, a dealer would relish a call such as this. To be able to turn a painting around in less than a week was miraculous. Sometimes it took years to match a painting with a qualified buyer.

But Con's Diebenkorn had come off the black market. He had purchased it at a bargain price from a pair of professionals who had stolen it six months before. To be safe, he knew he should hold it for at least a year. The more time that elapsed between the theft of a work of art and its reintroduction into the marketplace, the less chance there was of the piece being traced and/or remembered.

But if Con were able to turn this painting around immediately, he would make back his money twenty-fold with no investment of time. And unless he was dreadfully mistaken, the trail to the Diebenkorn was already cold. It was a tempting proposition, but risky. One wanted to be quite sure of one's buyer.

"Yes, I may be able to help you, Miss . . . Van Patten, did you say?

"Yes, Caroline Van Patten."

"I'm sorry. I'm afraid I don't recognize the name. Have we met?" Con had been careful to keep suspicion from his voice. No point in putting this woman off so early in the game. Two hundred thousand was not bad for a week's work, if he could pull it off.

"I'm representing a collector from the East who prefers to remain anonymous," the voice had said. "I can assure you we have the funds available for such a purchase. I can give you the name of our local bank, should you require a reference."

"If you don't mind."

"It's World Security Bank in Beverly Hills. The account is in my name as a signator for HFD, Inc. which is a holding company for a Swiss corporation. Would you like the account number?"

"That won't be necessary," Con had assured her, knowing full

well he could get that information from the bank when he
checked. But he was also aware that tracing the roots of the Swiss
corporation would be difficult since such information was not part
of the public record. This could be suspect, yet many of the biggest
players operated through clandestine shell companies. He had decided to risk it. "Shall we make an appointment then?"

"Yes, please. If it is at all possible, I would like to come in tomorrow, as I am only in town for the week."

CON ARRIVED at his small but elegant Canon Drive office in
time to take care of a few phone calls before the meeting with Caroline Van Patten. For the past several years, he had successfully
trodden a thin line between legitimacy and illegality, burning the
wick at both ends and getting away with it. His mode of operation
was simple but dangerous. Through his contacts in the black market, he would obtain a stolen painting which he would buy for perhaps one-tenth of its value. Instead of selling it, he would have it
expertly forged, a process which had become increasingly simple as
computers became more sophisticated and talented artists more
desperate to earn a livelihood.

Keeping the original safe and secure in a storage room dug into
the hillside under his home, Con would orchestrate the sale and resale of the fake at auction, a process called "whitening," which created a legitimizing history for the work, a provenance. This
documentation gave a potential buyer pseudo proof of past ownership, hence, 'evidence' that the work was not stolen. The only
problem was that whitening took time, forestalling the moment
when the work could be sold.

But ultimately Con would attach the newly-created provenance
to the forgery and quietly slip it back into the market. If it was identified as a fake, he could point to the provenance as proof that he had

been duped as well. Or, if things really got hot, he could switch the fake with the original and chalk it up to the cost of doing business.

The intercom buzzed and the temporary secretary his regular girl Anna had brought in to cover while she was on vacation told him Caroline Van Patten had arrived. Anna had already been gone a week and he missed her terribly. It was the first time in seven years she had deserted him. And to make matters worse, she'd gone off camping or some such thing, and was completely incommunicado.

"Yes, send her in."

The door opened and he stood to greet Caroline Van Patten, automatically assessing her credibility. She looked to be about forty, and she carried herself with confidence — or it could be false bravado. It was hard to tell. She wore an expensive dark blue wool suit belted in thick, red leather which matched the shade of her pumps. Her jewelry was minimal, but she was wearing an important diamond ring. It looked to be at least five carats, a brilliant cut. He'd have to look at it with a loop to know its true value, but guessed it was real because of the intricacy of its setting. Normally zircons were set simply, commensurate to their value. And yet, you never knew.

"Miss Van Patten, I'm Con Uttrell." He motioned to the woman to sit, and when she did, he perched on the corner of the desk so that from the cloying plushness of the soft chair she had to look up to him. Advantage, Con. "May I offer you some coffee or perhaps a glass of sherry?"

"Neither, thank you, my time is rather limited."

Con was glad she had declined his offer so he could dismiss the temporary girl; the less she knew about his business the better. He waited until she closed the door before he continued.

"Please then, tell me how I can help you. You're looking for a Diebenkorn?"

"Yes, as I mentioned on the phone, my employer is eager to acquire a painting from the Ocean Park Series," she said.

Con pretended to mull this over. "As you obviously know, there are some one hundred forty paintings in the series. Can you be more specific?" The black market painting now being copied was numbered eighty-four. If she specified it by number, he would know she was on to him.

"We would prefer something from the middle years, less geometric than the early work, with an opacity of color," she replied. "My employer admires the work of Matisse and Rothko and he finds the same brilliant qualities in this period of Diebenkorn's work."

Con nodded and smiled to himself. She had cleverly avoided mentioning a number or a year, but had aptly described the painting he had in his possession. "I see," he said, staring off into space to give the impression that he was trying to think where he could locate such a work.

"Ah, yes," he said finally. "If I remember correctly, I have seen something of that period in the collection of one of my private clients. But I doubt that it's for sale."

"I am willing to pay top price," Miss Van Patten said. "I assume you checked with the bank?"

"Yes, your account does seem to be in order," said Con.

"You do understand, we would be talking in the area of . . . two hundred thousand."

"That would be acceptable," she replied without batting an eye. "Depending on the piece and its condition, of course."

"Of course," said Con, the friendly expression in his eyes belying his mistrust of this woman. "It may take me several days to arrange for you to see it."

"The sooner the better."

"Very well. May I know where to contact you?"

"I stay at the Sheraton Miramar when I'm in town, but I'm leaving tomorrow and will be moving around quite a bit," she said. "You can leave a message for me there if you are able to acquire the painting, and I will make plans to come back to town to sign the papers and pick it up."

Con looked puzzled. "Don't you carry a cellular phone?"

She shook her head. "We've found the circuits lack the privacy we require . . ."

Con nodded and stood. "Well, then, I'll be in touch."

They shook hands and she exited. Con closed the door behind her and sat at his desk, tapping his fingers on the suede arm of his chair. Then he leaned forward and buzzed the intercom.

"Yes, sir," came the temporary girl's voice.

"Get me Willie Wilson," Con said. He waited impatiently, listening through the intercom to the rustling of pages as the girl leafed through the Rolodex for the number.

"Mr. Wilson? One moment please for Mr. Uttrell."

Con picked up the phone. "Wilson? How's it coming?"

"What's the rush? I've only had it two days. It'll be done when it's done," Willie's voice responded.

"I may need it soon, by the end of the week."

"You want it good, or you want it fast?"

"Both," Con said, and hung up.

IN AN ANTEROOM to his studio, Willie Wilson sat in front of a state-of-the-art computer. On its screen was an abstract image, horizontal bands of blue-violet, turquoise, buff, and sandy yellow-gray. A brilliant blue rectangle was partially drawn in the blue-violet band.

"Fucking asshole," he said to a scruffy dog curled up on a pillow on the floor. The dog wagged his tail hopefully. But Willie looked at the screen and then at an easel standing next to it. On it was an oil painting which bore an uncanny resemblance to the image on the computer screen. He looked from the original painting to the screen, put his fingers on the keyboard, and continued building the blue rectangle.

TEN

LUNCH AT the South Shore Cafe was Nick's favorite meal of the day. It wasn't so much the food — plenty of restaurants in town could dish up a plate of chili and a beer. It was more the atmosphere. At night the place was invaded by tourists dressed in baggy Japanese trousers and black shirts buttoned to the neck, and wannabe artists who thought talent would rub off if they hung around the fortunate few who'd made it.

But lunch was for the local creative types — painters, sculptors, filmmakers, art directors. They didn't come for the scene; they *were* the scene. Newcomers congregated around the bar for brews and endless cups of espresso, while the more established staked their claims on the booths, reading newspapers or contemplating the afternoon's work in public privacy. The hierarchy was unspoken but understood, a caste system based on creative repute rather than birthright.

Nick and Willie frequently shared a booth, but they had been friends so long that neither waited for the other to arrive before ordering. So Nick was well into his chili before he heard Willie's three-note prelude. He watched Willie ricochet across the room like a pinball, his pupils the size of Grape Nuts, his skin as chalky as an old Hershey bar. He slid into the booth, and when he doffed his magenta and chartreuse baseball cap, Nick noticed that his paint-splattered hand was trembling.

"What's the matter with you?" Nick asked between bites. Supposedly Willie had sworn off drugs — too many close calls in the old days. But Nick had his doubts.

"Rough night," was all Willie said.

The waitress came to take Willie's order and then disappeared again.

"Women or work?" Nick asked, knowing it had to be one of the two.

"Women are work, aren't they?" Willie replied. "Hard ass labor." He pulled a green Marks-a-lot out of his pocket and began scribbling furiously on his linen napkin.

Nick ate, waiting for Willie to continue, knowing he would.

"My one man show at Rave," Willie said finally, "it got aced, man."

Nick pushed his plate aside. "What happened?"

Willie shook his head. "They told me my new work's not cutting edge. They called it 'decorative.'" This last word he spat out with disgust. "Decorative!" he repeated as though trying to get the sour taste of it off his tongue. "Where do they come off laying that shit on me? If the show doesn't sell out, the work's not commercial. If people buy it and hang it on their walls, they say it's decorative. I'm too old for this crap, man. I want to bail."

Nick nodded sympathetically. An artist sweated to create a body of work, starving and scraping by on the generosity of art world patrons who either pitied his poverty or were willing to pay for his company. Then, if he was lucky, a dealer would waltz in and deign to offer him a show. If the work sold, the dealer pocketed a whopping forty percent. If it didn't, the artist and his canvases faded into obscurity.

Nick knew what it meant to Willie to lose his dealer at this point in his career. Thirty years ago he had been one of the first California artists to make it big. Rather than imitate the dark and static work being done in Soho in the '60s as so many young artists had done, Willie painted ebullient watercolors, paeans to the dazzling L.A. light. They evoked the airiness of a day at the beach, the colors of summer, the rhythm of a palm frond lapping at the breeze.

When California Art became It, Willie was considered one of the dozen artists who had started the trend. But he had become a victim of his own success; like Orson Welles, he had done his best work in his early twenties and now, nearing fifty, he could only imitate himself. If Rave dropped him, the best he could hope for would be some sales at auction, maybe a retrospective in an obscure Midwestern museum, and finally, a burst of interest in his work when he made the final sacrifice for it and died.

"Excuse me, who's paying today?" a waitress named Cindy asked. She'd been at the South Shore as long as Nick could remember, but she was still in wide-eyed awe of the artists.

"This will cover it, babydoll," said Willie, and presented her with the sketch he'd been drawing on his napkin.

"Willie! Those napkins cost four bucks each. Jason will have a shit fit."

"Add it to my tab," said Willie, pushing the bill away with a gesture of disdain.

"Sorry, cutie, your tab is tapped out," she said.

"Says who?" Willie demanded.

"Jason. He does own the place after all."

"I'll get it," said Nick. He pulled out a crisp fifty. "I'm flush for a while." He gave Cindy the money and she disappeared. Then he offered Willie a cigar, using his fettling knife to manicure the end of his own.

"Who died and wrote you into the will?"

"I got a commission," Nick admitted.

"No shit? Who from?" Willie's affection for Nick was deep but he couldn't hide his envy. It had been a while since he had been so lucky.

"A client of Con Uttrell's." Nick drew on his cigar until the tip glowed red. "Some foreign guy. Uttrell wouldn't tell me his name. But hey, his money's green, so it's fine by me."

"Oh, man, don't do it." Willie pulled his cap down over his eyes and shook his head.

"What?"

"Uttrell. Don't let him get his claws in you."

"You were the one who said I needed a dealer."

"Not Uttrell. He pay you cash up front?" Willie asked.

"Part of it," Nick replied. Willie nodded knowingly. "Why?" Nick asked.

"You know that pet python he's got? I think the two of them's blood brothers. Take my advice and stay as far away from him as you can. Unless you wanna get snake-bit."

Nick flipped the knife nervously in his hand. He had his own doubts about Con Uttrell and wasn't at all happy to have them echoed by Willie. "I didn't know you knew him."

Willie didn't meet Nick's eyes. Looking over his shoulder he said, "I did some work for him, coupla things I'm not so proud of. That's all I'm gonna say."

"Sonofabitch, Willie, what does that mean?"

"I'm just trying to warn you. Don't let him get your nuts in a wringer." He leaned closer to Nick. "I can tell you for a fact he's got more than a little to do with Rave canceling my show, and there's not a damn thing I can do about it."

"That's bullshit."

"Is it?" He grabbed the knife out of Nick's hand and pointed it at a piece of corn bread. "Picture yourself as that piece of bread."

"So?"

Willie stabbed the crust with the knife, pinning it to the hard wood. "That's what Uttrell will do to you if you screw up, and he won't give a flying fuck about it."

"Christ, Wilson, what the shit are you doing?" Jason Stark, chef and owner of the South Shore hurried out of the kitchen wiping his greasy hands on his Grateful Dead T-shirt. He grabbed the knife and jerked it out of the table. "First you ruin my linen and now you're out to destroy my table. I only got so much tolerance, man, and you're pushing it." Jason was not known for his love of the artists who congregated at the South Shore. But it was they, not his cooking, that drew in the rich suburbanites from Encino and Brentwood. So he tolerated them, but only to a point.

Willie held his hands up over his head. "What? Like I'm the first dude to ever put a nick in your damn piece of shit plank? Gimme a break man. At least read me my Mirandas before you crucify me."

Nick fingered the small niche made by his knife. "This is no problem, Jason. I'll have one of my guys come over here and patch it. You'll never know it's there."

Jason refused to be mollified. "What about this?" He fluttered the napkin with the green drawing in Willie's face.

Willie grabbed it from him and scribbled his signature in the bottom right corner. "Here, frame it. In ten years you can sell it and put your snot-nosed kid through college."

"Who do you think you are, Picasso?" Jason fumed.

"Who do you think you are, Wolfgang Puck?" Willie shot back.

"Hey guys, cool it," Nick said. "Look, I'm adding five bucks to the bill, see?" With a flourish he crossed out the figure on the receipt and wrote in a new one, signing his name to the bottom. "Okay?"

"Cindy, did they clear his plastic yet?"

"He paid cash, actually," Cindy said, holding out the change. Jason took a five and allowed her to give Nick the rest. Nick and Willie rose from the booth and left the restaurant, going their separate ways, no more said.

Willie took the shortcut through Breeze Park back to his studio, keeping his eyes peeled for a score. He was hungry for blow, desperate enough to risk buying off a twelve-year-old park rat, even if it was risky. One of them had pulled an Uzi on him last month, the little fuck. So since then Willie began packing a weapon — nothing serious, just a little self-defense. Today, he'd filched Nick's fettling knife when nobody was looking. He dug his hand into his pocket and toyed with it. The sharpness of the blade felt good against his fingers. Wouldn't he just love to test its honed edge against the neck of his ex-dealers at Rave?

And that made him think of Con Uttrell. He'd accused Willie of screwing up on the Rothko, and as punishment he'd pulled some strings at Rave and gotten Willie's show canceled. Well, the tables were going to turn. Soon enough Willie would get back at Uttrell. He could hardly wait for the chance to skewer the bastard.

NICK STROLLED BACK to his studio nonchalantly, in no hurry since Tory Hartman was not due until three. The beach was nearly deserted this spring day, but the Boardwalk's Korean vendors all had their stalls open — T-shirts, sunglasses, novelties, arts and crafts for sale — nearly the same assortment in every one. A few mangy cats poked at the scraps of garbage and debris on the footpath. Pigeons fought with sea gulls for the remains of somebody's Jody Maroni sausage sandwich. A homeless woman swept at the clutter in front of her bench, clearing the spot like a diligent housewife sweeping her front porch. When she was finished, Nick sat down.

Willie's warning about Con Uttrell had disturbed him. He didn't trust Uttrell either, but it was too late to back out of the deal now. He'd already spent the $5,000 Uttrell had given him, paying past due bills. And besides, he was eager to begin work with the new girl.

He let his thoughts drift to the arduous task of beginning a new statue. He hoped the girl had the stamina to stick with it, for although he'd made it sound easy, posing was physically and emotionally exhausting for both model and artist.

He had never worked with a subject as young as this one and wondered if her age would be a hindrance. Most of his models were spoiled brats in the bodies of goddesses, women foolish enough to think they could get their way just because of their physical beauty. Was it possible that this teenager would be easier to work with, simply because she hadn't yet learned how to use her womanly wiles? Or would she be more difficult because she didn't know how the game was played? He couldn't wait to find out.

ELEVEN

SPONTANEITY IS what makes this photograph a success," the teacher was saying, holding up the photo of Nick Stone Tory had taken two days before. "The conspiracy of light and angle and opportunity create an image that draws us in because it cuts right to the quick of the subject." He smiled at Tory. "This shows a marked improvement, Victoria. I suggest you try more work in this vein."

The bell rang and Tory rose with the rest of the class. "Remember, those of you competing for the École Photographique summer scholarship, your *completed* portfolios are due in three weeks." He smiled at Tory as she passed. "You're definitely in the running, Miss Hartman. Keep up the good work."

"Thanks, Mr. Lempke."

Buoyed by the praise, Tory hurried down the hall to her locker. She wanted to avoid Keri and Lily because she hadn't told them about the modeling job yet. The truth was, she hadn't been sure she wouldn't chicken out at the last minute.

A thousand dollars was more then she'd ever dreamed she could earn, and she'd need it to pay for the airfare to Paris. But she was definitely not thrilled about the idea of actually standing there naked while a strange man stared at her. What if he was some kind of pervert? What if he didn't like what he saw? What if he laughed at her?

She had been shocked that her mother hadn't objected, had actually encouraged her instead. "I don't get it," Tory had protested. "Last week you practically made me wear a chastity belt because I was taking pictures of Brad McMurphy's thigh. Now you don't care if I take off my clothes in front of a complete stranger? What's the dif?"

"Oh, there's quite a 'dif,'" Charlotte had replied in that supercilious tone Tory hated. "This is A-R-T."

Who was to say what was art and what wasn't? As far as Tory could see, getting naked was getting naked, regardless of what snobby label you put on it. But her pride wouldn't let her back down, especially after Charlotte gave it her stamp of approval.

She turned the corner and saw Keri and Lily leaning against the wall waiting by her locker. Damn, there was no way to avoid them now. Tory took a deep breath and approached.

". . . and then he asked me if he could drive me home," Keri was telling Lily. "As if I would ever set foot in his Volkswagen. I'm sure! I'd spew all over the upholstery!"

Tory fumbled with the knob of her combination lock. "God, Tory, be a spaz or something," Keri whined. "We'll be here all day."

"You guys go ahead," said Tory. "I've got to go somewhere anyway."

"But we're supposed to watch the guys trying out for the track team. I already told John and Tyler we were coming," Lily said.

"I can't today," Tory replied. At last the combination clicked into place. She swung open the locker door and stuffed her books into it.

"But we told them you'd take pictures of them like you did of Brad," said Keri. "We can't just, like, show up there without you."

Tory shut her locker and turned to her friends. "Look, I'm really sorry. I've got to motor. I'm like late already." She started down the hall. "Catch you later."

"So where do you have to go that's so happening?" Lily demanded.

Thinking fast Tory blurted out, "To the doctor. I told you my mom is totally twisted about the thing with Brad. I've got to go and get it over with."

Lily and Keri shook their heads, commiserating.

"Bummer," Keri said.

"Maybe you can get him to give you an IUD," Lily suggested.

"I'm sure, Lily," Keri rolled her eyes. "Like her mother will be right there."

"Well maybe she'd want her to have one," Lily insisted. "Belinda's mom did."

"Yeah but Mrs. Milland was desperation city. Belinda's already been knocked up twice."

"No way," Lily scoffed.

"I'm serious," insisted Keri. "She had two abortions her sophomore year. You can ask . . ."

Tory saw her chance to escape. "Look guys, I'm history. See ya." She turned and ran down the hall and out the double doors before they could stop her.

Now what? Nick had said he'd send someone to pick her up, but she had no idea who or what kind of car they'd have. She prayed it wouldn't be some old bogus clunker that would make her the laughingstock of the school. Maybe she should have offered to take a cab. But a cab to Venice would cost a fortune.

And then she saw it. An excellent stretch limo parked in the red, right in front of the school, as though its very elegance allowed it special privileges. She stopped, unsure. No way. This couldn't be for her, could it? But the driver, a guy barely older than she was, seemed to be looking in her direction.

She approached, wary. He smiled at her. "Are you Tory Hartman?"

She nodded.

"My name's Rod, as in Hot Rod. Nick Stone sent me to pick you up." He opened the passenger door and stood aside for her to get in.

"You're not serious."

"Yeah, I am. He likes to do it right for his models."

Tory had never ridden in a limousine before, and the prospect was awesome. The kids around her were whispering and staring. She felt like a celebrity. Now she wished she hadn't hurried away from Keri and Lily. She'd love for them to see this. And Brad Mc-Murphy too. Especially Brad McMurphy. She glanced over her shoulder. What luck! Lily and Keri were just coming out of the building. They spotted the limo immediately and stared at Tory, dumbstruck. She waved at them and got in, beaming with pleasure. Maybe this modeling job wasn't going to be so bad after all.

Rod shut the door and went around to the driver's side. The engine started with an expensive hum. As they peeled away from the curb, Tory couldn't resist turning to look out the rear window. They were all still watching her, like she was Madonna or Cindy Crawford. She decided to take a picture to document the moment. She raised her camera and snapped, but it clicked emptily. Damn, out of film.

Tory settled back into the velvet seat and began checking out the car's appointments — a minibar with real crystal glasses and decanters for booze, unfortunately empty; a small television, which she tried and got only ear-shattering static; a bank of controls for air conditioning, heat, sun roof, moon roof and lighting. She pushed another button with no name, and the glass partition which separated her from the driver went down. Oops.

"Can I help you with something?" Rod asked politely.

Flustered, Tory didn't know what to say. Then she had an inspiration. "Do you know a camera shop on the way? I need some film."

"Gotcha," he replied, and Tory settled back into her seat, prepared to enjoy the ride.

THE VENICE CAMERA SHOPPE WAS a small neighborhood operation housed in a dilapidated building; it had remained in limbo because the city would not grant the owners funding for renovation, and the Historical Society would not allow them to tear it down. Which was fine with Bud. The place was shabby enough that it didn't get a lot of nuisance traffic, which meant less work for him. And he liked the setup — the shop in the front, right on Rose Avenue, and out the back door, a patch of dirt yard fenced in for Marge's mutt, separating the store from the house they shared. It wasn't a palace, but hell, it was an easy commute to work, he joked. And he'd talked Marge into fixing up the old garage out back for her idiot brother Eli so the lamebrain stooge didn't have to live with them like he had in Culver City.

Talk about wacko. Eli was as weird as they come, like that guy Dustin Hoffman played in "Rainman." If he'd been Bud's brother, Bud would have had him the hell committed. But not Marge. She doted on Eli like she did that mangy mutt of hers, letting him fix up his tacky room with all those sick pictures he took of roadkill and maimed animals. Bud shuddered to think of it.

"Excuse me, can I have some help out here?"

Bud tipped far enough back in his chair to see a white-haired troll waiting impatiently in front of the cash register. "Marge!" he yelled, "We got a customer."

"I'm on the phone," a woman's smoke-scarred voice rasped back. "Can't you take care of it?"

He lowered the volume on the TV, and shouted, "I'm doing inventory like you said."

"So it'll still be there after you do the customer," the voice replied.

Bud took a final swig of beer and hoisted himself out of the chair, not bothering to silence a rumble of gas. Marge hated it when he farted back there since the close space seemed to retain the odor for hours. Well, she shouldn't buy him those frozen burritos for lunch. It wasn't his fault he had a delicate stomach.

"Please, may I have some assistance!"

"Hold your horses, Pops. I'm on my way." He took his time just to annoy the old geezer. "Yeah? What can I do you for?"

"I'm interested in purchasing a Polaroid camera," the man said. "Can you suggest a model? I'm not terribly good with mechanical devices. I don't want anything complicated."

Bud reached to the wall behind him and pulled out the most expensive Polaroid model. "This is your best bet," he said. "Automatic focus, auto flash. Even an idiot could use it." Even an old goat like you, he added to himself.

The man took the camera and fumbled with it, unable to open the case. Dumb fuck, Bud thought. Probably couldn't find his dick with both hands. He heard the bell at the entrance jingle as the door opened.

Tory entered and looked around. Ignoring the old man, Bud strutted over to her and gave her a lecherous smile.

"Hello, beautiful. Anything I've got, name it, it's yours."

"Some film, please. 400 ASA color print," Tory replied.

"That's too easy," Bud teased. He leaned on the counter and said seductively, "Ask me, and I'll give you something hard."

"Excuse me, I'd like to see that other one, over there." The old man pointed to a model on display for 25% off.

"Hold your horses, Jack. Ladies first."

"He was here before me. It's okay," said Tory, repelled by Bud, wishing she hadn't come in.

"But I'd much rather wait on you," Bud said. "Eli?! Get your butt out front," he yelled.

A man burst out of the storeroom, not so much walking as scuttling along in short, jerky steps like a giant crab. His hair was buzz cut to the same length as the stubble of his beard, so his head appeared to be a ball of fuzz, vacant of expression with a curved line of a smile and two dots for eyes. He was dressed in a misbuttoned plaid shirt and huge corduroy pants — Bud's castoffs no doubt — which were bunched up beneath a tightly cinched belt.

He looked at Bud, then at the old man, and finally at Tory. Seeing her, his smile broadened, and he shuffled in that direction.

"He walks, he talks, he's almost human," Bud joked.

"Bud!" a woman's voice warned, and he turned to see Marge peering out from the back. The curlers in her hair matched those in the top knot of the poodle lovingly cradled in her arms. "Eli will help the girl with the film," she snarled. "You sell the camera."

Bud leaned closer to Tory to whisper, "How was I to know when I married her that her brother was a zombie? The guy's got the brains of a six-pack."

"Bud!"

Tory stepped back, mortified, but Eli seemed not to have heard. She smiled at him and he smiled back. "I just want a couple rolls of film," she said.

Eli muttered incoherently.

"You gotta tell him what kind. He can't talk for shit."

"Two rolls of 400 ASA, please, twenty-four exposure color print," she said, carefully articulating the words.

Eli nodded and found the film, fumbling it around in his hand until the price was visible. He thrust it towards her. Tory reached into her purse for the money and gave him a ten dollar bill. Eli shuffled to the cash register to make change, taking out each coin separately and placing it on the counter. It was a painstaking process. Tory reached for the coins and he covered her hand with his own withered extremity, mumbling again.

"What? I'm sorry," said Tory, easing her hand away. She knew he meant no threat, but still he gave her the creeps.

"He asked if you were a photographer?" Bud interpreted.

"Yes, I am," she replied.

"Me too," Eli said, and grinned at her so happily that she stopped being afraid and grinned back.

"Oh, yeah, right. A real Ansel Adams," said Bud. "You should see his stuff. He likes to take pictures of roadkill, don't you, Eli? Squirrels, cats, dogs, bugs, snakes, you name it. If it's dead or dying, he'll take its picture."

Tory saw the hurt expression on Eli's face and wanted to say something to make him feel better. "Sounds cool," was all she could think of as she backed out of the store.

Rod had kept the motor running, so as soon as Tory got in, he gunned it. She sat back and watched the neighborhood change as they neared the beach, storefront businesses and bungalows giving way to soft-drink stands and bikini shops. Palm trees lined the streets. People on bicycles and rollerblades shared the streets with them.

"How much further?" she asked.

"We're there," Rod said without warning.

The limousine veered off the main drag, into a garbage-strewn alley, and stopped before an unmarked metal door with no handle. Rod turned off the engine.

Tory looked out the window. The limousine was parked next to a decrepit building, scarred and covered with graffiti. The street around it was littered with the refuse of a transient population: greasy paper wrapped around the gangrenous remnants of fast food meals, torn and stained shreds of clothing, dried vomit in a variety of colors and textures, a shriveled condom. A bag lady sat next to the metal door which led into the building, cataloguing her worldly possessions — the contents of three shopping carts. Tory heard a dog barking and, through the mesh of a chain link fence attached to the building, a German Shepherd bared his teeth at her.

Could this be the place? It was hardly the environment Tory had expected for the studio of a famous sculptor. Maybe this was some kind of a joke. Or a scam. For the first time in years, she wished she had allowed the Wicked Witch of Westridge to come with her. Charlotte would never have let her set foot in a place like this without a tetanus shot. Maybe it wasn't too late for Tory to reconsider.

But Rod had already opened the door and was reaching inside to help her out. When she didn't take his hand, he bent down to peer inside. "This your first trip to Venice?" She nodded. "Don't worry, it's a lot better inside."

Reluctantly Tory let him pull her from the car, and followed him to the door, trying not to see the festering sores on the bag lady's legs or smell the pervasive odor of urine hanging about her.

They entered a hallway with cement floors and plaster peeling off the walls. The stench from outside was still faintly apparent, even though Rod had shut and triple-bolted the door behind her — another ominous sign.

"Hi, you must be Tory Hartman. I'm Leslie, Nick's secretary. Come on in."

Tory followed a girl a foot shorter and ten years older into a cramped office whose clutter of magazines, paperwork, books, and cast-off clothing was comfortingly like her own room at home.

"Don't mind the mess," Leslie was saying, "I'm one of those people who can't throw anything out. My mom was totally anal retentive and I guess this is my way of getting back at her, or at least that's what my shrink says." She eyed Tory curiously. "You're very young."

"How old should I be?" Tory snapped, regretting it immediately.

Leslie seemed unfazed. "Old enough to sign these release forms without a parent's consent." She handed Tory a stack of papers.

"Is seventeen old enough?"

"Nope." Leslie shook her head. "So you'll have to have somebody at home sign them. It's no big deal, just to cover us in case there's a crackdown on child labor laws." Then, seeing the concern on Tory's face, she added, "Just kidding. They're for insurance, in case you fall or get sick or something. Don't worry about it." The phone rang. "Damn, it never ends," she said, and then into the phone, "Studio? Oh, hi, Cassie, just a sec." She put her hand over the receiver and turned to Tory. "I have to take this. Why don't you go on back? It's just through there." Leslie motioned through the hanging strips of fabric. "I'd buzz Nick, but he'd never hear it over the welder. Just follow the decibels. Okay?"

"Okay," said Tory. Only she wasn't so sure.

"You can leave your stuff, here," Leslie added.

"Thanks," Tory said, and set her books on the floor. But she kept her camera around her neck, just for security.

The studio was cavernous, cold, and crowded with art and junk. There were no windows, but the room was bathed in light that streaked in through a skylight above Tory's head. Around her, statues of female figures soared on tall pedestals. Fragments of bronze, mounds of clay and smaller statues were cluttered on huge wooden tables amidst books and magazines, stray papers and a jumble of wires.

At one side a camera was set up facing a white backdrop. She gravitated towards it, something familiar in this alien world. It was a Hasselblad with a 90mm lens. She had never even seen such an expensive camera up close. A series of 8 x 10 photos was tacked hastily to the wall beside the backdrop, shots of a voluptuous woman, standing in various somber poses which exposed her body parts from all points of view — thigh, foot, elbow, chin, rib cage, shoulder. Despite the woman's very sexy body, the photos were static and without emotion, merely a documentation of her limbs and curves. Except for the last one. Tory stared at it, embarrassed to look but unable to tear her eyes away.

It was a picture of the same woman, but Nick was in it too. He was touching the curve of the woman's bare breast with his fingertips. His head was so close to her flesh that he could easily have licked the erect nipple. And he was grinning, like this was not work to him, like he was enjoying every sexy second.

"There you are." Leslie's voice pulled Tory out of her trance. "Hey, come on, Nick's waiting."

Reluctantly, Tory followed Leslie deeper into the studio. "Does he always take pictures like those?"

Leslie nodded. "As a matter of fact that's probably where you'll start. He'll want to get the feel of you on film before he starts to work on the clay."

Tory stopped walking. 'Feel' was not a word she wanted to hear. Leslie saw the apprehension in her eyes. "Look," she said. "It's not so bad. I lost six pounds when I saw what I looked like."

"He did a statue of you?" Tory asked.

"Not the whole thing," Leslie admitted. "He needed a detail for a back in the fountain frieze, and I was handy. Come on."

Reluctantly, Tory followed her to where Nick stood, or at least she assumed it was Nick; it was hard to tell since his face was covered by a welder's mask. He was intent on the work before him, watching two muscular assistants chip solder a small statue onto a bronze base. The jet of blue flame licked cruelly at the tiny feet, which were so lifelike Tory almost expected the figure to cry out.

"NICK!" Leslie shouted, but her voice was drowned out by the sound of the generator. She moved up behind him and tapped him on the shoulder. He turned, nodded, and snapped off the welder. The crew took this as their signal to stop working and all three men stared at Tory with undisguised curiosity.

"Hi," said Nick, lifting his mask.

"Hi," said Tory. She felt a flush burn her cheeks.

"Tony, Zago, knock off for today. We'll do the patina tomorrow morning." Nick spoke to the workmen over his shoulder, keeping his eyes trained on Tory, starting at her feet and moving slowly upward.

Nobody had ever looked at Tory the way Nick was looking at her now. The hungry intensity of his gaze made her heart beat so fast she could feel the pulse pounding at her temple. She squirmed uncomfortably, tugging her sweater tightly around her as though it would protect her from Nick's stare. But it didn't. She wished she could stop him or move out of the way, but like a deer frozen in the headlights of an approaching car, she seemed unable to move, pinned to the spot.

As his eyes traveled upward to her breasts, Tory unconsciously crossed her arms, desperate to shield herself. She felt naked, exposed, like the woman in the pictures on Nick's wall. God, would he never stop staring!

Finally his eyes reached her face and rested there. She brushed back a lock of hair and stared back. But he refused to meet her eye to eye, instead taking in the details of her ears and her forehead, her hairline and the flare of her nostrils.

At last he gave her what passed for a smile and turned to Leslie. "I'd better get cleaned up a little before we start. Get her set up for the Hasselblad." And he walked away.

Tory exhaled deeply. She hadn't realized she'd been holding her breath, but now her body seemed desperate for air. She felt dizzy and a little weak in the knees. "Whew! I feel like I just ran a marathon. Without my clothes on," she added.

Leslie put a comforting arm around her. "He's not a bad guy. He's just an artist. They're kinda different."

"Does he always stare like that?"

"Yeah, as a matter of fact." Then, seeing the concern on Tory's face she added, "But don't worry about it. He's not really looking at *you*, per se. He's like a doctor looking at a patient, wanting to find out where it hurts. Come on, I'll walk you through the routine."

Leslie took Tory to a partitioned area near the camera setup and pointed to a thin silk robe hanging on a nail. "You can undress back here, and put the robe on. Bring a pair of sandals or else I can buy you some floppies on the Boardwalk, because the floor's pretty cold. The bathroom's by my office. If you need to wash up or anything you can do it there. You should tie your hair back so he can get the shape of your head. He'll do the hair at the end, so you should keep it out of the way until then. Any questions?"

"Yeah, how do I get out of this?"

Leslie laughed, thinking Tory had meant it as a joke. Then realizing she hadn't, Leslie's expression softened. "Look, don't worry. I know it seems scary right now, but once you get started, it's no big deal. You'll see."

She gave Tory's shoulder a squeeze and turned to leave. "Nick should be ready in a second. I'm just in my office if you need anything. Okay?"

Tory tried to smile. What could she say? That it wasn't okay, that she was totally freaked about what this man might ask her to do? That even if he was ready, she wasn't, not in the least?

NICK TOOK HIS TIME cleaning up, and even changed into a fresh work shirt. Starting with a new model was always a turn-on, not knowing what he would find when he saw her body for the first time, or what they would learn about each other as they became more relaxed.

At first he had barely recognized Tory. In her school uniform and saddle shoes, she looked achingly young — a typical teenager from suburbia. Had he made a mistake?

But then the sensation had eddied around him. It was not a visual impression, not something he got from looking at her. It was something he *felt*, a mysterious quality that always drew him to his models.

She seemed particularly uptight and nervous, but he should have expected that because she was just a kid. He would have to try not to push her too hard, to let her open up gradually.

But he had less than a month to complete the statue. It wasn't as though he could twiddle his thumbs until she finally got with the program. Maybe he should suggest they work together every day instead of three times a week.

"Tory? Are you ready?" Nick's voice was low and relaxed.

"Coming," she said. It was impossible to buy any more time. With lead weights in her shoes she walked out from behind the partition, still dressed, clutching the silk robe to her chest.

Nick's back was to her. He was adjusting the camera lens. Finally he turned and looked at her, and his smile faded. "You were supposed to take your clothes off and put the robe on. Didn't Leslie tell you?"

"Yeah, she told me." Her voice was a whisper.

"Well then?"

"So, I didn't do it."

"Damn it, why not?" Nick was impatient, eager to get started.

"I've changed my mind," Tory blurted out. "I don't want to do this, okay? Can you have the car take me home? Or I'll take a cab. I don't care how much it costs." She dropped the robe. "This was a really bogus idea. There's no way. I must have been crazy to say I'd do it. I'm outta here." Backing away too quickly, she stumbled on a cord and fell, grabbing hold of a spotlight on the way down. It crashed to the floor beside her, pulling along an empty tripod, a reflector, and a stool. Nick caught the Hasselblad just as it too began to topple.

For a moment Tory just lay there in the jumble of electrical equipment, afraid to look at Nick, afraid to move. But Nick's frustration had turned to amusement. Tory's clumsiness was a perfect expression of her youth. He started to laugh, but stifled it. Her pride was already wounded; if he damaged it any further, he'd never win her over.

"Are you okay?" he asked.

"Yeah."

"I have an idea. Why don't we take a walk on the Boardwalk? There's a frozen yogurt place about a block from here."

Tory looked at him, curious, surprised and a little wary.

"What, and then come back and take the pictures? No thanks."

"I mean forget the pictures. It's no big deal. Yogurt sounds much better, doesn't it?" He held out his hand. "They've got these great waffle cones in chocolate and almond."

"Well, okay," Tory replied with relief. She took his hand and let him pull her up.

An hour later when Rod, the limousine driver, came to take Tory home, Leslie told him Nick and Tory were on the Boardwalk and she expected them back any time. It was just like Nick to hire a limo at $50 per hour, and then make the driver wait. But thanks to this new commission, he had the money to pay for his extravagance. For a while, at least.

NICK LEANED AGAINST the wall, sketching Tory as she glided by on a pair of rented rollerblades. She was in her element, relaxed and happy again, in harmony with the strollers, skaters and bikers. He wasn't surprised. The Boardwalk had a childlike quality to it, a Red Grooms carnival of bright colors and bold images. He saw a woman stuffed into an orange T-shirt, purple pants and turquoise tennis shoes, a rollerskater in an Indian headdress strumming a battery-operated electric guitar, a dog wearing sunglasses and a visor, a guy juggling chainsaws. It wasn't the real world. It was a kid's fantasy. And that's what Tory was. Just a kid.

Sweater tied around her waist, hair streaming behind her like a kite, she was all instinctive movement and grace, slaloming through the crowd, giving Nick a perfect opportunity to see how her body flowed and fit together. Since he'd promised not to take the stills he usually worked from, he drew as fast as he could, memorizing every nuance of her body as it streaked past him. His artist's eye collected the images: the muscles in her calves as she dipped to stroke a passing collie, the arch of her neck as she threw her head back in the sunlight, the long, slender strength of her arms as she twirled around a light post, her square white teeth as she opened her mouth to eat her yogurt. When she saw that he was looking at her, she ducked her head shyly and turned away.

To get the portrait of Tory he was after, as she was at this moment, he'd have to get her to overcome this self-consciousness. Or, he'd have to capture her when she wasn't aware he was looking. Maybe a hidden camera would work, a video setup. Then he could watch the way she moved and study her body in different aspects. He could even make stills from the video.

It was an interesting thought. So often he felt his presence intruded, creating unwanted tension in his model, a kind of violence inflicted on her body, distorting the way she presented herself.

Yes, it made sense. He should physically remove himself from the process so she would be completely relaxed and abandoned, alone with her body. He made a mental note to tell Leslie to arrange it. But first he'd have to convince the girl not to quit before they got started, and he'd somehow have to cajole her into taking off her clothes.

Tory rolled up to the bench and flopped down next to him. Her presence made him tingle with the desire to sculpt her. He wanted to tell her about his excitement, but what if it scared her off again? He couldn't take that chance, so he just sat there and waited for her to speak.

"I want to model for you. I really do," she said at last, concentrating her eyes on her yogurt. "I just have to get used to it, you know?"

"Yeah," he said. "I know."

II

TWELVE

NICK'S PATIENCE WAS at a low ebb. He was itching to get started on the new statue of Tory. But he'd wasted the first session tolerating her hesitancy, and today he had to wait for the new video equipment to be installed. The two men had been at it since morning. He had stayed out of the studio as long as he could, but he was getting anxious. Tory would be arriving in a few minutes.

Nick hadn't realized installing a hidden camera would be so technically complicated. To mount it meant creating a baffle on the ceiling with a hole in it through which the lens would poke. Then a remote switch had to be wired so he could trigger the camera whenever he wanted. They'd decided to mount the switch with the lights, making the two-gang outlet for the east spots a three-gang. That way Nick could activate the camera when he turned on the lights, and no one would know.

"Let's see what we got," the worker named Bud said as he lumbered down the ladder, his low riding 501s abundantly exposing his rear cleavage. "Eli, punch the lights when I tell you."

The other worker shuffled over to the light switch and jabbed at it with the knuckle of his hand. The room darkened.

"Not yet, numbnuts. When I tell you!" Bud turned to Nick. "My brother-in-law, he's got a few lights out up here," he said, tapping his head.

The room became light again and Bud motioned to Nick to follow him. He led the way into Nick's bedroom and turned on the television, flicking the remote to channel three.

"Okay, douse 'em," Bud called.

The room darkened again. "Now check this out," Bud said to Nick. "Lights, Eli."

When the lights went on again, the television screen showed Nick's sculpture platform shot from a high angle. Bud played with the zoom. The picture cooperated by closing in on the platform, and then pulling back as he pushed the reverse. "See? Whenever those spotlights are on, this'll record automatically, long as you have a blank tape in. You can use it just like a normal video you rent at the Wherehouse — only I bet you don't need to get them X-rated ones since you got your own private dancer." He jabbed Nick in the ribs.

"You can give my secretary your bill on your way out," Nick said flatly, and walked away.

Back in the studio, Nick found Eli staring open-mouthed at the sketches he'd made of Tory on the Boardwalk.

"She's beautiful, isn't she," Nick said.

"I know her," Eli said, but his reply was so garbled that Nick didn't understand.

"Eli, get your ass in gear. The guy wants us outta here."

Nick unpinned one of the sketches and handed it to Eli. "Here, you can have it."

"Thank you," Eli struggled to enunciate properly, but the words were unnecessary. Nick could see in his eyes how pleased he was. And that pleased Nick.

"WHAT'LL YOU HAVE?"

"Coors," Bud said, and before Eli could say anything he added, "and a Shirley Temple for the retard. That's about as close as he gets to girls."

The bartender chuckled and went off to get the drinks, and Bud got up to put a coin in the jukebox. As soon as he was gone, Eli pulled the sketch out of his pocket to look at it. He had been thrilled when he'd recognized the girl in the drawing, the same one who had come into the shop last week to buy film. She had smiled at him, had been patient while he'd forced his crippled hands to work the cash register and extract change. She had even defended him to Bud, something no one but his sister Marge had ever done for him.

That was how he'd known he was in love with Her. Although he didn't really know what "in love" meant, he had seen movies, and Marge had read stories to him about men and women who were "in love." And always it involved a smile like the one the girl had given him, and a special sense of happiness blossoming from the inside like a flower, which was what he felt now.

He put the drawing back in his pocket. He wouldn't tell Bud about it. Bud might make fun of him, or worse, take his treasure away. No, it would be his secret and he would show it to no one.

Bud lowered himself back onto his stool as the Rolling Stones began to sing "Satisfaction." He took a long swig of beer. "You're not sayin' a word 'bout this to Marge, right pal?"

Eli shook his head and sipped his drink.

Two young black girls sauntered up to the bar on the other side of Bud. They were wearing bicycle shorts and bra tops and high heeled clogs.

"Licorice, my favorite," Bud said, loud enough for them to hear. "Sweet and juicy and baaaaad for you." The girls rolled their eyes and looked away.

"Two Miller Lites," one of the girls said.

"Got I.D.?" the bartender asked.

"Aw, shit, man, we only want beers."

"Sorry, I'll lose my license."

"Bartender, another beer for me." Bud winked at the girls. "Make it two," he said, nodding at Eli. "Miller Lites this round."

To Eli's surprise the girls sidled up to Bud like wary cats, wanting to be petted but staying just out of reach. He wondered which one had the licorice Bud had mentioned.

"What's happenin'?" the taller one said to Bud, making it sound like an invitation.

"Nothin' yet," Bud drawled, "but could be something real fine, a coupla girls like you and a guy like me."

"What kinda jive you talkin', white bread?"

"I'm just offerin' you two beautiful ladies a brew. Nobody as beautiful as you should go thirsty. Come on and sit yourselves down. Or I'll tell you what, I got a van parked outside. We'll buy us a six pack and hit the road. I'll take you anywhere you wanna go and back again."

"LaVerne and me, we live in Carson. You gonna drive your honky van all the way t'there?"

"Lady I'd drive to the moon if you gimme a kiss."

"A kiss? What's it worth to you?"

"Hey, if I was gonna pay for it, I'd expect more'n a kiss."

"Honey, you kin expect all you want, but if you're talkin' 'bout pussy, you're gonna hafta put more'n a Miller on the line."

For a while Eli watched the girls' red-rimmed lips forming around the words, but he couldn't understand what was being said. Finally, bored and completely ignored by Bud, he rose and went to the door. He could see the artist's studio a block away. Maybe the beautiful girl was going to come back there. Maybe he would see Her. Just in case, he would stand outside and wait.

NICK STARED at the length of raw clay before him. It was formed into a column about three feet high, molded around a thick wire that was attached to a turntable base at one end, and to an armature at the top. This system allowed him to rotate the column of clay on the base as he worked, to examine it from all angles and in all levels of light.

The more he stared at it, the more Nick's idea of what he wanted to sculpt crystallized. But he couldn't start until Tory arrived, and when she did it would no doubt take him some time to cajole her into taking off her clothes so they could begin. He smiled to himself, thinking how very like a sexual seduction it was to convince a woman to model. Nothing, not even the act of making love was as erotic to Nick as his work. The feel of his hands on the clay, shaping it into a portrait of the female body before him, created a physical response in his own body. Julia had been right when she'd accused him of getting off on his work. It was his most satisfying form of release.

He began to pace, but saw that he was telegraphing his tension to Attila, who was chained near the sculpting platform, watching him with alert, feral eyes. Maybe music would help them both relax. Nick flipped through the CDs heaped on the modeling platform. He always let his models choose the music, and their tastes ranged from Guns 'n Roses to Ray Charles. Nick never paid much attention. Usually when he was working, he was so focused on the visual and the tactile that he ceased to be aware of the aural, and when he was not working, he wanted complete silence. But right now he needed to fill the void created by Tory's absence.

At the bottom of the pile he found an old re-recording of a Frank Sinatra record from the '50s. Just for the sake of perversity, he jammed it into the ghetto blaster, and Nelson Riddle's cotton candy orchestration billowed through the cavernous studio. Then Sinatra began to sing, his voice still dulcet at the time of this early recording, articulating the chaste longing and bridled lust of the postwar generation.

Suddenly Nick realized what drew him to Tory, what he wanted to put in the statue. It was the embodiment of unrealized sexual longing, the image of a virgin who had a romantic vision of sex, and who was waiting eagerly for someone to introduce her to the physical sensation. Yes, that was it. Unlike Julia and most of his other models who radiated carnal sensuality, Tory's statue would be about purity. But not in a prudish sense. She would represent the profound beauty of a girl at the brink of womanhood. Nick's hand began to twitch with eagerness to translate this idea into clay.

Unable to restrain himself any longer, he picked up his file. He gripped it firmly in his right hand and with his left he caressed the clay column, letting his fingers play over the cool, wet mass until they found a spot near the center. Unconsciously moving in sync with the heartbeat rhythm of the music, Nick applied file to clay and stroked downward, deftly excising a large slice. Seconds passed, then minutes, and as the music crested and fell, Nick continued to stroke at the column, giving it the first rudimentary shape of a human figure.

LESLIE OPENED the door to the studio. "You're late," she scolded Tory. "He's been waiting for you."

"Sorry, I had to stay after school."

Leslie hid a smile. She could tell by looking at the girl that she'd spent the time slathering her face with makeup. And where had she gotten those clothes! Well, she'd find out soon enough that it would all have to go. "Go on in. He's in back."

Tory followed the retro sound of the Sinatra CD to its source at the rear of the studio where Nick was working. His back was to her and he was totally engrossed in the enormous hunk of clay suspended before him. She stood quietly, watching him work. His left hand moved haltingly over the surface of the clay as though he were blind. And then when he felt the spot he wanted, his right hand quickly applied the file to it, gouging out a chunk. She was fascinated and would have been even more impressed if she had seen that Nick's eyes were closed.

Tory heard a low growl and saw Attila lying under the table. His brown eyes had darkened to black, his ears were alert and twitching, his complete attention riveted on her. She smiled in delight and dug into her backpack to find the sandwich she'd saved from lunch; she'd eaten nothing all day so her stomach wouldn't bulge.

"D'you like tuna on rye?" she whispered and offered a piece to Attila. He gulped it down and stood, nosing her for more.

At that moment Nick stepped around the clay column to get a different perspective, and suddenly he saw Tory kneeling next to Attila, her head practically in his mouth. All he could think about was the dog's powerful jaws destroying her perfection before he even started to sculpt it.

"Attila *FREEZE!*" he shouted.

Confused, since he hadn't been in an attack mode, the dog nevertheless dropped to the floor, his head cocked to one side.

"Get away from him," Nick commanded. "Now!"

"It's okay, I'm cool with dogs." Tory couldn't imagine why Nick was so upset. Usually people were pleased when you showed affection to their pets.

"Stand back!" he bellowed, and finally she did. "Never touch him again. He doesn't know you and he's a Schutzen."

"What's that?"

"He's trained to attack."

"Why?"

"For protection."

"From what?"

"People who get too close to me."

"Oh, well, I didn't know I was getting too close," Tory said sarcastically and looked at Attila. His tail thumped the concrete floor in response. "I think he wants to be friends, don't you, boy?"

"He's not supposed to be friends with anybody, okay?"

"Yes, master."

Nick breathed a sigh of relief. He was probably insured, but wouldn't it be a bitch to have her disfigured before he'd even begun to work.

Now he looked at Tory, really seeing her for the first time today. She was wobbling on three-inch heels which tilted her body forward unnaturally. The diaphanous patterned sundress she was wearing was hiked up unevenly, revealing the lace border of a slip at the hem. Linebacker-size shoulder pads and a plunging neckline further obscured and parodied her natural shape.

Likewise, her face was so caked with makeup that it looked like one of his clay figures. And her hair had been teased so that it stuck out on all sides.

"What is this? What did you do to yourself?" Nick managed at last.

Tory squirmed uncomfortably. "Nothing, I — I just put on some makeup," she stammered.

"Yeah, well, how do you expect me to sculpt your face when it's buried under two tons of crap?"

"I just thought it would make me look . . ."

"What?"

"Nothing."

"*What?*"

"Older, you know, more mature."

Nick shook his head. Most of the women he knew were desperate to look younger. He was going to have his work cut out for him with this one. He cleared his throat, trying to keep his frustration in check. "Down the hall is my room, and through there's a bathroom. Go in there and wash that crap off your face. All of it."

"But —"

"Just do it, okay?" His voice was louder than he meant for it to be. There wasn't time for this foolishness.

Tears flooded Tory's eyes. "You don't have to yell," she cried, running in the direction Nick was pointing.

"I wasn't yelling," Nick yelled. But she had already slammed the bathroom door behind her. "Way to go, asshole," he muttered to himself, and sent the file flying into the target on the wall. Bullseye.

TORY FUMBLED for a moment trying to lock the bathroom door, before she realized there was no lock. Great. She looked at herself in the mirror. God, he was right. She did look awful, especially with dark rivulets of mascara running down her cheeks. She turned on the water and splashed it onto her face, scrubbing as though she could wash off her embarrassment. Maybe now that she'd made a fool of herself he wouldn't want to sculpt her any more. She didn't know if that thought made things better or worse.

She groped for a towel and pulled one off the rack, rubbing her face in it. The last of the makeup left an ugly brown streak across the terrycloth. Nice move, Tory, she thought guiltily. She looked around the small bathroom for a place to hide the dirty towel, finally finding a clothes hamper which was already overflowing with towels, shirts, and ohmygod, she couldn't help but see — underwear? Tory had never seen used men's underwear before, unless you counted the boxer shorts her father wore. What was in the hamper was the kind of thing they had in the Victoria's Secret catalog, tiny black briefs that looked more her size than his.

No way. They had to be women's panties, unless Nick was into lace bikinis. She wondered whose underpants they were and why they were in Nick's hamper.

A knock on the door startled Tory and she let the lid slam shut.

"Hey, I'm sorry I yelled at you," Nick's voice filtered through the door. "I didn't mean to be such a jerk. I'm just hot to get started. See, I only have two weeks to sculpt this piece. Usually, I spend months on a statue. But I don't have that luxury on this one. So it's not you I'm yelling at. It's the damn deadline hanging over my head. It's driving me nuts!" He paused. "Are you about finished in there? Please?"

"Just a second," she called. She felt stupid. He was paying her to model and here she was acting like a baby. She finished drying her face with the ruined towel and opened the door.

"Sorry," he said again.

"It's okay," she replied without looking at him. "I guess I'm a little nervous."

"Me too," he said, and then he realized it was true.

He took her hand and led her back into the studio, guiding her up onto the sculpture platform.

"Do I have to stand up here?" she whined.

"Yes," Nick said. "Please," he added quickly. "I need the perspective." He walked to the side wall, flipping the two switches which illuminated the overhead lights and the third which activated the hidden video camera. The lights glared hotly on Tory, casting her shadow against the white screen behind her. In his mind he imagined the tape rolling in the camera.

"Does it have to be so bright?" She shaded her eyes.

"For now, yes," said Nick knowing that he needed the light to get a good video image. "You'll get used to it."

He waited for Tory to be ready, able to be patient now that he was looking at her. Scrubbed clean of the grotesque mask of makeup, she looked achingly young and vulnerable, a fawn, all awkwardness and endearing shyness, with the seeds of the elegant adult she would become cunningly implied in the details of her body.

"How do you want me to stand?" she asked.

"However you want, for now."

Tory took a deep breath and let it out slowly.

Nick faced her fully, waiting. "So let's start."

"Whenever you're ready," she said bravely.

"I *am* ready," he replied.

"Okay."

It was now or never. She slipped out of her heels, and took a long moment to arrange them neatly at the edge of the platform. Then she wriggled out of her pantyhose and lay them on top of the shoes. She looked down at her feet. "I forgot to cut my toenails," she apologized, stalling.

"It doesn't matter," Nick replied patiently. He'd heard it all before.

Tory told herself to stop thinking, to stop feeling anything. She reached back to unzip her dress. But she could only get it halfway down. Damn! Before she could say anything Nick jumped up on stage to help. She shivered from the closeness of his hand, the intimacy of his presence. Oh God, oh God, was he going to touch her? She'd die if he did.

For a moment neither of them moved. Then slowly and carefully, Nick pulled down the zipper. And much to her relief, he stepped down off the platform and went back to his stool. Then he waited.

She waited too, holding the dress against her chest.

"Why don't you just take the dress off now, Tory," he said softly.

"Oh, right."

Before she could think anymore about it, as though she were ripping off a bandaid so the adhesive wouldn't hurt, she stripped off the dress and threw it on top of the shoes. Then she straightened, smoothing the too-large silk slip to her body. One of the straps slid off her shoulder and she quickly lifted it back into place.

"I borrowed this from my mother," she explained.

Nick said nothing, waiting.

Tory sucked in her stomach. "I guess I shouldn't have eaten so much last night."

"You look fine," was all Nick said. At least she was like the others in this — they all thought they were too fat.

She looked at him, hard. His eyes were glued on her. "It makes me feel weird to have you watch me."

Nick smiled. "Would you feel better if I took off my clothes too?" He started to unbuckle his belt.

"*No!*" Tory yelped. And then they were at a standoff again. "I mean 'no,'" she repeated softly.

Nick walked to the edge of the platform and sat down. "Come here," he said, and patted the boards next to him. Tory plopped down a few feet away, still self-conscious, shivering in the slip, but relieved for the momentary reprieve.

"What's wrong?" he asked softly.

Tory couldn't speak at first. Then the words spilled out of her mouth in a whisper. "I'm so ugly. I'm embarrassed for you to see me."

Nick sighed. "I know this is very hard for you and I respect that. What you said isn't true, but it isn't wrong that you feel it. It's part of what I'm trying to put in this piece." He could see by Tory's expression that she didn't understand what he meant, so he tried again.

"What do you think is the most beautiful thing in the world?" he asked.

Tory reflected. "A lot of things," she said.

"Name some."

"Sometimes when I have to get up early and I see the sun coming up, it's awesome."

"Good. What else?"

She thought again. "My neighbor has a new puppy. A Golden Retriever. It makes me feel really good to hold her, especially when she falls asleep in my arms."

Nick nodded. "What else?"

"Well, there's this bush in our garden. I don't even know what it's called. But when I saw it yesterday, I noticed it had these great little flowers on it. Blue with yellow centers. I can't describe it. It was just really pretty." Tory stopped, unsure, but Nick was smiling.

"Do you see what's the same about all those things? The sunrise, the puppy, the flowers?"

Tory shook her head.

"Part of what's beautiful about them is that they're new, they're just starting out. There's freshness and innocence and purity about them. It's not just how *they* look, but it's how they make *you* feel. That's what I see in you. That's what I want to put in this statue. The newness, the glow, all of it.

"So it's okay that you're embarrassed and not sure what to do. It's the right thing to feel. It's what I want. But don't let it stop you from thinking you're beautiful."

"I'm not . . ."

"Oh yes you are, I promise you. I can see it. And when the statue is finished, you'll see it too. Okay?"

"Okay," she agreed.

"Then let's get to work."

Nick stood and went back to his stool and waited, hoping the pep talk would work. He'd never had to explain himself to a model before, but saying the words had made it all that much clearer to him what he was going for, what he hoped to achieve.

Finally Tory rose and went back to the center of the platform. So what, she asked herself, so what? One at a time, she lifted the straps of the slip off her shoulders, and let it drift to the floor in a satiny glissando. And there she stood at last, fully exposed.

Naked.

It was done.

To her surprise, instead of being embarrassed, she began to realize a sensation of lightness and power. She had Nick's rapt attention and awe all focused on her. It was the first time she'd felt the strength of her sexuality and it was not a bad feeling. Not bad at all.

Nick's face betrayed no reaction to Tory's naked body. But he took it all in, the fragile pink of her skin in the places where the sun had never touched it; the faint tan lines left over from Easter break; the surge of her bosom, endearingly tight at this tender age; nipples thrusting upward like flower buds reaching for the light; the deeply indented collar bone; the angelic shoulder blades.

His eyes moved hungrily over her body, learning it, memorizing its form. He remembered the camera and was glad of its conspiratorial silence. He went to work.

THIRTEEN

TORY SAT CROSS-LEGGED on her bed, a Sociology text and notebook propped against her knees, a portable Sony television nestled amongst the menagerie of stuffed animals mounded at the foot of the mattress. "Roseanne" was on, her favorite show. But she wasn't really watching it. She couldn't concentrate on anything tonight. Her mind kept going back to Nick's studio, the moment when she took off her clothes.

She could still feel the throbbing intensity of his eyes. He'd been the first man ever to see her naked and she couldn't help wondering what he'd thought of her body. How did she compare to the other women he'd seen? Did he think she was too fat or too hairy? Were her arms long enough? What about her breasts? Had he seen the little scar near her left nipple where she'd had a mole removed? Probably. His eyes seemed to notice everything about her.

She sighed and got up, drawn by some invisible force to the full length mirror on her closet door. She stared intently, mesmerized by the sight of herself. Then, unbidden, her fingers moved to the buttons of the old jumpsuit she was wearing, slowly unfastening them one by one until the cotton fabric fell open, revealing the bare flesh of her torso.

However many times Tory had undressed and seen her body in the mirror, before it had always been a completely private act, a girl looking unself-consciously at her own reflection. But tonight it was different. Tonight she was looking at herself through Nick's eyes.

She stared straight ahead, concentrating on the way her collarbone stretched the skin taut against her throat, her square shoulders and too long neck. What was he looking for? What had he seen? Then, of their own volition, her eyes strayed downward to her breasts and settled there.

The potency of her own curiosity was strangely erotic, and as she looked at herself in the mirror, she could actually see the coral-colored nipples harden until they were sternly erect against the flesh of her bosom. Had they done that during the modeling session? She'd been too numb to feel it and too shy in his presence to look down to examine herself. She took a step closer to the mirror, and saw tiny bumps like gooseflesh on the aureole surrounding the nipple, even a few slender, blonde hairs, almost invisible against the pale skin.

She raised her hand and gently touched herself, cupping her hand under her breast to feel the springy weight of it. Held this way, it felt larger, more shapely than she had imagined. Her fingers found their way to the nipple, and she pressed it between her thumb and finger, gently at first but then, spurred on by a rush of pleasure from the sensation, harder.

Now she was aware of a squirming, damp heat between her legs, and her other hand was achingly drawn there. With one hand she lightly kneaded her breast and with the other she dipped between the folds, shocked at the sticky wetness. She raised her finger to examine the secretion. It was almost transparent, more felt than visible. She rubbed her fingers together, spreading the liquid like cream into the skin.

A throbbing began low inside her, a robin's heartbeat, and she pressed her finger inside once again to find its source. This time she let her fingers explore, moving upward toward the fleshy pulse. When she touched it, the sensation surged so intensely it made her knees buckle, and she had to grab hold of the door to keep her balance.

Suddenly she thought about Brad McMurphy, and the day she took pictures of his thigh. She had wanted so badly to touch his body, to reach under his jockstrap and lock her hand around what was hidden there. At the time she'd forced herself not to think about it, to concentrate on the job at hand. But now her imagination exploded with fantasies. Instead of taking the picture, she imagined that she set the camera down and slid her hand under the elastic waist of the ribbed cotton fabric covering Brad, easing it slowly lower, further and further until . . .

"Tory?"

Her father's voice and his knock on her door were simultaneous. In the instant it took Tory to react, she imagined him bursting through the door, finding her standing just so in front of the mirror, with her jumpsuit around her ankles, a finger thrust up into her body and her breasts swollen and exposed. Somehow it would be even worse than if he'd caught her with a boy.

But then to her immense relief, she heard him say, "Honey, are you decent?"

"Just a second, Daddy."

Gathering up the jumpsuit and buttoning it hastily, she hurried to the door, opened it, and peeked out. "Yeah?"

"Can I come in for a minute?"

"Well, okay." She stood aside for him to enter. He seemed awkward, too big and mannish for her room. And once he was inside, neither of them knew what to do. Then to Tory's horror, he walked over to the mirror and stood before it. For a split second she was sure her own reflection was still there, indelibly etched into the glass. But when she dared look, she saw only her father's image as he scratched at a stain on his shirt.

"Spaghetti sauce," he said apologetically. "Your mother will kill me."

"Maybe I can get it out," said Tory, glad for an excuse to leave the room. In the bathroom she quickly washed the sticky guilt off her hands and, carefully avoiding looking at herself in the mirror over the sink, she ran cold water on a washcloth and took it to her father, dabbing at the stain with the wet cloth, concentrating on the effort.

"I didn't know if you were doing homework or just watching TV," said Arthur, groping for words.

"Both, I guess," Tory replied.

Arthur looked at the textbook lying open on the bed. "*Interpretations of Abberant Adult Alternatives*? What happened to good old trigonometry?"

"This is for my Social Values class. It's an elective."

"I would hope so." What Arthur really hoped was that Tory wouldn't misunderstand what he was about to say to her. It was difficult enough for them to find a common language these days; to discuss what he had on his mind tonight would be close to impossible.

"There. That's the best I can do." Tory stood back to admire her work. The stain was not completely gone, but it was significantly reduced. She sat on the bed, curling her feet up under her, waiting.

"Thank you, sweetheart."

"No sweat. I mean, you're welcome."

Arthur looked down at his daughter. She seemed so young snuggled there on the pastel comforter amongst the stuffed animals. He remembered how thrilled she had been on her twelfth birthday when he had brought home the little white unicorn with the satin horn and silken strands of tail and mane. Had that really been five years ago? It hardly seemed possible. Looking at Tory now, hugging the soiled toy to her chest, waiting patiently to hear what he had to say, she was still that precious, untouched twelve-year-old.

"I wanted to talk to you about, about this modeling thing for the artist."

Tory rolled her eyes. "Daaad!" She drew out the syllable in a childish whine.

Arthur flinched inwardly. "I just wanted to make sure you knew . . . it's not something you *have* to do."

"It's no big deal, Dad. All I do is stand there."

Without your clothes, he thought, and knew she was thinking it as well. He was a little surprised and somewhat disappointed that she didn't seem to be uncomfortable about it. Did that mean she was used to taking off her clothes in front of boys? Or did it mean she understood the place of nudity in art and accepted her role as a muse? He didn't have a clue.

"I'm worried about you, Midget," he said, unconsciously reverting to his long-discarded pet name for her. "I don't want you to try to grow up too fast. You're still a little girl."

"Daddy, I'm seventeen-years-old."

That's what I mean, he thought, but didn't say. He just stared at her, unable to speak because his emotions were getting in the way.

"I can handle it."

He sighed. "Okay, just you be sure. There's nothing to be ashamed of if you decide not to go ahead with it."

"It's no big deal."

"Good." He stood and looked in the mirror at the damp spot on his shirt. The stain had disappeared. "Hey, you did great. She'll never know."

He reached for the door, and to his surprise Tory rose and gave him a hug. "I love you, Daddy."

"I love you too, Midget." He stroked her cheek with fatherly fondness, and left.

CHARLOTTE WAS ALREADY in bed when Arthur came in. She peered at him over her reading glasses, a *Vanity Fair* open on her lap. "Well?" she asked.

"She says she can handle it. I think she *wants* to do it."

"I told you," said Charlotte and picked up her magazine. "You worry too much."

"I'm her father. Isn't worrying my job?"

He wondered why Charlotte wasn't more concerned. Usually he was the one telling her not to worry. But they had completely reversed their normal roles on this issue. Charlotte turned out her light and reached over to give him a kiss. "I'm surprised at you, Arthur. You've got to let go. Let her grow up, sweetheart. After all, it's not every day we get a chance like this. Just think of it, we'll have an original Nicholas Stone sculpture of our own daughter! Who else do you know who can say that?"

Arthur was shocked. "You mean it's worth it to you to trade Tory's innocence for a piece of art?"

"She isn't sleeping with the man, she's posing for him! Heavens, Arthur, I never knew you were such an old fuddy duddy."

And because Arthur had no reply, the conversation ended.

Long after Arthur began to snore, Charlotte lay awake, too excited to sleep. At the monthly meeting of the Art Museum Council, she'd let word of Tory's modeling job slip to Nancy

Cartwright, knowing that the entire group would hear the news before the morning was over. And sure enough, at least half a dozen women had sidled up to her during the coffee break, eager to hear the details, their envy aroused by the knowledge that she had something their money couldn't buy. Charlotte had almost felt a physical sensation as her social status rose.

Why someday maybe I'll even donate the statue to the museum, Charlotte thought. 'Gift of Mrs. Arthur Hartman' it would say on a bronze plaque attached to the base. No, no, 'Gift of *Charlotte* Hartman.' Not only would Her daughter be immortalized in museum catalogs and by art history classes, but She, Charlotte, would be remembered as a generous patron of the arts.

And now that she was Nick Stone's patron, she saw no reason why she couldn't just drop by his studio, to say hello and check on the progress on the statue. Yes, of course. That's what she'd do. She'd drive down to Venice while Tory was in school and surprise Nick. Maybe even let him take her to lunch at that restaurant down there where all the artists went. They could have a glass of wine, or two or three, and discuss Art. Her heart warmed at the thought.

With a sigh, Arthur snuggled close to her in his sleep, and she imagined it was Nick beside her. After their lunch together, their wine, their tête-a-tête about Art, who was to say what might happen? And who would know if it did?

FOURTEEN

Roz GOT INTO the elevator at work in a state of contemplation, the memory of Adrian's body enveloping her like a prayer. It was the one week anniversary of their first night together, and they had been together nearly every night since. She was happy for the companionship, and she'd been soaking up the sex like a dry sponge. She should have been walking on air. But something was keeping her pinned to the ground. And she knew what it was.

It was the damn memory of Rick and how crazily in love she'd been with him. After ten years, she could still remember it vividly, and she couldn't stop herself from making comparisons. Adrian was a nice guy, no doubt about it. But he didn't inspire the kind of passion that made her head spin and her skin tingle. And when it came right down to it, sex without that passion was only one step up from aerobics. The question was, would she ever find that depth of feeling again, or should she just settle for second best?

"Morning, Diana." She smiled at the receptionist as she passed through the big glass doors at Century Insurance.

"Hi, Roz." Diana handed her two pink-slipped messages. "Two

calls for you this morning. And Mr. La Salle wants to see you."

"Thanks." Roz hurried through the side door to her office. At least the specter of her boss would take her mind off of her personal problems.

Nelson was at his desk reading *Computer Weekly* and eating a bagel, his size thirteen feet resting comfortably on Roz's chair.

"Morning," Roz said, noticing the feet but keeping her mouth shut. "Got any Red Zinger?"

"Nope," Nelson replied, taking a sip of his own tea.

No doubt he was still hurt that she'd canceled their Friday movie date. Well, how was she to know Adrian was going to enter her life just when she was scheduled to go out with Nelson? Roz dumped her purse and briefcase onto her desk. As nicely as she could, she lifted his feet off her chair and set them on the floor, brushing off the seat before plopping down into it.

"La Salle wants to see you," Nelson taunted.

"That's what I heard," replied Roz, glancing at her messages. One was a callback from Joe Miller, her contact at the Treasury Department. She'd asked him to check FINSEN, the Financial Crimes Enforcement Network, just to make sure there'd been no recent calls about the Diebenkorn. But Joe's message was short and sweet. "Nada on the D," it read.

The other message was from Lieutenant Drake at the L.A.P.D.'s Art Theft Division, returning her call. He was her best bet. She'd get back to him after she ran a few more files.

Roz put both messages aside and accessed her computer. The little grey screen blinked and bleeped at her, and came up with her main menu. She went into the Stein file and started to work. For days she'd been loading data she'd gotten from Richard Diebenkorn's estate, hoping to find the owners of every other painting he'd sold in his forty-odd year career, on the off chance that one of those collectors might have coveted "Number 84." It was a long shot, but Roz knew that sometimes art collectors became obsessive about certain artists, and would go to any lengths to obtain a given piece of art.

Diebenkorn had been prolific; his collectors numbered in the thousands, in the United States, Europe and Asia. She had her work cut out for her. She pushed "Print" and waited while the machine spat out a hard copy of the file. At least she could show La Salle that she was doing something.

She glanced at Nelson who was again buried in his magazine. "Any idea what La Salle wants?"

He didn't look up. "No doubt it's about Stein. That's what you're supposed to be working on, isn't it?" he snapped.

Roz sighed. "Nelson, could we just get past this . . . this whatever it is between us? It's making me crazy."

"What d'you mean?" His voice was slightly muffled by the magazine in front of his face.

"I know you're angry at me because I canceled our date last Friday, but you never let me explain."

"You don't have to explain anything to me." His tone implied that nothing she could say would be explanation enough.

She ignored him. "I canceled our date last week because I met a man."

"What am I, a wildebeest?"

He had a point. Nobody liked being told they were second string. She decided to try an appeal to his rationality. "Look, I like you a lot. I wouldn't last a week here without you. But Nelson, you don't really think there could be anything more than friendship between us, do you?"

"Why not?"

"Well, for one thing, our ages."

"I like mature women."

"I'm 'mature' enough to be your mother!"

"What's wrong with that? I love my mother," he persisted.

Roz sighed. This was going to be harder than she'd thought. "Look, why don't we have lunch today? I want to talk to you about this but I've got to see La Salle before it gets any later. Okay?"

Nelson hesitated, as though he had to think about it.

She knew how to get to him. "California Pizza Kitchen. I'll make a reservation. One o'clock?"

"I suppose I could pencil you in."

Roz picked up a notebook and tried three pens before she found one that worked. "My treat," she said as she went out the door.

"Damn right," he replied to her retreating back.

FOR THE SECOND TIME in a week, Roz found herself in the hot seat facing David La Salle over his massive desk.

"I'm eager to hear about your progress on the Stein Case," La Salle said, getting right to the point. "What do you have?"

Roz squirmed in her chair, adjusting her skirt to cover her knees. "I've been compiling a file of all the current owners of Diebenkorn's work." She held out the computer printout, but he ignored it so she went on. "My theory is that maybe one of them coveted that particular . . ."

La Salle leaned across his desk, his gold Masonic pin glinting in Roz's eyes. "*Ms.* Weeks," he said, emphasizing the Ms., "you don't seem to realize that we're fighting for our lives here. This is trench warfare. Working on a computer file just isn't going to win the battle. We need action!"

"I'm also trying to get some hard evidence on Con Uttrell." Roz hoped she sounded optimistic.

"And?"

"I haven't been successful yet," she admitted. "But I haven't given up. I just need a little more time."

"I assume you like working here at Century Insurance," La Salle said, his voice thick with menace.

"Oh, very much, sir," Roz replied.

"Well enjoy it while you can, Ms. Weeks, because the Steins are demanding restitution by the end of the month, which is next week. If we have to pay them off, I'd be hard pressed to justify your salary. We can't carry a slacker indefinitely, you know."

Roz bit her lip. She was furious that the big twerp would ignore her past record in auto claims and fire her over this one case, but it was within his power to do so. "I'll do my best," she said.

"Oh, well then, I guess we can all stop worrying." La Salle's sarcasm lopped another chunk out of Roz's self esteem. She tried to think of a retort, but no inspiration was forthcoming. And then La Salle's door burst open. A short, hirsute man in an expensive hand-tailored suit stormed through it.

"Mr. Harrington!" cried La Salle. He leapt to his feet so spontaneously that Roz rose as well. She'd never met the Big Boss, but recognized him from his photo in the company newsletter. Although he was diminutive in stature, he didn't waste any time in living up to his nickname of 'Dirty Harrington.'

"We've got a problem, La Salle, and you're it," he shouted, ignoring Roz, who stepped out of the line of fire and tried to blend into the wallpaper.

"Mr. Harrington . . ." La Salle began.

"Shut up and listen to me," Harrington spat. "You know damn well the claim on the Michelangelo Giant is going to blow this company out of the water. Why haven't I heard back from you on it?"

"Mr. Harrington, the whole world has been looking for that piece for months with no success."

"La Salle, you are so lame, it pisses me off that you were even born."

"I assure you I'm doing my best to . . ."

"Your best, my ass," Harrington roared, much to Roz's delight. "Or should I say *your* ass, because it's going to be in a sling, La Salle, unless I see something concrete on my desk pronto. Have I made myself clear?"

"Perfectly clear, sir."

Harrington spun on his well-polished heel and strode toward the door, but he stopped and glared at Roz who was hovering close by La Salle's ficus tree as though its sparse branches could hide her. "Who the hell are you?" he sniped.

"Roz Weeks, sir," she said.

His face remained blank. There was no reason why he should know her; Century Insurance employed nearly two hundred people, and Roz was only a face in the peanut gallery.

"I work for Mr. La Salle, in Art Recovery," she added limply.

Harrington looked at La Salle, then back to Roz. "Let me give you a word of advice, Roz Weeks. You and your boss both better start typing up your resumés because this bomb has a short fuse, and if it explodes, it's taking the whole department with it."

"Yes sir, Mr. Harrington," Roz stifled her impulse to salute as Harrington stormed out of the office. When the door slammed behind him, La Salle melted into his chair, eyes glazed, expression blank.

"That'll be all, Ms. Weeks," he said without looking at her. "Oh, and Ms. Weeks. We should keep this little incident to ourselves. In fact, the whole topic of the Michelangelo is off limits. Understood?"

"Not really, sir. Mr. Harrington said . . ."

"You report to me, Ms. Weeks, and I say stifle it." He motioned her close and said in a low tone, "I have reason to believe there may be an internal connection, so it's in our best interests to keep the investigation quiet. Is that clear?"

"Yes, sir," Roz replied meekly, and nearly tripped in her eagerness to get out of the office. As she hurried back to her office she tried to remember what she'd heard about the disappearance of the Michelangelo Giant.

"A SOUTHWEST BURRITO PIZZA, hold the guac, and a veggie, no cheese."

The waitress set the pizzas down in front of Roz and Nelson. "Anything else I can get you guys?"

"I'll have another Diet Pepsi. Want anything, Nelson?"

Nelson shook his head. He was already stuffing his mouth with a pizza, its mottled surface a mirror image of his complexion. "That's all, thanks," Roz replied to the waitress.

Roz watched Nelson eat, her appetite gone. "Nelson, do you know anything about the Michelangelo Giant?"

He shrugged. "I read a memo about it a few weeks ago. Century stands to drop a bundle if they have to pay off. Something like four zillion." He picked an olive off his pizza, examined it, and ate it.

"Well, why aren't we all breaking our necks trying to find it?" Roz asked.

"I dunno. Maybe someone higher up's trying to get the reward."

"What reward?"

"The four hundred grand for whoever finds it."

"How come I never heard about that?"

"Because the memo I read was never circulated."

"Then how'd you see it?"

"I accessed La Salle's secretary's computer file."

"What? How?"

"I know her password. It wasn't very hard to figure out. It's 'dalmatian' as in black and white spotted dog, as in the twenty snapshots she's got pasted all over her wall."

Roz picked up her knife and fork, cut a piece of her pizza, and began to chew.

"What're you doing?" asked Nelson.

"Eating my pizza."

"Roz, nobody eats pizza with utensils. It's un-American."

"Pizza's not American, it's Italian."

"No, it's not," Nelson insisted. "Actually it's a completely American invention, like chop suey. Somebody just took an ethnic idea and gave it that good old American twist."

"If you know everything, tell me who stole the Giant."

Nelson chewed thoughtfully, then swallowed. "Idi Amin was known to pay thieves to steal specific works for his private collection. He had a French connection, took stuff out of Marseilles."

"You don't really think the Michelangelo Giant is in Uganda, do you?"

"Probably not. Especially since General Amin is dead." Nelson smiled at Roz. "Do yourself a favor. Forget about the Michelangelo. Concentrate on the Diebenkorn. That's what they're paying you for, isn't it?"

Roz sighed. "La Salle is all over me like a rash. I just can't seem to make any headway. And there's no trail. I don't know where to go with it."

"You've gotta think like Uttrell. Say you're sitting there with a hot painting, and you wanna get rid of it. What do you do?"

"Put an ad in *The Recycler?*"

"I'm serious. What do you do?"

Roz sighed, "You either warehouse it for a long time while the trail cools, or you move it out of the state or country."

"Right. So in this case, which is Uttrell going to do?"

"You tell me."

"You really want to hear my theory?" Nelson asked.

"I'm asking you for it. Yes."

"This may sound a little off the wall, but here goes. Con Uttrell's made a fortune in this business, recession or not. I've been asking myself how he's done it." He leaned over close to Roz, as though to impart some secret wisdom. "I think he's got more up his sleeve than just a measly Diebenkorn."

"A painting worth a quarter of a million isn't so measly," Roz noted.

"Yeah, but what if he had two paintings worth a quarter of a million each, or three or four?"

"I'm not following."

"If Con Uttrell has an original Diebenkorn, what's to stop him from having a forgery made of it? He's got practically every artist in town under his thumb. Who's to say he can't get one of them to copy a Bengston or a Moses or a Diebenkorn? If he sticks to the contemporaries — art that hasn't got a lot of age to it — he can buy the same paints, have his canvases stretched by the same art shop, whatever. By photographing a print and transferring it to a lithograph or silkscreen, a forger can make a duplicate that is virtually indistinguishable from the original. Then he can circulate the fake and keep the original."

"That's taking a lot of risks."

"Yeah, but it would work. The way I see it, L.A. is a very savvy art community, especially where a local boy like Dick Diebenkorn is concerned. But Uttrell could take his copy out of the area, out of the country, even. The chances of somebody catching a fake Diebenkorn in Argentina or Australia would be slim. He'd make some money, and he'd still have the original."

Roz thought about this. It did make sense, in a twisted sort of a way. "So you think I should stop looking for the original and try to find the forgery?"

"I'd look for the forg*er*, hit as many artists' studios as possible — paper the city with your cards."

"You think a forger's going to confess?"

"Think about it, Roz. You know how jealous these artists are of each other. Would you really be surprised if one of 'em ratted on a competitor?"

Roz nodded. "I suppose it's worth a shot."

"I'd also go out to LAX in case Uttrell's already trying to move the painting. Show 'em pictures of the Diebenkorn. Those guys don't know a Picasso from a pizza. You gotta spell it out for them."

Roz looked at her watch and smiled. "I'm way ahead of you there. I already have an appointment with the head guy, at three o'clock."

FIFTEEN

CON'S STRETCH MERCEDES screeched to a stop at The Bradley Terminal at LAX. Rocco ran around to open the door. "We're here, Mr. U," he said.

Con didn't respond. He sat for a moment, preparing himself to deal with the onslaught of people, noise and confusion that made coming to the airport so exhausting. He hoped this foray was going to be worth the effort.

"Wait here," he instructed Rocco.

"Yessir, Mr. U."

Con entered the building, glad for the automatic sliding doors which made it unnecessary for him to touch the filthy glass. He asked directions and followed them to a door that said 'Department of Inspection and Control.' There was no response to his knock, so Con opened the door gingerly, using his handkerchief to turn the knob.

It was a typical government office, too much cheap furniture crowded into an unventilated space, manned by a politically correct staff — an Oprah-sized black woman in a Whitney Houston-sized uniform, and a beautiful Asian whose extravagantly long hair hung down her back like the pelt of a slain animal.

"I have an appointment with the Director of Inspection and Control, Arthur Hartman," Con said.

"He's on the floor," the black woman replied, not looking up from her magazine.

"She means the baggage check," the Asian said.

Con turned his attention to her. "I would be most grateful if one of you could direct me. I'm in somewhat of a hurry."

"I'm on my break," the black woman said, cracking her gum.

"You're always on your break, Lucille," the other sneered.

"Break this, Kimberly," she threw back, illustrating her meaning with a raised middle finger.

"Oh, I'll show you," the Asian girl said. When she stood, Con saw that the long hair was an unsuccessful attempt to camouflage her hideously misshapen spine. Like some freak in a Ken Russell movie, she was beauty and the beast all in one. As she led him from the office, her body heaved from side to side with the effort of manipulating her tortured body. A bad omen, it seemed to Con. But he followed her back into the hall.

"Turn left at the end of the corridor, and take the elevator down to the basement, then go . . ."

Con found Arthur Hartman standing behind two-way glass, watching a Customs officer inspecting luggage. Beside the glass was a video monitor showing an x-ray of the bag.

The two men shook hands. "I had no idea your operation was so sophisticated," Con said politely. In truth, he was unnerved to realize how ignorant he'd been.

"Travellers are getting bolder and much more ingenious at hiding undeclared goods," Arthur explained. "You'd be surprised how many otherwise honest people lie about their purchases. So we're really cracking down. From now on, people who try to cheat the United States government are going to get caught."

Con nodded somberly and watched through the glass.

An expensive Gucci suitcase was splayed open on the conveyor, revealing a slovenly jumble of clothes: wadded up underwear, wrinkled slacks and shirts, a damp bathing suit, toiletries in crumpled and crushed containers. With poorly disguised trepidation, the bag's owners watched the Customs officer poke through the bag, as though he were trying to identify an animal by examining its spoor.

"What happens when you catch someone?" Con asked.

Arthur Hartman shrugged noncommittally. "They're thoroughly searched. The undeclared items are confiscated, of course, and there is an inquiry. When it's just a matter of some items of clothing or a camera, we usually let it go with a fine. But when we catch a smuggler, we prosecute to the full extent of the law."

The men watched as a Labrador Retriever nosed the luggage on the carousel.

"Guess what he's looking for?"

"Drugs?" Con asked.

Arthur smiled. "That too, but if you can believe it, fresh fruits and vegetables."

"What for?"

"Medfly control. The Animal and Plant Health Inspection Service trains them."

"Too bad they can't sniff out stolen goods as well," Con mused, thinking he was making a joke.

"It's not out of the realm of possibility," Arthur said seriously. "I've read about tests done whereby valuable objects, art pieces even, have been imbued with an odor as a kind of security. Not anything detectable by humans, of course, but something an animal can recognize, in case the object is stolen."

The thought of it brought a chill to Con's blood. "And these tests have been successful?"

Arthur shrugged. "The jury's still out. I don't know if it's actually being put into practice, but anything is possible."

"I've heard there's a list of some sort," Con said, following Arthur out of the terminal and into an elevator, "of people who have been caught with undeclared items."

Arthur pushed the button for the basement and the doors enclosed them. "Ah, the famous list. It's simply a computer record of everyone who has tried to cheat the government out of its import duty. You people in the art world must have some sort of computerized method to keep track of individuals who don't abide by the rulcs."

"Yes, we do, but it isn't very accurate or helpful. The problem is compounded because identifying stolen works of art is so difficult. There are no serial numbers on art, no comprehensive system of identification. Even experts have trouble telling the fakes from the originals."

The two men got out of the elevator and Arthur led Con into the employee cafeteria. "I hope you don't mind our talking here," he said. "Since they've been remodeling the airport, office space has been cramped. And not very private."

"I understand," said Con. "I appreciate your taking time to see me."

Arthur was flattered, and a little uncomfortable. He rarely had visitors, and never before had anyone as sophisticated or impressive as Con Uttrell made the trek down into the bowels of LAX. "I must admit I was a bit surprised to get your call."

Con nodded, adding a packet of Equal to his coffee. The brown liquid was the consistency of sludge. It must have been percolating for hours. His stomach gurgled in anticipation of the acid. "Francis Thornton was kind enough to give me your name," he explained. "Apparently you've been a great help to him in the importation of his art works."

Arthur took a sip of his coffee. "It's my job," he said simply and smiled at Con. "So how can I help you? You said something about a piece of sculpture?"

Con nodded. "An artist I represent is creating a bronze statue which I need to ship to a collector in Japan. The problem, of course, is protecting artwork when it's traveling long distances. You wouldn't think so, but bronze is quite fragile. The metal has a memory of the stress it suffers, and once there is a blemish, or a distortion of the surface, the piece loses value."

"I didn't know or care very much about bronze, until recently," Arthur admitted, somewhat embarrassed. "You see, my teenage daughter is posing for an artist in town. He's making a statue of her."

"Oh, really," said Con politely. "Who is it, if I may ask?"

"Actually we met him at the party at the Thorntons', where we met you," Arthur said. "His name is Stone, Nicholas Stone. You probably know him." He looked hopefully at Con. "My wife arranged it. She's very keen on getting a piece of sculpture for our house and made some agreement with this artist that if we gave Tory — that's our daughter — permission to model for him, he'd give us a copy of the sculpture."

Con set his coffee down carefully and tried to keep a neutral expression on his face. This was a preposterous coincidence, a glitch in his plans that nobody could have foreseen. How on earth had Nick Stone met the Hartman's daughter? Then he remembered the incident at the Thorntons' unveiling. "Your daughter — she was the one who fell into the pond at the party?"

"Yes," Arthur admitted. "I'm not altogether sure how that happened. You know how young girls are."

Con did know quite a bit about young girls. But that was another subject and certainly not one he wanted to get into with the father of one of them. He tried to read Arthur's thoughts, toeing the line between opportunity and disaster.

"Do you know him?" Arthur asked.

"Nick Stone? Yes, I do," said Con. "In fact, he's the very artist whose work I am shipping to Japan."

"No kidding! You don't think . . . it wouldn't be the statue he's making of my daughter, could it be?"

"I haven't seen the statue yet, but I will certainly find out."

"It would mean a great deal to me," said Arthur, his tone suddenly confidential. "I'm not crazy about this business. Tory's just seventeen. I don't know how he convinced her mother to go along with it. Charlotte is usually so strict where Tory is concerned. Anyway, I'm sure you can appreciate my feelings."

"Of course," said Con.

"I'd be grateful if you could talk to him, make sure that my little girl, how can I say this, is still my little girl when she's finished."

"Don't say another word. It's done," Con replied. Perfect, he thought. Now Arthur Hartman owed him one.

"And what can I do to repay the favor?" Arthur asked, as though reading Con's thoughts.

"A statue by one of my artists is, in a small sense, as precious to me as your daughter is to you," he said. "Traveling such a long distance, frankly I'd prefer not to let it out of my sight. But I'm hardly eager to ride in the baggage compartment."

Taking his cue, Arthur replied, "I can arrange for you to take the statue on board the aircraft, if that's what you'd like. And I can get you cleared right through Customs on the other end as well. Would that help?"

"Immensely," said Con. "I would be very thankful for your assistance."

"It would be my pleasure," said Arthur, relieved. "After all, we may be talking about a statue of my daughter. I'd certainly want to see that she got first-class treatment."

WALKING BACK TO THE STREET, Con congratulated himself, pleased with the turn of events. He was confident Hartman would do everything in his power to eliminate the red tape from the transport of the statue to Japan. And taking the statue on board would lessen the danger of theft.

It only remained for Con to live up to his end of the bargain, to ensure that if Nick Stone was using the Hartman girl as his model, that he did not abuse his relationship with her, at least not until the statue was safely out of the country.

ROZ WAITED IMPATIENTLY for the light to change so she could cross from the parking lot to the Tom Bradley Terminal. She felt the excitement around her, people dragging suitcases or pulling them on little carts, excited children running ahead of their parents to meet Grandma and Grandpa's plane. It had been years since she'd gone on a trip. Wouldn't she love to just step up to a counter and purchase a one-way ticket to a new life?

Unconsciously she patted the totebag hanging at her side. In it were a dozen 8 x 10s of the stolen Diebenkorn painting. She'd set up a meeting with the Director of Inspection and Control to alert him that it might be passing through his jurisdiction, and to ask him to distribute the photos to his staff so that they would be on the lookout for it.

The light turned green, and she joined the other pedestrians in the crosswalk. Roz had to hop the last step onto the curb to avoid being mowed down by a limousine, which cut across two lanes of traffic and skidded to a halt just in front of her. The driver, who looked like the heavy in a James Bond flick, jumped out and ran around to open the passenger door.

Roz couldn't believe her eyes. None other than Con Uttrell stepped through the automatic doors of the terminal building and walked toward the waiting car. What was he doing here? Did it have something to do with the Diebenkorn, or was he just returning from a trip? He didn't have any luggage, so that was unlikely.

On impulse, Roz ran to intercept Con Uttrell before he ducked into the car. "Mr. Uttrell," she called. "May I have a minute?"

He glanced at her — through her it seemed — and got into the car.

"Mr. Uttrell don't answer questions," said the driver. He blocked Roz's way with his huge body and closed the door behind his boss. Helplessly, Roz stood and watched as the limo merged with the traffic, her heart beating wildly.

FIVE MINUTES LATER she was showing the Diebenkorn photos to Arthur Hartman.

"Yes, I did meet with Mr. Uttrell just before you came, but he didn't mention anything about a painting," he assured her. He was holding the photos of the Diebenkorn upside down. "We were discussing a piece of sculpture Mr. Uttrell wants to ship. A bronze statue."

Damn. Roz couldn't believe she'd hit a dead end. Her instincts told her there had to be a connection between the Diebenkorn and this statue. But what?

"Who's the artist?" Roz asked.

"A fellow by the name of Nicholas Stone. Maybe you know him," Hartman added hopefully.

"By reputation, but not personally." Roz said. Nicholas Stone. He was fairly well known. Roz thought she'd seen his name somewhere recently. Then it came to her. He was one of the artists listed on the invitation to the Venice Art Walk, a community charity event which she attended each year. It was coming up in a few days.

She stood. "I hope you will let me know immediately if you see any artwork that resembles this photo." She turned the photo rightside up in Hartman's hand.

"If it's a stolen painting, I presume it wouldn't come through looking like this," Arthur commented.

"What do you mean?"

"Smugglers are a very ingenious bunch, Ms. Weeks. Once we had a painting come through, a landscape, quite nice really, but nothing of value. Then one of our men noticed that the paint was not entirely dry in one spot." Arthur chuckled. "That made him suspicious because the paperwork said it was painted in 1985.

"At any rate it turned out that someone had just painted over the real painting, which was by somebody named Alexander. Stolen, as it turns out."

"Peter Alexander?"

"Yes, I think that was it. It was worth about $50,000." Arthur scratched his chin. "And then there was the Chinese scroll painting. Now that was really clever."

"How so?"

"It was hidden inside a piece of pottery. Literally. The smugglers had made a hollow bottom on the thing and actually fired the clay with the scroll inside. There was no way to tell it was in there, no way at all."

"How did you find it?"

Arthur chuckled. "Sheer luck. The officer who was examining it wasn't paying attention, and he dropped it. The damn thing broke all over the floor, and this scroll wrapped in plastic fell out. That was one for the books!"

SIXTEEN

"ARE YOU OR ARE YOU NOT using the Hartman girl as your model?" Con demanded. "It's a simple question, requiring a simple answer."

It was early morning; Leslie hadn't even arrived. Nick had just started unwrapping the wet paper from around the mold when Con Uttrell had appeared unannounced. As yet the clay had only the rudimentary shape of a human figure, an artwork in an embryonic stage. But Nick still treated it with sensitive hands, giving it his full attention.

"What if I am?" he answered without looking at Con.

Con tried to remain calm. "Why, may I ask, did you chose her?"

"What business is it of yours how I choose my models?" Nick asked.

"The girl is a minor, Nicholas. If you get her into trouble . . ."

Nick wheeled around to face Con. "*You're* the one who gets girls into trouble, Uttrell. I sculpt them."

Con burned with anger, but knew better than to let it melt his icy restraint. "There are a thousand prettier girls out there on the beach. Why not pick one of them? What difference does it make?"

"What difference does it make to you?"

"I'll tell you. The girl's father is . . . a friend. He is concerned about preserving her . . . innocence. I warn you, if anything is done to compromise her, you will be jeopardizing this commission, and your career." As he spoke, Con approached the partially molded clay.

"I'm going to sculpt her, not seduce her." Nick moved protectively between the clay and Con Uttrell. He hated for a work-in-progress to be seen by anyone, let alone so hostile an audience.

"You do have a reputation, my boy," Con said, circling wide to get closer to the clay. "If she gets it into her schoolgirl head that you are taking advantage of her and goes crying to Daddy . . . I'm telling you, Nicholas, the consequences will be dire. There's no time to waste. The statue must be cast and ready to ship in three weeks." He casually picked one of Nick's sculpting files up off the work table and stroked it as he circled the clay. "I must say, I'm not very impressed so far. Can't you give her a little more," he made a lewd gesture with his hands, "maturity?"

"Don't tell me how to do my work!" Nick erupted. "I'm the creator. You're just a salesman. Without me you'd have nothing."

"Without me perhaps you'd have many things, but they would all be worthless," Con replied, reaching out with the file to prick the clay pubis.

"Son of a bitch — get out!" Nick was beyond anger now. He surged forward, pushing Con away from the statue. Con raised his hand to fend off Nick's advance and that slight movement incited Attila to do what he had been trained to do. Although chained to the floor, the dog hurled his massive body at this intruder who had threatened his master. But the line jerked him backwards to the floor, and his bared teeth clamped shut half an inch from Con's jugular. He tried to scramble to his feet, but Rocco leapt forward and stepped on the chain, choking the dog. Quickly he drew his gun and delivered a crushing blow to the animal's skull with the butt end.

"You bastard!" Nick lunged at Rocco but stopped short when Rocco pointed the gun at him.

"Oh, put it away, Rocco," Con said, struggling to regain his composure. "He's an artist. He's not going to hurt anyone."

Reluctantly, Rocco got to his feet and holstered the gun. Attila lay still, breathing hard.

"Keep away from the girl, Nicholas. If you so much as lay a finger on her, you will wish I'd let you off as easily as I did that animal." Con walked a few paces, then turned back to Nick. "Don't think I won't know what you're doing," Con said ominously, and he was gone.

CHARLOTTE HARTMAN DROVE around Venice for twenty minutes, looking for a proper parking place for her Buick. Squinting through her new contact lenses, she'd seen several AP-COA lots, but the attendants looked unsavory and the parking spaces too close together. God forbid she should get a ding in the door of her pristine little Skylark.

Finally she spotted a dilapidated VW van backing out of a space on the street. It had a one-hour parking meter and she hoped she'd be with Nick longer than that. But she'd rather risk getting a ticket than relinquish her car to some miscreant in a public lot.

Slipping into the spot, she locked the gearshift in park, activated the alarm, and stepped onto the street. Immediately she was assaulted by the moist beach air, heavy with the aroma of frying hamburgers and coconut oil. Her first thought was of her hair. She hoped the dampness wouldn't cause it to frizz. She should have worn a scarf or a hat.

She raised her foot to step up to the curb, but a string of bubble gum held the slingback pump to the pavement, and she lost her balance, falling, nearly landing in the lap of a vagrant who had staked out his territory against the wall of Nick's studio.

"Howdedoodie," he yodeled at Charlotte, baring his blackened gums in a pathetic parody of a smile. He reached out his hand.

"Aagh!" she gasped, recoiling and struggling to get to her feet. Her shoe was broken but she ignored it and limped toward Nick's door as fast as she could. When she looked over her shoulder, the vagrant was scooting towards her. To her horror she realized he was legless, the blunt stumps of his thighs balanced on a skateboard, which he maneuvered with amazing agility and speed. Frantically, Charlotte pummeled Nick's metal door with her shoe.

"Somebody help me, please! Help!"

Inside the office, Leslie heard the pounding and the cries. "I'm going to have to call you back, Dr. Jensen," she said into the phone. "Some weirdo's about to break down the door." On the way out of the office, she picked up a canister of mace. You never knew what errant life form might try to wander in off the Boardwalk. When she pulled open the door, Charlotte stumbled forward.

"Oh, thank God," she panted. "You saved my life." She limped inside and slammed the door shut behind her.

The woman didn't look like one of the local street denizens, but in Venice you never knew. Leslie kept a firm grip on the mace. "What happened? Did you get mugged?" She peered through the peep hole in the door and saw nothing out of the ordinary.

"Yes . . . no, not exactly. There was a man with no legs. It was horrible!"

"Shorty?" Leslie peered out the hole again, this time aiming her eyes downward. And sure enough, Shorty scooted by on his board, his elongated arms substituting for both legs and feet. "Oh, he wouldn't hurt anyone. How could he? The poor guy got his legs chopped off by a doped-up surgeon in Viet Nam." She looked at Charlotte as if she were to blame for Shorty's misfortunes. "What can I do for you?"

Prickling with annoyance, Charlotte slipped on her pump and did what she could to smooth out her soiled dress. "I've come to speak with Mr. Stone. I'm Charlotte Hartman, Victoria's mother."

Leslie eyed her with suspicion. Anyone who called Nick 'Mr. Stone' didn't know him very well, and who the hell was Victoria? She drew herself up to her full 5' 2" height. "I'm Nick's secretary, Leslie Woods, and I'm sorry, I don't recognize your name. Did you have an appointment?"

"No, but he *will* see me. Just tell him I'm here, please."

"He's working now, and can't be disturbed."

"Nonsense! I've come all the way from Westridge." There was a tremolo of frustration beneath Charlotte's bravado. Then she seemed to catch herself and regain her dignity. "It's very important I speak to Nick about Victoria. In fact, if I don't see him, I'm afraid I won't be able to allow her to continue modeling for him."

"Wait a minute. Victoria? That's Tory! Tory's your daughter?"

"Yes, that's what I've been saying," Charlotte snapped.

"Oh, God, I'm sorry. I didn't realize it was a nickname. She never told us. Tory, Victoria. Of course! I'm Leslie Woods. Oh, I already said that, didn't I?" Leslie giggled. "Tory's a sweetie, she really is. And I think the statue is going to be beautiful, Mrs. Hartman. Nick seems to be very excited about it already."

Charlotte held her head high. "Well, there's not going to be a statue unless I'm able to speak with him. Her father and I are . . . I really must talk to Nick about it," she finished imperiously.

"Well, sure," Leslie's tone was now accommodating and eager to please. "I'm sure he'll see you, Mrs. Hartman. Let me just tell him you're here. Would you like to . . . freshen up a bit while I get him?"

"That would be good, yes," Charlotte replied.

"The bathroom's through that door over there, where it says, Tête. It means . . ."

"I know what it means," Charlotte snapped, already on her way. "Thank you." She stepped into the bathroom and closed the door behind her.

Leslie heard the deadbolt turn. "Thank you too, bitch," she muttered under her breath, and went off to warn Nick.

Charlotte looked around for a clean place to set her purse. The surfaces were grimy and damp, the sink a deep, free-standing basin that looked like it belonged in a laundromat, not a powder room. Charlotte slung her bag over her shoulder and bent toward the mirror. Her image was blurred and somehow distorted in the cloudy glass. From what she could see, her face and hair looked salvageable, nothing a comb and a bit of powder couldn't fix.

But her new dress was another story. The Nile-green bodice was badly wrinkled, and the hem was torn in back. Something sticky seemed to have attached itself to her sleeve as well. With vigor, Charlotte set to work. Soap and water would have to do for now, with the help of a safety pin for the hem. There should be one in her purse; she usually carried a few in case of emergency.

NICK WAS BENT OVER his work table, using a heliarc welder to solder two fragments of cast bronze together. He wore a shield over his face and enormous gloves to protect his hands from the intense heat of the welder. Usually his crew did this labor, but Nick had dismissed them today. He needed the distraction of hard, physical work as an antidote to the anger that had been gnawing at him since Con Uttrell's surprise visit. He had been at it nonstop all morning, trying to funnel his rage into something productive. But the anger had not gone away.

Leslie made sure she was in his line of sight so that her sudden appearance would not startle him. When he saw her, he turned off the welder and pulled up the shield.

"What's the word on Attila?"

"Dr. Jensen thinks he's going to be okay. I'll go over there on my lunch break to see him."

Nick nodded and turned back to his work.

"Charlotte Hartman is here to see you," Leslie said.

"Who's that?"

"Charlotte Hartman. Tory's mom."

It took a second for Nick to focus on this. "What does she want?"

Leslie shrugged. "She says she and her husband are concerned about something and she needs to talk to you."

Nick sighed. He was in no mood for this. But what choice did he have? Charlotte could forbid Tory to model if she chose, and he wasn't about to risk that — not when the piece was progressing so well.

"Okay, send her back," he said reluctantly.

"I was going to go to lunch and the vet's. Do you want me to wait?"

"No. I can handle it."

"I'll put the phones on hold."

CHARLOTTE PICKED HER WAY carefully through the studio, awed by the towering statues on pedestals, the myriad fragments of figures, and the works-in-progress — all jumbled together chaotically. How incredible that Nick's exquisitely serene artwork was born of such aesthetic anarchy. Wouldn't she love to bring Radiance down here and set about organizing and cleaning the place.

Then Charlotte saw Nick, dishevelled from his work and disoriented by the interruption. She ached to tidy him up as well. She had to stop herself from reaching out to smooth down his hair and refasten the mismatched buttons of his shirt.

He was staring at her, unsmiling, wordless. She couldn't tell whether this was a good sign or not, but clearly he was waiting for her to break the silence.

"Nick, how good to see you again." She thrust out her just-washed hand, but when he reached to shake it, instinct made her recoil as she did from anything dirty, and his work-soiled hand was left hanging in midair. Slowly, he let it drop to his side.

"I-I-I'm sorry," she stuttered. "You're . . ."

"Not used to being interrupted while I'm working," he finished.

"I've come to see how the work is progressing on Our Statue," Charlotte said boldly.

"It's coming," Nick replied, trying not to let her use of the possessive pronoun anger him.

"May I see it?"

"No."

His sharp reply flustered Charlotte, but she persisted. "Now Nicholas, Tory is my daughter. I think I have the right to . . ."

"I don't let anyone see a work-in-progress. Ever. Even if they do have the right," Nick interrupted. "That's just how I operate."

"But I've come all this way!" Charlotte tried to recover herself.

"Nobody asked you to."

She was stunned by his rudeness. "If I could just take a tiny peek at . . ."

"It's out of the question. End of subject."

"Couldn't we at least have lunch or . . ."

"No. I can't leave the studio while my secretary's out."

"Oh."

"Besides, I'm not hungry. I have to work."

"I see." Her whole body seemed to deflate. She looked so disappointed and beaten that Nick softened. He hadn't meant to be so harsh. Besides, he needed to have her on his side. "I guess you can stick around awhile if you want, as long as you're here. I don't care. It's up to you."

"Thank you," she replied meekly. "I will."

He nodded to the stool in the photography area. "You can sit over there. I'm going to get a beer. Do you want one?" he called over his shoulder, heading for his living quarters.

"No, no beer, thank you," said Charlotte.

She picked her way over to the photography area and when she was sure Nick couldn't see her, dug her handkerchief out of her handbag. It was still moist from her bathroom ablutions, and she used it to dust off the stool. Just as she'd expected, it came away smeared with grime. She worked at it until she was satisfied it was clean, and sat delicately, just on the edge, and waited.

Then the photos on the wall caught her eye. She got up to look at them. They were pictures of a nude body, a female body. A dozen photos documented the woman's appendages and orifices and curves. Charlotte had never seen female nudity so casually displayed. She was shocked, but at the same time she couldn't stop looking.

All of a sudden, it dawned on Charlotte that these could be pictures of Tory! She did not recognize a breast or a thigh, but then it had been years since she had seen Tory without her clothes. Could her daughter really be this voluptuous? She moved closer to look for some identifying mark.

And as she did, she started to think about her own body. How would she compare? Granted, the woman pictured was much younger than she, but then Charlotte never visualized her body as it was. In her mind's eye she saw herself as she had been at twenty-five, when her breasts had not succumbed to the inevitability of gravity, and she had proudly boasted that her waist measurement was smaller than her age.

She was still proud of her body, but even so, how would it feel to have pictures of it just tacked up on the wall for anyone to examine? The thought was surprisingly titillating.

Nick approached Charlotte unseen and watched her pouring over the photographs. It was amazing, he thought, how fascinated women were by other women's bodies, more so than men, who were aroused to be sure, but needed only glance at a picture to satisfy their interest. Women could stare at the pictures on the wall all day long. And now, as he watched Charlotte, she reached a tentative hand toward one of the photos of Julia, as though to touch the beautiful breast. Nick was stirred by the scene, and in a calculated way that was second nature to him, he knew that if he interrupted her now, catching her in this private erotic act, he would always have the upper hand with her.

"She has beautiful breasts, doesn't she?" he said, and Charlotte jumped, startled, embarrassed, guilty.

"You frightened me," she said cvasively.

"I didn't mean to," he replied, moving closer.

All Charlotte could think about was that he was seeing her with the same eyes that had photographed all that nakedness, eyes that saw everything. "I was just looking at your pictures."

Nick nodded but did not speak. "Let her do the work," he said to himself. "Let her come to me."

"Is this one of your models?"

Nick nodded again.

"Is it Tory?"

He smiled, detecting a note of jealousy in her voice. He wasn't surprised that she was curious about what was going on between him and Tory, but he hadn't expected her to be so obvious. "No, that's the model I used to use."

"Why do you take pictures when you can have them here in the flesh?" she asked.

"It's how I get to know them. It creates a bond between us." A puzzled expression interrupted his face and he stepped closer to Charlotte, staring into her face.

Her breath caught in her throat. What flaw had he detected? What horror had she left uncorrected? Or could he be admiring her?

"I didn't realize you had one blue eye and one brown," he said at last.

"Oh." She was let down. "It's my contact lenses. I must have lost one outside. Maybe that's why I feel so disoriented. I should go look for it, I suppose."

Nick touched her chin with his fingertips and gently turned it so he could stare into her eyes. "Your daughter looks very much like you," he persisted. "I wouldn't have said so from a distance, but up close I can see the resemblance."

To her surprise, tears of disappointment sprang into her eyes and she lowered them so he wouldn't see how wounded she was. Tory was completely unlike her, gawky and inelegant, completely without grace. Is that how he saw her too? Usually such a thought would have infuriated her. But instead she felt meek and vulnerable, completely consumed by Nick's mesmerizing presence. She closed her eyes to focus on the touch of his finger tracing her jawline, and on the smell of soap still fresh on them. "Oh, Nick," she breathed, "you have such gentle hands."

Casually, so as not to arouse her suspicions, he flipped the switch that activated both the lights and the video camera. He'd had the idea when he'd passed the TV in the bedroom, on his way to get the beer. He hoped it wouldn't be necessary, but if she gave him any more grief about Tory, or threatened to pull the plug on their modeling sessions, this tape would be a very good insurance policy.

His voice was quiet, hypnotic. "Would you like to pose for me?"

"Oh, yes," breathed Charlotte. This was exactly what she had hoped would happen. But then she realized what she was agreeing to and opened her eyes. Nick's face was only a heartbeat away from hers. She drew back. "But I couldn't."

"Why not?"

"I . . . I'd be too embarrassed."

"Why?"

"I'm not that kind of a girl," she said with a simper.

"What kind is that?"

"One that would be so free with her body."

Nick smiled. He knew from experience that this kind of 'no' meant 'yes.' Did she even realize how blatantly she was begging for his permission to let down her guard? "I'll bet you can be pretty free with your body when you want to, and that's nothing to be embarrassed about." He meant her to take this as a compliment, and she did.

Charlotte laughed nervously. "But I'm so much older than this girl." She gestured to the photographs on the wall with a deprecating sweep of her hand.

"It's not a matter of age," Nick said. "It's a matter of beauty."

"You think I'm beautiful?" Charlotte held her breath.

"I don't know. Let me look at you and I'll tell you," Nick challenged.

"I mean my face," Charlotte sputtered.

"There's no such thing as a beautiful face without a beautiful body. It's all part of a whole. Show me."

"But your secretary . . ."

"She's at lunch. Show me," he repeated.

"What if somebody else comes in?"

"I'll go make sure the door is locked."

"Nick . . . Are you sure we're alone?"

"I'm sure."

And as he walked away, he noticed with satisfaction that Charlotte had already started to undo the belt of her dress.

SEVENTEEN

FOR THE UMPTEENTH TIME, Roz looked up at the clock over the Sergeant's desk. It was two thirty-seven. She'd spent an hour in traffic to get here and now she'd waited thirty-four minutes to speak to Lt. Leo Drake, the one-man Art Theft Division of the L.A.P.D. It was a long shot at best. But she was desperate to come up with some cold, hard evidence against Con Uttrell.

Besides, she'd always wanted to meet this Lt. Drake in person. Although they'd phoned, faxed, and interfaced their computers to transfer information in the past, there had never been a reason for her to make the trek downtown to meet the man in person. She hoped that if they could build up some modicum of rapport, maybe Drake could give her a lead that would be the break she needed.

And while she was here, she could ask him about the Michelangelo Giant. She'd sent out some feelers through her network of contacts, but she'd come up dry. Even at Century nobody was talking about it. There wasn't any gossipy inter-office chatter, none of those jokey faxes secretaries and junior executives sent to each other. La

Salle hadn't been kidding when he'd said the topic was off limits.

But surely Lt. Drake would know something. The problem was getting him to tell her.

When she again raised her eyes to the clock, another fourteen minutes had ticked by. Why on earth was Drake keeping her waiting so long? She pushed her way between a doped-up teenager who looked like an extra from "*Night of the Living Dead*" and a derelict who had recently vomited down his shirt, until she was standing in front of the Sergeant's desk.

She mustered a smile. "Excuse me, Officer." Considering she was holding her breath so she wouldn't be asphyxiated by the stench of the vomit crusting like overcooked oatmeal on the derelict's shirtsleeve, the words came out quite pleasantly, and the Sergeant pointed at her.

"You," he snapped.

"I'm sorry to bother you again, but I've been waiting for Lt. Drake for nearly an hour. Is there some way I can . . ."

The Sergeant flipped through his tattered manual for the extension and punched it into the phone. "Yeah, this lady's still waiting on Drake." There was a pause and he turned away from Roz, mumbling so she had to strain to hear him. "I told you practically an hour ago! What? When? Yeah, yeah."

He turned back to Roz, a little less gruff, a little more contrite. "Seems he went to lunch. He should be back in about fifteen minutes. You can go up and wait back at his office if you want."

Roz brightened. If she could wait in Drake's office, perhaps she could sneak a peak at his files before he returned.

"Terrific. How do I get there?"

"Down the hall, take the elevator up to seven, then down to the end of the hall. 717. Next, you," he barked at the derelict. "You shoot your cookies at me man, I swear I'll be back atcha!" He rested his hand threateningly on his gun.

The elevator doors were just closing. "Hold it, please," Roz called, but of course nobody did. So she jammed her purse between the doors at the last second and, using all of her strength against the dumb force of the machinery, was able to slip inside. The passengers were mostly cops, a rowdy bunch, ethnically mixed, the most macho of males. Roz kept her head down and ignored their wisecracks, wedging herself in between two uniforms as the doors closed and the elevator rose.

Quite suddenly Roz was assaulted by a familiar smell. It was the cloying aroma of Aramis, her ex-husband Rick's cologne of choice. Could Rick be in this elevator? Her heart lurched. It was certainly possible. He was a cop, and technically he worked in the building, or at least he used to.

But Aramis was a popular product. Probably half the men in L.A. used it. She had to be overreacting. Or was she?

She strained to see around the hulk behind her and succeeded only in getting an elbow in her bosom. The cop who owned the elbow leered at her and whispered something to his buddy that Roz could not hear. But obviously everyone else on board did, because a chorus of guffaws echoed through the car.

An eternity later, the car rattled to a stop at the seventh floor. Eager to flee the possible implications, to say nothing of the memories they were dredging up, Roz flung herself out of the door and hurried down the hall.

"Roz?"

The familiar voice stopped her cold.

"I thought I recognized the back of your head."

Roz turned around slowly. There was Rick, leaning against the wall, his arms folded across the chest of his ecru linen suit. Where was his uniform? And where did he get the money to dress like an Armani mannequin, she wondered, taking in the high gloss on his wing tips, his silk jacquard tie, his crisply ironed shirt. No wonder he'd divorced her. He needed a valet, not a wife, and she couldn't iron a dress shirt if her life depended on it. Obviously wife number two, the child bride, was an expert.

She walked slowly back to him. "Hello, Rick."

"What brings you to Hill Street?"

"I'm meeting with Leo Drake."

"Art Theft?"

Roz nodded. "I'm investigating a case for . . ."

"Century Insurance," Rick supplied.

"How'd you know that?" She was shocked.

"Hey, I'm a cop. I've got my sources."

Roz blushed, trying to hide her surprise that he had been keeping tabs on her. "I didn't know you cared."

"You never did."

"What's that supposed to mean?"

He looked her up and down. "It means you look great." He gave Roz the kind of smile that used to be the prelude to a much more intimate application of his lips. Ten years later and she could still remember the signs. She shook her head and took a step backward, trying to compose herself.

"Am I missing something here?" she asked. "Last time I ran into you I got the distinct impression you would be eternally grateful if the next time you saw me I had a little I.D. tag wired to my toe — name, age, cause of death. Now I find out you've got a file on me. Should I be flattered or pissed off?"

Rick shrugged again. "It's your call," he said. "Come on, I'll walk you to Drake's office. It's on the way to mine."

Like the couple they used to be, they turned and walked down the wide, empty hall together. She liked how familiar it felt, matching her stride to his, taking two small steps to his one long one. She reveled in the incense of his Aramis which enveloped her like a protective bubble.

"What're you seeing Drake about?" he asked.

"A stolen Diebenkorn — that's a painting," she clarified. "It disappeared about a year ago. Now supposedly it's surfaced on the black market and we're trying to track it down. What about you?"

"Same old things — murder, mayhem and misdemeanors. But I'm off the street now. I made detective three, four years ago. I can't say I lack for things to do."

Rick stopped in front of a door. The name on the opaque glass read Lt. Leo S. Drake, O.I.C., L.A.P.D. Art Theft Division. "What does OIC mean?" Roz asked.

"Officer in Charge," said Rick, knocking on the glass and opening the door at the same time. "He's also the *only* officer in the division. There's not a lot of extra change in the city coffers for investigating luxury crimes like art theft." They both looked in. The office was empty.

But it was immaculate. The metal desk was not only cleared of all papers and personal effects, but it was waxed to a mirrorlike finish. Who would have thought government issue furniture could look so good? Behind the desk was a credenza, consisting of three rows of shelves and a cupboard below. Books, magazines, and computer files were neatly arranged. Roz would bet money they were in alphabetical order. A surprisingly healthy fishtail fern squatted in the corner under the blinding white glow of a Gro-Light. Framed museum posters were on the wall. Roz had rather liked Leo Drake over the phone; his clipped businesslike manner was always a relief from that of the ego-driven art crowd she dealt with.

But now that she'd seen his hermetically sealed work environment, she was beginning to distrust him. It was just too clean.

Apparently, Rick felt the same way. "He's probably in the men's room sterilizing his badge," he said. "You wanna wait in my office?"

She was torn. If Rick left, she could look through Drake's files. But she realized she didn't want him to leave. And he didn't seem to be in a hurry to go. "They told me he was due back in a few minutes. I think I'd better wait here."

He gave Roz that smile again. "We should get together for dinner some night. For old time's sake. What do you say?"

Roz was stunned. The last thing she would have thought was that Rick would want to remember old times.

"You mean, you, me, and Tracy?" She was glad she remembered not to call Rick's second wife Spacy, the way she had during the divorce.

For a second Rick looked perplexed, like he couldn't remember who Tracy was. Then he recovered enough to say, "She left me. About six months ago."

"I'm sorry. I didn't know."

He shrugged. "It had been coming on for a long time. A coupla years. She just seemed to need something I couldn't give her. I can't blame her for that. Know what I mean?"

Roz nodded. She knew exactly what he meant. That was how she'd soothed her own ego when Rick had left her, by trying to convince herself that their divorce had not been due to a failing in herself, but to a gaping hole in him that she couldn't fill. The truth had probably been somewhere in the middle.

"Besides, I can be an asshole — I guess I don't have to tell you that! But it is weird, living alone. I'm not really cut out for it, you know?"

Rick looked so vulnerable. On impulse, Roz reached out and squeezed his hand, feeling the familiar strength of his short stubby fingers as he squeezed back. Ten years and still her heart leapt at the touch of him.

"So, what about it, Roz? You probably got guys standing in line ten deep and a mile long. You got a night for a sorry sap like me? I'm pretty free for the next twenty years or so."

Roz blurted out, "I thought you went for teenyboppers. Aren't I a little old for you?"

Rick shrugged and smiled. "I guess maybe my tastes have changed, because you look real good to me, Roz."

The office door opened and a man entered. He looked like a cross between Donald Duck and PeeWee Herman, wearing an absurd bow tie made of the same print fabric as his shirt. For a moment the three of them just looked at each other. Then Rick spoke up.

"Drake. Good. We've been waiting for you."

Drake looked from Rick to Roz and back again. "Detective Weeks. Yes, what can I do for you?"

Roz summoned her composure and stepped forward. "I'm Rosalind Weeks, Lt. Drake, from Century Insurance." She stood uncomfortably in front of him, unsure whether to extend her hand to be shaken or to salute. She decided on the shake.

He looked confused. "Oh, Miss er, or is it Mrs. Weeks?"

"It's Roz," she said.

"Roz," he repeated. "I was expecting you much earlier."

"I know. Actually I was here, but there was a mix up downstairs. I guess they didn't get the message to you that I was waiting."

"No, I had no idea."

"Could we talk now? Do you have time?"

Drake looked at Rick, unsure. "Oh, don't mind me," Rick said, backing towards the door. "Roz, good to see you." Awkwardly he offered her his hand. "I'll call you," he said, and was out the door before Roz could respond.

Left alone with Drake, she felt compelled to explain. "Rick — Det. Weeks is my ex-husband. I ran into him in the hall. By coincidence."

"I see," said Drake.

She wondered if her association with Rick would help her case or hurt it. "At any rate, that's not why I'm here. I hope you can help me, Lt. Drake," she said.

He looked at his watch. "I suppose I can give you several minutes now. It's unfortunate, but I have a meeting beginning at 3:00." He turned a dial on his watch and pressed a button on the side. "A timer," he explained. "The alarm will go off at four minutes to three so I won't be late."

"How ingenious," said Roz, and how insanely anal, she thought. "What I wanted to talk to you about was . . ."

"The Stein Case," Drake finished for her. "That's what you said on the phone. And as I told you then, I really don't have anything I can add to your investigation."

"Yes, but what I was hoping was that we might work together, to find out if indeed Con Uttrell . . ."

Again Drake interrupted. "Mrs. Weeks, Con Uttrell is a prominent citizen and a force to be reckoned with. I suggest it would be in your best interests not to harass him."

"I'm not concerned with my best interests," Roz insisted. "I am concerned about my company, Century Insurance. We have reason to believe . . ."

"'Reason' isn't enough. You need evidence, hard evidence," Drake said. And they both listened as the alarm on his wristwatch informed them that her time was up.

EIGHTEEN

WHEN THE CLAY SCULPTURE IS complete, the figure is divided by metal shims where the mold will later be separated into sections. The clay is then covered with a thick layer of rubber to preserve its surface precisely. Once set, the rubber is encased in a plaster cast for support. When the casts are dry, they are broken away from the clay and reassembled. Any questions?" The docent looked at her audience, relieved that none of them expected more information. She was only a volunteer after all, not an art expert.

The Venice Art Walk was an annual tour of artists' studios benefitting the Venice Family Clinic. The artists cooperated because it was for a good cause, and because it was good for business. And because the chairwoman of the event was one of those dynamic, hard-driving volunteers who wouldn't take "no" for an answer.

Nick watched the group lap up the docent's spiel. Their rapt attention was gratifying but frustrating. They always wanted gritty information — statistics about how the art was made, what it weighed, how long it took to create — to appreciate it. It was like needing to dissect a woman, revealing the layers of muscle and bone and blood in her gut, in order to pronounce her beautiful.

The group was the usual mix, young couples looking for an inexpensive way to 'experience art'; older singles who had nothing better to do and would partake of any activity rather than spend the weekend alone; a smattering of aging yuppies who, having determined that it was time to get their feet wet in the art market, were testing the waters before making their first major investment.

Mostly they were interested in gathering facts and figures. Rarely did a person come out of pure love of art. But that one person made the whole thing worth it.

Nick took a healthy pull on his bottle of beer — his fifth, sixth or tenth, he'd lost count. He wished Leslie were here to help handle the crowd. But she'd begged off — it was Sunday, after all. He couldn't force her to work seven days a week. And she'd said she had one of those poetry workshops to attend.

He burped, and the sound echoed, bruising the stillness of the room. Poetry? Leslie was no more of a poet than she was a Pomeranian. But what could you do? Everyone wanted to be an artist. It was better than being rich.

The docent moved to a work table on which a plaster-encased torso lay like a corpse. She tilted it so the group could see the network of red veins running through its center, giving it the blood and guts appearance of human anatomy.

"After the molds are reassembled, the hot wax is painted or poured inside." She pointed to the red 'veins.' "A system of wax 'gates' is attached to the inner surface, which will enable the bronze to flow evenly to all parts of the figure. Before the waxes are removed from the mold, they are filled with a core of plaster and sand. Then the molten bronze is poured into the mold, melting the wax and creating the final metal impression. Any questions?"

"So the final statue is hollow?" Roz called out, turning up the volume on her tape recorder.

"Yes," the docent told her. "With bars supporting it across the larger expanses. Of course you could never tell it was hollow after the piece is completed and welded to its base."

This was just what Roz had hoped to hear, because her meeting with Arthur Hartman and his story about the Chinese scroll had sparked an idea: what if Con Uttrell planned to hide the Diebenkorn inside the bronze statue he was shipping? If the statue was hollow that meant it was possible, depending on the size of the statue, of course. She would have to find the statue and see if it would fit.

Aside from this angle, her attempts to get evidence against Con Uttrell had so far been fruitless. She still couldn't believe she had bombed out so badly with Lt. Drake. Why had he refused to help her? Certainly he would benefit as much as she if Uttrell were caught. Or maybe he didn't want Uttrell caught. Could he be protecting the art dealer?

In any event, since he had offered no help, all that was left for Roz to do was to follow the thread that lead from Arthur Hartman in Customs to Nick Stone in Venice, and hopefully catch Con Uttrell somewhere in the middle.

"Now if you will all follow me, we'll look at the dipping room, where the actual bronzing takes place," the docent was saying. "Remember, this is Mr. Stone's personal living quarters as well as his studio. Please be respectful of his privacy, and don't wander off."

Like dutiful children, the group traipsed after the docent toward the far end of the studio. Roz lagged behind until the group had moved away. This was the perfect chance to find the statue and do some measuring. All she had to do was look for a work-in-progress, a figure of a young girl. She'd brought her camera — even though it was against the Art Walk rules to take pictures — and a tape measure. The painting measured 81" x 90". It would have to be rolled and folded to fit. Once she knew the size of the statue, she could calculate her theory's viability.

She looked around, curious about this Nick Stone, now that she'd seen his studio. She'd always admired his art, but she hadn't realized that the guy was obsessed! It was spooky; everywhere she looked, there were female figures and fragmented body parts made of wax, clay, rubber, and bronze. Some were on pedestals, dancing high above her head. Others lay shrouded in dust and grime on the filthy cement floor. Some had the hard, muscular bodies of athletes, others were busty and built like Playboy Bunnies.

She imagined how it would feel to pose nude for an artist knowing that strangers would stare at the finished likeness, could possess and touch your body without your knowledge or participation. On one hand, it would be humbling, the ultimate surrender of self. On the other, being the focus of attention, a catalyst for people's fantasies, would give you an extraordinary sense of control.

And then she saw it. Not far from her, near a platform surrounded by lights, a tarp was draped over a column about the size of a person. A wire led up from the top, suspending it from an armature. It must be a work-in-progress. She started walking towards it, already pulling the measuring tape from her purse.

But suddenly, there was Nick Stone, half hidden behind a column, watching the departing group, grimacing like a kid kept after school. She recognized him from his picture in the Art Walk catalog, but he was even more gorgeous in person.

Knowing she wasn't supposed to be here without the group, Roz ducked down low so that she was hidden by a large wooden table, and in this hunkered down position, she crawled closer to Nick. She wanted to get a better look at him, and, if she was lucky, maybe ask him about the statue.

Beneath the work tables was a netherworld of junk and debris. It reminded Roz of accidentally looking under the bed in a cheap motel room. You'd rather not know what was down there, but once you looked, it stayed in your memory.

She dared to raise her head above the level of the work table to make sure she was moving in the right direction. And it was a good thing she did, for Nick was just disappearing through an archway. Should she follow him? Why not? She'd already be in trouble for leaving the group. What could they do to her anyway?

Roz flattened herself against the wall and turned her head just far enough to peer through the archway. The coast was clear, so she eased her body around the corner into the hall. It was short, maybe twenty feet long. Slowly, carefully, quietly, she made her way toward the open door at the far end. The floor was cement and she was glad she'd worn her Reeboks.

Just outside the door she stopped and peeked in. There was a bed strewn with clothes, a small lamp, a T.V., a couple of ratty chairs, and a low table.

Nick Stone was sitting on the bed with his back to her, facing the television, a beer in his hand. On the screen a videotape played soundlessly. She moved closer to see the picture. It was a home video shot in Nick's studio, of a very young, very naked girl standing on the modeling platform.

Nick seemed mesmerized by what he was watching, and the utter absorption of his gaze made Roz's skin prickle, imagining how it would feel to be studied so intently. Then she, too, looked at the screen.

The young model could not seem to stand still. She scratched her leg, brushed her hair back from her face, chewed on a fingernail. A moment passed and she twisted her hair around a finger, then pulled it forward to examine the split ends. She spent some time plucking off the stray wisps, patiently working strand by strand. Clearly, she was not aware of the camera recording her movements.

Watching her made Roz think back to her own adolescence. Unlike this swan of a girl, she had been a lumpy, unlovely child, so chubby at ten that her mother had dragged her to a special department store which specialized in sizes fourteen through twenty-four, a humiliation to them both that had left an indelible impression on Roz.

She had not had a real boyfriend until she'd met Rick the summer after she had graduated from high school. He had been the first man she'd kissed, the first man to whom she'd revealed her body. She'd been a size eight by then, but she'd remained deeply self-conscious, trapped in the vision of herself as the chubby child she'd been. That is, until Rick had pronounced her desirable. The joy he had taken in her body had given her the courage to look in the mirror and see that she had indeed outgrown her adolescent self-image.

"Who the hell are you and what are you doing back here?"

Nick's voice, low and emotionless, startled Roz. She had been so caught up in her daydream she had practically forgotten him. Now she saw that he had swiveled around to face her, his fists loosely clenched by his side, obviously annoyed that she had invaded his privacy.

Caught off guard, Roz thought fast. "My name is Rosiland Weeks. I'm on the Art Walk, and I need . . . You wouldn't happen to have a tampon, would you? It's kind of an emergency." It was a shameless lie, but men usually backed off when a woman referred to her monthlies.

This man stared at her long and hard. Then at last he said, "The bathroom is over there. Look in the cupboard. But make it quick."

Roz nodded her thanks and walked away. She was stunned that

he'd believed her. But then what was the guy going to do, turn her in to the Art Walk police? She found the bathroom and closed the door behind her, glad for a chance to collect her thoughts.

When she stepped out again Nick was leaning against the opposite wall, arms crossed over his chest, waiting. He was a little unsteady, tipsy perhaps. She smiled bravely. "Thanks, I appreciate it."

Nick didn't smile. "What do you really want?"

"What do you mean?"

"You didn't come back here to look for a bathroom."

"But . . ." How did he know? Did he have a hidden camera in there too?

"Are you a reporter?"

"No way." She was glad she didn't have to lie.

"An artist?"

"Nope."

"An art student?"

She smiled and shook her head.

"I got it. You want to model for me."

"No!" Roz cried. And then she realized he was being sarcastic, and she felt hurt.

Nick scratched his chin. "Then you must be a cop. I dunno what I did." He held out his wrists as though to be handcuffed. "But you might as well take me in. That's one way to get the hell out of here."

She shook her head. "No, really. The truth is I just came on the Art Walk, and I really liked your work, so I thought I'd look around." Was he going to let her off with this flattery or did he see through it? To distract him she asked, "Do you think I could have a glass of water?"

Nick stared at her for a moment. "Follow me."

She followed him into the bedroom. The video was still on, but he ignored it and opened a small refrigerator. In it were some beers and a bag of bagels. Nick reached for two bottles and pulled them out by their necks. "Coors all right?"

Roz hated beer. "Great, thanks," she said, accepting a bottle and trying to unscrew the cap with her hand as Nick did. It wouldn't come off. When he realized she was having trouble, he handed her his open bottle and unscrewed hers, taking a long swig.

"It's so nice of you to let us — the Art Walk — come here," she said.

He made a derisive sound. "I feel like a baboon in the zoo."

"Then why do you let them — us — come?"

Nick shrugged. "The money goes to the Venice Family Clinic. It's an amazing place. They really provide a service to this community. And besides, all the artists do it. They'd think I was an asshole if I didn't."

Roz smiled. "I don't know you at all, but I'm surprised you care what anyone thinks about you."

"I don't really. Not the public anyway. But peer pressure is something else. I gotta live with these guys." He finished his beer and took another one out of the refrigerator, looking first to see if Roz needed one too, but she hadn't even taken her first sip.

"They always promise me no one will come back here where I live. But someone always does." Nick wasn't smiling. "So, are you gonna tell me what you were looking for? It sure as hell wasn't a bathroom."

"You're right. I shouldn't have left the group. But I was so curious about the person who created these statues. I mean, they're incredibly beautiful, and the workmanship is incredible. You obviously have a very intimate relationship with your models."

He stared at her, unblinking, like he'd heard all this before. "You mean, do I fuck them all? Is that it?"

"No." Roz took a moment to phrase her words precisely. "It doesn't seem to me that it's a sexual connection. The statues don't seem to know how erotic they are."

Nick cocked his head in surprise. "Strange. Most people just assume all this," he gestured with a dismissive sweep of his arm to the studio around him, "is about sexuality."

"I don't think that," Roz said defensively. His eyes bored into her, making her blush violently.

"You're right," he said. "That's not what I'm getting at all. It's funny. No actually, it's a bitch how most people can't get past the idea that these sculptures are nude. They just see them as a bunch of bodies. I watch people staring at them, like it's some kind of peep show. But my statues aren't meant to be sex toys. If I've tried to accomplish anything, it's to glorify the female body, not debase it."

Nick sipped his beer. Clearly the booze was loosening his tongue. "Once a shrink asked me if I put my women on pedestals in real life too. And I thought about it. What I realized was that I do and I don't. I worship them, for sure. Because they're all so damn beautiful. Short or tall, fat or thin. It doesn't matter. Because I do love them. But in order to get the art to work I usually end up being hard on them. Why? Because in order to get to what's inside I've got to break down all their defenses, and it's painful. For them and for me. They end up hating me. I don't want to do it, but I have to. Because, see, all I want to do is get the art right, whatever it takes."

"So what happens when you get one that doesn't respond?" Roz asked.

Nick stroked his chin thoughtfully and turned toward the television. The video was still playing. "She's different. I don't know. Maybe it's because she's so young. I haven't been able to break through to her yet, to get a fix on what she needs to relax and be herself in front of me."

"She looks pretty relaxed to me," Roz said.

"It's not how she looks, it's how she feels, and I know she hasn't let go yet, because her body is holding too much tension. But I'm working on it." He shook his head. "Problem is I've only got two more weeks to finish her."

"Why the rush?"

"Who the hell knows. It's probably just Uttrell's way of getting the upper hand, by making me work on his timetable."

"Con Uttrell?" Roz leapt on the name. She knew it! The girl in the video was the model for the statue Uttrell wanted to ship to Japan.

Suddenly Nick seemed sober. "How do you know Con Uttrell?" he asked warily. "Did he send you here?"

"No. I never even met him. I've just heard his name."

Nick stared at her. "Shit," he said, and stood, listing slightly to the right. "What am I doing? I don't even know who the hell you are and here I am spilling my guts out. Jesus, I must be wasted. You're probably one of his spies."

"No, we were just talking about how you do your work. I only asked about Con Uttrell because he's a famous art dealer. I didn't know he represented you."

"He doesn't. I'm just doing a commission for one of his clients."

Roz let a moment pass. Then, as nonchalantly as she could, she said, "I'd love to see it."

Nick snorted. "Yeah, you and everybody else. What the hell is so fascinating about seeing a piece of art before it's finished? Nobody sees my work before it's done. Nobody. Not even the client. Not even the model." He was angry now. He picked up the remote control and snapped off the video.

Damn, she'd blown it. "Sorry," Roz backpedaled, "I didn't mean to . . . I only was curious, that's all."

"Yeah, right. Well you're not supposed to be back here. So why don't you split and take your curiosity with you."

"Okay, sure. I'm sorry if I upset you. I didn't mean anything by it."

"Just go away, okay?"

"Okay. Thanks for the beer." Seeing no trash can she set the untouched bottle on top of the refrigerator and went to the door. "It was really an honor to meet you."

"Yeah, I'll bet."

Roz heard the bedroom door slam behind her. Now was her chance. The statue Nick was making for Con Uttrell had to be the one under the tarp she'd noticed earlier. And now that she had seen the video and knew what the model looked like she'd only have to peek under the cover to know for sure.

Recklessly, she approached the figure and whipped the sheet off it. Immediately she saw that she had been right. Even though the statue was unfinished, the resemblance to the girl in the video was incredible.

"Now if you'll follow me into the studio, I'll explain the procedure this artist uses to make his bronze statues."

Roz saw the docent lead the next group into the studio. There wasn't time to measure, so she set her purse next to the figure and quickly snapped a photo. When she got home she'd use the bag's measurements to calculate the proportion. Then somehow she'd build a model to size, and figure out if and how you could stuff a rolled up canvas inside it.

III

NINETEEN

TORY EXTENDED HER ARMS above her head and tossed her hair in a bad imitation of the Guess Jeans ad from the April *Vogue*. Of course she knew she didn't have Brigette Hall's lush body, but then Brigette was only a two-dimensional fantasy in a black and white photograph. She, Tory, was flesh and blood, and only an arm's length away from Nick, who she was trying shamelessly to seduce.

During the first few modeling sessions, she had been paralyzed by his presence, hypersensitive to his hyperintense observance of her body. But gradually she'd realized that he was scrutinizing not just the flaws or the sexy parts, but every detail of every inch of her, even her earlobes and her fingernails, the backs of her knees and her shoulder blades.

And his eye was not critical but entirely accepting of whatever it saw, seeking only to clone her into clay. So she'd stopped being embarrassed by her nudity and began to enjoy the attention. And then because Nick was completely and utterly dependent upon her, and so endlessly fascinated by her every movement, she began to feel a sense of confidence in herself and the way she looked. She started to welcome his scrutiny, letting it bubble around her like the water of a jacuzzi, making her feel warm and buoyant.

But then a weird thing happened. One day Nick stopped looking at her. And after that, he began to ignore her altogether, not even speaking to her. Instead, he focused completely on the clay figure which he refused to let her see. When she complained, he said she wouldn't understand the evolving form of the statue; she might be turned off by some imperfection at this intermediate stage, and it might affect the way she held herself.

By the beginning of the second week, without Nick's eye on her, the very act of taking off her clothes had become a dull ritual, no better than brushing her teeth. So she had begun to do anything and everything she could think of to draw his interest.

Today she was pretending to be the Guess Girl, the blonde bombshell in the advertisement who sold jeans by selling sex. Tory imitated the photo in the magazine, making her lips pouty and leaning over so her breasts bulged. Nick continued to ignore her. She tossed her head and arched her back. Then she thrust out her pelvis and rotated her hips. Still nothing.

Nick just stood with his back to her, so close that she could see the muscles in his neck twitch when his arm got tired of its constant strokes, shaping and reshaping the figure. How could he act as though she and her nude body didn't even exist? Weren't men supposed to lose control in the presence of a naked woman?

Not Nick. It had been an hour since he'd even glanced her way. And yesterday he had spent half of their time together on the phone, just staring at the figure and talking to someone named Donnigan, something about wax and molds and she didn't know what.

But then, just when she had decided she'd had enough of being treated like the invisible woman, he'd hung up the phone and stood, staring at her, and told her not to move. And she'd frozen, holding her breath until she'd practically turned purple, until her head had started to swim. Still, he'd just stared.

Finally, days later it seemed, he'd lifted his hand to the top of her head and with his eyes closed, he'd gently traced a fingertip down the center of her face, over her nose and mouth and chin, down her neck over her Adam's apple and between her breasts to the center of her belly.

Then she'd watched him take the same finger, and with his eyes still closed, trace the same invisible line down the statue's body. As he'd touched the clay, she had felt the sensation of his fingers on her flesh so vividly that the path from her forehead to her belly button had burned.

It had been the single most erotic experience of her life.

But today, again, he was acting as if she didn't even exist. It was so frustrating! She desperately wanted him to look at her and touch her and make her feel that buzz again. It didn't even occur to her to consider what it could lead to. All she knew was that she wanted to feel it.

The Guess Girl ploy was a bust, so Tory decided to try something else. Nick had encouraged her to move around all she wanted, saying that motion was what this statue was all about. But the one rule was that however she moved she must stay on the modeling platform.

She flipped through the CDs and found a tape she liked. It was called "Swan Lake." The music was soothing, much more conducive to all the standing around than the usual music she listened to. Plus, the 'swan' part reminded her of how she and Nick had met at the Thorntons' party.

As music filled the studio, she tried to flow with it, visualizing herself as a downy, plumed, long-necked bird floating lazily on a pond. She allowed her head to fall to one side, imagining the feel of the cool water beneath her. And then she closed her eyes and leaned into the music, letting it drench her whole feathered body.

When she dared open one eye she saw that Nick was still oblivious. Well, screw him! She stepped off the plinth and danced over to the statue so she was directly in Nick's line of sight. When he did not acknowledge her, she began to rub her hands over her body, imagining that she was rubbing the music into the pores of her face and arms and shoulders. How could he ignore her now?

As the music built to a crescendo, she began to twirl faster and faster, hugging herself, letting her hands find the nuances of flesh and form, playing up and down her body as though it were the instrument of the sound. Eyes closed, she fell back over one of Nick's work tables and thrust her legs into the air, flexing and kicking in tempo.

The music ended, and Tory let her legs relax onto the table. She felt good now, energized by the endorphin rush, satisfied by the musical climax. She took a deep breath and opened her eyes.

Nick was standing over her, staring at her with an odd expression on his face, as though he was trying not to laugh. Oh God, she thought, I've made a fool of myself! She tried to sit up, but his hand shot out and pinned her to the table.

"Let me up, please," she begged. "I'm going to spew, I swear it."

"Just relax," he said, his voice low and solemn. And he kept staring at her, stroking the hair off her damp forehead. "Your dance was beautiful."

Tory clamped her eyes shut. "I'm so embarrassed," she moaned, covering her face with her hands.

"Why?"

"Because I'm such a klutz. I didn't think you were watching."

"That's what made it so beautiful. It's the first time in two weeks that you forgot about me and acted completely natural. That's what I want. That's what I need to see." He stopped stroking her hair. "Tory, open your eyes."

"I can't."

"Why not?"

"Because I think you're laughing at me."

"I wouldn't laugh at you. Ever."

Tory just lay there, limp, eyes shut. Now that she'd finally gotten Nick's complete, undivided attention she didn't want it. All she could think of was escape and she didn't know how to get away. A tear slipped out of her eye and trickled onto the rough wood table beneath her. God, she had never felt so mortified, so completely humiliated.

"Hey, open your eyes, please?" Nick's voice was gentle now, as delicate as his finger tracing the wet trail of the tear on her cheek.

"You think I'm ugly! I *am* ugly!"

"That's not true," Nick protested.

"Then how can you just let me stand there for hours making a fool of myself. How can you just ignore me when I never . . . you are the only . . . I hate my body! I hate it!" Tears choked her voice. She didn't know why she was crying, or how she could explain that she felt something in the air that wasn't there before, something that made her heart hurt.

"Don't you understand? I've been ignoring you so you would forget that *I'm* here. I wanted you to be the way you are when you're alone."

"I don't get it."

Now she felt his hands on either side of her head, gripping it in a tender vice, his thumbs rubbing gently at the throb in her temples. And then she felt his lips at her throat, his murmured words tickling the hairs in her ears.

"Sweet Tory, don't you know you're the most beautiful woman on the planet? You're so beautiful I don't need to look at you to see it. I can feel it just being in the room with you. Please open your eyes. I want you to look at me so you will believe what I'm saying. Please."

Finally she allowed her tear-matted eyelashes to part. Nick's face was so close she could see the tiny bristling hairs of his beard and a minute scar above his cheekbone. His smirk was gone and in its place was a look of indescribable tenderness. He stroked the hair off her forehead and planted a chaste kiss just at the hairline.

"You've got to understand the process, baby," he said.

"Baby?" she repeated the word to herself rapturously. It was the first time he'd used any term of endearment and, although baby wouldn't have been her first choice, it was better than nothing. Especially the way he'd said it, a very grown-up and sexy 'baby.'

"Over here, there's this lump of clay, cold, lifeless, godless. And over here is you, warm, beautiful, and vibrant. My job is to transfer your spirit into the clay and bring it to life."

"But how can you do that without looking at me?"

"You think I don't look at you?" He shook his head. "Babe, I know you better than you know yourself. I know every inch of your body. I know *inside* your body, places you never even thought of. And you know why? Because I have your soul in me. You came here that first day and I started to absorb it through my eyes and my hands and my skin. What you are and who you are is all around me. I live you. I breathe you. I eat you for breakfast. There is nothing but you in my life. Do you think I have to look at you too? That would just dilute what I feel."

Tory's head began to spin with Nick's solemn flattery. She was dazzled, ready to burst with joy and adoration for this man who was saying all these wonderful things, pouring out his heart to her. Was this love? It had to be! How could it be anything else?

My God, she thought, I'm in love with Nick Stone! It was a relief to give a name to the feeling that had been ricocheting around inside her, and it gave her a new sense of confidence. She didn't want to break the mood, but she finally had the courage to ask him the question that had been burning inside her.

"Nick, what made you pick me?"

He pulled back a little and stared off into space, remembering. "When I first saw you that day by Thorntons' pond, there was a quality, a gracefulness. No, it was more a sense of harmony, just this point where your neck arches into your collarbone, the narrowness of your wrist, the curve of your cheek. . ."

Tory closed her eyes. She felt the caress of his words as though his hands were on her face and body. Nothing else existed except the two of them and what Nick was saying.

". . . this captivating kind of openness. I wanted to touch you, and I felt you wanted me to. But at the same time, I was held off by a sort of animal shyness, saying 'stay back, don't spoil me.' Something pulled me toward you and at the same time pushed me away. If I can get that paradox in this piece I'll really have something."

It was like a curtain descending with a crash between them. The *piece* again, the damn statue. Couldn't he just for once see her, without thinking of her as a means to an end? The tears started again. She couldn't help it. His words were so beautiful. He was so close. But he wasn't thinking about her. All he was thinking about was the damn statue.

"What is it? What's wrong?" His voice was soft with concern.

"Nothing."

"Tory, come on. What did I say? Tell me."

"You treat that statue like it's alive and you treat me like I'm made of clay."

Nick was incredulous. "What are you talking about? This could be my best work."

"See? That's exactly what I mean. What about me? Don't you care about me?"

"Of course I do. That's what I'm saying."

"But that's not the way you're acting."

Nick threw up his hands. "I don't get it. Please, help me understand!"

"I never took off my clothes in front of a guy before, okay?" Tory blurted out. "And you act like I'm not even here!"

Nick was taken aback. "I'm working on the figure. What do you want me to do?"

"I want you to . . ." She stopped. It was so hard to say it out loud. "I want you to make love to me."

"What?" Nick finally began to understand. "Hey, wait a second. Is that what you think this is about? Jesus Christ. You're only seventeen. And a virgin, right?"

Her face burned with shame. Why did he have to say that word? How did he know? Did it show? She composed herself. "It's not a matter of age. Or experience." Her voice quivered with emotion. "It's about feelings, isn't it? I don't turn you on, do I?"

Nick threw up his arms in exasperation. "If that were true, would I have picked you to be my model? Would I? If that were true, I couldn't work. What I feel for you is what my art is about. Tory, you're everything to me right now. I swear. Yes, you turn me on. Is that what you want to hear? Jesus, you're the only damn thing that does!"

And that was all the encouragement Tory needed. She threw her arms around his neck and before he could object, pulled his mouth down to hers. She kissed him gently, experimentally, then drew back, shyly savoring the taste of his lips.

Nick was stunned. He pulled away, gripping her by the shoulders and staring into her eyes. Then in a burst of passion he drew her to him, crushing his mouth against hers, forcing her lips to part.

The kiss built and deepened until Tory was a slave to it. She tasted the bitter tang of saliva as Nick's tongue thrust into her mouth, and she felt the pressure of his long lean torso against her. For every movement on Nick's part, there was a corresponding explosion inside of her. She knew he was going to make love to her now. She just knew it. And she wanted it. She was ready for it. Silently through the kiss, she begged him to relieve her of her damned virginity.

But abruptly, Nick pulled back, withdrawing so suddenly that she felt as though her flesh was tearing. He looked dazed, confused, angry. At her? What had she done except offer herself to him?

"We can't do this," he said.

"Why not?"

"Because. You're too young."

"But it's *okay* with me. More than okay. I want to." She didn't want to sound like she was begging. But hell, she *was* begging. "Nick, come on!"

She tried to pull him to her again, but he shrugged her arms off of his neck and stepped back. Physically, he was only a few feet away, but emotionally, she could tell, he had moved into another galaxy.

"I've got a deadline. In two days I've got to be finished with this statue. Tory, it has nothing to do with you as a person, but right now I can only let you be real to me in that figure. Anything I feel

I've got to put there. Please, don't be angry. Don't be sad. It's not your fault. It doesn't have to do with feelings. It's just the way things are. If we were to . . . it would spoil the balance. See, I have to put everything into my work."

"Oh Jesus, Nick, can't you even think of a new line?"

Both Nick and Tory turned to see who had spoken. There, standing in the doorway, watching them with hatred so intense it warped her beautiful face, was Julia.

When she saw that she had their attention, she walked toward them, an actress making the most of her entrance.

"Don't you know he says that to all the girls? Did he give you the one about 'I've got to feel what it's like to be inside your body?' It's just bullshit. He's just trying to turn you on so he can use it for his quote-unquote *work*."

"Shut up, Julia."

"That's the whole point of it, don't you see? He strips you down to your soul and makes you pour out your guts. But it's not for *him*, it's for the *art*, the glorious bronze statue that will be immortalized for eternity."

Nick grabbed Julia's arm and whipped her around. "How did you get in here?"

"I have a key, in case you forgot." She leaned around Nick to face Tory. "Did he give you a key yet? No? Too soon probably. It comes next, after you screw. Oh, but then you're so young, maybe he's afraid you'll lose it. Maybe he should pin it to your dress. Or better yet pin it to your scrawny excuse for a tit. That would be practical *and* trendy. Don't you think, Nicky?"

"Shut the fuck up!" The cold cruelty in Nick's voice only stopped Julia for a second. She jerked her arm away.

"Guess who I'm having dinner with tonight."

"I could give a shit."

"Con Uttrell. Willie invited me."

Nick said nothing, but his interest was piqued.

"Willie said you're taking it in the ass from Connie-boy."

"Keep it clean, Julia," Nick warned, stealing a glance at Tory. She averted her eyes.

"What, the little baby girl doesn't wanna hear these big bad words? Well, wash my mouth out with soap. I'm only trying to warn you. You mess with Con Uttrell, you're gonna get screwed, booed, and tattooed. He's got a mean streak that's longer than his dick, honey. You suck on it, sure it tastes good going down, but sooner or later it'll choke you. Preferably sooner."

"Shut up!" Nick grabbed a hunk of her hair and held it tight.

She tried to pull away. "Let me go! I came to get my earring."

"Then get it and get out of here." Still holding her hair he marched her toward the door.

"I've seen your statue," she called over her shoulder to Tory. "It's a piece of crap. He's made it as ugly as you are and the whole world is going to see it."

Nick and Julia disappeared through the door, and Tory let her body deflate against the table, a puppet whose strings had just been cut. She could still hear Nick and Julia's angry voices but she couldn't understand the words. Her mind was numb. She felt beat up and empty, bereft of any emotion except the hot, spewing lava of self-pity.

She should have known it all along. What Nick had said to her, it was all just words. The truth was, he was using her the way he would a bank account, making withdrawal after withdrawal, and no deposits.

She slipped the silk robe up around her shoulders and cinched it tightly around her waist. She couldn't think about this any more. Instead she tried to concentrate on something happy. "When I get home, I'll take a bath and then it'll be time for dinner," the voice in her mind said. "Radiance was going to make my favorite, lasagna with three kinds of cheese. It's really fattening, but who cares? No way I'm going to be over here taking off my clothes, that's for sure. Never again. No way."

When Nick returned Tory was putting on her clothes. He watched her buckle the belt of her jeans. "I want you to understand something," he said.

She couldn't look at him. "I'm cold and I'm tired. Can't I just go now, please?"

"Tory, look at me."

Gently he turned her towards him, forcing her to look into his eyes. They were sad and pleading. "Julia was my model, no more than that. I thought I saw something in her, but when I started the work, it wasn't there. It wasn't there! I couldn't even finish it."

Tory could hear the pain in his voice but she refused to let herself feel sorry for him. Her own pain was so much worse. "It was only on the surface," he continued. "It didn't go deep enough. That won't happen with you. I swear it."

"How can you tell?"

He stared at her for an endless moment. Finally, he took her hand and walked her around to the front of the statue and whipped off the tarp, letting her look at it for the first time.

"This is how I see you," he said.

Tory stared at the figure, mesmerized by it. It was like looking in a mirror, only the clay statue before her was so much more beautiful than she was. She saw ripeness and passion in its face, exuberance bursting from its body, arms reaching, legs grasping. It was sensually alive, yet remote and pure. It was unlike any image she had ever seen of herself and yet it was her identical twin.

"Is that what I look like?" Tory managed to ask. Nick nodded.

"But it's so, so . . . beautiful!"

"Because you are beautiful."

"No way."

"Yes you are. You just don't know it yet." He hugged her and she hugged him back, this time feeling not passion, but relief. Nick pulled her to him again. "Please," he said, burying his mouth in her hair, "I can't lose you now. Let's finish this together and then afterwards we'll see what happens. Can you do that? Can you wait and believe in me just a little while longer?"

Tory didn't have to speak to let him know her answer was yes. She only hugged him a little harder, pressing her body into the comfort of his, saying a silent prayer of thank you to whatever spirit was watching over her.

Nick reached into his pocket and pulled out a small bronze medallion on a delicate gold chain. "I made this for you."

"For me?" Tory grasped it greedily and held it up to the light. It was about the size of a quarter, with a woman's profile indented into it in several angles, creating an abstract impression of movement.

"Can I put it on you?"

Tory nodded, and Nick surrounded her neck with the chain, letting the medallion dangle against her chest. "I love it," she beamed. "I'll never take it off."

"Good." Nick grinned. "Now can we please get back to work?"

TWENTY

CON LOOKED AROUND the room. As usual, Spago was jammed — a noisy, neurotic frenzy of sycophants kneeling at the altar of celebrity. Con saw it as the Hollywood caste system in a microcosm. At the top of the pyramid were superstars like Madonna, Liz Taylor, and Michael Jackson, who came here to be adored, the same way the Pope appeared on the balcony of the Vatican at Easter. On the next tier were celebrities such as David Hockney, Cher and the Governor, people who were definitely famous, but who needed an occasional public airing to keep their ratings up.

The next strata, broader and always in flux, included people who *thought* they were celebrities, Joan Collins, José Eber, the star of any hot television series, and people on their way down from the higher levels. It also included a smattering of the super rich, who felt their net worth alone bought them celebrity status.

At the bottom of the heap were those who admitted they had come to gawk, who insisted they didn't care about the famous clientele but had come for the food — the same sort of people who swore they bought *Playboy* and *Penthouse* to read the articles — and those who just wanted to tell the folks back home that they'd had dinner with the rich and famous at L.A.'s most star-studded restaurant.

By token of being an independent art dealer whose clients were impervious to the fluctuations of the economy and so famous that they shunned fame, Con considered himself above classification. The super elite knew him and the lesser luminaries knew *of* him. The rest of the world was immaterial. His reputation was not about celebrity. It was about anonymity. He preferred being the man behind the curtain pulling the strings rather than the puppet dangling at the other end. And because he generally knew exactly which strings to pull, he was able to call the Maitre d' at Spago at three o'clock on a Friday afternoon, secure a seven-thirty reservation for four people, and, when he arrived, be seated immediately at a good table.

Con did not come here often. He saw the scene as performance art, a term he considered a euphemism for exhibitionism. But Spago was his venue of choice for certain social occasions, particularly for business meetings at which it paid to be publicly pretentious. Tonight was a case in point.

Caroline Van Patten was back in town to consummate her purchase of the Diebenkorn, which would net Con two hundred thousand dollars. Con wanted to sign the papers and close this deal in a very public place so no one could later accuse him of trying to defraud an unsuspecting buyer. He would make a show of celebrating her purchase with champagne and a designer dinner, introducing her to members of the art community whose presence at the table would lend greater credence to the authenticity of her purchase. She would never know that art historian and former Director of the Los Angeles County Museum of Art Wendell Niles was well-compensated by Con to say whatever Con told him to. Or that his other guest, Willie Wilson, was all flamboyance with no substance, that despite his celebrity, his sales had been steadily declining for years. Ideally, the two would make a perfect balance — Wendell's pomposity and Willie's fame together would distract Caroline Van Patten from thinking too much about the business she was transacting.

As usual, Con was the first to arrive, the consummate host, anxious to reconnoiter the room and approve the location of the table before the others arrived, to order the wine and remove the flowers from the table — he detested flowers, particularly in proximity to food.

After choosing an '84 Cakebread Chardonnay and a '73 Stag's Leap Merlot from the sommelier, Con sat to wait for his guests. Not a great crowd, he scowled, noticing Morgan Fairchild, all hair, at one table, and Sean Connery, balding, at another. An Arab family was ensconced at a large table in the center of the room — chic over-dressed wives, black-veiled mothers, unruly children, servants and all. Their presence distorted the trendy ambiance of the restaurant, creating a scene like something in a Salvador Dali painting.

While he waited for his guests to arrive, Con let his mind drift to Thornton and the Michelangelo Giant. There must be some way for him to sweeten the deal, even to keep the statue for himself! Once he had it in his possession, who was to say he couldn't blackmail Thornton with the threat of exposure, and sell it for a record-breaking sum?

No, that wouldn't work. If he threatened Thornton, Thornton would only have to snap his fingers to have Con snuffed out like a match. And then what good would it do him to have the statue?

Perhaps he could find an artist to copy it, the same way he did paintings, and pass off the forgery to Thornton's people in Japan. It would take them time to recognize the fraud, and by then Con would be long gone, and in possession of the original, to do with what he pleased. Yes, that would be the ideal plan.

To pull it off he would have to find a way to make the copy look five hundred years old. But that was not an insurmountable problem. All marble was hundreds of centuries old; it was only the work of the sculptor's chisel that could be dated, and there were dozens of craftsmen at every site of ancient civilization — Egypt, Tunisia, Greece — who specialized in making newly carved objects appear antique, for sale to the tourist trade. He could fly one in at a moment's notice.

But first he would have to find a sculptor who could actually do the carving, who could create a reasonable facsimile of the Michelangelo. What about Nick Stone? No, definitely not. It would require the talent of a real artist and Con did not put Stone in that category. Sure, he was facile with his bronzes, but marble was a much more difficult medium. One slip of the chisel and a piece was irrevocably ruined.

Besides, he didn't trust Nick Stone, not for a minute. Stone might go right to the authorities, or worse, to Thornton, and Con would be dead in the water. Literally.

He shivered. No, as tempting as it was to imagine cheating Thornton and getting away with it, it was an impossible dream. Better to leave well enough alone, to perform the task that was demanded of him and be done with the obligation.

Con's musings were interrupted by the sight of Wendell Niles arriving. Poor fool, Con thought, watching the old relic stumble across the room, searching for a familiar face. How mortifying to be past your prime, grasping at an invitation to dinner as though it were a summons from royalty. Con waved and Wendell's relief was pathetically obvious.

"Hail fellow, well met," Wendell called, still some distance away. Con rose and extended his hand to draw the old man around to the worst seat at the table. Con himself would sit where the light was less harsh and where he would have an omniscient view of the room.

"I hope I'm not late," Wendell said, and with audible relief, lowered himself into the chair.

"No, no, you're first to arrive," Con assured him, hoping the others were not too far behind. Wendell was an insufferable bore and Con had neither the patience nor the interest to indulge him tonight. "Have a drink." Con nodded at the waiter.

"What are you pouring?" Wendell asked.

As though it makes a difference, you old drunk, Con thought.

As the waiter patiently described the qualities of the two wines Con had chosen, Con heard an off-key whistle. Just as Willie had intended, his aural introduction turned heads, and conversation in the restaurant faded to a low hum as he crossed the room. Not surprisingly, he was dressed in flagrant disregard for social decorum. Tonight's costume consisted of pleated red pants, a Hawaiian shirt that boasted buxom hula girls on surfboards, a very natty bowler hat, and high heeled cowboy boots.

But what outraged Con more than Willie's appearance was the fact that he was not alone. A gorgeous woman was on his arm. In contrast to Willie's informal attire, the woman was dressed to the nines. A black silk dress hugged her thighs, the décolletage of its bodice emphasizing the fullness of her breasts and the ivory softness of her skin. Her hair was a lusty red, teased and lacquered to a gravity-defying height. She walked with the confidence of a woman who was used to being gaped at, who reveled in the spotlight.

Con knew her intimately, if not well; she was Nicholas Stone's former model and mistress, Julia Richaud. At one of Con's parties, she had separated herself from Nick and attached herself to Con with breathy promises of what she would do to him if allowed to participate in a private 'post party' party. Never one to forgo such a generous offer, Con had immediately squired Julia into the master suite and allowed her to make good on her promises, not waiting for his other guests to leave, because it was more titillating to screw her behind Nick's back, while he and the others were steps away in the living room. He didn't know if she had ever told Nick about their liaison. But it didn't matter. After he'd had her, he'd known Nick couldn't have really cared for her. How could a man love a woman who was a self-proclaimed sex object? That kind of woman begged to be used and then discarded.

But tonight, seeing her on Wilson's arm gave Con pause. Con had purposely invited the two men stag to allow Caroline Van Patten the pleasure of being the only woman at the party. To add another female to the table — a gorgeous, sexy one at that — fouled the balance. Wendell would be dazzled at the sight of Julia, and Caroline would no doubt be intimidated. Damn Wilson. He had purposely sabotaged this dinner party and he was obviously very pleased with himself. Con would have to settle the score later.

But for now he focused his attention on Julia, introducing her to Wendell and seating her next to him on the dark side of the table. Let her play footsie with the old buffoon all night.

"My man," said Wilson, extending his hand to Con. Con did not shake it, making his anger obvious. But Wilson's expression was defiant, and Con sensed trouble. Most likely it was due to drugs — either an excess or an absence of them. With narcotics, achieving a balance was crucial, and Wilson's was notoriously precarious. Con ought to know; he was Wilson's primary supplier.

"I didn't realize you were bringing a guest," said Con, signaling to the waiter to set another place at the table.

"Say what? I thought you dug the bitches, man. What's a party without pulchritude?"

"Unfortunately, this is not just a party, I do have some business to transact, as you know," Con said, looking at Julia. Her eyes seemed focused on his crotch and he felt an answering twitch in his groin.

"Business should always be a party. Isn't that what you think, Mr. Uttrell?"

Her formal "Mr. Uttrell" was unnerving in its juxtaposition to her very personal knowledge of him. But he brushed it aside.

"I'm sure anywhere you are is a party, my dear, but tonight I hope you will let me set the tone."

"You always do, don't you, Mr. Uttrell?"

The animosity in her reply irked Con, but he let it pass because he saw Caroline Van Patten entering the restaurant. He waved and went to greet her.

In contrast to her businesslike attitude and attire at their first meeting in his office, tonight she was dressed like someone out of a Jackie Collins novel, in a combination of sequins and spandex that was more costume than couture. It always bewildered Con how otherwise fashionable women floundered when confronted with the Los Angeles social scene, and apparently Caroline Van Patten was no exception.

"Miss Van Patten," Con smiled, extending his hand. "You look absolutely ravishing."

"Thank you," she said and shook his hand with a strong, businesslike grip. Con was confused. It was not the greeting of a beautiful woman in a sexy dress, but that of person who used her hands for some sort of work, a professional mud wrestler or a masseuse perhaps. But an art consultant?

She apparently saw or sensed his reaction, because her hand instantly relaxed in his, becoming as soft and demure as a debutante's. Con brought it to his lips, and in courtly fashion, kissed the air just above it.

"I hope I'm not late," she said.

"No, not at all; the others have just arrived."

The Maitre d' led them to the table and Con made the introductions, seating Caroline between himself and old Wendell who was, as expected, dazzled and delighted.

"My, my," he clucked like an old hen. "How fortunate I am to be nestled here between two such beautiful women."

"No shit, man. You're talking a primo pussy sandwich," said Willie.

"Caroline, what would you like to drink?" Con snapped his fingers for the sommelier. "Some of our California wine?"

"The red, please," she replied and Con poured some into her glass, also replenishing Wendell's.

"Love your dress," Julia hissed. "Is it Bob Mackie?"

"Actually, I got it in Paris," Caroline said. "My work takes me there several times a year."

Julia stiffened, then she shrugged her shoulders, which had the effect of letting her dress slip down to reveal another inch of cleavage. She didn't have the budget to buy Paris couture, but she had a body money couldn't buy.

"I understand you are a curator," Wendell said to Caroline. "How amazing to find a work of art actually working for art." He sat back, pleased with himself.

"I'm more of a consultant, really," Caroline admitted, ignoring the compliment. "My employer is quite knowledgeable himself and very involved in his collection. There are several of us who just do the legwork to acquire the pieces he wants."

"Might we know the name of your employer?" Wendell asked.

"Actually he prefers to remain anonymous," Caroline replied. "He's a bit eccentric," she admitted.

"Aren't we all?" said Con under his breath, watching Willie stir a spoonful of mustard into his glass of wine.

AT HOME LATER that night as Con sipped Absinthe, he listened to the rain begin and watched his pit viper stalk a furry meal, reflecting on the evening. More specifically, he thought about Caroline Van Patten. She had certainly seemed knowledgeable enough about the art world, and in particular, the piece she was acquiring for her employer. But there had been something in her manner that bothered him. He'd spent half his life sucking up to curators and consultants, with their MFA's from Yale and Mt. Holyoke held reverently aloft like the Holy Grail. Certainly this one knew her stuff, able to chat with Wendell about everything from Irving Penn's flower photographs to James Turrell's volcano. She had even responded with equanimity to Julia's pointed barbs about the current demimonde of Venice, and had graciously accepted Willie's invitation for a private tour of his studio. Con shuddered to think where that could lead.

The snake had cornered its prey and was waiting. Con obliged by blowing the silver whistle, and the snake struck, crushing the mouse and consuming it whole.

Con was reminded of Caroline Van Patten's strange, viselike handshake, the way it had consumed his hand. In her firm grip Con had felt callouses on her palms and at the tips of her fingers. Certainly she could be an athlete of some sort, an equestrienne or a tennis player. But in a whole evening of conversation, she had never alluded to any sport or physical activity. And that dress! Con felt certain it was not couture at all, but some celebrity cast-off from a resale shop.

Nevertheless, in front of everyone, she had handed over her cashier's check and signed the papers. As soon as the check cleared, Con would turn over the painting — the forgery, that is. The original he would get back from Wilson and keep for himself. It wasn't worth a hundredth of what the Michelangelo could bring, but the risk involved was small in comparison.

The phone rang. Con picked it up. "Yes?"

"Boss?" It was Bryant's voice, on the car phone. "We've got a situation."

The Absinthe soured on Con's tongue. "What is it?"

"We dropped her off at the Miramar, and waited, like you said. But she just came out, and now she's getting into a cab."

Con thought fast. It might be nothing. Maybe she was just going out for a late drink, or to a club. But it was one in the morning. And hadn't she said she had an early flight? Something was not right.

"Stay with her," he said. "And keep in touch."

TWENTY-ONE

THE FIRST CRACK OF THUNDER bolted Roz into wakefulness. Rain always filled her with anxiety bordering on panic; ominous, dark clouds of it were building inside her already. She dreaded having to go to work. Since most of the houses on the canal, hers included, had no garages, it would be a soggy schlep to her car, and the freeways were bad enough even on a sunny day.

Thunder again, and then a flash of lightning. In its glow Roz looked at the clock. It was only four-thirty, but she'd never get back to sleep now. She slipped quietly out of bed. Adrian was still snoring softly, oblivious to the change in the weather. Why should he worry? He'd probably never lived in a house that leaked like a sieve when the rain came out of the north, or by a canal that sometimes overflowed, flooding the basements of the houses on its banks. At least the storm would keep the ducks quiet and the pert blonde jogger at home.

Cinching her robe around her, she padded into the kitchen. The first thing she saw when she turned on the light was her drawing of the male model from art class. Adrian had insisted she hang it, so she'd tacked it to the refrigerator, like a kid with a prize finger-painting. She touched the small tattoo on the model's buttock, a perfectly articulated snake's head. It wasn't a bad drawing, even if she did say so herself. And it was kind of a turn-on to see that glorious body each time she came into the kitchen.

After setting the tea kettle on to boil, she made a tour of the house, closing windows, putting bowls and towels in the places where the dripping was the worst, glad she owned nothing of real value which could be ruined.

Circling back into the kitchen, she made tea and set out the snapshot she'd taken of Nick Stone's statue, her purse, a tape measure, ruler and calculator, and several pieces of drawing paper, which she taped together to make one long rectangle the dimensions of the Diebenkorn canvas. This she rolled into a tube.

When she was finished, she took the measurements of her purse, and assessed the height and width it was in the photo. She also measured the size of the statue in the photo. Then she set the pencil down.

She knew there was some mathematical formula for figuring the size of the statue and the actual area inside of it, by comparing the size of her purse in the photo and in reality. But for the life of her she couldn't remember it. Nelson would know! He was a whiz at math. But it was only five a.m. — too early to call.

"What are you doing?"

Roz turned around and her heart clutched. Adrian looked like a nine-year-old, endearingly caught in between wakefulness and sleep, standing bare-assed on the linoleum. The left side of his face was still crushed from sleep, his black hair matted, his voice distant, defenseless, out of a dream.

She gathered up her papers and covered the photo. "I couldn't sleep so I was trying to work. Want some tea?"

He shook his head and scratched his belly unself-consciously. "Why couldn't you sleep?" he yawned.

She shrugged. "I have a phobia about rain."

"How come?" He came to sit beside her, flinching when his bare skin touched the cold seat of the canebottom chair.

"Didn't they teach you in nursery school that rain is God's teardrops?"

"In Bali, the rain is sacred. We worship the rain because it makes the rice grow. There can never be too much. On the other hand, even a short drought at the wrong time can cause a famine. Speaking of which, is there anything to eat? I'm starving."

"I can probably scrounge up something. How about an omelet?" She opened the cupboard to get out her favorite mixing bowl, then remembered she was using it to catch the rain by the front door.

"Can I help?"

"As a matter of fact. . ." She handed Adrian a plastic container, saved from a Häagen Dazs binge. "Can you put this where that bowl is by the door and bring me the bowl?"

Roz watched Adrian's butt recede into the living room. He had a great body, lean and limber, with soft skin the color of creamy peanut butter. And he was so comfortable with his nakedness, completely unself-conscious. She looked down at her own heavy robe and socks. His lack of modesty made her feel priggish.

What the hell. With a giggle she stripped off the robe and replaced it with her favorite apron, a gag gift a friend had given her when she turned forty. It was a frilly thing, with a cotton piqué bib, a wide chiffon sash, and a tiny, square bottom edged in three colors of rickrack, something the French parlor maid in a Noel Coward play would wear.

She caught her reflection in the rain-spattered window, her breasts exposed on either side of the apron's bib, the sash perched atop her rump, the linen bottom barely covering her crotch. Pretty sexy for a middle-aged insurance claims adjustor, even if she did say so herself.

She opened the refrigerator and bent over to find eggs, cheese, mushrooms, and onions. Was it too early in the morning for onions?

The thunder cracked again, like a door slamming.

"Roz?"

"Umm?" She was still thinking about the onions as she turned to face Adrian, butter in one hand, eggs in the other.

But it was not Adrian who stood in front of her. It was Rick.

Rick! Reality check: had she been with Rick all this time? No, there was Adrian, standing sheepishly behind him, shielding his private parts with the mixing bowl.

"I hope I'm not interrupting anything," Rick said.

"What are you doing here?" was all she could manage.

"I know how you freak out in bad weather, so I thought I'd stop by, make sure you were okay."

"After ten years you just stop by, at five in the morning?" she wanted to scream; the slow grin spreading across his face was infuriating. "I got over that years ago," she lied.

"Really? I guess a lot has changed. I sure don't remember you wearing that apron, for example," he said, trying to keep a straight face.

Roz gasped. She'd forgotten the apron and her body bulging out on all sides. Automatically her hands moved to shield her nakedness and she dropped the egg, spraying yolk, albumen, and shell all over the floor.

"Let me get that," said Rick, reaching for the dish towel.

But Roz beat him to it and held the towel to her chest, covering her exposed breasts. "Just hand me my robe, will you please?"

"Whatever you say," said Rick. There was a carnal twinkle in his eye which she was glad Adrian couldn't see. Fortunately he'd disappeared — to find his pants, Roz hoped.

Rick picked up her robe and took his time walking across the kitchen to hand it to her. "Sorry if I'm busting up a party," he said.

"You're not one bit sorry." She knew he was loving every minute of this.

"Maybe not," he grinned, looking around the kitchen. "The old place looks great." His eyes stopped on the sketch Roz had tacked up on the refrigerator, and he winked at her. "Nice," he said.

"You should see it in the daylight," Roz snapped. Rick looked puzzled. "The house, I mean. It's barely standing. Termites, dry rot, water damage."

His brow furrowed with concern. "No kidding? Well, I supposed it's inevitable, this close to the beach. I miss the beach," he said wistfully.

"Is that why you came by? Because you miss the beach?" asked Adrian, now fully dressed except for his shoes.

He padded directly to the stove and set the tea kettle on to boil again, then busied himself pouring coffee beans in the grinder, setting out the filter and cups like he owned the place.

Roz looked at Rick to see if he was picking up on the subtext, Adrian's subtle hint that he was the man in residence, not Rick.

If anything, Rick looked amused. "No. We're investigating a homicide in the neighborhood. It looks like there's a connection between the victim and someone in the art world, and I thought Roz might be interested."

"Why would Rosiland be interested in a homicide?" Adrian persisted.

Rick deliberately turned his back on Adrian and faced Roz. "It may be a coincidence. I don't know. But the victim had some papers on her, something about a painting by that guy you mentioned, Deban, Diebur . . ."

"Diebenkorn?"

"That's the one."

"Mentioned when?" Adrian asked.

"When she came down to headquarters," Rick replied.

Roz didn't want to look at Adrian. It would take too long to explain. "Let me get dressed. I'll just be a second."

Roz threw on jeans and a turtleneck, and opened the closet to get a coat. The first one she grabbed was bright purple, something she'd bought to cheer herself up last winter. She shrugged into it and pulled on her rain boots, still damp from the last storm.

She picked up her umbrella and gave Adrian a peck on the check. "I won't be gone long. Will you stay?"

"No," he said, looking at Rick. "Obviously it's time for me to go."

"I'm sorry," Roz said. "But this is . . ."

"You don't have to explain. Goodbye, Roz."

"'Bye."

"Nice to meet you." Rick thrust out his hand but Adrian declined to take it.

"Will you be in class next Wednesday?" he asked Roz.

"Of course."

"Then I'll see you there."

Roz ran through the rain, following Rick to his car. Her umbrella was blown useless by the force of the wind, her gaudy coat flapping open at her sides. What was she doing running after him like this, so willing to cast Adrian aside, the way she had been cast aside ten years ago? No wonder he was upset.

They drove in silence for a few blocks, punctuated by the static of an occasional coded message off Rick's radio. Roz glanced at him out of the corner of her eye. Somehow he'd managed to get out of his raincoat and put it in the back seat. He was sitting there, dry and elegant, like something out of *GQ*, while she was still bundled in her coat, dripping all over the seat. How did he do that?

His attention was focused on the road ahead which was slick with mud and rain. He had always been a careful driver. That had been one of the things she liked best about him — the way he made her feel safe. The light reflecting off the wet pavement bathed his face in a warm glow. He looked so confident, so handsome, so in control. Roz didn't know if she was more annoyed with him for knowing she would follow the instant he beckoned, or with herself for not hesitating a heartbeat to run after him.

He turned to her and smiled. "What?" Roz asked.

"I was just thinking. This is some funny coincidence. You mention the name of an artist to me, and within twenty-four hours it comes up again in connection with a homicide in your neck of the woods."

"Tell me about the . . . homicide," she said aloud. Why was it so hard to say the word murder?

Rick sighed. "She died sometime between midnight and two this morning. Strangulation, multiple stab wounds, mutilation. It's not a pretty picture."

"And you think it was done by an artist?"

"Too soon to tell. She was *found* by an artist, that much we know, a black guy by the name of Wilson. Do you know him?"

"Willie Wilson? I know of him. He's pretty famous."

"Yeah? He dresses like a two-bit transvestite. Those guys, they love wild colors." He looked at her and smiled. His smile became a chuckle and then full-blown laughter.

"What's so funny?" Roz demanded.

"That coat." He nodded at her raincoat.

"What about it?"

"It's as bad as Wilson's getup. The color's so loud I can hardly hear the radio."

"Shut up! This cost me a fortune." Leave it to Rick to make her feel like a fool. "Just because you hide behind Brooks Brothers pin-stripes and white button down shirts. It takes courage to wear col-orful clothes."

"I don't doubt it takes a lot of guts to wear that," Rick laughed. "Oh come on, I'm just kidding."

"No you're not. I can't believe it. We're divorced ten years and you're still nagging me about the way I dress. As though you've cornered the market on style."

"Well," said Rick, brushing an invisible speck of lint off his im-maculate sleeve, "I don't get too many complaints."

"Yeah, and how many compliments?"

"A few."

"I guess you weren't getting too many from Tracy."

"Ouch. That was a low blow." Rick gave Roz a quick, pained look, then regained his composure. "But you're right. And I apol-ogize." He reached across the seat and put his hand on Roz's. "To be honest with you that's probably one of the reasons I wanted to see you. The way I treated you . . . I was an A-one asshole, and I need to apologize, to try to make it right. Because now I know how it feels."

She wanted to tell him he'd never know how it felt to be dumped at thirty-five, and alone at thirty-seven, then forty, then forty-two and now forty-five, a middle-aged woman whose hips were spreading in direct inverse proportion to her prospects for love and remarriage. But instead she said, "Hey, we had our good times."

"Yeah we did. And I've been thinking about them a lot recently.

Actually, I'm in therapy, and we're rehashing the whole business."

"Therapy!" Roz was incredulous. "You? For how long?"

Rick shrugged. "A few months. Seems like longer. I always thought shrinks were just a self-indulgence. But they're hard work. Anyway, like it or not, I'm learning some things about myself that I guess I need to deal with."

"Well, wonders never cease. I'm impressed, Rick," Roz said, and she meant it.

He squeezed her hand and looked at her, grateful, relieved. They were driving along the Grand Canal now. Rick pointed to some kids in a small boat, furiously bailing rain out of the hull to keep it from swamping. "Remember that rowboat we used to go out in when there was a full moon?"

"The *Ringy Dinghy*. I remember."

"D'you still have it?"

"No." There was no point in telling him that she'd made a ceremony out of sinking it the night of the first full moon after he'd left her.

"You didn't mention you had a friend," Rick said.

"Why should I have? It's none of your business."

"Maybe it wasn't, but it is now. What's his name?"

"Adrian Ambulu."

"What does he do?"

"He teaches art; a class I'm taking."

"Yeah, he looked like the sensitive type," Rick said sarcastically.

"Sensitivity isn't a bad thing, in case you still haven't figured it out. It's one of Adrian's best qualities, as a matter of fact."

"At least he's got that going for him."

"What's that supposed to mean?"

"Well, don't forget, I did see his equipment back at the house, and I hate to say it Roz, but it looked like you were sending a boy in to do a man's job."

"I don't believe you said that! How old are you, fifty-six or fifteen?"

"And that's another thing. He's an awful lot younger than you."

"Wait just a minute. Tracy was twenty-seven when you ran off with her, and you were forty-six."

"And look where we ended up."

The car slid to a smooth stop next to half a dozen other squad cars that were blocking the road at the entrance to Breeze Park. Rick turned to face Roz. "I'll tell you from experience, Roz. This midlife crisis business — it's not all it's cracked up to be. Take my advice, younger is not better, new can't replace old." He paused. "And, darlin' save the last dance for me." He gave her a light kiss on the forehead. "Now let's get to work."

THE CRIME SCENE WAS straight out of "*Hill Street Blues,*" with the black and whites, the curious crowd, the proscenium marked by yellow tape, separating the actors from the audience. Roz was dazzled by it all, and just stood for a moment to take it all in.

"Roz!" Rick held the tape for her to duck under. Somebody handed her a cup of coffee. It was steaming and bitter, the perfect antidote to the damp air and emotional chill of the scene. "They got an I.D. on the victim," he said. "Her name is — was — Caroline Van Patten. Know her?"

"No, I don't think so," Roz said quietly. "Maybe if I saw her I might."

Rick scratched his head. "I kind of doubt it. The guy made mincemeat out of her face. It's not something you'd want to see." He corralled another officer. "Is Drake here yet?"

"He's on his way," the man replied.

Someone handed Rick a sheaf of papers in a plastic evidence bag. "Thanks," Rick said, and handed it to Roz. "This was on her."

Gingerly, Roz took the bag from Rick. Raindrops had stained the clear plastic, but she could see that it was a bill of sale. She made out the words "Ocean Park, Number 84, by Richard Diebenkorn," and part of a short description that aptly characterized the Steins' painting. Con Uttrell's name was typed in the space for the seller's name, and the name HFD Inc. was written in for the name of the buyer.

"Does that ring a bell?" Rick asked.

"It looks like a bill of sale for the painting I'm looking for, yes," said Roz. "But I've never heard of HFD Inc."

"Neither have we, but we'll trace it."

"Well, I guess this knocks my theory out of the box," Roz sighed.

"What theory?" Rick asked.

"Oh, I found out this same dealer, Con Uttrell, is shipping a bronze statue he commissioned to Japan, and I had this silly idea that he might be trying to hide the painting inside it to get it out of the country. But obviously he sold it to this woman instead. Do you know where the painting is, by the way?"

"She didn't have it on her," said Rick dryly. "But we'll find it."

"Good. I'll need to know if you do, because it's stolen, and my clients have claim."

"Yes, Ma'am. I'll get right on it."

"So what do you do first?"

"We start questioning suspects."

"Who?"

"Classified," Rick said. Then with a twinkle in his eye he added,

"But if you'll cook up a batch of your famous pot roast and invite me over for dinner, I may weaken and bare my soul."

"Pot roast! Nobody eats pot roast anymore. Skinless roast chicken is more like it."

Rick looked hopeful. "Anything you want to cook sounds good to me. What do you say?"

"I'll have to check my calendar," Roz said. But her smile made it clear she'd be expecting him.

Rick smiled back. "DeVane, drive the lady home, will ya?"

"Yessir." The young rookie officer frowned like he'd just been demoted, but grabbed the keys Rick threw at him.

"See you tonight. I'll call you later and let you know what time. Oh, and Roz. . ."

"Yes, Rick?"

"It's okay with me if you want to wear that apron you had on this morning."

TWENTY-TWO

NICK SWUNG OPEN the door to his studio, ready to crucify whoever had rung the bell at this ungodly hour. But before him stood two uniformed officers of the law, somber and sober in the drenching rain, the strobe on top of their squad car backlighting them with an ominous glow.

Bleary-eyed and hung over from the excesses of the day and night before, Nick tried to read the time on the clock atop the all-night market across the alley. It was either twenty-five minutes after eleven at night or five in the morning; his vision was too blurry to tell. But he reasoned that it must be morning because he was too hung over for it to still be the middle of the night.

"Nicholas Stone?" one of the cops asked.

"Yeah."

"There's been a homicide in Breeze Park. We'd like you to come downtown with us to answer a few questions," the first cop said.

"What the fuck are you talking about?"

"Which word didn't you understand, Mr. Stone?" the second cop asked with measured politeness.

"What I don't understand is what you're doing knocking on *my* door at five in the morning. I don't know shit about any homicide."

The first cop persisted. "Do you know a guy named William Wilson?"

"Willie Wilson. Yeah, I know him. Why?"

The two cops looked at each other and smiled smugly. "He gave us your name," said the first one.

"He said you could corroborate his alibi about where he was last night," the second one added.

"If it's no problem," his partner finished sarcastically.

Nick shook his head to clear it. "Just give me a second to get my shit together." He started to shut the door but thought better of it. "You can wait inside," he said.

The cops stepped just inside the door, their huge wet presence filling the hallway like a noxious gas.

"This guy's some kind of an artist?" he heard one cop ask the other as he retreated to his living quarters.

"Supposedly," he replied. "Looks like he works for *Penthouse* or something."

"Not bad work, if you can get it."

Nick shook his head and fought back a wave of anger. Before he dressed he took a second to sweep his stash of pot and a small pipe into a drawer. Then he splashed water on his face and used his fingers to smooth down his hair. He put on his boots and gathered up his jacket, and, as an afterthought, grabbed a hat, which he pulled low over his eyes.

Damn Willie. What did he have to do with some homicide in

Breeze Park? And what did he expect Nick to say about it? For some reason he felt guilty as hell, guilty of what he didn't know.

Moments later he was stuffing his long legs into the back of the police car. It was an eerie sensation, being caged in a black and white. He hadn't been in one since he was sixteen, but the memory was still crystal clear. It had been the day his father had been killed.

Mitchell Milton Stone had been a diamond cutter, working for an Israeli gem merchant in the downtown jewelry mart. After spending eighteen years at minimum wage cutting stones without incident in an unventilated workshop the size of a closet, he had been shot in the head during a robbery when he'd refused to hand over the seven carat stone he was faceting.

Nick's mother was dead, and he had no other relatives living in Los Angeles. So it had been up to Nick to identify the body. The police had come to get him at school. He had been in gym class, swimming laps. When he surfaced after twenty, still breathing hard, the cops had been standing by the edge of the pool. They didn't even wait for him to get out of the water before they told him what had happened. "Your father was shot in a robbery," they'd said. "He's dead." Nick never swam again.

NOW, REMEMBERING that day, he felt the same shortness of breath, the same sense of unreality. He looked for the handle to roll down the window of the patrol car to let in some fresh air, but, of course, there were no handles on the rear doors.

He leaned toward the screen separating him from the cops in the front and tried to speak calmly. "Could you give me some air? It stinks like hell back here."

The cop didn't look at Nick, but sighed and cracked his window a quarter of an inch. Nick took a deep breath and allowed himself to sink back into thoughts of the past, anything to avoid acknowledging the present.

AFTER HIS FATHER'S FUNERAL, Nick had accepted a job from his father's employer, Harry Bloom, who pitied the boy and put him to work as a janitor. But Harry was kind-hearted and sometimes he allowed Nick to watch the diamond cutters at work. On occasion, he took time to teach him a few tricks of the trade.

Nick had shown an immediate aptitude for sculpting faceted gems out of unpolished stones. His hand was true and his eye astute at discovering how to free the beauty from the raw chunks of rock. In a matter of months he was carving gems. Harry saw a great future for the boy, and gave him every opportunity to learn the business. But Nick had other ideas. Although he loved to sculpt, the frustration of working with such small pieces of rock was stifling. He yearned for a larger canvas to test his talents, and applied for an art scholarship to San Jose State College.

Four years later, when he returned to Los Angeles, he found that his patrons, the Blooms, had closed up shop and gone back to Israel, leaving him $1000 and their address in Tel Aviv, should he ever been traveling in that part of the world.

He used the money to rent the studio in Venice because Venice was where art was happening, and in 1972 space was still dirt cheap. For the first year he'd paid his bills by selling tiny wooden carvings of bathing beauties for ten dollars each on the Boardwalk. There was always a crowd around Nick's card table with its forest of wooden sirens, but even on a good day he could only sell seven or eight, barely enough to cover his costs, with a little left over for cigarette money.

At that time Willie Wilson had been at the height of his career.

His dazzling watercolors had made him successful, and his personality had made him the darling of the California art scene; his tastes started trends, and everything he did was imitated. One day after lunch at the South Shore, he happened to stroll past Nick's Boardwalk table. He was impressed by the little wooden ladies, and the two men got to talking. Since Nick's sculptures posed no threat to his monopoly of the watercolor market, Willie took him under his wing. He treated Nick like some kind of art pet, raving about his work, parading him around town, and introducing him to buyers, dealers, and curators.

So Nick had gotten his start by grabbing onto Willie's coattails. He'd always wanted to find a way to show his gratitude to his mentor and friend. And now it looked like he was going to have his chance, in a way he'd never imagined.

NICK FOLLOWED the two cops into the station. "You can wait here," one told Nick. "The Detective'll be out in a minute." He ushered Nick into a small office which contained a gunmetal grey desk, two chairs and a waste basket. The only light in the cubicle glared from a row of bare fluorescent bulbs in the ceiling. Nick sat down to wait, trying not to let panic engulf him.

Fortunately, he didn't have to wait long. A well-dressed man almost as tall as Nick but with the huskiness of a fitness freak, strode into the room. "Rick Weeks, Homicide," the Suit said, offering his hand.

Nick took it. "Nick Stone," he said.

"We know," Weeks smiled. And then he wasn't smiling any more. "We'd like to ask you a few questions about a homicide, took place about half a mile from your residence, early this morning."

"I don't know shit about it."

Rick perched on the edge of the desk. "You can talk to me, Stone, or I can put you in a cell until you decide to cooperate."

"On what charge?"

Rick shrugged. "Possession, tax evasion, drunk driving, accessory to murder." He let his mouth linger on this last horrifying word. "Pick one. Or two. It's all the same to us."

Nick's fists tightened involuntarily. "What do you want from me?"

"Your pal Willie Wilson mentioned your name," Rick said. "He was at the scene, drunk and disorderly. His blood/alcohol level was off the charts, and I won't be at all suprised if we don't find narcotics in his apartment, when our search warrant comes through." He looked at Nick. "We started asking him questions, and your name came up."

"In what regard?"

"He says he was with you last night and you'd corroborate."

"We had a drink together. Late."

"How late?"

"I don't know. I don't wear a watch."

"Take a guess."

"One-thirty, two, something like that."

"Where were you?"

"At the South Shore."

"Anyone see you?"

"Anyone who was there." He stood up. "Is there anything else or can I go?"

"As a matter of fact, there is something else." Rick threw a small plastic bag on the desk.

Nick didn't have to move to see that one of his fettling knives was in it. There was a thin film of blood on the blade. "You use this kind of tool in your work, don't you?"

"Yeah, but so does every other sculptor in town."

Rick nodded and put the baggie back in his pocket. "But not a whole lot who live in Venice and whose fingerprints are on the handle."

Was he being accused of murder? Nick broke into a sweat. What was scary was that he couldn't remember how he'd gotten home last night. "Hey, wait a fuckin' minute. Just because some chick is killed with one of my tools, why does that mean I did it?"

"We're not saying you did." A long silence passed as he stared at Nick. "Did you?"

"Hell no!"

"I didn't think so. Because this isn't the murder weapon. Did I give you the impression it was? Sorry. She was killed with a blunt instrument, coroner says about so big." He measured a distance of about four inches between his hands. "We haven't recovered it yet. This was used later, to make it harder for us to identify the victim."

There was a knock on the door. Another Suit stuck his head in.

"Drake, where the hell've you been?"

"I just got back from the scene," the man said nervously. "We've got to talk."

"I'm almost done here."

"We've got to talk *now*."

"Okay, okay." Rick stood and straightened his tie. "This won't take long. Do you mind just waiting?" Without giving Nick a chance to answer, he left the room.

TWENTY-THREE

"IT'S A DETECTIVE RICHARD WEEKS, Mr. Uttrell." Bryant was holding out the cellular phone to Con as though it were radioactive. Then he added the single, ominous word, "Homicide."

Con opened his eyes and pulled himself into a sitting position against the pillows. "What time is it?"

"Seven a.m."

Carefully, he took the phone from Bryant. "Uttrell here," he said in a businesslike tone. And then he simply listened.

Thirty minutes later, riding down to County General Hospital to meet Detective Weeks, Con tried to sort through the dominoing events. It had all started with Francis Thornton's incredible demand that Con arrange to have the Michelangelo Giant secreted to Japan. No, before that even, had been Thornton's revelation that he knew the Rothko he had purchased from Con was a fake. The demand about the Giant came later, when Thornton had the leverage to manipulate him.

Con thought about this for a moment. How had Thornton

known? Wendell Niles had been the mutually agreed upon expert who had authenticated the painting as a condition of its sale. Thornton must have called in another expert who disputed Niles' conclusion. What would have given him the clue to question Niles' report, Con's word, and the exhaustive provenance?

Or perhaps the question was not 'what' but 'who?' Somebody must have tipped him off.

The only other person besides his private secretary Anna who knew about it was the forger himself, Willie Wilson. But what could Wilson have hoped to gain from admitting his crime to Thornton? And why had Thornton gone ahead and bought the painting if he knew it was a fake? The money he'd paid Con for it had certainly been real.

Next came this Caroline Van Patten person, with all her phony credentials, and her desire to obtain a specific Diebenkorn, just when Con had procured one from the black market. It was clear now that she had been out to get him; if his judgement hadn't been impaired by anxiety over Thornton, he surely would have seen it earlier.

But where had she come from? Who had she been working for? Normally, he would have had Anna trace her. But Anna was still on her camping vacation. She wouldn't be back for days, and there was no one else he could trust to ask for help.

The limousine pulled off the freeway at Soto Street and stopped at a red light two blocks from County General Hospital. Ahead, Con saw a pack of reporters standing vigil on the hospital stairs — rabid dogs, eager to accuse and castigate. Con's mind reeled. He needed to be at the top of his game for what was coming. He pushed the button that lowered the interior window.

"Rocco. I need a stimulant."

"Yessir, Mr. Uttrell," Rocco replied and flipped an unmarked toggle switch on the dashboard which released the catch on a hidden niche in the armrest of the left passenger door. From it Con took a small silver vial and a tiny spoon and snorted two full spoonfuls of the white powder into each nostril before returning the container to its hiding place.

Hyper alert and back in control, he let Rocco lead the way through the gauntlet of reporters into the hospital where this Detective Weeks was supposed to be waiting. It was imperative that Con deflect his questions, for a police inquiry into his business practices would destroy him. No, he would play dumb. What was the old adage? Better to keep your mouth shut and be thought an imbecile than to open it and remove all doubt.

The detective was waiting for him at the end of a shabby hallway. As he approached, Con rearranged his features into a tortured look of bereavement. The detective extended his hand. "Detective Weeks, Mr. Uttrell. Thank you for coming at this early hour."

"It's no problem," Con replied. "Actually, I never went to bed last night. I was wide awake after dinner, so my assistant helped me go through some paperwork — things I hadn't been able to get to during office hours. We worked through the night." Satisfied that he had established a believable alibi, Con smiled.

"Sorry about the press out there. The pack instinct makes them crazy when they get the scent of a homicide like this."

"This came as such a shock, Detective," Con said soberly. "We'd just had dinner together! She was a lovely woman, although I only knew her slightly," he hastened to add, brushing his hand over his eye in a gesture of sadness.

"I'm sorry we have to ask you down here to identify the body, but we're having trouble tracking her family. Perhaps you could help us in that regard."

"I . . . really, I know nothing about the woman. As I said earlier, she was a client, a new client, representing a collector from the East."

"Do you have his name, perhaps?"

Con shook his head. "She didn't offer it and I didn't push her." When he saw the detective's raised eyebrows he added, "That isn't as unusual as it sounds. Many wealthy collectors prefer to remain anonymous."

The two men got into an elevator and rode down to the basement in silence.

When the elevator door opened, the smell of formaldehyde blasted Con's senses. His eyes began to tear and his breath came short. Seeing this, the detective pulled an immaculate handkerchief from his pocket and handed it to Con. "You'll do better if you keep this over your nose and mouth," he said.

The draped gurney was rolled out, and the stench of death overpowered even the formaldehyde. Con was indeed grateful for the handkerchief. Even so, he tried not to breathe. The detective waited for Con's nod, then took a deep breath himself and lifted the sheet.

If the body on the cart did belong to Caroline Van Patten, it was impossible for Con to tell. Its facial features had been so mutilated that it looked more like a ghastly abstraction of a corpse than the remains of an actual person. But rather than be repulsed by what he saw, Con was, thanks no doubt to the cocaine, fascinated. What had once been a woman's face had been transformed into a cubist sculpture of a face, with the actual body parts used to create the image.

The woman's nose and ears had been severed and her eyes plucked from their sockets. One ear had been stuck messily into the cavity in the middle of the face where the nose had been, the other crammed in the mouth. The eyeballs decorated the vacant ear holes, from which bits of cartilage and brain matter dangled like dreadlocks. Con wondered where the nose was. Rick lifted the sheet a little higher and Con saw it protruding from her vagina. Grotesque as it was, Con had to stifle a smile.

"Can you identify this woman?"

"It could be Miss Van Patten, but I'm sorry, I can't be sure."

"I understand."

He lowered the sheet and nodded to the attendant to wheel the cart away. In silence the men returned to the elevator. After a respectable amount of time, Con thought it appropriate to ask, "Do you know who did this?"

Rick shook his head. "We don't have enough evidence yet to charge a suspect. But the press is crawling all over us because of the mutilation thing. Sick as it is, people eat this stuff up. We're following up on all possible leads. Any thoughts?"

"I couldn't begin to think of anyone who would commit such an atrocity."

Rick nodded his head as though this was the answer he was expecting. "I'd like to ask you to stop by headquarters, Mr. Uttrell," he said pleasantly. "Would that be a problem?"

"Now?" Con stalled. "I am a businessman, Detective. I should be thinking about getting to my office. My driver's waiting outside."

Rick smiled pleasantly, the expression of a man who knew he was holding all the cards. "I'm sure it's on your way. You can have your driver follow us. We'll go in my car."

A ROOMFUL OF PEOPLE AWAITED them at Police Headquarters, among them Nick Stone, Willie Wilson, and another man wearing a polka dot bow tie, who Rick introduced as Lieutenant Drake, Art Theft Division.

Con felt his chest tighten with paranoia. The pertinent clues of the case, the accusing eyes of the people in the room, his own fascination with the dead body, all swirled about him in an ever-constricting circle. He stood immobile in the eye of the storm.

"The victim is a female Caucasian. Age, forty-two. Height, 5' 6". Weight, one hundred twenty-one pounds. We've identified her as Caroline Van Patten. We have no current address on her yet." He turned to Willie Wilson. "When you found her in the park off Breeze, she was dead. Is that correct?"

All eyes focused on Willie. Con could see that he was agitated, perspiring freely.

"I was walking home from the South Shore, late. Nick and I'd been hoisting a few." He looked to Nick for affirmation of this and Nick nodded. "I came up Sailfish and cut across the park. I always do. It's shorter. And I was about halfway through when I saw this kinda light flash up ahead, like lightning. But then there was another flash right away."

"And then I heard someone running, heavy, like, I dunno, they were dragging something. I was scared shitless. You know what it's like at night. So I hid over in the bushes, to wait for whatever it was to pass. But then I didn't see anything, so I came out and kept going. I could've gone back and around, but it was longer and I just wanted to get home. Y'know what I mean?

"Anyway, I went a ways, and I was about outta there when I tripped on something, took a header right on top of it." He buried his face in his hands, and when he continued his voice was muffled. "It was her. I was lying right on top of her."

"That could explain why we found your fingerprints on her face and neck." Rick spoke matter-of-factly, but the accusation was clear. "She was bludgeoned to death before she was cut, before her face was mutilated. We haven't found the murder weapon yet, but we think the murderer used this to cut her." Again he held up the plastic bag with the fettling knife in it and showed it around, then tossed it onto the table in front of Nick.

"It has your fingerprints on it," he reminded Nick.

Nick squirmed uncomfortably in his chair. "Yeah, so what? I've got about a hundred of those. Anybody could have walked out of my studio with that in their pocket. People are in and out all day."

"Of course they are," he said in a voice that implied he was leaving it open for Nick to name some names, but Nick had said all he was going to say.

"She also had this on her." Rick set a paper sealed in plastic in front of Con.

Con swore softly to himself. He knew what the paper was without looking at it. But everyone in the room was waiting for him to react, so he picked it up. Indeed, it was the bill of sale for the Diebenkorn, with Con's name and that of Caroline Van Patten on the appropriate lines for buyer and seller.

"Did you sell a painting, entitled 'Occan Park, Number 84' by Richard Diebenkorn to a Caroline Van Patten?"

"I think I'd prefer not to answer any questions until my attorney arrives," said Con.

"That's your privilege, of course. But you're not being accused of anything. We're merely trying to clarify a few issues."

"Just the same. I'd like to call my attorney and have him here."

TWENTY-FOUR

THE MINUTE ROZ WALKED into the office, Nelson leapt to his feet. "La Salle wants to see you. He's practically foaming at the mouth. I hope you have something for him."

"I do, but not enough." She'd spent the morning at home, documenting what she'd learned at the crime scene and writing up her report. There was just one piece still missing, a big one: the Diebenkorn painting itself. The phone rang and she picked it up, grateful for the diversion, hopeful that it was Rick, confirming dinner. Even with all that she had on her mind she couldn't stop thinking about him.

"Rosiland Weeks," she said.

"Willie Wilson."

Willie Wilson! According to Rick, he'd been the artist who found the corpse. But why would he be calling her? "Yes, Mr. Wilson. What can I do for you?"

"I'm lookin' at a business card someone dropped in my box, has your name on it. Says you're looking for information about a forged Diebenkorn."

"Yes, I am."

"So, look no further."

"I see." Roz tried to keep the excitement out of her voice. She pulled the pad and pencil closer to the phone and scribbled on it. "Yes, I can be there at noon. Yes, I remember where it is. No, I won't. I'll be alone. Thank you for calling. Thank you very much."

She hung up and stared at the phone, not believing what she'd just heard. Then she jumped to her feet, gathering up her purse, her coat, and her umbrella.

"Well?" Nelson demanded.

"Your idea about going to the artists for leads might be paying off. Will you do me a favor?"

"Who is it? Tell me!"

"I'm not sure yet. When I get back." She started for the door.

"What about La Salle?" Nelson called.

Roz sighed. "I forgot." She smiled at Nelson. "Will you cover for me?"

"You want *me* to talk to La Salle?" He was incredulous.

"Just stall for me."

"But, what will I say?"

"Fake it. Tell him I called in sick. Tell him it's female problems. Help me out, please?" She planted a kiss on the top of Nelson's head and walked out the door.

"This is going to cost you more than lunch at the Pizza Kitchen," he called, but Roz was gone.

ROZ WAS ELATED, but her excitement had an edge to it. She remembered going by Willie Wilson's studio when she was making the rounds two weeks ago, one of dozens of studios she'd visited. She'd gotten into the building easily enough; the street door hadn't been locked. But she had been stopped cold at the entrance to his studio by a barking dog and a disembodied voice which had refused to open the door, had barely allowed her the privilege of stuffing her card through the mail slot. The card must have gotten to him though, because here she was, on her way to his studio at his summons. What a lucky break. Or was it? Rick had mentioned Wilson's name in connection with the corpse in Breeze Park. Could it be only a coincidence that his name had come up again in the space of six hours?

She turned onto Sailfish and slowed, looking for a parking place; it was always tough this close to the beach. But she was in luck, because a Mazda pulled out of a spot just across the street from Willie's studio. Roz nabbed it and hurried across, slipping between two parked cars to get to the sidewalk. Out of the corner of her eye she noticed two men sitting in the rear car — a beat-up tan Chevy with no license plate. They stared at her as she passed in front of them. Visions of the dead woman in Breeze Park were still fresh in her mind. She averted her eyes and hurried to the blue door of Willie's building.

Today it was locked, but on the right jamb was a note that said "*Doorbell*" with an arrow pointing down to a button. She pushed it. It didn't ring, but she heard a dog's high yipping, and then the door buzzed open. Roz entered.

She remembered the interior from her previous visit. It was an older building and the hallway was spacious, beautifully tiled in a checkerboard of red and turquoise, and very clean. Willie's studio was on the second floor. There was no elevator, just a broad staircase with a wooden rail painted egg yolk yellow.

Willie's magenta door was at the top of the stairs. This was as far as she'd gotten last time. She raised her hand to knock but before she applied knuckle to wood, a voice from inside called, "Come on in, but be careful where you step."

Gingerly, Roz opened the door. Before her was a long, high-ceiling studio flooded with fluorescent light. Directly inside the door an eight-by-twelve foot canvas was stretched out over the floor. Willie Wilson stood beside it. She recognized him from pictures she'd seen, but in person he looked diminished, sick in fact — dilated pupils, sweaty forehead, shaking hands, black skin as pale as cigar ash. Clearly, something was amiss.

"Rosiland Weeks. Sorry it took me so long," Roz apologized. "One of those days."

"Tell me about it," Willie replied. He bent over a small Benji-type terrier, forcing each of his four paws into a different dish of colored paint. As Roz watched, he lifted the dog and set him on the canvas. "Okay, Vincent, do your stuff."

He tossed a ball in the air and the dog romped across the canvas, leaving colorful pawprints in his wake. "Most people send their dogs to obedience school. I sent mine to art school," Willie said. "A little more left hind in the corner, Vince. Thatta boy."

Willie offered Roz a box of Crackerjacks. "I had a late breakfast," she said. "No thanks."

"Don't blame you," Willie shuddered. "Wouldn't touch the stuff myself." He tried to rip open the carton but his hands were shaking too hard. Again he held out the box to Roz. "Do you mind?"

She tore off the top and handed it back to him. He sprinkled the candy liberally across the canvas. "The perfect touch," he said, and stood back to admire his work. "That ought to be worth five grand."

"You can really get five thousand for that?"

Willie's expression darkened. "I can get that much for my signature," he boasted, his expression challenging Roz to disagree.

She tried to make light of it. "What's Vincent's cut?"

Hearing his name, the dog trotted over to Roz and jumped up on her, leaving one blue and one green paw print on her skirt before Willie could pull him away.

"He gets a free ride, which is more than most artists. Don't worry about your skirt. It's just watercolor. It'll wash out."

"I wouldn't dream of it. I'll bet it'll be worth a fortune someday."

"Damn right."

Holding Vincent at arms' length, Willie walked across the studio, opened a door just wide enought to toss him through it. But before the door shut, Roz saw an impressive computer setup inside, a scanner and at least three interconnected terminals. Odd, she thought, for a painter to also be a computer hacker. Or was it? It seemed everything and everybody was wired into a mainframe these days.

"Hey, you don't have to lock him up for me," Roz said. "I like dogs."

Willie was busy rummaging through a cardboard box on the floor. "Naw, he's done for the day. What d'you want — a toke, a snort, or a sip?"

"Er, nothing thanks," Roz demurred. "My drug of choice is adrenalin, and I'm way over my limit today."

"Me too, but that never stops me." Willie picked up a joint and lit it, holding the smoke in his lungs for longer than Roz thought anyone could hold their breath. He motioned to her to follow him into an alcove where two ponyskin Le Corbousier lounges sat side by side. He collapsed into one, and motioned to Roz to make use of the other. Then he took another long hit off the joint and closed his eyes.

"Mr. Wilson, on the phone you mentioned something about the Diebenkorn I'm looking for."

He turned to her drowsily and stared. Suddenly his eyes focused and he bolted upright. Roz was so startled that she practically fell off of the armless lounge.

"Jesus!" he said. "For a second I thought you were someone else." He shook his head as though to clear it. "I keep seein' her face."

"Whose face?" Roz wondered, but was afraid to ask.

"What did you say your name was?"

"Roz, Rosiland Weeks," she said. "You called me about the Diebenkorn. I left my card . . ."

"Yeah, yeah," he said, getting to his feet. "I knew I was forgetting something." He strode out of the room. "I'll be right back. Don't go away."

When he was out of sight, Roz sighed in relief and looked around. The studio was neat and sparsely furnished — spartan almost. Some boxes were stacked by the door. Except for the painting on the floor, there was no evidence of work-in- progress, and except for the two lounge chairs, no creature comforts.

Willie came back into the room holding a stretched and mounted canvas. He turned it around to face her. "Know what this is?"

Roz's heart leapt. "The Diebenkorn. Number 84."

"Ha! Fooled you. This baby's an original, but not by Big D. It's not too shabby, if I do say so myself."

This was a forgery? Roz's eye was untrained, but she'd spent a lot of time looking at photographs of the missing painting and the canvas in front of her certainly looked authentic. "If this isn't the Diebenkorn, do you know where it is?"

"Con Uttrell has it."

So Nelson had been right. He was operating a forgery ring and keeping the originals for himself. She felt the brass ring slip from her hands. To settle the Stein case, she needed the original, and she wanted to find it in Uttrell's hands so she could put him behind bars. This fake was no good to her unless she could tie it to him. "Where'd you get this?"

"Uttrell paid me to do it. Not bad, is it?"

Was Wilson admitting that he was a forger? "It's incredible," Roz agreed, playing along.

"He was going to pawn it off on this chick from out of town," Willie was saying. "But she found out he was trying to stiff her." He leaned close to Roz. "She threatened to go to the cops, so he killed her, snuffed her out in Breeze Park last night."

Roz froze. "Con Uttrell killed the woman?" she whispered.

Willie nodded. "She was definitely dead, very dead. I found her, you know. But I didn't kill her. Like I said, Uttrell was responsible."

"You mean, you saw him do it?"

Will shook his head. "He's not that dumb."

"Then how do you know he's responsible?"

Willie smiled. "I know what I know," he said cryptically.

"Have you told the police?"

Suddenly, Willie looked agitated. He backed away from Roz. "There's a lot of stuff going down. I don't wanna get in the middle of it."

"Then why are you telling me?" Roz's pulse was racing.

"You want to bust Con Uttrell, don't you?" He thrust the painting into her hands. "Take this. Good riddance. I hope you and the cops screw him to the wall. Just leave me out of it. That's all I got to say."

Roz didn't hesitate. She had no use for the forged painting, but it was her ticket out of the studio. She took the painting from him and started for the door.

"Make sure they skewer the bastard!"

"I'll do my best."

Roz hurried down the stairs holding the painting by its wooden frame. It was heavy and she had to set it down to open the door to the street. Outside, she hoisted it up again to carry it the final few yards to her car. She noticed the men in the tan Chevy watching her.

Then she heard a three-note whistle and looked up. Willie was leaning on the windowsill one story above the door. "Oh, by the way, I could be wrong," he called down.

"About what?"

"That could be the real Diebenkorn. I did such a damn good job copying it, I may have given Uttrell the fake by mistake!" He laughed, and closed the window.

That ought to confuse her, Willie thought as he watched Roz cross the street, the painting tucked under her arm. Had she bought his story about Uttrell? At least maybe it would obscure the issue temporarily, and give him a little space.

He watched her walk right in front of the two plainclothes cops in the tan Chevy who had followed him home from police headquarters that morning. Giving her the painting had served two purposes. It was hard evidence against Uttrell, and more important, the dumb-fuck cops were so stupid, they'd follow her for sure and get off his back.

Just as he'd predicted, one of the men got out of the car and the other hung a U-turn and sped after Roz. Willie would have no problem ditching the sucker on foot; he could slip out the back before the guy even knew he was gone.

TWENTY-FIVE

IT HAD TO BE love. For the last twenty-four hours Tory had thought of nothing except Nick and the way it had felt when he'd kissed her. Her life had begun at that moment. Nothing would be the same ever again.

Fingering the bronze medallion Nick had given her, she looked out the window of the taxi. In a few minutes she'd be at his studio. She had a lot at stake here, ditching school, missing a French test, sneaking the taxi money from her father's top drawer. But it was the only plan she had been able to come up with to get Nick's attention.

Her idea was to show up when Nick wasn't expecting her, not to work, just to visit him. Then maybe he would see her as a normal human being, a friend, a *girl*friend. And maybe, if she was lucky, he would allow her to come behind the wall he'd built around himself.

So she wouldn't appear so obvious, she'd brought her camera on the pretext that she wanted to photograph him for a class assignment. The film! She had almost forgotten. God! If she showed up with an empty camera, for sure he'd suspect.

"Excuse me." She leaned forward to the cabbie.

"Yeah?"

"Could we please stop at the camera shop. Over there."

She pointed to the old storefront building ahead about a half a block on the left.

"We can do anything, kiddo, long as the meter's running."

He pulled a U-turn and screeched to a halt in front of the Venice Camera Shoppe.

THE BELL ON THE DOOR TINKLED, announcing Tory. Eli was sweeping the aisle in slow, inefficient strokes, his lips moving as he sang to himself. When he saw her he grinned and began to sweep faster, like a dog wagging its tail.

"Look out!" Tory called.

But it was too late. The broom connected with a Kodak display and a pyramid of little yellow boxes collapsed onto the floor.

"Jesus Christ! You are as clumsy as a ballerina with two club feet!" Bud shouted from his perch in the storeroom. "Don't just stand there. Clean it up!"

Eli knelt among the strewn boxes like a child playing with yellow blocks. One by one, he picked them up, but instead of stacking them, he carefully set them in a circle. Tory bent down to help him. Eli was so absorbed, he seemed to forget she was there. Suddenly his face flooded with pleasure.

"Beautiful," he said in a garbled voice. He pointed to a large cockroach scuttling within the circle of boxes.

"Aah!" Tory recoiled.

Eli lunged forward and made a grab for the beetle. But he was too clumsy and it skittered away. Before he could reach for it again, Bud's enormous booted foot crushed it into the linoleum.

"Damn cockaroaches. Musta come from the Chink place next door."

Immediately Eli bent to scrape the bug off the floor.

"Oh, gross!" Tory cried.

"See? He likes 'em dead. The more squished up the better. Can you believe this guy?" Bud went on. "A bowl of refried beans has more brains. I don't know what's lower, his I.Q. or his sperm count."

"You shouldn't say things like that," Tory snapped. "He's a person too."

"The jury's still out on that one," Bud countered, amused at her spunk. "Anyway what's a pretty little thing like you doing sticking up for a retard? Wouldn't you rather have a real man?" He took a step nearer to Tory, pinning her against the counter. "Give me your hand," he demanded.

"What for?" Tory was afraid now. His beery breath was choking her and she couldn't move.

"I got a present for you, here in my pocket." He patted the bulge in his pants and pressed against her. "Doncha want it?"

"No!"

"Aw, come on, I've been saving it just for you."

"Let me go!" she cried, but he only laughed.

Suddenly Eli charged at Bud, brandishing the broom like a sword. In one sweeping stroke he knocked a whole shelf of picture frames to the floor and caught him full in the groin.

"Aagh!" Bud grabbed the brush end of the broom and wrested it free from Eli. "Damn retard! I'll teach you . . .!"

He raised the broom and was about to bring it down on Eli's head when a large woman in curlers and a housecoat appeared.

"BUD!" she screamed, diverting his attention long enough for Eli to scramble to his feet and escape out the back of the store.

"This is it, Marge. He's got to go. Look what he's done to the store!" He used the broom to gesture to the broken picture frames and Kodak boxes still littering the floor.

"He didn't start it," Tory interrupted. She pointed at Bud. "*He* did. The other one was just protecting me."

"From what?" Bud accused.

"From you!" Tory said. She turned to the woman. "He tried to make me touch him!"

"What are you saying?"

"He told me he had a present for me in his pocket and he tried to . . ."

"Marge, don't believe her. She's nuts too!"

Marge stared from Tory to Bud and back to Tory again. "What do you want here?" she demanded.

"I came to get some film," Tory said.

Marge picked up a Kodak box and thrust it into Tory's hand. "Here, take it and go." Tory reached for her purse, but Marge shook her head. "Just go! And stay away from my men." Then she directed her fury at Bud. "And you! As long as you've got that broom in your hands, use it!"

From the dirt-streaked window of the garage, Eli watched Tory run to the taxi and get in. As it pulled away from the curb, he hurried outside and mounted a dilapidated moped with a sidecar attachment, clumsily kick-starting it. By the time the taxi had U-turned back toward the beach, Eli was in hot pursuit.

NICK'S STUDIO WAS LOCKED, but Tory knew that the key was hidden behind a loose brick in the wall. She unlocked the metal door and went in.

"Hello?" Her voice echoed emptily. She went into Leslie's office. It was deserted, but there was a note taped on the door jamb in Leslie's loopy handwriting that read, "*Nick, where are you? I'm at yoga and then to vet to get Attila. Back by two.*"

Tory wandered into the studio, considering her options. She could chicken out and go home, and no one would be the wiser. But she was going to be in trouble anyway. She might as well stick around. She looked around the room. What if she was just, like, there, in Nick's bedroom, waiting for him when he came back. It was only 12:30. They'd still have more than an hour before Leslie returned. That is, if Nick showed up soon. An hour would be enough time, wouldn't it?

She slipped out of her clothes and got into Nick's bed. The sheets felt heavy and unfamiliar. Her own bedclothes at home were an easy care percale, slick against her skin. These felt softer, like an old favorite shirt, something Nick would wear. She shivered nervously at the strangeness of being nude in bed, his bed, in the middle of the day. It was decadent and kind of thrilling.

The remote control for the TV was sitting on the bedside table and she could see that a tape was plugged into the VCR. Curious to see what Nick watched when he was alone, she flicked it on. The TV was old, and the sound started before the picture faded in.

"Is that better?" a woman's voice asked. A shiver of confusion racked Tory's brain. The woman's voice sounded horrifyingly familiar, yet impossibly out of place.

"Much," Nick's voice replied. "Now let me look at you." Tory gasped in shock as the picture came into focus. On the screen was something she had never in a million years imagined she'd see: her mother's naked body!

That in itself was startling enough. But added to it was the appalling fact that Charlotte had been naked *here* at Nick's studio, standing on Tory's platform.

"Jesus, relax," Nick's voice was saying. "You look like you've got a rod up your ass." And Charlotte giggled. "I just have good posture. I won a prize for it in grammar school, you know."

Tory beat her fists on the bed. "This isn't happening," she told herself. "It can't be!" Nick was *her* artist. *She* was the model, not Charlotte! She cried out, "Mother, you hypocrite! Nick, you liar! How could you do this to me!" But her voice rang emptily. There was no one to hear her or reply.

The tape continued to run. In appalled fascination, Tory watched it, studying her mother's naked body. Charlotte was shorter than Tory by perhaps three inches, but in the armor of her conservative shirtmaker dresses and stalwart suits she had always seemed to be looking down at Tory. Now, fully exposed in the raw light of Nick's studio, she looked shrunken, a pygmy compared to the figures which soared serenely on the pedestals around her.

Her face, hardened into a mask by age, makeup, and the harsh light, looked foolish atop a body that had softened and given way to gravity. Without the support of a brassiere, her breasts drooped, and without their fashionable padding, her rounded shoulders slumped into fleshy arms. The sad pouch of her tummy was slashed by a vertical scar from navel to pubis, a reminder of Tory's birth by Caesarean in the days before bikini cuts, and the skin on her thighs was puckered and strafed with varicose veins.

Then Nick moved into the camera's eye. He picked up a sketch pad and started to draw.

"You're not drawing me, I hope," Charlotte simpered, coquettishly protecting her privacy with her hands.

"Would you rather I took a picture?" Nick asked, and moved toward the camera.

"God, no!"

"Then how am I going to compare your body to your daughter's? That's what you said you wanted me to do, isn't it?" He put down the sketch pad and took a few steps closer to Charlotte, extending his hand across the distance that separated them. "I suppose I could do it by touch."

Charlotte stopped giggling and frowned. "You're not telling me you and Tory. . ."

"No, no, I haven't laid a hand on her. And I won't, either."

"Why should I believe that?" she taunted him. "You obviously aren't the kind of man who is inhibited by morality."

Nick turned away from her and towards the camera, his contempt clear on his face. "I don't do virgins."

"Oh why not?"

"They're too much work, too much responsibility."

"I would have thought you would see a virgin as a chance to take something unformed and mold it," Charlotte teased. "Like you do your clay."

"I like a woman for who she is, not for what I make her. And when my work is successful, it's because it captures something that's already inside her, not something I put there. Now do you want me to do this or don't you?"

That was it. Tory couldn't watch any more. She snapped off the video, quickly put on her clothes, and slipped out of the studio. She was still dazed by what she had seen, so overwhelmed that she didn't notice Eli when he slipped out from behind the dumpster in the alley and began to limp along behind her.

He followed at a distance until they reached the Boardwalk, at which point his pursuit was camouflaged by the crowd. Then he walked faster, getting closer and closer until he was only inches away. He was so close that he could smell Her special scent. And he was about to reach out to touch Her when a derelict in ragged bedroom slippers grabbed his arm. "Got a quarter, buddy?"

Eli flailed his arms, trying desperately to shrug him off. But by the time he'd freed himself from the gnarled fingers of the derelict, She was gone from sight. Eli was disappointed, but not discouraged. He'd seen Her come out of the door on the alley. Surely, She would return to that place sooner or later. His job now, his destiny, was to follow the Girl and make Her his own. He would wait.

TWENTY-SIX

LESLIE WAS JUST ABOUT TO close up the studio office for the evening when she remembered she needed to take out the trash. Nick had refused to eat the veggie burger from The Fig Tree she'd brought him when she'd come back from the vet. If she didn't put it outside tonight, she was sure to find her office crawling with vermin in the morning.

As she walked through the darkened studio she could hear the shower on in Nick's bathroom. Good, he'd pulled himself together to get ready for the party. She'd heard him talking to Con Uttrell in the afternoon, trying to beg off, but Con had insisted. After all, the party at the Thorntons' was being thrown in celebration of the completion of the statue. Apparently Francis and Margaret were friends of the collector who'd commissioned it and had made the initial connection with Con. Leslie had been all set to arrange for the statue to be taken to the Thorntons' house so that it could be shown to the guests. But for some reason, at the last minute they had decided not to have an unveiling. It was just as well. It saved Leslie the effort of organizing it, and now the staff could finish the last minute patina in the morning, rather than rush to finish it tonight.

Leslie let herself out the back door into the small gravel-bedded yard where Attila lived at night, and locked it behind her. She had been surprised to find the dog in relatively good shape when she'd picked him up at the vet. His head was bandaged and he held it cocked to one side when he walked, but he had wagged his tail vigorously and barked when he'd seen her. The doctor had given her tranquilizers to keep him quiet, but other than that he was fine.

He was by the back gate, growling and circling, his attention focused on the dumpster in the alley. He probably wanted to go for a walk. Leslie took the leather lead off the hook by the door and snapped it onto his collar. When she unlocked the gate he charged out, dragging her toward the dumpster.

She jerked on the lead. "Attila, heel. Heel!" she commanded.

Reluctantly, the big dog fell into step beside her, still whining and sniffing around the dumpster. She tossed the garbage into the open bin and pressed on. She had to use all her strength to pull Attila away from it, practically dragging him down the alley to the Boardwalk, toward the setting sun.

The moment they were gone, Eli stepped out from behind the dumpster. Hidden in the shadow of the building, he watched until they turned the corner onto the Boardwalk. Then he let himself in the open gate and snuck around to the west side of the building. He saw that the chain-link fence was close enough to the side of the studio that he could climb it and pull himself onto the roof. Then, when She came back he'd be able to watch Her through the skylight. It wouldn't be as good as being *in*side, but much better than being locked *out*side the fence. And the dog would never be able to get him up there.

He began to climb.

NICK STOOD under the pulsating stream of water, clean, but not absolved of the gritty film of apprehension, palpable as bruises on his body. He'd felt dirty since the cops had appeared at his door at dawn, and no amount of scrubbing seemed to help.

He hadn't known the dead woman, so he could hardly mourn her. But the fact that one of his fettling knives had gotten to the scene of the crime chilled him to the bone. He had dozens of knives and he often carried one with him, the way some people carry a rabbit's foot or worry beads. Had he left one somewhere? Or had the murderer taken it from his studio? Was someone trying to implicate him? If so, who?

For the hundredth time, he retraced his actions of the past twenty-four hours. He and his crew had been welding the figure until about eleven, when Willie had called from Spago and asked Nick to meet him at the South Shore.

By the time he got there, it was near to midnight. They'd had some drinks on top of the weed Nick had smoked while he worked — a nasty mixture for him. He knew better, but he'd needed the release. He must've passed out in the head, because he had a vague recollection of Cindy, the waitress, shaking him and telling him to wake up, that it was two a.m. and that the restaurant was closing. That was all he remembered until the cops at the door had awakened him at five. There had to be more to the story. How had he gotten home? What had happened to Willie?

He decided to stop by the South Shore on his way to the Thorntons' party. Surely someone there would remember seeing him and be able to fill in the gaps in his memory. But first he'd swing by Willie's and try to rouse him. They hadn't spoken since Nick left him at the police station late that morning. Nick had been calling him every fifteen or twenty minutes all afternoon, but there had been no answer, not even the machine. He had no idea if Willie was still in custody, or if he was just not answering his phone.

Nick stepped out of the shower, wrapped the towel around his waist, and walked into the studio to look at the statue one more time. It was finished — well, almost. The figure was cast, and he'd sanded the welds when he'd come back from the police station. All that was left was to apply the final patina. It was scheduled to be picked up by Con Uttrell's men in the morning and taken to the airport for the flight to Japan.

He should have been feeling relief that he'd made the deadline, and pleasure that he was going to be paid a hell of a lot of money. But he didn't. He felt frustrated, like he needed more time. It was always hard for him to let go of his work, and in this case, he'd only lived with it for a month. Less than that, really. Unbelievable as it seemed, he'd only met Tory three and a half weeks ago.

Tory. He'd planned to surprise her when she came in for their final session that afternoon, by inviting her to come with him to the celebration at the Thorntons'. It would have been his way of thanking her for being his muse and his model, a kind of closure to their relationship. And he'd been anticipating her pleasure at being asked to be his date.

But his day had started with the cops at five a.m., and then in the afternoon Tory hadn't shown up. He'd had Leslie call her house, but she hadn't been there either. The maid had said something about a soccer game, but that couldn't be right. Nick knew Tory was supposed to come down to work with him one last day.

Nick approached the statue. She was lying face up on one of the work tables, staring up at the skylight, a sleeping beauty. Nick ran his fingers along the smooth bronze thigh, up past the curve of the buttocks to the arc of the waist. He would have liked nothing more than to lie down next to her and share her serene slumber.

But his reverie was distracted by the rusty slam of the back gate, followed by a creaking sound on the roof, and Attila's ferocious barking.

"Attila, cut it out, damn it!" It was Leslie's voice.

"What's the problem?" he called.

"I dunno. Attila's acting really weird. Maybe we should give him one of the tranks the vet prescribed. I hate to give him drugs, but since . . ." Leslie stopped, obviously taken aback by the sight of Nick's bare torso and the towel around his waist. "Oh, sorry, I . . ." she fumbled. "What do you think about the tranks for Attila?"

"Whatever you think. And maybe he should stay inside tonight. No point in leaving him outside if he's drugged to the gills."

"Good idea," Leslie said. "I'll chain him."

NICK DROVE by Willie's, but the studio was dark and no one answered his knock. He walked around the building twice, but saw nothing, no clue to Willie's whereabouts.

It was six-thirty when he got to the South Shore. He was supposed to be at the Thorntons' at seven, but to hell with it. He'd get there when he got there. He slid onto the last empty stool at the bar and motioned to Lionel, the bartender.

"Hey, man, look who rose from the dead." Lionel wiped the counter in front of Nick, his eyes glinting with amusement. "After what you put away last night, I thought you'd still be out like a light."

"What was I drinking?"

"You don't remember?" Lionel laughed. "I don't know why I'm surprised. You and Wilson were knocking back straight tequilas 'til closing. Killed a whole bottle. You were really out of it, man. Missed the excitement."

"Yeah? What went down?"

"Ask Cindy. She was waiting on you."

Nick turned around on his stool and saw the waitress balancing a platter of french fries and a Caesar salad on her arm. When she'd set them down and turned back to the kitchen, Nick caught her eye and waved her over. But she frowned and went to the waiters' station instead to add up some bills. That was strange. Cindy was usually glad to see him.

He walked over to her. "Hi Cindy."

"Hey Nick. How d'you feel?" Her words were cautious, measured.

"Better than I should, apparently. Lionel says I was in here raising hell last night and I can't remember a damn thing about it."

"Just as well." She smiled nervously. "Willie started that routine with that ice pick thingie, stabbing at the table."

"You mean my sculpting file?"

"Yeah. Like he did the other morning. Only this time he whacked it up good before we could stop him. Jason went crazy. You can imagine. It was like he was on PCP or something. We just couldn't control him. It took four of us to get him outside."

"Where was I?"

"In the head. The woman just sat there and watched us wrestle with him."

Nick stopped breathing. "What woman?"

"I never saw her before. She came in after you went to the head, just before Willie went berserk."

"What'd she look like?"

Cindy shrugged, trying not to look at him. "Tall, fortyish, maybe even older. She had that horsey look, like the women in *Town & Country*. I was kinda surprised, actually. Not Willie's type at all."

Perspiration broke out on Nick's forehead. Willie had one of his files. Could the woman Cindy was describing have been the murder victim? He had to find Willie.

"After she left, Willie made a phone call. And then he really started to get crazy, shouting like a loonie off the Boardwalk," Cindy continued. "That's when we decided we had to get him out of here. You were still passed out in the can, but you weren't causing any trouble, so we let you stay for a while." She smiled weakly. "Jason's still holding your bill, by the way. So unless you've got some cash in your pocket, I suggest you split before he comes in."

"What happened to the woman?"

"She left, right after Willie."

Nick got up to leave. "Thanks, Cindy. Tell Jason I'll settle up tomorrow."

"Nick," she stopped him. "You should know. The police were here this afternoon asking questions." She took a deep breath. "They told us about the woman who bought it in Breeze Park. They think it was the same woman."

So that was why Cindy was acting strange. Nick should have realized that the police would have covered all the bases. "What did they want?"

"They were asking about you and Willie and last night."

"What did you tell them?"

"Just what happened. I'm not going to lie for anyone."

"Nobody'd expect you to, Cindy."

TWENTY-SEVEN

IT WAS DARK when Tory got home. She'd spent the afternoon walking on the beach trying to decide what to do with her anger. And then the sun had gone down, and it had gotten cold, and she couldn't find a cab. So she'd had to wait for the bus, which made her even more angry, stopping at practically every street corner between Venice and Westridge. It had not been a good day.

She let herself into the house through the back door and dumped her books on the kitchen counter. The table was set for one. That meant Charlotte and Arthur were going out. Hopefully, they'd left already.

She opened the freezer and got out a carton of frozen yogurt. "Hello," she called. "Anybody home?"

"In here," Arthur answered.

She followed his voice to the den. He was alone, reading the paper. Thinking about what she'd seen on the video, Tory was embarrassed to even look at him. She fiddled with the zipper of her sweatshirt and avoided his eyes. "Hi, Dad. Where's Mother?"

"Upstairs," he replied. "Do me a favor and tell her to hurry. There's a lot of traffic this time of night."

"Where are you going?"

"To another one of your mother's art parties," he sighed.

Tory found Charlotte at her dressing table, her head bent low over the arsenal of beauty supplies. She blinked violently and raised her head to study her reflection in the mirror. One eye was brown, the other, Paul Newman blue. Oblivious to Tory's angry presence, she bent again and inserted the other contact lens. Then both eyes were blue, but teary. She reached for a tissue and saw her daughter.

"Oh, hello, dear. You're so late, I was beginning to worry."

"How touching," Tory muttered, and took a huge spoonful of yogurt. Charlotte was so intent on her reflection in the mirror that she ignored Tory's triple sin — eating frozen yogurt out of the carton, before dinner, and in Charlotte's bedroom.

"How was the game?" Charlotte asked, leaning closer to the mirror to pat a last coat of powder on her face.

"Pali won, three to two," Tory lied. She had no idea what the score really was because she'd been at the beach. She flopped down on the bed and propped her tennis shoes on the pristine coverlet, another no-no. But still Charlotte refused to take the bait. "I'm quitting the team," she added.

"What?" Charlotte asked.

"Volleyball's a kid's game." Tory sighed and set the drippy yogurt carton on top of the neatly stacked magazines on the bedside table, admiring the ring it made on the top cover. This usually sent Charlotte into a rage, but all Tory got was a distracted warning glance.

"What do you think about my new lenses?" Charlotte smiled expectantly.

"Neon is my favorite color," Tory deadpanned. She yawned and burped at the same time, determined to take this as far as Charlotte would let her.

But Charlotte only frowned. "Please pick up that carton. It's dripping all over my *Town & Country*."

She got up and went into the closet to select a dress. Tory did not pick up the carton. "What are you going to wear?"

"My blue Donna Karan."

"Don't you think the green dress is sexier?" Accusation was thick in Tory's tone; she'd seen the green dress lying on the chair beside Charlotte in the video. "The blue one looks like something Grandma Hartman would wear," Tory persisted.

But cither Charlotte hadn't heard her comment, or she didn't make the connection. "The green's got to go to the cleaners. And the blue matches my new lenses."

"Where's the party?"

"At Francis and Margaret Thornton's. I'm sure you remember them."

Tory sat up straight. "Will Nick be there?"

"Of course," Charlotte said. "It's to celebrate the completion of the statue."

"*My* statue?"

"The statue you posed for, yes."

"How come nobody told me?" Tory's voice was shrill, almost a scream. "There wouldn't even be a statue without me. Why wasn't I invited?"

Charlotte stopped and turned to Tory with an expression of condescension. "Just calm down. You weren't invited because it's a party for adults. Now come here and zip me."

Enraged, Tory jumped to her feet. It was the last straw. She wanted to rip the dress right off her mother's back, anything to let this anger out. But before she could react, Charlotte noticed the chain around Tory's neck, and she reached for the bronze medallion Nick had given her.

"What's this?" she asked.

"A necklace. Nick gave it to me," Tory replied triumphantly.

Finally Charlotte flared. "He gave you jewelry?"

Tory nodded. "He made it especially for me."

Charlotte grabbed Tory by the shoulders and shook her. "What else did he give you, young lady? Tell me!" Her tone was jealous and accusing. It was obvious what she meant.

"Why don't you just ask me, Mom?" Tory said the word "Mom" like a threat.

"Ask you what?"

"Whether he fucked me, the way he fucked you. Well, he didn't because he respects . . ." A stinging slap across the face cut her short. Angry tears sprang into her eyes, but she held them back, refusing to give Charlotte the satisfaction of seeing her cry.

"Don't you ever, *ever* utter that word in my presence again!" Charlotte cried. "Do you hear me?"

"Which word didn't you like, Mother dear, 'fuck' or 'respect?'"

Charlotte gasped. "I am shocked, Victoria. Absolutely shocked. What's gotten into you?"

"Why don't we talk about what's gotten into *you*, Mother, like Nick, for instance."

"I don't know what on earth you're talking about. Shame on you!"

"No, Mother, shame on you!"

"Charlotte! If we're going, let's go. Theres going to be traffic this time of night," Arthur's voice broke in, and Tory ran from the room before her mother could stop her.

She raced down the stairs and out the door, and was half way to Brad McMurphy's house before she even knew where she was heading.

When Brad opened the door, he didn't look surprised to see her, or particularly happy. He leaned nonchalantly against the door jamb. "Hi," he grinned. "What's up?"

"You said I should come over some time to take more pictures. Well, here I am."

"Cool," he said, and stood aside to let her in.

Neither of them mentioned the fact that she hadn't brought her camera.

TORY KNEW she should get out of bed and go home, but she couldn't force her body to move. She watched Brad rise and go into the bathroom, the muscles of his butt tensing with each flat-footed step.

Once they'd gotten started, the whole thing had taken less than a minute. And, amazing as it seemed, she'd had time during that sixty seconds to become bored with the rhythmic pumping of Brad's body on top of her, the ludicrous moaning sounds he made, the pained expression on his face.

Oh, she wasn't disappointed. In fact she was triumphant, lying on top of a towel that was stained red, her badge of initiation into womanhood. It was only a few drops of blood, nothing like she'd expected. The pain had been one sharp stab, and then it was done. It reminded her of getting a shot at the doctor's, all the anxiety and fear of what it would feel like, then the whole thing was over with just the shortest prick of the needle.

She watched Brad soaping *his* needle over the tub, cupping it and stroking it with foam. It looked like he was enjoying this private act more than what they'd just done. But she couldn't blame him.

It hadn't been the thrill she'd expected either. And she, too, was looking forward to having a good wash.

Brad appeared in the doorway, the light from the bathroom silhouetting his broad shoulders. She had to admit he did look good. But so what? She'd kept her eyes closed the whole time; he could have been anyone. Even Nick. Only she was certain making love with Nick would have been a lot more exciting.

"Hey," Brad said, "Lauren's coming over to study tonight. It'd probably be better if you weren't bare assed in my bed when she gets here."

"Are you going to nail her too?" Tory was surprised that she didn't feel jealous or hurt, only annoyed that she was getting shoved out before she was ready to go.

"Maybe. What do you care?"

"I don't." And she was surprised to realize she didn't. She swung her legs off the side of the bed, and using the soiled towel to cover herself, slipped past him into the bathroom. "What do you want me to do with this towel?" she asked.

"Just leave it there. I'll keep it for my collection."

BY THE TIME Tory got home, her parents had long since left for the Thorntons' party, and Tory had the house to herself. Radiance had kept her dinner warming on the stove; it was leftover lasagna, but Tory had no appetite. She dumped it in the sink and turned on the garbage disposal, enjoying the sight of it getting sucked down the drain.

Now that the narcotic of her first sexual experience had worn off, the hurt and sadness of the afternoon crept back in. There was a dull ache in her chest. She hated Charlotte right now, but what was worse, she hated Nick too. And only this morning she'd thought she was in love with him.

She couldn't believe that he would hurt her this way, after all the time they'd spent together working as a team, and his implied promises about how they would get together once the statue was complete. Had he been doing it with her mother all that time?

Well, fuck him. Fuck, fuck, fuck. She found a can of Budweiser in the refrigerator and pulled the tab, purposely leaving it on the sink to be found later. Then she went upstairs, sipping the bitter liquid even though she hated the taste.

Now what? She could blab to Arthur — Dad, your wife is spreading her legs for Nick Stone. That would fix Charlotte. But it would hurt her father too, and the poor guy was only an innocent bystander to this sordid intrigue.

What she should do was move out. Pack her bags and be gone when they came home. She could move into an apartment. Sure, Tory, with what? Monopoly money? Nick owed her for modeling, but that money was for the trip to Paris. If she won the contest.

She could go hang out at Lily's or Keri's until summer, they'd let her stay with them, at least until Nick paid up.

She took the stairs two at a time. Yeah, she'd go to Lily's. Keri's mom was really strict; she'd call Charlotte for sure. But Lily's mom was divorced and seemed more sympathetic. She might let Tory stay there without a hassle until she decided what to do.

But maybe that was exactly what Charlotte wanted, to get rid of Tory so she could have Nick all to herself. No. Before Tory went anywhere, she had to stop that train dead in its tracks. But how to do it?

Tory stood at the door and looked into her parents' bedroom. Charlotte's robe was still lying on the bed. Tory set the beer can down and put it on, enjoying the slick feel of the silk against her bare arms.

Suddenly, she knew what she could do. She would crash the

party — put on her Mother's green dress and crash the Thorntons' party! She'd show Nick and her mother that she was not a child, that they couldn't just trample her feelings and forget about her. They'd know she knew without her having to say a word. And then Nick would have to decide.

She dug the dress out of the dry cleaning hamper and laid it on the bed. It was wrinkled and the hem was pinned in the back. Nothing a little steam and a needle and thread couldn't fix. But she'd have to hurry.

"Land sakes, what you up to, girl?"

Tory wheeled, startled, guilty. Radiance stood at the door, wearing her hat and coat. "Radiance, what are you doing here so late?" Tory asked.

"Your Mama asked me to stay 'til you got home. She said you was upset and she was worried. You okay, sweetie girl? What you doing in your Mama's closet, wearin' her robe?"

Tory couldn't think fast enough to come up with a lie, so she just started talking. "There's a party tonight to celebrate my statue, and I'm supposed to go. But I was late after the game, and they went without me. Can you believe it?" Tory's eyes brimmed with tears. "I need to be there. Don't you think I should be there?"

"Well of course I do, honey, but nobody cares what old Radiance thinks."

"So anyway, I'm going to take a taxi and meet them there. And Mother said I could wear one of her dresses because I don't have anything grown-up enough."

Radiance shook her head. "Oh, child, you sure she said that? That don't sound like your momma to me. She'd be mad as a wet hen if you spilled somethin' on one of her dresses."

"This one was in the laundry already. She already got it dirty." Tory tried to smooth the wrinkles out of the dress. She knew Radiance didn't believe her, but she couldn't give up now. "Radiance, don't you see? I have to go. I have to! Please don't stop me. This is the most important thing in my whole life."

There was a long silence, then Radiance sighed. "Well you can't wear that dress all wrinkled, lookin' like Lawrence Welk could play a polka on it. Come on, let Radiance press it out. You go on and take your shower."

"Thanks, Radiance!" Tory threw her arms around the maid, then ran into Charlotte's bathroom, stripping off her gym clothes. "Could you do me one more favor and call the taxi company?"

Moments later, Tory let Radiance zip her into the dress. She'd washed her hair and it was still wet. So she pulled it back from her face into a tight bun, making her cheekbones even more prominent. And, resisting the temptation to slather on makeup, she put just a touch of blush on her cheeks, and a single layer of mascara on her eyelashes. She bit her lips a few times to make them redden, and as a final touch patted her face with powder from her mother's compact.

Then she stood in front of the mirror to see the effect, and when she saw her reflection, she smiled. Before she began modeling, she'd always felt like a shapeless hulk, and she'd dressed to camouflage her body. But now, swathed in designer silk, she was transformed into an elegant and shapely woman. But it was more than just the dress. The weeks of modeling for Nick, making peace with her body and learning to accept his scrutiny had given her a sense of confidence which showed in the way she carried herself and in the way she moved. She was beautiful, and she knew it.

"So, what do you think?" she asked Radiance.

Radiance stared at Tory for a moment, her expression inscrutable. Then she said, "Well Missy, I gotta say it, you look like one of them fancy girlies in *Cosmo-Pol-i-tan*." She smoothed the skirt and adjusted the shoulder pads. "Don't you go tellin' your Mama, but she can't hold a candle to you in this dress."

"Do you really think so?"

"Honey, I know it." She gave Tory a little hug. "And I think you know it too."

Tory smiled and turned back to the mirror. "Good."

"You be careful lest you spill something on that silk I can't get out," Radiance warned.

"Don't worry," Tory assured her. "I'll take real good care of it."

"And I didn't see nothin' tonight, did I?"

"No, not a thing. You weren't even here."

"Now don't you go sayin' that. I'm supposed to be here. I just didn't see you go out in that dress!"

THE CABBY LEANED against the car waiting impatiently. He'd already honked three times and in another minute he was going to drive off. But when he saw the stunning young woman hurrying towards him, his frown turned into a wide smile, and he was glad he'd waited.

He jumped out and opened the door for her. "Where to, Miss?" he asked.

"To Beverly Hills," Tory said. "Ariel Drive. I don't know the exact address, but I'll know the house when I see it."

IV

TWENTY-EIGHT

DESPITE THE DEBILITATING FATIGUE that had plagued Con for the past twenty-four hours, he felt the familiar fire of adrenalin begin to burn. The exhilaration caused by the realization that the game was in play and all was at risk was as good as a drug rush. In the end, pushing fate to the limit, pitting his luck against the combined forces of his adversaries and the law, was what he lived for, what kept him alive.

He tugged at his tie, making the infinitesimal adjustment which distinguished perfection from mere precision. Then he stepped away from the mirror, let Bryant throw a silk scarf over his shoulders, and strode through the open door to his waiting limousine.

"Ready?" he asked Rocco.

"Yessir, everything is in place."

Rocco tipped his hat, and Con ducked into the limousine. Bryant opened the rear door of the weathered van parked next to it. On its side was written "Bobo's Twenty-four Hour Pet Grooming A GoGo." But instead of a bathing tub and grooming table, it held a portable welding arc and small generator, a pair of overalls, a welder's mask and gloves. Bryant stashed the small dufflebag he was carrying next to the generator, then climbed into the driver's seat and waited, watching the limo negotiate the sharp turns on the long driveway.

The limo slowed slightly at the foot of the drive, waiting for the gates to close behind it, and then it turned left onto the public street. Immediately, a beat up Pontiac Firebird, parked up a neighboring driveway, turned on its lights and followed.

When he saw that the two cars were gone, Bryant drove the Bobo van through the gate and turned right on the main street. He kept his eyes on the rearview mirror just in case, but he was not followed.

FROM HABIT, Margaret Thornton checked the dining room table before ringing for Neville to bring her first Manhattan. Her inspection was cursory since the staff had assumed, as it always did, complete responsibility for the dinner party — menu, table settings, and floral decoration. Francis had issued the invitations, and Margaret's secretary had done the seating. So really, all that was expected of her was to show up, which seemed to be all she was capable of lately.

At least three years had passed since Margaret had lost control. She couldn't pinpoint the exact date that it had all begun to unravel, but she knew why. Her spiralling depression was directly related to her realization that Francis didn't love her any more.

When she had become suspicious that his trips to Japan were altogether too frequent and prolonged, she'd hired a private detective to follow him. Sure enough, the man had returned with evidence of a mistress in Kyoto, an ex-geisha who worked at a karaoke restaurant where Japanese businessmen entertained their

American associates. How beneath Francis it was to philander with such a woman! And how insulting to Margaret. She prayed nothing would come of this relationship because she would die from public humiliation if Francis left her. He and the art collection they had amassed together were her whole life.

The secretary appeared. "The guests will be arriving in a few minutes, Mrs. Thornton. Shall we go over the list?"

"Of course, dear, as soon as I get my drink." She tinkled the tiny silver bell she had been clutching in her hand, and Neville appeared in a flash with her cocktail centered on a small silver tray.

"Has anybody seen Francis?" Margaret asked, taking the drink.

"I believe he's in the upper suite," Neville replied, referring to the private annex that housed most of the Thorntons' treasures.

Margaret fortified herself with a healthy swallow of alcohol. With Francis occupied, she could finish this Manhattan and start on another one before the guests arrived.

As she left the dining room, she sensed rather than saw that something was missing. She looked about the room, trying to summon the spirit of the meticulous hostess she had once been. The table looked fine, the flowers, the Brice Marden triptych, the sideboard with its magnificent eighteenth century silver candelabra, and — ah, Francis' humidor. It always sat in the center of the sideboard, so that his Cuban cigars could be offered at the end of the meal.

"Neville, where is Mr. Thornton's humidor? You know how unhappy he will be if it isn't in place after dinner."

"I'll check into it, Madam." The butler bowed stiffly and left the room, promptly putting this promise out of his mind. By the time she finished her drink, she would have forgotten about the humidor, and he didn't need the extra work of looking for it.

BEHIND THE LOCKED and alarmed door of his upper office, Francis Thornton carefully removed the Cuban cigars from the humidor and placed them on a shelf in the large cooler where he stored the unopened cases of tobacco. Then, with a linen towel he'd brought upstairs for this purpose, he gave the inside of the humidor a thorough wiping, brushing out every shred of loose tobacco.

Taking care to close the cooler behind him, he approached the safe, whose door was cleverly disguised as a Davidoff crate.

Francis uncovered the numerical pad and punched the codes that disarmed the fiber optic camera, infrared motion detector, and ultrasonic sensor. Then he pushed a button that opened a side compartment housing a dial. With practiced fingers, he twirled the dial and unlocked the safe, using both hands to pull from it his treasure, the Michelangelo Giant.

With the solemnity of a priest bearing the blood of Christ, Francis carried the small stone carving out of the cooler and placed it on his desk, where he could consume its beauty one last time.

Again he marveled at the ethereal radiance emanating from the marble. Like the works of Rembrandt and Turner, whose paintings seemed illuminated by a magical internal glow, this small piece of sculpture appeared to contain a source of light within it, so that the curves and angles and smooth surfaces appeared incandescent.

Francis stroked the statue as he would caress a lover, and he thought of Mariko, in Kyoto, waiting for him and this artwork, which he was sending on ahead as his emissary, a token of his love and commitment. How strange that he would so willingly part with the object he treasured most in the world. And yet, wasn't that what love was about, conferring on the loved one that which was most difficult to give?

Besides, very soon, he would be joining his beloved and this treasure, to start a new life in Japan. He had bidden his time and planned meticulously to extricate himself from the entanglements here, both financial and emotional. But the goal was now in sight.

ROCCO ACCELERATED into the turn onto Ariel Drive, throwing Con against the door. "Slow down," Con barked. "This is not the Grand Prix."

Rocco stepped on the brake. "Sorry, Boss. I guess I'm kinda wired 'bout the job tonight." In the rearview mirror he saw the plainclothes police following in the Pontiac. When he slowed, they slowed as well. Rocco shook his head, amazed that the cops were so inept. He'd have fun with them later, after he dropped Mr. Uttrell at the party.

"I'm only going to say this once, so listen well," Con said. "It's a very simple operation. The only way something can go wrong is if you make a mistake. And if you do, your life won't be worth the gonads of a eunuch. Is that clear?"

"Yes sir, Mr. Uttrell," Rocco replied, slowing to thirty to make the final turn into the Thorntons' driveway.

"You know where to go after you drop me?"

"Round to the back and Thornton's man Hans'll give it to me. I put it in the trunk, in the compartment where the spare tire was and then I go . . ."

"You *wait* until Nick Stone gets here before you go anywhere."

"That's what I meant."

Con felt beads of perspiration at his hairline. Was it a mistake to rely on a cretin like Rocco? But what choice did he have? He dabbed at his forehead with his handkerchief and motioned to

Rocco to let him out. Rocco put the limo in park and ran around to open Con's door.

"You can trust me, Mr. Uttrell. I swear. I'll do the job or I'll die trying."

"That's true, Rocco, there is no doubt about it."

AS SOON AS HE SAW the Boss entered the house, Rocco got back in the limo and drove around to the rear door. He got out and knocked. Just like Mr. Uttrell had told him, the German goon Hans was waiting there with a box which looked like one of those fancy cigar cases you saw in a haberdashery. Under Hans' watchful eye, Rocco opened the trunk and turned back the carpet, revealing the indented space where the spare tire usually lay. With the care and concern he would have used in handling a newborn baby, Rocco placed the box in the empty niche, arranged the carpet back in place, and slammed the hood shut. "Thanks, pal," he said to Hans, and got back in the car. But to his surprise, the man opened the passenger door and he got in too.

"What's up?" Rocco asked.

"I go to make sure the job is done."

"Says who?"

"Herr Thornton."

"I only take orders from 'Hair' Uttrell and he didn't say nothing."

Hans casually unbuttoned his jacket and showed Rocco his shoulder holster. "If there is problem I can be of aid."

"I don't need no aid."

"So to you I am the observer."

"I gotta ask Mr. Uttrell."

Hans shrugged. "I wait."

Rocco got out of the car and slammed the door. Without bothering to knock, he barged into the kitchen.

CON HANDED Margaret Thornton a Manhattan — her third — off the tray and then took his own drink, water splashed with scotch. He was trying to listen to her prattle, something about the new director of the Norton Simon Museum in Pasadena, but he was finding it difficult to be attentive. The murder of Caroline Van Patten had raised the stakes of this operation significantly. Every detail was crucial, and now there was another problem. Nick Stone was late. They could not proceed until he arrived; this whole party had been orchestrated in order to get him out of his studio for a few hours. What if he didn't show up at all? When would there be time to do the cutting and welding necessary to secrete the Giant inside his statue before tomorrow's departure?

Out of the corner of his eye Con saw Francis Thornton follow his butler into the hallway where Rocco was standing, hat in hand. Con's heart stopped. Another snag? He excused himself from Margaret and joined the men, trying to cover his concern with an air of polite interest.

"What seems to be the problem?" he asked.

"Your man objects to my man accompanying him," said Thornton in a tone that accused, judged, and hung Rocco on the spot.

"No sir," Rocco insisted. "All I says was nobody tole me he'd be coming. I'll do whatever you want, Mr. Uttrell. You know that."

Con cursed under his breath. This had not been part of the plan, and Con had no idea what it meant. But there was no way he could object now without inciting Thornton's suspicion. "You did the right thing by checking," he told Rocco, "but it's perfectly all right

with me. I'm sure there will be no interference with your work."
He looked at Thornton for confirmation.

"None whatsoever," Thornton replied. "Think of Hans as my
eyes and ears, just to see that the job gets done."

With their backs to the door, neither Con nor Francis Thornton
saw that Nick Stone had entered the room. But as Nick passed
through the hall to the living room where the other guests were
gathered, he noticed them in conversation with the Uttrell's driver.
It occurred to him to wonder what they were discussing in such
hushed tones, but he dismissed the thought in favor of finding a
drink.

AT 8:05 P.M. the limo reconnoitered Bobo's Twenty-four
Hour Dog Grooming A Gogo van on a darkened stretch of Walgrove Avenue in Palms. Rocco flashed his lights once to let Bryant
know that he was sure he had lost the police escort on the way
over, and Bryant opened the side door of the van. Rocco and Hans
got out of the limo, transferred the humidor to the van and got in.

Ten minutes later, the three men pulled up in the alley behind
Nick's studio and parked. The alley was dark and still. They got
out. Rocco and Bryant were wearing overalls with the BoBo logo
on them. In case anyone saw them, they would say they had been
called to groom Nick Stone's German Shepherd. Bryant sprung the
lock on the back gate and opened it gingerly. Supposedly, Rocco
had put the dog out of commission when he and Mr. Uttrell had
visited the studio days ago. But just in case, he'd brought a tranquilizing gun. It would also come in handy if any two-legged guards
were around.

But there was no barking, no sign of a watchful canine to hinder
their entrance, and no people around, save the homeless denizens
of the Boardwalk who paid them no heed.

The rear entrance to the studio was also locked, but using the tools in his bag, Rocco was able to open it in less than twenty seconds. The door slid back and the three men entered the studio. Once the door was closed behind them, Bryant turned on his flashlight. It would have been easier to find the statue with the lights on, but they knew better than to risk it.

Rocco nudged Bryan and pointed to a dark shape on the floor. Bryant swung the light around and illuminated the ferocious attack dog. The dog saw them and struggled weakly to its feet, growling and whining. Bryant made quick use of the tranquilizing gun, and the men went about their business.

By 8:37 p.m. the job was done. The men left the same way they'd come in, relocking the door and the gate behind them. Mission accomplished.

Hans drove the van the sixteen blocks back to Walgrove where they'd left the limo. Bryant got out, dressed in Rocco's chauffeur clothes, and Rocco slid over into the driver's seat of the van. "I suppose you're stayin with me?" he asked Hans.

"I stay," replied the German.

They waited while Bryant steered the limousine off in the direction of Beverly Hills. Then Rocco hung a U-turn and headed back to the site they'd chosen in the alley a block from Nick's studio, where he and Hans would spend the night watching, to make sure no one disturbed the sleeping Giant.

FROM HIS ROOFTOP PERCH, Eli watched these comings and goings. He didn't know why the men had come to the studio, or what they had done while they were bent over the statue of His Girl. But it didn't matter to him. She wasn't here, and that was all Eli cared about. He settled back to wait for Her return.

TWENTY-NINE

ROZ WAS EXHAUSTED. She had spent the entire afternoon carting the Diebenkorn around town, from the Museum of Contemporary Art downtown to the County Museum on Wilshire, and finally out to the Getty in Malibu, trying to determine if it was real or fake. Willie Wilson had been so spaced out that she didn't know what to believe, and the painting certainly looked genuine to her. But judging the authenticity of a contemporary work required an expert's eye. Hence the afternoon roadshow.

Of the four curators she'd talked to, two voted for fake, one thought it was an original but didn't want to be quoted, and one said he would have to use gas chromatography or mass spectrometry in order to make a determination, and both of those methods would take time.

Before she left the Getty, she dialed the office, hoping that Rick had called to confirm dinner and to tell her what time he would be coming.

"No calls," Diana at the front desk told her, and Roz felt even more tired than before.

"Put me through to Nelson, please," she said.

"I got you until tomorrow morning, but let's just say I wouldn't walk in asking for a raise if I were you," Nelson said. "Unless you've got the Diebenkorn tucked under your arm."

Did she? There was no point in bringing in the painting until she knew if it was real or fake; La Salle would have her head if it wasn't the original. So she was back where she started, with an artwork of unknown provenance stashed in her trunk and her job in limbo. And was Rick coming to dinner or wasn't he? Roz considered stopping at the market, but when she reached Gelson's, she drove on instead. Why should she knock herself out to prepare a meal for him when he hadn't even had the courtesy to call? To hell with him.

When she got home she made a circuit of the house, picking up the towels and the bowls half filled with rainwater. For the first time that day she thought about Adrian, the look in his eyes when she'd hurried out the door after Rick. He hadn't said it in so many words, but she knew he wouldn't be back. How could he, when given the option, Roz had chosen Rick? And now Rick had left her high and dry. Again. Would she never learn?

Roz took a long, scalding shower and put on her old chenille bathrobe; the one nice thing about being alone was not having to worry about how you looked. She took a Lean Cuisine out of the freezer and nuked it, then settled herself on the couch in the living room with her files spread around her and the Diebenkorn painting propped against the television. She stared at it between bites. Was it the real thing, or a fake?

The phone rang and she picked it up, still thinking about the Diebenkorn. "Hello?"

"Roz? It's Me." Rick's tone capitalized the personal pronoun. "Look, I'm sorry I didn't call you earlier. Things got a little hairy. I've been up to my ears."

He sounded just like the old Rick, making excuses, his damn busy schedule. "Yeah, sure you have," she said.

"I know it's late, but can I come over now?"

"Now?" God damn it, she wasn't about to let him fall into the old patterns again. Besides, she couldn't let him see her looking like a bag lady at a slumber party. And the thought of rallying the effort to get dressed and primped was debilitating. "I've already eaten," she began. "Do you know what time it is? It's nearly . . ."

But he didn't let her finish. "Actually, I'm already here, just outside in my car. I didn't want to surprise you again, in case your 'friend' was still around."

"No, no, he's gone for good, thanks to you," Roz told him. She turned around on the couch and pulled back the curtain. Sure enough, a nondescript Dodge was pulled up behind her Toyota with its motor running.

"Good. I'm on my way . . ."

"Give me a minute!"

"Okay." He hung up.

Roz ripped off her robe, threw on a pair of jeans, dragged a comb through her hair, and dusted her cheeks with blush. And then, almost as an afterthought, she stashed the real/fake Diebenkorn in the closet.

Already Rick was knocking on the door, announcing his impatience in sharp raps. Roz made him wait another full minute, plastered a smile of simulated languor on her face, and opened the door. She was already mouthing the words, "You caught me by surprise," when she saw that he truly had.

Standing at the door very close to Rick was an attractive woman at least ten years younger than Roz. Not again, Roz groaned inwardly, hoping her face did not betray her dismay.

The woman gave Roz a smile which was as phony as her capped teeth and then looked back at Rick. Next to him was Leo Drake from the Art Theft Division. And behind them was the young officer named DeVane who'd driven Roz home from the crime scene that morning. So much for Roz's fantasy that Rick had come for a date.

"Hi, Roz," Rick spoke for the lot of them. "Sorry to drop in on you like this. Can we come in?"

Speechless, Roz stood aside and let them troop in, all but Officer DeVane, who tipped his hat at Roz. "I'll wait out here, Ma'am," he said.

Rick took charge, ushering the woman into the living room. Drake followed them.

"Can I talk to you a minute?" he asked Roz, and nodded toward the kitchen.

"Yeah, if you're going to tell me what's going on."

Roz led him into the kitchen. "I see you fixed the crack," Rick said, fingering the wall next to the stove.

"Yeah, about seven years ago," she replied.

"Oh, well, you did a good job," he said awkwardly.

"Thanks," she said.

"What ever happened to . . ."

Roz stomped her foot impatiently. "Rick, what's going on? And who's your female friend?"

"I'll introduce you, but before we go in there, I just want to say . . . now don't have a conniption fit, but I've got to tell you. I ran a check on your friend Adrian and he's . . . did you know he's an illegal alien?"

"It doesn't matter. He's gone."

"Where?"

"Probably back to Bali," she said sarcasticly. "How should I know?"

"Good." Rick looked relieved. "He . . ."

"Not that you had any business poking your nose into his private life — or mine!" Roz interrupted.

"Sorry."

"No you're not."

"You're right, I'm not. I'm glad he's out of the picture. Let's keep it that way. Come on." Rick took her hand and led her back into the living room.

Drake and the woman were still standing, waiting for them. "Roz, you know Leo Drake. And this is Anna Winetsky," Rick said. "Con Uttrell's secretary."

The woman extended a limp hand. "What a cozy little nest," she said in a condescending tone.

There was something about the way the woman carried herself — the way she sat in the chair farthest from the men and wouldn't look at either of them — that made it clear to Roz she was here against her wishes. She was dressed in a conservative but expensive suit and low-heeled shoes. Despite the hour, her makeup was flawless. Not a hair was out of place. Roz wished she'd taken an extra minute to at least put on some lipstick.

Anna lit a cigarette, and then almost as an afterthought said, "I hope no one minds if I smoke."

Roz minded, but she went to the cabinet anyway and took an ashtray from the drawer, setting it on the table next to Anna.

"We're sorry to barge in on you Roz, but this couldn't wait," Rick apologized. "Drake, why don't you start."

"So, Mrs. Weeks," Drake began.

"Roz," Roz said.

"Roz," he amended, and then hesitated. "This has all become so complicated. I don't know where to begin."

"Spit it out, Drake," Rick interjected, "or I'll do it for you."

Drake sighed. "My division has been watching Con Uttrell for some time now, with the help of FINSEN. That's the Treasury Department's . . ."

"Financial Crimes Enforcement Network," Roz finished. "I know them."

"Yes, of course you do. Sorry," Drake apologized. He went on, "So with the help of FINSEN, we have been following Uttrell's illegal activities, but we've been unable to pin an arrest on him." He looked at Roz guiltily. "I didn't mention this to you when you came in last week. I couldn't. FINSEN insisted it all remain top secret. But now . . ."

"Now that the shit's hit the fan, he thinks you might be able to help us," Rick finished for him.

Drake dragged his finger around the too tight collar of his shirt and continued. "As Mr. Uttrell's secretary for the past seven years, Miss Winetsky has been a witness and an accomplice to Mr. Uttrell's crimes."

"I was only doing the job I was paid to do," Anna Winetsky insisted.

"And so were the guards at Auschwitz," Rick pointed out. That shut her up.

Drake continued. "So, after a bit of, er, negotiation, we convinced Miss Winetsky to throw in with our side. She told Mr. Uttrell that she needed a vacation and we planted our own girl as a temporary secretary in the office. Then we sent in Officer Litton."

"Who is Officer Litton?" Roz asked.

"A.K.A. Caroline Van Patten. The dead woman," Rick explained. "That's where I come in."

Roz shook her head to clear it. "Sorry, you've lost me."

"Caroline Van Patten was not an art curator. She was an under-cover plant. Art Theft borrowed her from Narcotics, since Drake's division is a one-man show," Rick said. "She was part of a sting operation. Without checking it with me, Drake set her up to catch Uttrell with his pants down." Rick was staring at Drake with un-disguised fury. "Only she got picked off, and he still doesn't have Uttrell."

"Officer Litton's assignment was to catch Uttrell in the act by consummating a business deal with him," Drake said.

"The Diebenkorn," Roz mumbled, her eyes straying to the closet.

"But she stumbled onto something much bigger, and that's why she got killed," Drake finished in a rush.

Rick sighed. "Now I've got a dead woman on my hands. A dead police officer."

"Do you think Con Uttrell was responsible?" Roz asked, re-membering what Willie Wilson had told her.

Rick shrugged. "The guy's a crook and a flaming asshole. But we don't think he'd go so far as murder, especially not something so grisly. He doesn't seem like the kind of guy who'd get his hands dirty with a mutilation like that, does he?" Roz had to agree. "What I think is that the real murderer has gone to a lot of trouble trying to pin the murder on him."

Again Roz thought of Wilson. "Who's the real murderer?"

"We don't know yet. We're following some leads," Rick said. It was obvious to Roz he knew more than he was telling.

"If Con Uttrell isn't the murderer, how is he involved?" Roz asked.

"You've heard about this statue, the Michelangelo Giant?" Drake asked.

"Of course," Roz replied. "Wait a minute, you think Con Uttrell has the Giant?"

"That's what Officer Litton stumbled onto. Apparently Uttrell has been retained to move the statue out of the country."

"By who?"

Drake looked at Rick as though unsure if he should tell her.

"What we know is how Uttrell plans to transport the Michelangelo Giant out of the country," Rick said, evading her question. "We have you to thank for helping us make the connection." He smiled at Roz.

"Me?" Roz asked.

Drake nodded. "I got a call from Arthur Hartman, Director of Inspection and Control at LAX. He said you'd gone to see him just after he'd had a visit from Con Uttrell, requesting special treatment for a bronze statue he was shipping to Japan. Your conversation bothered him, and he called us. This isn't the first time he's flagged a piece of art going through LAX.

"But this time, we put together what we knew about the Giant with your theory that Uttrell was stashing the Diebenkorn inside the bronze he commissioned from Nicholas Stone, and bingo!"

"You had the right idea, just the wrong piece of art," Rick said. "We think," he added.

"Of course we can't be a hundred percent sure until we open up the bronze," Drake explained.

"Hartman told us the statue is scheduled to leave LAX on board a flight to Japan tomorrow morning. Con Uttrell will be traveling with it himself. When he gets on the plane, we'll grab him and the statue."

"If you know where the Giant is now, why don't you just pick it up?" Roz asked.

"We want to catch Uttrell with it in his possession, in the act of taking it out of the country. The only way to do that is at the airport," Drake explained.

"Once we have Uttrell's balls in a vice, pardon my French, we think we can get him to point the finger at whoever he's working for, and that, we hope, will be Officer Litton's killer."

Roz let this sink in.

"What about the Diebenkorn?" Drake asked.

Roz's head jerked up. She looked at Drake, then at Rick.

"What about it?" she asked.

"We know you've got it here," Rick said. "That's why we brought Miss Winetsky. We need her to take a look at it."

"Why do you think I have it?"

"You were followed leaving Willie Wilson's studio this afternoon. We had a tail on Wilson. When they saw you leave with the painting, one of them tailed you." He smiled. "You put in a lot of miles this afternoon."

Drake was impatient. "We need for Miss Winetsky to identify it as the stolen Stein painting, so we'll have something to hold Uttrell on, if the smuggling charge on the Giant doesn't hold, and until we catch up with the murderer. So if you can just . . ."

"I did bring a painting home from Willie Wilson's. But I don't think it's the original Diebenkorn. I think it's a forgery."

"Why?"

"Wilson told me it was, sort of."

Drake looked at Roz. "Please, Mrs. Weeks, if we could just *see* the painting. . ."

She opened the closet door, and pulled out the painting. Holding it carefully, she walked across the room and set it against the sofa facing Anna.

They all studied it. "Well?" Rick asked.

Anna Winetsky rose and approached the canvas, then tipped it forward and ran her finger along the wood frame backing on which the canvas was stretched.

"This is the original," she said.

"How can you be sure?" Rick asked.

"Here, on the top left of the frame, there's a carved 'D,' for Diebenkorn. You can feel it."

Drake touched the back of the canvas where Anna had indicated. He nodded at Rick.

"Mr. Uttrell always marks the original," Alice explained. "The forgeries are so good, sometimes it's the only way to tell which is which . . ."

THIRTY

NICK EXCUSED HIMSELF from the table, unaware that both Francis and Con were watching him. All he could think about was getting away from the stifling small talk and being alone.

He let himself out onto the porch overlooking the garden. It was a windless night, crystal clear for a change. He noticed that there was no moon, but nevertheless, the sophisticated outdoor lighting system made the garden appear as though it were bathed in a celestial glow. Nick shook his head. Nothing was real; even the moonlight was fake. His eyes went to the pond where the black swans floated like feathered props. Was it less than a month ago he'd met Tory here? So much had happened since then. So much, and nothing at all.

Nick took the stairs down into the garden two at a time. His shoes made silver footprints in the dew-dampened grass as he crossed to the water. Then he settled himself against the trunk of the willow tree to watch the swans and think of Tory.

He remembered her emerging from the water, the cloth of her

light dress clinging to her body. How embarrassed and miserable she had been, and yet how beautiful and defiant. What he had felt at that moment, what he still felt when he thought of her, was not sexual arousal, not a physical thing at all, but an emotional charge. He was amazed that the feeling was still there after three weeks of scrutinizing her body, studying it and doing his best to recreate it from the outside in. Usually when a work was complete, he lost interest in the model who inspired it. But this was different. Tory was different. He sensed there was unfinished business between them, more work to do, more to know.

Now that the statue was done, he wondered if he would ever see her again. Of course he could always call her, invite her out to lunch or something. But wouldn't he feel like a fool, a thirty-eight-year-old man with a seventeen-year-old girl? Would that be a date or babysitting?

And then, as though his imagination were orchestrating the scene, an apparition appeared at the far edge of the lawn. It was a woman walking toward him. She was backlit by the glow from the house, and he couldn't see her features. But he knew instinctively it was Tory. It had to be. The moment was too perfect for it to be anyone else.

INSTEAD OF RINGING the Thorntons' doorbell, Tory followed the drive around to the rear, as she had that other day, in that other lifetime. Being here was like being in a dream, a vision made all the more romantic by the memory attached to it.

Of course, it was different now. It was night, and although the yard was well lit, it seemed dark with the weight of unexpressed emotions. Tory let herself be drawn to the pond, but with each step, the dewy lawn seemed to grasp her feet, sucking at the three-inch satin pumps she'd borrowed from her mother's closet. So she slipped out of them and ran barefoot the rest of the way, her feet hardly touching the grass.

Near the pond the ground was muddy, so she jumped onto a flat rock and stood staring across the lawn at the house where the dinner party was still in progress. Jealousy burned inside her as she imagined her mother at the table, talking and laughing with Nick, the two of them toasting Nick's creation without even acknowledging the role she had played in it. Well, she was here to change all that. She wasn't going to let Nick ignore her any more.

In the silence she could hear the water cascading over the fountain, and pouring into the pond. Carefully, she stepped across the rock and stood next to the emerging figures, her sisters, forever imprisoned in bronze. She was one of them. She must break free! Tentatively, she stuck her hand into the flowing water and felt an infusion of power in its cold rush.

"Tory."

The familiar voice startled her. She jerked her hand out of the water and stepped back. Nick? She turned, and there he was, standing so close that she could feel waves of heat radiating from his body. Her heart pounded.

All the way over in the cab she had thought of the things she wanted to say to him, hurtful words to vent her anguish, hateful words to make him feel the pain that he had caused her, loving words to let him know how much she cared. But now that she was here, she fell back into the familiar pattern of letting him capture her and silence her with his eyes.

He spoke again. "You look like an angel." His voice was reverent. "I want to sculpt you, just the way you are right now."

"No!" She was startled by her own vehemence. "I'm not going to model for you any more. I'm through with that. Anyway, I thought the statue was finished."

"It is. It was. But I can see now that I missed the essence. I got it all wrong." He seemed mystified. "I don't know what happened. You're different."

He reached out to her, but in a burst of anger she pulled violently away, stumbling on the wet rock. "Of course I'm different. Because you stole something from me."

Nick seemed baffled. "What did I take?"

"My secrets. Who I am inside. You took that away and put it in your statue."

Nick was defensive. "Damn it. It's not a competition between you and the statue!"

"It is, because making me into a bronze statue was your way of controlling me, forcing me into an image that you had in your mind."

He thought about this. "I never meant to hurt you."

"You mean you didn't think it would hurt me that you were fooling around with my mother?" Tory shook her head. "Nice try."

"What? I didn't . . . Did she tell you that?" Nick was angry now.

"She didn't have to. I found out."

"Well you're wrong. Your mother came to see me. She threatened to forbid you to model for me so I had to . . ."

"Screw her?"

"No! I needed some leverage on my side, so I offered to let her pose for me, just so I could get it on video."

"I don't believe for a second she would let you film her nude."

"She didn't know. I used a hidden camera. It's connected to the lights so that I can turn it on when I turn on the spots."

Tory was even angrier now. "Does that mean you've been taking home movies of me all this time as well?"

Nick's shoulders slumped. "I did it so I could study how you moved. I had to be able to look at you and we both know the camera made you nervous."

"So you shot film anyway, but it's okay because you didn't tell me? God, I feel so violated."

"Tory," Nick sounded desperate, "I didn't think about it like that. It was only a means to an end. But you're right. I can see it now. I'm truly sorry if you feel like I used you. All I wanted was to give you something. I thought that's what I was doing."

"Oh, you did. You taught me how to look at myself honestly."

Now Nick was confused. "Then why are you so upset?"

"Because I'm like a prisoner. You made me this, this *thing*, and then you left me hanging there. I'm not a little girl any more, and I'm not a woman yet. Not until you make love to me."

He stepped back. "You don't really want that."

"Why do you keep trying to tell me what I feel? I know what I want. Nick, stop putting me on a pedestal like a piece of art. I'm a real person, damn it!"

She jerked away and lost her footing on the slippery rock. But before she could fall, Nick's strong arm swept out and caught her. For a moment he held her suspended between the girl she had been a month ago and the woman she had become. And then he gently pulled her to him, kissing the hot tears that streamed down her cheeks.

Then he took her face in his hands and looked deeply into her eyes. His expression radiated love. "Precious Tory. Are you sure this is what you want?"

"Oh, Nick, I'm so sure."

He wrapped his arms around her and kissed her full on the mouth, a real kiss, lips, teeth, tongue. And then he swept her up off her feet and carried her back across the lawn. As naturally as though they had practiced this embrace, she circled his neck with her arms and nestled her head into his shoulder. Avoiding the house, Nick carried Tory to his car, set her in the passenger seat, and drove off.

CON TRIED to concentrate on the banal chatter of his dinner partner, Charlotte Hartman, but all he could think about was Nick's empty chair. Where the hell had he gone?

The door to the dining room opened and Con's hopes rose, until he saw it was only the butler, who bent to whisper something to Thornton. He watched the smile on Thornton's face freeze over and crack, and he felt a chill. Thornton looked out the window and then his eyes locked into Con's, icy with rage.

ELI HEARD the throaty rev of Nick's car as it cornered into the alley and settled into its spot behind the building. Crouching low, he crawled to the edge of the roof and peered over the side. The girl, His Girl, was getting out of the car. She appeared angelic to Eli, the embodiment of every dream he had ever had. He wanted to go to Her, but She was with the man, the artist who had given him the drawing. So he waited, lying still against the gravel and tar paper, his heart beating hard.

The man led Her through the back door into the studio. A light went on inside, throwing bright beams up through the skylight. It seemed to Eli that they were beacons radiating from his True Love.

A dog barked. A skateboard rolled by. Somewhere off in the distance, a police siren wailed. Eli settled into his place by the skylight to watch the drama unfold beneath him. When the time came, he would take Her to his secret place, and then he would have Her all to himself.

NICK TURNED ON a spotlight and trained its heavy head up to the ceiling, so that the studio was bathed in reflected light. It was the first time Tory had been there at night, and in the low light it looked like a fairyland. The bronze figures on pedestals, so formidable in the harsh light of day, were magically transformed by night into benevolent muses. They seemed to be dancing to silent music, presiding over this moment. As Nick led her through the studio, her feet didn't seem to touch the ground, she danced above it like the statues, floating outside of her body.

He stopped at the modeling platform, and turned to face her. Here? Naturally she had assumed they would make love in the bedroom. But she'd do whatever Nick wanted; he was still the teacher and she the willing disciple. She stepped up onto the platform and reached around to undo her zipper. But he caught her hand in his, training it back down to her side. And then, very slowly, he unzipped the dress. It slid to Tory's feet in a sizzle of silk, and she stepped out of it.

Nick's hands moved to her hips and grasped the elastic waistband of her pantyhose, gently rolling them down, smoothing them lower, past her thighs, her calves, her ankles, until she could step out of them as well.

And then she was naked. She had been nude before him so many times, but this was different, and they both felt it.

Now Nick started to take off his own clothes. Tory watched with shy curiosity as his fingers worked each button of his shirt, starting from the bottom and moving up. He shrugged out of it and flung it aside, his eyes never leaving Tory's face. But she could not stop herself from looking at his bare torso. His skin was so pale and his arms, though strong and taut, had nothing of Brad McMurphy's superfluous bulk. He looked much smaller without his shirt, more vulnerable, fragile even. The web of thatched hair across his chest trickled into a dark stream which led her eye down his torso to his belt buckle which now hung open. She caught her breath and looked away. Suddenly she realized with surprise that she was no longer intimidated by him. She was ready.

Quickly Nick unbuttoned his pants and let them fall to the floor. Now naked, he moved towards her and mounted the platform. The first sensation of his body against hers gave Tory such an intense rush she cried out from the joy of it. His touch was so gentle, his skin against hers soothing and warm. She marveled at how naturally their bodies fit together, how right it felt to have his hard flesh crushed against the softness between her legs. Following his lead, she used her hands to satisfy her curiosity about his body, tracing the jutting bones of his shoulder blades, exploring the lean length of his back, pressing the flat of her palm into the small indentation above his tailbone. His flesh felt deliciously new to her touch, and at the same time completely familiar.

Without warning, Nick swept Tory up in his arms. She clung to him as he carried her off the platform, and laid her gently atop the nearest worktable. She felt the scratch of wood as she lay back, but it didn't register as pain. All she felt was pure joy, rushing at her from all sides and enveloping her like Nick's arms.

NICK LOOKED DOWN at Tory and paused long enough to realize that he had lain her down next to the completed bronze statue, the Tory Figure. For a brief instant he was struck by the perfect symmetry between the sculpture and the young woman in his arms. His hands, which had so often caressed the damp clay and cold metal during the various stages of creation, at last felt the reward of Tory's warm flesh. He was intoxicated by the heat of her and by her beatific expression, so trusting, so full of love. His heart swelled, and very gently he covered her body with his.

Suddenly, above them there was a cracking sound, like ice breaking. And then a shower of glass rained down on Nick's back.

In the next instant a huge weight crashed down onto the table. Nick pressed himself protectively against Tory, and then darkness enveloped them both.

TORY'S FIRST SENSATION WAS one of motion: the hum of wheels under her, travelling over a hard surface, the cool night air blowing against her face. Her second sensation was one of fear: she was not alone. She struggled to put the pieces together, but her brain was muddled. She felt as though she were in a dream.

With a sudden jolt, the movement stopped. But the fear continued, a black thrill of horror, choking the scream in her throat. She tried to escape the crushing darkness but could not open her eyes. Nor could she move her hands or her feet. And then the movement began again, steady and slow. She could hear the noise of traffic, somehow muffled, but familiar. It comforted her to hear the swooshing sound of a passing car and the honking of a distant horn. She must still be in the city. But how had she gotten here? Where was Nick? Who was propelling her into this foreign twilight? And most important of all, why?

Eli saw that his precious load was beginning to stir beneath the heavy blanket in the sidecar, and he leaned forward, trying to make the moped go faster.

Finally he saw the camera shop up ahead. He turned down the alley to enter his little house, the converted garage, from the rear. It would take a few seconds longer, but it meant he would not have to pass by the main house where his sister and Bud lived. He did not want to see Bud, but especially he did not want Bud or his sister to see Her. Once he got Her inside his room, everything would be okay. Better than okay. It would be his dream come true.

THIRTY-ONE

NICK WAS TOO TERRIFIED to open his eyes; the throbbing ache in his head was excruciating enough with them closed. But as his consciousness returned in gradual increments, curiosity won out over fear and pain, and through sheer will he forced his eyelids apart.

He was in a dark room, but it was not his studio. Somehow he knew this, because the air was thick, too thick to breathe. He blinked rapidly, trying to accustom his eyes to the lack of light. It wasn't until he tried to raise his hand to rub them that he realized that both his arms were bound to his body. That accounted for the tightness in his chest. He tried to loosen the binds by squirming slightly. No dice.

His mouth was gagged, he realized, and there was something cold and metallic taped between his lips; he had no idea what. He wriggled his tongue, tried to dislodge it, and in exerting the necessary pressure, breathed out heavily. The thing between his lips made a muffled trilling sound and he realized it was a whistle. Con Uttrell's whistle, the one he used to command his snake. Oh, God.

The events of the night came back to him in fragments, slashing like shards of broken glass against his mind — the Thorntons' dinner party, Tory's appearance, the feel of her body under him on his studio work table. And then nothing, until now.

Suddenly Nick sensed movement and looked around him. He prayed he was wrong about what it was, but his eyes had become attuned to the lack of light, and he saw the long, thick cylinder of reptilian flesh slithering in excruciatingly slow esses in his direction. He was inside the terrarium with the snake!

Frantically he racked his brain for a way out. He thought of the pathetic mouse, scratching hopelessly and helplessly against the heavy glass of the terrarium seconds before it was killed. Would that be his fate as well? He remembered that the snake would not strike unless the whistle blew. With every fiber of his being he thought of stillness and tried not to breathe.

When the overhead light flickered on, its brilliance blinded Nick, disorientating him again.

"Good morning, Nicholas." It was Con Uttrell's voice, oddly distant through the thick glass. "I hope you're not too uncomfortable. But then, you've put yourself in this snake pit, so to speak. It was all going so well until you made a botch of it."

When Nick's vision cleared for the second time, he saw Uttrell across the room. He had opened a false panel in the wall and was twirling the dial of a small safe.

Nick took a quick look around. He was indeed propped up against the glass wall of the reptile terrarium in Con Uttrell's basement office, his hands and feet tightly bound. Already his ankles and wrists were raw from his attempts at movement. The wall of glass on which he leaned was smeared with blood — his blood, no doubt — there was a sore spot on his head and minute cuts scoring his back and arms.

The snake was stretched languorously a mere two feet away. Nick ached with its nearness. He was well within its striking distance, but because he had not blown the whistle, the snake had been obediently patient. It was waiting.

Con was removing some cash and documents from the safe. "I see you've reintroduced yourself to Jaws. I believe it's been twenty-four hours since his last meal, and it was such a tiny mouse at that, just an hors d'oeuvre. Imagine his self control. He certainly has a lot more restraint than you, my dear boy."

Con shook his head. "I know how tempting these young girls are, believe me I do. But if you had only kept your libido in check for another few hours you wouldn't be here now. It's a good thing my associates were watching your studio, and that they saw the man on the roof fall through the skylight. If they hadn't, you'd probably be dead.

"I suspect you're wondering where the girl is. To be honest, I really don't know. Or care. Whoever fell through the skylight took her out the front while my men were coming in the back." Con chuckled. "He was clever and quick. But he made the stupid mistake of taking the girl and leaving the statue. A very costly choice.

"Have you figured it out yet, Nick? Or have you been too wrapped up in your Art with a capital A?" Con's tone was cold and derisive. "I know you artists live in a fantasy world, but even so, I was surprised you were so easily fooled. Did you really think some anonymous collector would pay one hundred and fifty thousand dollars for one of your statues, sight unseen?" He shook his head. "You have a lot to learn about art, my boy.

"If you could have seen the Michelangelo Giant! It is a true work of art, not some metal welded together by a two-bit craftsman, but the work of a genius, pure beauty made tangible."

Con put his papers into an attaché and the money in his pocket.

"I must admit, it did fit perfectly inside the statue you made. At least you accomplished that task properly. And Rocco did a fine job of soldering your statue back onto its base. No one will ever guess that the *real* art is hidden inside the bronze.

"Bryant will be back from taking me to the airport in a few hours. If you're very careful and don't blow the whistle for another . . ." Con checked his watch, "eleven hours, he will let you out. By then I will be in Japan with the statue and there will be nothing anyone can do." He opened the door. "I'm sorry, Nick. But as I told you, there is no point in playing the game unless you can control the outcome."

Nick threw his body against the thick glass, hoping that by sheer weight he could shatter it and use a shard to cut himself free. Con watched with amusement. "Dear boy, that glass is an inch thick. Don't waste your energy." He turned off the lights and left.

After Con was gone, Nick sat motionless in the semi-darkness. The snake seemed to be watching him. Robotic and insensate, its unblinking eye was trained on Nick's face.

Suddenly Nick realized how like the snake he was, self-absorbed and insensitive to all but his own needs, programmed to react to certain stimuli. Even his art the contrivance of an automaton. How could he even call it *his* art when the art was really just working through him, using his hands as tools and his brain as a computer to facilitate its creation? Uttrell was right. He was no more than a craftsman. As lowly as the snake.

It was moving closer now, its body undulating across the terrarium floor until its dry skin grazed Nick's bare leg, rubbing against it like a cat. Only instead of contented feline purring, the serpent was deadly silent. It lifted its head and its forked tongue flicked rhythmically in and out, only inches from Nick's face. But still it did not strike. Helpless, Nick surrendered to the moment and, like the snake, waited.

Time passed.

Nothing happened.

Then suddenly in the vacuum, Nick heard a metallic click and a scraping sound. He was only marginally aware of it, numbed by the nearness of the instrument of his death. But the snake's head whipped around to the source and its cold eyes seemed to glare at the warm light pouring in from the opening door. Then cowed by the sudden brilliance, the snake slithered into a corner, instinctively keeping its options open. Nick couldn't move, but he shifted his eyes to the light and tried to steel himself for the intruder.

Putting the tool he had used to jimmy the lock into his back pocket, Willie Wilson tried to whistle, his usual three-note greeting, but he couldn't seem to force a sound through his dry, cracked lips. And then he entered the room.

Relief flooded through Nick's body. It was all he could do to keep his breathing even, and the whistle pursed between his aching lips silent. But then he realized Willie hadn't seen him, was ignoring the terrarium entirely. And since Nick couldn't move or make a sound, there was no way for him to get Willie's attention.

As Nick watched, Willie started rummaging through the drawers of Con's desk, his movements jerky, desperation drawing sweaty circles under his arms and around the neck of his fuchsia shirt. With furtive jerks of his head, Nick tried to catch Willie's eye, but Willie was totally engrossed in his search, muttering to himself.

"Fuckin' guy. Gets me hooked on the white rock. Shit, I'm a drug addict, a junkie, man. Isn't that old news? I mean, drugs went out with hula hoops..."

Willie jostled the bottom drawer of the desk with growing frustration. It was locked. Barely hesitating, he picked up a paper-weight and pounded on it, becoming more agitated as the drawer refused to break. Nick heard the faint rustle of the snake, disturbed by the noise, tensing its body to strike. His heart beat wildly.

"Damn!" Dropping the paperweight, Willie kicked savagely at the drawer with his booted foot. And at last the wood splintered. Willie reached inside and removed a silver-capped vial filled with crystalline rocks of cocaine. He did a little dance, hustling over to the couch. "Success! I knew the fucker was flush. This stuff better be good. The shit I got on the street was laced, man . . ."

Suddenly, he saw Nick. He stopped dancing and stood there staring in disbelief. "Nick! What the fuck are you doing here? Hey, man, you look like a Cristo all tied up like that! Jesus, look at you. Didn't I tell you not to let Uttrell get his hooks in you?"

Then to Nick's utter shock, he sat down on the couch, and, piece by piece, began to assemble the paraphernalia to create his own brew — the tiny bunsen burner, the round-handled spoon, the syringe, the rubber strap.

Nick squirmed uncomfortably. He couldn't understand why Willie hadn't untied him, but he could do nothing except listen to Willie's monologue and watch him perform his ritual.

"I'm outta here soon as I get my roadie. Mexico, man. Mazatlan. The light's good, the dope's everywhere. Food's for shit, but who the hell needs to eat? Can't stay here anyway, they're getting too close, too damn close." He knocked a rock of cocaine into the spoon and jiggled it over the flame, watching it with glazed eyes.

"She came to the South Shore and told me she knew it all, about the forgeries, about the Giant, everything. She told me she'd turn me in unless I told her who was behind it. I was scared, man. What was I supposed to do? I panicked, and called The Man. He told me he'd have his goon take care of it. Fine with me, I just wanted outta there."

At first Nick didn't know what Willie was talking about. But then it dawned on him. The woman who was murdered! She *had* been the one with Willie at the South Shore.

"It wasn't my idea to kill her. The Nazi did it. But I saw it happen. I was just going home through the park. She came after me, askin' me one more time to come clean to the cops. Before I could say anything, he grabbed her, and BOOM! Twice he bashes her over the head."

Willie was sweating fiercely. He had to put down the spoon to mop his face so he could see what he was doing.

"The weirdest thing was how normal it was. She died, man. I saw it and I didn't feel nothin'. Like when you start to paint, and suddenly something gets hold of the brush, something inside. You don't control it, you just sit back and watch, and the painting becomes art. That's how it was.

"Only problem was that damn runt dog hadda start barkin'. The guy hadda pick that motherfucking time to walk it. He sees me running, damn near trips me with the friggin' leash. And then I started seeing lights flashing and I dropped the fucking file."

Willie rolled up his sleeve and wrapped the rubber strap around his arm, tapping at his inner elbow. "Anyway, soon as I get fixed I'm outta here. You can come man, I could use the company." He sucked in a breath as he stuck the needle in his arm. "Find us some signorinas, set us up on a beach and he'll never. . . find . . . us."

As the syringe emptied, Willie wound down like a Walkman with a dying battery. He stared at his arm in fascination, as though he could see the drug moving through his bloodstream. Then, gradually, as the narcotic hit, he came back into focus, all his good humor and enthusiasm restored tenfold. He looked at Nick as though he were seeing him for the first time.

"Jesus H., Stone, speak up man! Lettin' me do the deed while you just sit there in the all-together, like the bad guy in a porno Clint Eastwood flick."

At last he walked over to the terrarium, unlatched the door and pulled himself in just far enough to touch Nick. But his trembling fingers couldn't untie the binding, so he reached in his back pocket and pulled out one of Nick's fettling knives. "Recognize this? Yeah, I got a bunch of 'em. Never missed 'em, did you? You oughta be a little more careful with the tools of your trade, man."

The knife was sharp, and in a matter of seconds Willie severed the rope. As soon as his hands were free Nick ripped the tape from his mouth, and the whistle fell to the floor.

"What you got? A whistle? Hell, that's what I need, t'give the old lips a rest."

"NO!" Nick's shout and Willie's first blast on the whistle were simultaneous. But before Willie could blow the second note the snake hurled itself at the back of his neck with the deadly speed of a heat seeking missile. Its fangs sank deep into the soft flesh and hung on.

Willie hadn't seen what had hit him, but the poison was already spurting into his blood stream. He staggered backwards out of the terrarium, trying to struggle free from the unseen assailant. But the weight of the snake was overpowering, and he couldn't wrest loose from the fangs without tearing a chunk of flesh from his neck.

Nick scrambled for the knife, and in a swift, instinctive movement, slashed at the reptile. The blade sliced through the flesh under its jaw, severing the head. It dangled ghoulishly, its fangs still imbedded in Willie's neck, while the decapitated body fell to the floor in a confusion of writhing gore. Willie dropped to his knees, then slowly collapsed onto the floor. He was unconscious.

Nick turned Willie over and shook him. "Hey, man, talk to me. Willie!" Willie's eyes were open but unseeing. His body convulsed as the poison joined the coke in his bloodstream. Nick bent his head to Willie's chest. His heartbeat was faint.

"I won't let him get away with this. I'll get Uttrell," Nick promised.

Willie shook his head and struggled to speak, whispering one word, "Thornton."

THIRTY-TWO

I T WOULD HAVE MADE more sense to transport the bronze statue in a crate, but Con had been afraid that some power-crazed airline employee would have overridden Arthur Hartman's authority and insisted that it travel in the baggage compartment. And Con was not going to let the statue out of his sight until he turned it over to his contact at Narita Airport in Tokyo. So his arrival at LAX made quite a stir, and by the time Rocco and Bryant had lifted the almost-lifesize bronze nude out of the limousine and strapped it onto a trolley, a small crowd had gathered.

Con was relieved that the end of the operation was finally in sight. The complications, first with the Van Patten woman, and then with Nick Stone, had tested his nerves. Fortunately, Rocco had used his brain for once, bringing Stone to Con while he was still unconscious. Even so, it was a miracle they weren't seen, or caught by the police who constantly patrolled Venice.

Now, at last, things were moving ahead on schedule. In a matter of hours the plane would land at Narita and Con would be free of the burden of his obligation to Francis Thornton.

The entourage entered the Bradley International Building. The terminal was unusually quiet, the flight representatives for Alitalia, El Al and JAL attending to the travelers checking in for their morning flights. Turning to Bryant, Con said, "Let them know we've arrived."

"Yes, sir." Bryant approached the JAL information counter and spoke to the immaculately uniformed employee. She made a call, then followed Bryant back to where Con was waiting. She bowed slightly in greeting. "Mr. Hartman will meet us at the security checkpoint," she said. "Will you please follow me?"

She led them to the escalator, and held the other passengers back. Rocco got on first, deftly wheeling the dolly around so that the figure appeared recumbent as it ascended, then Con stepped on with his attaché, and finally Bryant, carrying Con's Hermes garment bag.

At the top of the escalator the wide passageway narrowed and veered sharply to the left, funneling the passengers into the security checkpoint. Con hoped Arthur Hartman would be there waiting, because it was only ten minutes to flight time, and although he was certain JAL would hold the jumbo jet — after all, he was paying a premium to bring the statue on board — he didn't want to prolong the agony. The sooner the plane was in the air, the better.

Con, Bryant, and Rocco turned the corner in concert. Con was relieved that there was not a long line of travelers waiting for their baggage to be scanned. In fact, the entire area was deserted, except for the security staff manning the equipment, and a half dozen other men in airport police uniforms standing with Arthur Hartman.

"I will make sure everything on board is in readiness," said the employee from JAL, and hurried on ahead.

Con smiled a greeting and walked toward Arthur Hartman. But Hartman did not acknowledge him. He seemed rooted to the spot, looking past Con to the statue. And then Con realized that it had to be a shock to him to see a bronze likeness of his daughter being wheeled through the airport. Con smiled inwardly. It was probably the first time the man had seen his daughter's nude body. No wonder he was stunned.

"Arthur, good of you to be here." He gave Hartman's hand a hearty shake. Hartman could not tear his eyes away from the statue. "Isn't she lovely?" Con asked, his voice carefully modulated to communicate appreciation without prurience.

Arthur was speechless. He didn't know what had been on his mind when he had allowed Tory to pose for this statue. But now that he saw the finished product, he was appalled. Thinking of Tory posing naked for an artist in the confines of his studio had been one thing. But seeing the result in public was something else entirely. It was not a bronze statue at all. It was his precious little girl, bereft of every shred of privacy. Without realizing it, he had allowed her to surrender the mystery of her femininity to an anonymous public. And to what end? Did it make her immortal or immoral? And what did it make him?

Arthur planted himself directly in front of the statue, instinctively trying to shield its nakedness. If he could have, he would have thrown his coat over her body and led her away from this audience. Instead, he nodded bitterly in response to Con Uttrell's praise of the statue and kept his anger in check.

"I'm sure it seems as though we are spiriting your daughter away," Con said, unable to keep a patronizing note from his voice. "But don't worry. She will be in good hands, and in impressive company. My client is one of the most important collectors of contemporary art in Japan."

Arthur remained mute.

"Perhaps we should go to the plane," Con urged. "I wouldn't want to cause a delay for the other passengers."

"Yes, of course," Arthur replied. And suddenly he was all business. He nodded to the guards still huddled by the security apparatus and two of them approached. "My men will take her through."

"That's not necessary," Con assured him. "Rocco can handle it."

"No, no, it's policy. You see, only ticketed passengers can go beyond this point. Ever since the damn Gulf War in '91, we've had to be sticklers for procedure."

It was ridiculous, but Con saw there was no point in arguing. He had hoped Rocco could stay with him until the last possible moment. But to force the issue would certainly draw suspicious attention. "Well, let's get on with it then." He motioned to Rocco to give the dolly to one of Hartman's men and allowed the other to help steer the statue through the metal detector, which screamed its outrage as the bronze passed through.

Con shook hands with Bryant. "I'll call you from Tokyo to let you know when the transfer is made."

"Yessir. I'll be at the house."

The waiting area for JAL Flight #108 was deserted; the other passengers were already on the plane. In just a few minutes Con would be home free. He patted his pocket for the tenth time to be sure his passport and boarding pass were there, and stepped up to the boarding desk.

Rocco clenched and unclenched his fists in frustration as he watched the Boss walk away. Where were all the other passengers? He'd never seen the airport so deserted, and it made him edgy. Something was wrong; he was sure of it. And it was up to him to do something about it. He started to walk toward the metal detector, to follow the Boss, but Bryant's hand on his arm stopped him.

"Where are you going?"

"I don't trust these guys," Rocco said simply.

Bryant shook his head. "You walk through there with what you're carrying, all hell will break loose." Up ahead they could see Con and his entourage disappearing through the gate. "Come on, it's over. I'll buy you a beer and we can watch the plane take off."

IN ANOTHER PART of the airport, on board Delta Airlines Flight #611 to Geneva, Francis Thornton buckled the belt of his first class seat. He was thinking about the woman who had been killed, how her death had forced him to accelerate his timetable, making his move today rather than after the Giant arrived at its destination.

At least Wilson had had the presence of mind to call him and warn him that she was on his trail, threatening to go to the police. And killing her had served a dual purpose. It had stopped her from connecting him to the Giant, and, as the last piece of the puzzle, it had provided an insurance policy: if Con Uttrell tried to blackmail him or didn't deliver the Giant as promised, Francis would see to it that the murder was pinned on him.

Hans still had the murder weapon — a marble paperweight that belonged to Uttrell. Thornton had arranged for it to be stolen from Uttrell's house weeks ago, as a precaution. Now, if Uttrell tried anything, Thornton would see to it that the murder weapon turned up with Con's fingerprints still on it.

If Uttrell did deliver the Giant as promised, Thornton would fly on to Tokyo immediately. Alternatively, if a problem arose, he would stay in Switzerland and send for Mariko. Either way, he was saying goodbye to the United States and his life here for good. He had no regrets. He leaned back and closed his eyes.

"WE'RE READY to move in, sir." It was Drake's voice on the walkie talkie.

"Wait for me," Rick said.

"But —"

"I said wait for me. I'm almost through here. Then I'm coming over."

Rick nodded at the Delta representative and she unlocked the door of the jetway ramp to Flight 611. The two officers with him drew their guns. Rick stopped them. "Hold your fire unless he resists. What we don't need is to cause a riot."

"WILL ALL GROUND PERSONNEL please disembark for our departure to Tokyo."

Con extended his hand to Arthur. "Thank you for everything you've done. I am in your debt."

Arthur nodded curtly at the statue. "Take good care of my daughter."

"I intend to."

Much to Con's relief, Arthur and his men finally turned to leave the aircraft. But at the same moment the beeper on Arthur's belt sounded. Con caught his breath, then let it out as Arthur silenced it and continued down the aisle. The flight attendant activated the control to lower the door behind him and it locked shut with a resounding slam. Con began to relax.

"I don't suppose your companion will want anything to drink," teased a flight attendant, nodding to the statue strapped securely against the seat next to Con. "But may I get you something, sir?"

"We will both have champagne," Con smiled, letting down his guard at last. "In one glass."

RICK AND HIS TEAM RAN down the passageway of the Bradley Terminal, stopping only to show their badges to the security staff in order to skirt the machinery. Then they raced down the corridor to the boarding gate. But the jetway had already been re-tracted and the jet was backing onto the runway. Arthur Hartman and his men, and Lt. Drake and his men, were watching through the window. They turned toward Rick.

"What's going on? I though I told you to wait." Rick looked at Drake, but Arthur Hartman answered his question.

"We have to let the plane take off or you won't be able to assert in court that he was actually trying to leave the country. I've alerted the tower to clear the air so the pilot can circle once and bring her down again. They'll dock back at this gate."

THE JAL JUMBO JET ROLLED down the runway, gathering speed until it had enough momentum for the lift off. Then it soared toward the sun, its wheels tucked up into its belly. Con lowered his seatback to a comfortable angle and sipped his champagne, congrat-ulating himself on his intelligence, his great daring, and his good luck.

But then suddenly, he felt the angle of the plane change, the wing dipping to the right. The Captain's voice sounded over the loudspeaker, "Ladies and Gentlemen, I regret to inform you that we must return to the airport. Do not panic. We are in no danger. But please keep your seat belts fastened until the aircraft has come to a complete stop at the gate."

Con flagged down a passing flight attendant. "What's wrong?" He couldn't keep the panic from his voice.

She shrugged, "They say it's a mechanical. The Captain will let us know as soon as we land."

THIRTY-THREE

THE STREET IN FRONT of Nick's studio was swarming with people — police, press, and passers-by, all drawn by the irresistible allure of the yellow tape police barrier. Reluctantly they moved aside as a Pontiac Firebird skidded to a stop just inches from the curb. Nick jumped out.

"Hey, not so fast," the cop who was driving called. But Nick ignored him, ducking under the tape.

He'd been lucky to find the undercover team prowling around the gate at Con Uttrell's. They'd rushed Willie to the UCLA Medical Center, but they'd been too late to save him. So they'd lent Nick some clothes and brought him home. On the way they'd filled him in on the excitement at the airport and the arrests, but they hadn't mentioned that the show had shifted venue to his studio, although surely they'd known. What was going on?

"Hold it, buster," the policeman in charge of crowd control warned as Nick pushed his way toward the studio door.

"It's okay, Matthews," Rick called from inside. He held the door open for Nick. Nick glared at him coldly and entered.

Leslie hung up the phone when she saw him. "Nick! Are you okay? They just called from the hospital at UCLA. Willie's . . ."

"I already know about Willie." He let her rest her head against his chest, and reached out to push aside the silken strands separating her office from the studio. It was a madhouse of activity, people taking pictures, measuring, making notes, combing the space for evidence. "What's going on?"

Leslie was beside herself. "It's a mess, just a mess. I tried to keep them out, but no one would listen to me."

"Do you have a search warrant?" Nick demanded as Rick swept past him.

"It's on the way."

"Then get out."

"Two people are already dead, Stone, and we don't want to find a third," Rick said. "Every minute counts in a case like this."

"What kind of a case is that?" Nick asked. But Rick had turned away.

Nick felt like a stranger in his own home. The investigation teams were going about their various arcane tasks, ignoring him as though he were invisible. They talked and laughed among themselves, making lewd jokes about the naked statues. Then, through the crowd of police, press and men in suits, Nick saw the statue of Tory, beatific amidst the chaos. At least *it* was safe.

But what about Tory? What had happened to her?

Nick glanced at the work table where he had lain with her just hours before. It was covered with glass and specks of dried blood. His blood. And hers? Above it where the skylight had been, the ceiling was completely open. Fresh air and the sounds of the Boardwalk filtered in.

Nick bent to pick up a shard of glass. "Good thing it was tempered," a policewoman said as she swept some fragments into an evidence bag, "or you'd've been chopped liver."

"Nick, I don't know if you remember me, from the Art Walk. My name is Rosiland Weeks."

Nick turned toward the woman who had spoken. She did look familiar, but it took Nick a second to focus. "The bathroom, right?"

"Right," Roz shrugged, embarrassed. "I'm with Century Insurance. I'm sorry to admit I was snooping around that day, investigating a claim about a stolen Richard Diebenkorn painting."

"I don't have it."

"I know. But well, now it's turned into something else." Her eyes swept the room. "I'm sorry about this circus, too." She looked at the statue of Tory. "I guess you know about the Michelangelo Giant."

"Yeah, I heard."

"My company wrote the policy on it." She sighed. "We're going to have to open up your statue, as soon as the curator from the Getty arrives. There's no other way. But believe me, I feel terrible about desecrating such a magnificent piece of art."

"Not half as bad as I feel about the whole damn thing," Nick said.

"Mr. Stone? We met yesterday, I'm Lt. Drake, L.A.P.D. Art Theft Division." Drake held out his hand, but Nick ignored it.

"We're looking for evidence that the Giant was planted inside your statue here, at this location."

"How are you going to get any evidence with ten thousand cops swarming all over the place?"

Nick saw someone unpinning the photographs from the wall. "Hey! Get away from there!"

"I didn't bring those people," Drake tried to explain, but Nick had already stormed off towards his living quarters. There men and women were combing the room, dusting for fingerprints, taking pictures, talking into microrecorders. Nick saw his stash of marijuana dumped into a large plastic evidence bag along with everything else in his nightstand drawer.

His bed had been stripped of its sheeting and two cops were sitting on the mattress, waiting as a video cassette rewound. "What the fuck is this!" Nick cried in exasperation and grabbed for the remote control. "You have no right."

"Yeah, we got a right," the cop replied, tapping his badge. "This little hunk of metal gives us all kinds of rights."

"Where is my daughter? Will somebody please tell me?" Charlotte's wail echoed through the studio, and for a moment the machinery of the investigation stopped. All eyes turned to Charlotte.

She was leaning against Arthur. Both of them looked drained and distraught. But when Charlotte saw Nick she drew herself up and ran over to him, her spike heels clicking angrily on the cement floor. "It's all your fault," she cried, each word a separate burst of anger. "You've done this to Tory!" She pounded her fists ineffectively against Nick's chest.

Nick pulled free and held her away. "What are you talking about? What's happened? Where's Tory?"

Charlotte's anger dissolved into helpless tears. "She's gone. Kidnapped. We don't know . . ."

"She never came home last night," Arthur explained. He stepped forward and gently removed Charlotte from Nick's grasp, pulling her close to him. "We called her friends, nobody had seen her. But then when our maid came in this morning, she told Charlotte that Tory had asked her to call a taxi last night. She told Radiance she was going to a party to meet you."

"She did. She came to the Thorntons' last night," Nick said.

"But we were there! We didn't see her."

"I guess she didn't go into the house. I saw her in the back. By the pond."

"What was she doing there?"

Nick shrugged. "Looking for me, I suppose."

"How did she know you'd be at this party?" Rick asked.

"I don't know. I didn't tell her. I didn't have a chance."

"I told her."

Both men looked at Charlotte, who exhaled a tremulous sigh and buried her head in Arthur's shoulder. "She asked me where we were going last night, and I told her," she whispered. "Was that so wrong?"

"How did she respond?" Rick asked.

"She was upset, I suppose it's natural. She thought she should have been invited, since she had posed for the statue. She was very angry at you," she looked defiantly at Nick, "for not telling her about it."

"I was going to invite her to come," Nick said, "but she didn't show up to work yesterday afternoon."

"But you did see her at the party last night?" Rick prodded.

"Yeah, I told you. I was out in the yard, back by the pond."

"What time?"

Nick shrugged. "About nine, nine-thirty, I guess."

"And then?"

"And then I brought her back here."

"You just left the party?"

Nick nodded.

"Without telling anyone?"

Nick nodded again.

"Why?" Rick asked.

"Because I didn't want to be there," Nick replied, and looking straight at Charlotte, added, "and neither did she."

"So you came back here and what happened?"

"What do you think?"

"Oh my God," wailed Charlotte, burying her face in Arthur's chest again. The knuckles of his hand, gripping her shoulder, were deadly white with tension.

"Sir?" One of the cops from the bedroom yelled. "We've got something here you'd better see."

"Why don't you get your wife a cup of coffee, Mr. Hartman. One of the boys can help you." He nodded toward the office area and then turned back to Nick. "You come with me."

"I want to see too!" cried Charlotte. "I'm her mother. If there's anything to see, I demand to see it. It's my right."

"Suit yourself."

Rick, Nick and the Hartmans crowded into Nick's bedroom.

The two cops looked at Rick. "Sir, I don't think . . ." one of them began.

"You heard the lady," Rick snapped. "Whatcha got?"

The cops shifted uncomfortably. "See for yourself, sir," one of them said somberly.

He pushed the play button and gradually the screen filled with Charlotte's nude body.

"You're not drawing me, I hope," her video self said.

"Would you rather I take a picture?" Nick's disembodied voice asked.

"God no!" came the reply.

"Then how am I going to compare your body to your daughter's?"

The real Charlotte emitted a pitiful moan and fainted.

"What the hell is this?" Rick demanded.

"My daughter *and* my wife? You sonofabitch!" Arthur lunged at Nick, but Rick grabbed him. With the help of one of his men, he held Arthur back.

"Hey man, she came to me, I didn't ask for it," Nick said. Arthur lunged at him again. "Besides, nothing happened, I swear it. With either of them."

"This isn't the part anyway." The cop with the remote control pushed the fast forward button, mercifully ending Charlotte's nude scene. "There's something after this."

"Then get the fuck to it!" Rick yelled. And to his aide he barked, "Get Mr. and Mrs. Hartman out of here. And call a paramedic for Mrs. Hartman." To Leslie he said, "Can you bring her some water?" Leslie nodded and went into the bathroom.

Rick turned to Nick. "What's the story with this tape?" he asked in a calmer voice.

"I usually photograph my models to help me understand their bodies, but Tory was too intimidated by the camera. So I had a hidden video installed," Nick explained. "It's activated by the light."

"Here it is," the cop with the remote said and switched the tape back to play. "Check it out."

It chilled Nick to see his love scene with Tory replayed on the small screen. What had been a passionate, private moment was, by the addition of this audience of strangers, transformed into pornography. He couldn't watch it.

"It's coming," the cop with the remote said. "There. It starts in the top right corner."

On the video, suddenly a shower of glass rained down onto Nick and Tory, and then the hulking figure of a man crashed feet first onto the table, pinning Nick on top of her. Before either could react, the man picked up a fragment of bronze and hit Nick over the head with it. When the man moved to free Tory from under Nick's body, he turned directly into the camera.

"Freeze it!" Rick called. "Do you know him?" he asked.

"Yeah, from somewhere, I dunno," Nick answered, not taking his eyes off the picture.

"Replay it to there," Rick called.

Nick rubbed the spot on the back of his skull where a lump had risen, watching the scene rewind, then jerk forward frame by frame until the face was again visible.

"Is he one of Uttrell's men?" Rick asked.

Nick shook his head. "I dunno. I've seen him, but . . ."

"I know that guy!" It was Leslie's voice. She was standing in the door of the bathroom, holding a glass of water and a wet towel for Charlotte. "That's the guy who installed the video."

"Yeah, yeah. I remember him now," said Nick. "I gave him a drawing I'd done of Tory. He seemed . . . oh, shit." The realization swept over him.

"What?" Rick prompted. "He seemed what?"

"It wasn't much of a drawing but he acted like it was the best gift anyone had ever given him."

Rick turned to Leslie. "Do you have an address?"

"Sure, the Venice Camera Shoppe, it's on my Rolodex."

"Get it."

Leo Drake stuck his head in. "The curator from the Getty is here. We're ready to open up the statue," he said to Rick.

"It'll have to wait," Rick replied.

ELI PUTTERED HAPPILY with his equipment, adjusting the angle of the light, repositioning the camera, studying the tableau he had created to determine how to make it perfect. Here in his private place, with all his precious things around him, his disabilities were less obvious. Like any artist involved in his work, he was totally absorbed, patient and competent. He hummed along with the dulcet tones of Johnny Mathis playing in his headphones.

Then he saw a flaw in the scene he had created and ran around in front of the camera to correct it, elevating Tory's chin another half an inch and gently brushing her hair back from her shoulder so that the heads of the two dead pigeons dangling on either side of her neck were fully visible.

Tory remained exactly as Eli had placed her. She didn't want to move, didn't want to think about the dead pigeons or about what had happened since last night. Above all, she struggled to stay calm so he wouldn't get upset. Because although he had been gentle with her, worshipful even, the evidence of his cruelty was hanging around her neck.

She tried to take her mind off her predicament by studying the photographs that filled the room, pictures of animals and insects and birds, living and dead, in juxtaposition to each other, just as she was juxtaposed to the pigeons. They were dead; she was alive. She prayed the balance was important to him.

Why was she here? What had happened last night? Suddenly her mind flooded with the image of Nick making love to her. Or at least starting to. And then she remembered the glass raining like stardust down on Nick's back, the body crashing down on top of them, and then the man rising and swacking Nick over the head. Finally, she remembered Nick's body becoming a dull weight, pressing all the air from her lungs. "Please don't be dead," she prayed silently. "Please be okay. Be okay, be okay," She repeated the words over and over like a mantra.

A light flashed, blinding Tory, and she blinked rapidly, trying to focus and hold back the tears. Then all in a rush, the door burst open. Men ran into the room. Some in suits and some in police uniforms. Two, three, maybe more, she couldn't see clearly. Before Eli could react, they grabbed and handcuffed him. He didn't resist, he didn't even seem surprised. From the headphones, Johnny Mathis sang softly, "I'm as helpless as a kitten up a tree . . ."

And then someone was untying her and wordlessly removing the pigeons from around her neck. A blanket was wrapped around her, and arms were holding her. There was something familiar in the touch. She looked up.

It was Nick. He had come for her. He had saved her.

EPILOGUE

NICK HAD ALWAYS HATED openings, the obligatory pandering to the art crowd, the gratuitous compliments and empty conversation. But tonight was different. He was here not as an artist, but as a patron of the arts, patron of a new artist, photographer Eli Creswell.

The gallery was jammed, and because the show was that rare commodity — a famous artist offering the spotlight to a new talent — the glitteratti had come out in force. The newspaper publicity surrounding the artist and his relationship to the arrests of renowned art collector Francis Thornton and art dealer Con Uttrell hadn't done the show any harm either.

Surprisingly, Eli's photographs of dead and maimed animals, insects, reptiles and birds were not macabre and depressing, they had a miraculous sense of life, and as one reviewer had stated, "the childlike boldness of his technique perfectly articulates society's obsession with violence and its attempt to reconcile the passage of life, to accept it as a natural process."

Among the photographs in the show were two taken at the

crime scene in Breeze Park where Officer Susan Litton, a.k.a. Caroline Van Patten, had been murdered. In the Grand Jury investigation it had been revealed that Eli was walking his sister's dog in the park that night and had taken the photographs moments after the murder had occurred, of the dog sniffing at the dead body.

The bright bursts of light from Eli's flash bulbs, which had temporarily blinded Willie Wilson, had in the end vindicated him, because they captured in the background another dark figure, later identified as Thornton's goon, Hans Lieberman, holding a bloodied marble paperweight. When he was apprehended, Lieberman had pointed the finger at Francis Thornton, solidifying the D.A.'s case. In a few months Thornton would be standing trial.

Although not directly linked to the murder of the victim, the discovery of the bill of sale for the Diebenkorn found on the murdered woman's body gave the police cause to arrest Con Uttrell. Uttrell's long history of fraudulent dealings, substantiated by his secretary Anna Winetsky, who had turned state's witness, and by tapes made by Officer Susan Litton before she was killed, virtually ensured that Uttrell would be removed from society for a decade, at least.

NICK CIRCLED the room, shaking hands with eager patrons and posing for the press. He saw Eli, presided over by his sister Marge and her husband Bud, who were accepting accolades from the crowd. Fortunately, Tory's parents hadn't pressed charges against Eli. After all, it hadn't been a real kidnapping, just a misunderstanding. The artist had chosen his model but he hadn't been able to communicate his wishes to her in any other way except by taking her forcibly. After this show, Nick thought to himself, he won't have to sweat convincing girls to model for him.

Nick nodded to the owners of the Rave Gallery, Willie's old dealers, who he'd invited as a professional courtesy. They'd seen to it that Willie's funeral had been the art event of the year. It had been held in the courtyard of the Contemporary Museum, which staged a coinciding retrospective of his work spanning thirty years. Rave had created a memorial catalog for the show, which had already sold more than 20,000 copies and was in its third printing. Nick had seen to it that half the profits went into an art department scholarship at Willie's alma mater, UCLA.

"Since when did you start dealing?" someone asked Nick.

"Since I saw something that turned me on," Nick replied.

"It's interesting, but is it art?"

"If it sells, it's art," Nick said, watching a gallery assistant apply a red dot next to the title of one of the photos.

"What about your own work?"

"It's on hold for the moment."

The art critic from *The Times* approached him. "Congratulations, Nick. I understand you discovered this fellow. Is he here?" He stepped closer to whisper, "They say he's a nut case."

Nick smiled stiffly. "Can you name an artist who isn't?"

"You've got a point."

Nick saw Rosiland Weeks from Century Insurance across the room and waved. They'd become friends in recent months, and since she'd played an integral part in the scenario surrounding this show, he'd invited her to the opening.

Roz waved back to Nick and tried to make her way over to him. Like everyone else in the gallery, she was dressed to the teeth. Including the teeth on some, he thought, inching past a woman with a diamond embedded in one of her incisors.

"I had no idea this fellow was so talented!" Roz said to him when they connected. "Rick and I may buy one for the new house. Did I tell you we bought a place on the Peninsula? It's right on the sand, near the jetty."

"Nice neighborhood. You get good morning light over there."

"Yeah. It's amazing what money can buy." Roz smiled. "I still want one of your statues, by the way. When will you start working again?"

"As soon as I find a new model."

"Well, I hope it's not too long. The new house took a big chunk out of the reward money, and Rick's campaigning for a twenty-four foot ketch to go with it."

"Hey, Boss!"

Nelson was pushing through the crowd eating a small designer pizza. Roz smiled. "Nick, you remember my associate Nelson Kravitz."

They shook hands. "Enjoying yourself?" Nick asked.

"Free food, free booze, and a room full of available chicks. What more could a guy want?"

Roz dabbed at a speck of tomato sauce on his lapel. "Maybe a napkin?"

Then Roz saw her own boss and waved him over. "Mr. Harrington, thank you for coming, sir. Have you met Nicholas Stone? He's sponsoring the show."

"Looks like you're having quite a success," Harrington said, shaking hands with Nick. "Although I must say I can't for the life of me see the appeal of these photographs."

"Art is in the eye of the beholder," Nick replied.

"Who knows," Roz smiled, "someday these may be as valuable as the Michelangelo Giant."

"Just check with me before you write a $40,000,000 policy on them!" Harrington chuckled, moving back into the crowd.

Suddenly Nick sensed a shift in the atmosphere of the room. He turned to find the cause and saw Tory entering the gallery with her parents. Her presence penetrated the space like a brilliant color, and everything around her appeared drab by comparison.

Nick was, quite simply, dazzled, and he excused himself from Roz and Nelson to watch her walk around the room. Conversation stopped and people stared as she passed; photos of the Tory Figure had appeared all over the world in newspaper articles about the recovery of the Michelangelo Giant, and she had become a minor celebrity. But she seemed unaware of the attention, concentrating on the photos, and nodding hello to the people she knew.

Though he'd thought about her every day, three months had passed since Nick had seen Tory, and his eyes drank in the details. She was thinner now, yet somehow more solid. Her hair was cut short, revealing her graceful neck and shoulders. She was wearing a simple white sundress, and her bare arms, pale in April, were now burnished bronze from the summer sun. But these were just superficial changes; there was more, a change inside that shone in her eyes. She'd become a young woman, confident of herself, grown up, and she was more beautiful than ever.

When she had completed a circuit of the room, Nick came up beside her and gently touched her shoulder. Startled, she instinctively shrank away. But when she saw him, a smile lit her face, and she held out her hand. He took it in both of his. For a moment neither of them spoke.

"Hi, Nick," she said at last.

"I wasn't sure you'd come."

"I wanted to see the show."

"And what do you think?"

She shrugged. "I dunno. I like it, I guess. I have to look at it some more."

"I'll walk with you."

They began to make another circle around the room, but neither of them looked at the photographs. Finally Nick said, "I called and called, but your mother . . ."

Tory interrupted him. "I know. I told her I didn't want to talk to you. I was . . . I needed some time. But since I'm leaving tonight for Paris. . ."

"You won the scholarship?"

Tory nodded. "With a picture I took of you working at your studio, as a matter of fact."

They stopped walking in front of the centerpiece of the show, the photo of Tory with the dead pigeons around her neck. The picture combined the best of journalistic reportage and aesthetic imagery, capturing the fear and horror on Tory's face, set against a tableau as intricately designed as a Cornell box.

Tory shuddered. "I can't believe that's me. It's weird. I don't even remember being there."

"He told me he wants you to pose again."

"No way," she said. "From now on I'm going to be the artist, not the muse."

"Who says you can only be one or the other?"

"No one, I guess."

They walked onto a small balcony. The July sun was just dipping into the ocean, and the sounds of the Boardwalk drifted upwards, surrounding them with the music of a summer evening.

"I've missed your face," Nick said softly. He reached out to stroke her cheek, and she leaned into his hand, lowering her eyes. "Maybe, we could get together some time, when you get back."

"I'm going to take my senior year abroad, in Paris," Tory replied, "so I won't be back until next summer."

"That's probably a good thing," Nick said. "I mean it is a good thing, for you. But it seems like a hell of a long time to an old guy like me."

"I'll be eighteen," Tory said. "When I get back, I mean."

"Eighteen's a good age," Nick said awkwardly. And then neither of them knew what to say.

Arthur appeared at the balcony door. He nodded curtly at Nick, then said to Tory, "Honey, we've got to get going if we're going to make the flight."

"I'll be right there, Dad." Tory waited until he left them alone before turning back to Nick. "Thank you for letting my parents have the artist's proof of the statue. I know it's worth a lot, since the original . . ." Her voice trailed off.

Then she smiled shyly. "Maybe some day my dad'll get used to it and let Mom take it out of the basement. Anyway, it was really nice of you to give it to them."

"You know why I could let it go?" Nick asked. She shook her head. "Because I always have you with me, in my mind, and in my heart."

Tory couldn't speak for a moment. When she finally got her voice back, she said, "I didn't like modeling, but I wouldn't have traded the experience for anything."

A teasing smile lit her face. "Next summer if you aren't too busy, maybe you'll pose for me."

"Just tell me when," Nick said.

Tory nodded. "Well, good bye then."

She turned to go, but Nick caught her hand and pulled her to him. Gently, he took her face in his hands, and with elaborate care pressed his lips to her forehead. She closed her eyes and tilted her face up to his, and he traced the outline of her mouth with his fingertip. Then, tenderly he bent to kiss her, savoring the sheer joy of it, letting his mouth linger on hers. There was affection and promise in his lips.

"When you get back," he murmured, "when you get back . . ."

ACKNOWLEDGMENTS

I am grateful to friends and family whose support and encouragement helped create this book:

To the agents, editors and publishers who read the manuscript at various stages along the way, offering encouragement and criticism, not always in equal measure.

To Robert Graham, John Deep, John Barber, Anne Kresl, Connie Linn and Angela Nichol, who gave generously of their time and talents;

To Mother and Dad, Lillian, dearest Roy, Susan, and Angelo, who celebrated my successes along the way and listened sympathetically when things weren't going so well;

And to Zazu, who was indeed a faithful companion, staying by my side each day from dawn to dusk . . .

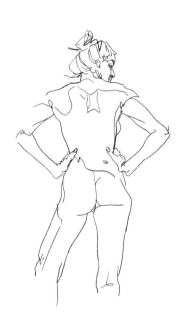